Book #3
Heal and Hart series

P9-CJQ-841

NOTE: Pages 277-282 "missing" in this copy. Author supplied the missing section via email.

Miller 9/23/13

SACRIFICIAL OFFERINGS

A LEAL AND HART NOVEL

SACRIFICIAL OFFERINGS

MICHAEL A. BLACK

FIVE STAR
A part of Gale, Cengage Learning

GALE
CENGAGE Learning

Detroit • New York • San Francisco • New Haven, Conn • Waterville, Maine • London

LIBRARY OF CONGRESS CATALOGING-IN-PUBLICATION DATA

Black, Michael A., 1949–
  Sacrificial offerings : a Leal and Hart novel / Michael A. Black.
  — 1st ed.
    p. cm.
  ISBN 978-1-4328-2618-5 (hardcover) — ISBN 1-4328-2618-2
(hardcover) 1. Police—Illinois—Chicago—Fiction. I. Title.
PS3602.L325S23 2012
813'.6—dc23   2012016207

First Edition. First Printing: September 2012.
Published in conjunction with Tekno Books and Ed Gorman.
Find us on Facebook– https://www.facebook.com/FiveStarCengage
Visit our website– http://www.gale.cengage.com/fivestar/
Contact Five Star™ Publishing at FiveStar@cengage.com

Printed in Mexico
1 2 3 4 5 6 7 16 15 14 13 12

For Shauna

ACKNOWLEDGMENTS

The road any author travels is often a lonely one, fraught with doubts and difficulties along the way. I've been fortunate that I've had so many people who have helped me on the arduous journey that was the evolution of *Sacrificial Offerings*. It's virtually impossible to recognize everyone so if you've been left out please don't feel slighted. I'll try to get you in the next one.

Certain people do stand out, however, who were instrumental in the production of this particular book, as well as my writing in general. I would like to extend a personal thanks to Ann Hemenway, who was my thesis advisor at Columbia; Patricia Pinianski, also of Columbia's teaching staff; Julie Hyzy, the best writing partner I ever had; Lt. Dave Case, CPD, who helped me in more ways than I could count; J. Michael Major, who read an earlier version of this novel and gave his suggestions; Ray Lovato, my best friend since childhood whose wise counsel saw me through many a rough period; Debbie Brod, my editor who once again shined the light and showed me how to improve my writing; Al Zuckerman, my agent, whose patience and help was always highly appreciated; Mr. John Helfers, who proved to be a good friend and ally; and all the men and women of law enforcement with whom I had the honor of working during my police career.

1
RIPTIDE

Taji sat in the driver's seat of his tricked-out Cadillac Escalade in the parking lot of the Riptide Motel contemplating how nice it was to be out of prison and doing work for Otha Spears on this fine summer night. Well, sorta doing work, if you could call sitting in the lot of this flea-bag shit hole and waiting while two hos finish up their trimming of some rich white john. Security, Otha had called it. But Taji wasn't gonna argue. Not with his main man Otha. Not after serving ten years for homicide and this last PCS bullshit, not to mention doing it all as a stand-up member of the Gangstas.

Otha had promised him a job when he got out, so Taji had kept his mouth shut and did what he was told inside. When he went in, he was known as Larry Barrow, which was still techni-cally his name, but when he came out, he was Oman Taji, and people respected that. Respected him, too.

The john was paying top dollar, so let him enjoy himself a little, Taji figured, as he fingered the pipe again. Efron James had set them up with the john, through some kind of actor friend of his. Taji had met the actor guy a few times to sell him some stuff. The dude had told him that this old white john was into show business big-time, and Taji was anxious to begin expanding his sources of income beyond the pimping and bodyguard duties he did for Efron's boss, Otha Spears. Maybe even start making some of them pornographic movies. Sitting back, he imagined seeing himself on a DVD labeled, *The Black*

Prince of Porno.

He wondered if he dared to smoke that rock he'd grabbed from the stash Chocolate had when he picked her up. Licking his lips, he took out the glass pipe and fingered it. Dumb to pick up such a bad habit now, but as long as he was controlling it, and it wasn't controlling him, he was cool. And what the hell, he was a free man, except for checking in with the parole officer every couple of weeks. He hoped the asshole wouldn't make him piss in the bottle. But he'd take that vial of clean juice with him next time just in case.

He fingered the pipe again and took out the plastic wrap that held the rock.

Yeah, I got time, he thought.

Then his cell phone went off and it was that bitch Chocolate telling him to get his black ass in there.

"Why? What's up?"

"This motherfucker's getting crazy. Trying to choke Janice with some rope."

"I am not!" He heard the john yelling in the background.

Shit, Taji thought, flipping the phone shut. He dropped the pipe into his shirt pocket and got out of the car. It wouldn't do to have someone calling the cops because of some rowdy shit. Otha wouldn't like that.

He quickened his pace to a fast jog, coming to the door of room thirteen, and rapped his knuckles hard on the wood.

The door opened a crack and he saw Chocolate's dark face stare at him. He could see her bare shoulder and the sweep of her brown hip as she stepped back. He moved inside and had to blink. What the fuck? A mess of bright lights—real bright lights—was shining right into his eyes. They were set up facing the bed.

"I'm not trying to hurt you," the fucking john was saying. The white ho, Janice, stood on the far side of the bed, her arms crossed in front of her tits, looking terrified. The john stood on the bed with some kind of noose around his neck. "See? It won't hurt. I'm doing it to myself, for Christ's sake." His hand grabbed the end of the rope.

Taji covered the distance from the door to the bed in two big strides, grabbing the john's wrist and pulling him from the bed to the floor in one motion. Taji figured a little show of force, just like he'd done in the joint, would straighten this chump out in a hurry. His powerful black fingers curled around the john's hands and with a sharp jerk pulled the man upward to his feet. The movement was quick and powerful, like just about everything else Taji did. The john's elbow slammed into Taji's chest, breaking the glass pipe and sending a sharp slash of pain through Taji's left chest muscle. He grunted and tightened his grip on the rope around the guy's neck.

"How you like it now, motherfucker?" Taji said. "Still think it don't hurt?"

He saw the john's face turning bright red, so Taji thought he'd keep the fucker like that for a while. Let him feel the fear. Show him who's boss. He looked at Chocolate. "He pay you two yet?"

She nodded, her dark eyes fixed on the scrambling john. "You best let him go."

"Relax, sweetcakes." Taji smirked and released the flabby white fucker, watching him slide down to the floor. "Now how about dousing those fucking lights?"

Chocolate's naked body moved over to the wall, and she pulled a plug out. The brightness ceased. Taji blinked a couple times, trying to focus. He'd known the john was setting up some video equipment. Shit, he'd even helped the guy set everything up when he'd first come inside to check the room out. And this white guy had some of the best video equipment Taji had ever seen. Knew how to use it too. Set it up just like a pro, and even encouraged Taji to try zooming with the remote, giving him pointers on just how he wanted the session videotaped, and hooking up a cable so they could see themselves on the TV monitor.

Taji had been surprised when he saw the guy sticking a small tape cartridge into the camcorder.

"You still using tape?" Taji asked.

"This camcorder's about four years old," the john had told him. "I take it with me when I'm traveling. I have a machine to transfer it to disk back in California when I edit it."

"I guess the whole world ain't gone digital after all," Taji said.

His vision was just coming back when he saw Chocolate still staring at the stupid john. "That dude ain't breathing right."

Taji looked down. The john was turning blue now, like he wasn't getting enough air, and he was making some kind of little, short snorting noises.

Taji crouched over the man, checking to make sure the noose was completely loose now. The guy's breathing was irregular and ragged, making a rasping sound with every breath. His eyes had a glazed look. Then he just sort of stopped breathing with a quick jerk, followed by a slow-sounding gurgle. Taji slapped the john's face twice, trying to revive him. When this failed he yelled at Chocolate, telling her to do something.

"What you want me to do?" she snapped back.

"Do CPR or something," he said.

"I don't know how to do that shit."

Janice, who was still looking buzzed from all the drugs she'd consumed in the last hour and a half, just sat there with a dazed and stupid look on her face.

"Me neither," she said after a few moments.

Taji looked at the guy again, then felt the man's neck for some kind of pulse. Nothing. He smacked his open palm down on the flabby pink chest a few times, like he'd seen on TV, then leaned over and put his ear on top to listen. Still nothing. Standing, he slipped the rope noose into his pocket, went to the window, and pulled the shade away from the glass, checking to see if anyone was outside.

"He dead?" Chocolate asked.

"Shut up," Taji said.

They'd chosen the Riptide Motel because it was cheap, and they usually didn't ask any questions. But best of all, the rear section faced away from the office toward a wooded area. Beyond that was the nearest body of water, the Cal Sag Sanitary Canal, from which the owner had apparently devised the name of the once quaint little place. But with the two larger hotels that had been subsequently constructed almost adjacent to the Riptide, the small establishment had been relegated to the dubious status of the no-tell-motel-four-hour-nap variety. Its main asset these days was that it was quiet and private. Nobody listened, or looked.

Taji had let the john rent the room, then just drove around the back of the motel so the clerk wouldn't see his ride or license plates. He'd been cautious because he was bringing the bitches and the drugs, but now he had a bigger reason. He was a three-time loser-plus. He'd done time a dime for homicide, armed robbery, and most recently three for delivery of a controlled substance. If he got caught up in this shit they'd lock him up and throw away the key. This was bad. Real bad. Then he realized how bad—the red light on that dude's camcorder was still lit up. Was the fucking thing still recording? Taji stepped over and pressed the button to turn it off.

"That thing still on?" Chocolate asked, her eyes wide open now.

"Get dressed and go put my car over in the Holiday Inn lot," Taji said. "I gotta think on how to handle this."

"You bleeding, baby," she said, reaching out and touching his chest.

Taji looked down and saw the red on the front of his shirt. Damn john had smashed the pipe right into his fucking chest.

Chocolate shuffled over to the foot of the bed and grabbed her pink halter top and red shorts. As she slipped on her shoes, she reached for the john's pants and felt for his wallet. Taji was on her in a second, twisting the wallet out of her hand, and then backhanding her across the face.

"Bitch, you only do what I tell you to do. Understand?"

Chocolate nodded, running her tongue over the inside of her lips like she was feeling where the cuts were. The sudden violence seemed to snap Janice out of her stupor. She leaned over and caressed Chocolate's bare shoulders.

"Wait a minute," Taji said, looking from one woman to the other. "You take my ride over and park it in the Inn," he said to Janice. "Nobody'd think twice about seeing a white girl walking around the lot over there. Then you get your ass back over here fast, understand?"

Janice nodded, the fear seeming to tug at her widening eyes. She jumped from the bed and began collecting her clothes. Taji started disconnecting the camcorder from the stand. He collapsed the telescoped legs and folded the stand into the carrying case. After setting the camcorder into the other section of the padding, he snapped the case closed and twisted the fasteners. He stood and looked at the set of lights. They were still too hot to take down.

Janice was slow getting dressed, so Taji gave her a shove as he stood up. "Take that motherfucking car over there now," he said. He took the keys to his Caddie out of his pocket and threw them on the rug in front of her.

Janice nodded and scurried over to grab the keys. She glanced from Taji to Chocolate, then back to Taji again, and left.

"You get right back here," Taji said as she slipped out the door. He slid a small automatic, a .380 Bersa Thunder, out of his jacket pocket and tucked it into his belt line. Then he began pacing.

"What we gonna do, babycakes?" Chocolate asked. Her voice was coy, like she was figuring the angles to get something on him.

"Shut the fuck up," he said. "I told you, I gotta think."

Taji licked his lips then picked up the john's wallet again. He opened the billfold and took out the cash, jamming it into his pants pocket without even counting it. Then he checked for credit cards and other IDs. He found a California driver's license issued to Richard Porter. He left that in the wallet, which he carefully wiped clean.

"Help me wipe down this room," he said. "Everyplace you touched. Make sure you don't miss nothing."

"Hey, baby, how much money was in there?" Chocolate asked.

"Just do what I fucking tell you, bitch," Taji said. He stepped into the bathroom and moistened two towels, then tossed one to Chocolate. They began to wipe all the smooth surfaces around the bed and the dresser. As they were finishing, someone tapped at the door. Taji snatched the gun from his pants and went to the peephole. Seconds later he opened the door and Janice came in. Her eyes widened as she saw the gun, and she handed him the keys.

"Where'd you put it?" he asked, gripping her arm.

"It's over by the front," Janice said. "Jesus, Taji, let go, would ya?" Taji released her, but there was still a fierce look burning in his eyes. "I gotta pee," Janice said, moving toward the bathroom.

"Just don't touch nothing," Taji said.

Janice closed the door and Taji scowled. He was over to the bathroom in three quick strides and shoved open the door. Janice was just dropping her pants when he jerked her out and threw her on the floor.

"I tell you not to touch nothing and what you do?" he snarled. "You touch the fucking door." He stood over her a few more seconds then turned to wipe off the doorknobs. Chocolate went over and helped Janice to her feet. The women exchanged worried looks. Taji came back in the room and threw the towel down.

"Okay," he said, exhaling through his flared nostrils. "This what we gonna do. Take this case and put it in the trunk of his car." He indicated the video equipment suitcase. "I'm gonna see if I can dress this dude and we'll drive him someplace. One of you can follow me in the Caddie."

Chocolate picked up the john's car keys and lugged the case to the door. Taji was picking up the rest of the scattered clothes.

"Man, this motherfucking case is heavy," Chocolate said. "Gimme a hand, girlfriend." Janice moved to the door and they both went out. Taji tried with great difficulty to pull the boxer shorts onto the corpse. He had pushed both feet through and was rolling and lifting the body when he heard the rev of the john's car, followed by the sound of the shifting of the transmission.

What the fuck? Those bitches be bailing, he thought.

Letting the left leg fall, he ran around the bed and yanked open the door, pulling out the Bersa as he saw the gray Chevy peeling by him. The tires squealed as they spun on the slick pavement, causing the rear-end to fishtail. This threw off Taji's aim a little as he pumped all seven shots at the diminishing rear-end of the vehicle. It whirled around the corner, skidding again, then it was gone.

Shit, he thought. That motherfucking tape is still in the camcorder.

Taji started to run toward the front of the motel to see which way they'd gone, then thought better of it and darted back inside the room. He grabbed one of the towels and wrapped it around the stand for the lights, and carried the lights with him. Using another towel, he wiped down the entrance door. Taji took one more look around to make sure he hadn't left anything, then closed the door. Handling it only by the edges, he slipped the plastic *Do Not Disturb* sign on the knob, then headed around the back toward the narrow expanse of grass that separated this parking lot from the Holiday Inn. On the way there he paused and dumped the light assembly into the Dumpster.

Be cool, bro, he told himself. Real cool. Ain't nothing more suspicious than a black man leaving someplace in a hurry and hawking and looking back over his shoulder.

He forced himself to walk slow, with an enforced nonchalance even though he could feel the sweat beginning to drip from his armpits and down his back. Just like moving in the yard after he'd shanked some motherfucker.

Be cool, he told himself again. Almost there now.

His eyes scanned the parking lot in front of the hotel looking for the familiar lines of his big Caddie. The sooner he found it, the sooner he could get on the street and start looking for those two bitches and make them pay for putting him through all these changes. He wondered if he'd hit either one of them as they took off. Probably not. Seemed like the rain spoiled his aim.

He saw the Cadillac parked at the end of an aisle, gleaming under the pale luminescence of one of the big mercury vapor lights and felt he was almost home free. But only almost, because as long as that motherfucking videotape was floating around out there somewhere, Taji knew he was only dangling by a thread above a lifelong 10 × 12 cell in Stateville.

2
URINALYSIS

Sergeant Francisco Leal struggled to produce more than the pitiful trickle of drops that only splashed into the bottom of the plastic cup. He spat into the blue plastic trough of the Port-O-Potty and watched the spit curl its way down the hole. The viscous solution in the bottom of the toilet portion was dark blue too. The color, he'd been told, was to prevent people from using it to augment or dilute their urine samples. Not that he'd be tempted to dip the cup down in there even if it hadn't been. He pulled open the door and told the nurse that he needed another drink of water. She was a tough-looking, middle-aged woman, rather stout around the waist, with a face like a scowling bulldog. But, then again, thought Leal, who would have a happy face with a job like she had, handling other people's excrement all day long?

The nurse glanced up at him with a sharp expression and nodded, then held out her gloved hand. Leal made sure the cloth robe they'd made him wear was closed before handing over the plastic cup.

No sense giving her the thrill of her life, he thought.

His bare feet padded along in the cloth slippers, occasionally sticking to the tiled floor. He didn't have to wonder what was causing the stickiness, imagining thousands of spillage incidents coupled with infrequent mopping.

Leal wondered how he appeared to her shuffling along in the robe. Just another Latino in his mid-thirties, around six feet tall with the rangy build of a boxer? Although he was half Irish, he'd taken more of his Mexican coloring. In anticipation of spring, he'd gotten his black hair cut shorter than usual and, with regret, had shaved off his mustache. But then again, what he looked like to some bored nurse was the least of his worries right now. He leaned over the fountain and drank. Standing, he waited for the cold rush of the water to hit his stomach, then took another long drink. He was heading back toward the nurse's desk when he saw his partner, Olivia Hart, handing over her cup to the bulldog.

"Success?" he asked as he approached the table.

Hart smiled at him. She'd worn her blond hair down today and it hung around her broad shoulders in a profusion of curls. Even the thin cloth robe that they'd given her couldn't conceal the powerful symmetry of a bodybuilder's physique. As he appreciated the attractive refinement of her features, it excited Leal to think that they were both naked under the robes, and that, in turn, reminded him how long he'd gone without having sex. Three months since his break-up with Sharon.

"Luckily this wasn't one of my running days," Hart said, "or I'd have been dehydrated."

"I guess that's my problem," Leal said as the nurse handed him his empty cup and he headed back toward the Port-O-Potty. "Although I didn't run this morning either. I just skipped that extra cup of coffee on the way here." He held up his empty cup as he stepped inside. "At least they gave you a glove."

"Anatomical differences," Hart called out. "I'll wait for you by the dressing rooms."

Leal closed the door and opened the front of the robe.

Maybe if I could just relax, he thought. But at least it wasn't as bad as the piss tests in the army, where somebody stood there and watched till you urinated. They only did that here on your second trip, if there was something suspicious.

19

He thought about Tom Ryan, the sergeant in charge of his section, standing in the hallway this morning swirling his coffee cup and grinning with his thin, waspish smile.

"You guys have to go pee in the bottles," Ryan had said.

He'd also introduced them to a college kid named Alfred Tims, who was doing his internship with the County Sheriff's Police.

Alfred Tims, Leal thought, looked like a refugee from one of those old *Revenge of the Nerds* movies. He was tall and gangly, with his hair long and slicked back on top, but crewcut length around the sides. Although he wore a sport jacket and tie, his clothes looked like they'd been draped on a mannequin. A malformed mannequin. But what got Leal the most were Tims's thick plastic-framed glasses. As if to punctuate the cliché of his nerd-like appearance, the center of the glasses had been reinforced with a band of neatly cut duct tape. To make matters worse, he was constantly playing with either his smart phone or his iPad, which he carried in some kind of modified fannypack man-purse thing. Leal shook his head.

"Al," Ryan said, patting the tall youth on the back. "You can go with them, but this is one test you can skip."

Tims looked up from his iPad screen and started in with a grating laugh that sounded like someone trying to prime a rusty pump. After several guffaws, Leal looked at Ryan and grabbed Hart by the arm. "Come on, Ollie. Let's go get this bullshit over with."

The tests were designated as "random urinalysis" because you never knew when your two-times-a-year were coming up. You were informed as you reported in for work on that given day, so, in theory, if you were a regular drug abuser, there was no way that you could abstain so it wouldn't show up in the test.

Leal wondered about this randomness, though. Was it because

he had spent several years working in the narcotics division? Or were they worried that Hart used steroids to achieve her remarkable muscularity? The test didn't irk him as much as the fact that he was senior to Ryan in rank, having more time in grade. But Ryan was a consummate ass-kisser, and spent almost all of his waking hours sucking up to Lieutenant Card. Thus, any time a shit assignment came along in investigations, Leal didn't have to wonder who was first in line for it. But that was all right. He'd rather get the shitty end of the stick than live like Ryan, with his nose so far up Card's ass that he had to breathe through a straw.

He chuckled at the thought, then wondered what the nurse would be thinking if she heard him laughing in the Port-O-Potty.

Probably thinks I'm really bad off, he thought.

He went back to ruminating about work. I'm surrounded by assholes on and off the job, he thought. Ryan and Card, another asshole, *el supremo.*

Then he got an idea: Maybe if he imagined that instead of a plastic urine cup, he was holding the lieutenant's personally inscribed coffee mug. The one that he'd gotten at some awards banquet that said in gold embossed letters:

> *LT. DEXTER CARD*
> *INVESTIGATIONS COMMANDER*
> *COUNTY SHERIFF'S POLICE*

Leal closed his eyes and could almost see the gold letters against the green plastic background, and the stream of urine began to flow.

Olivia Hart unlocked the padlock that they'd given her to secure all her clothes and possessions in the locker. She stripped off the robe and took a deep breath before gathering up her underpants and bra. Her muscles danced under her taut skin as she dressed. She was in her late twenties . . . her very late twenties . . . almost at twenty-nine and holding, as her trainer, Rory Chalma, put it. But she felt good. Physically at least. She was doubly glad that she hadn't listened to Rory, who was always trying to get her to do a cycle of Deca-Durabolin or HGH to bulk up a little. That would look real good showing up on some urine screening. Sometimes Rory was such a jerk.

Hart slipped on her socks and then grabbed her blue jeans. One of the nice things about working in investigations was that she could wear whatever she wanted, within reason. And blue jeans suited her just fine. Why wear a dress when you might be crawling around some filthy crime scene or chasing some asshole down a city alley? And the jeans allowed her to wear her Smith and Wesson Model 19 strapped to her waist. She notched the belt in place and pulled on her white Reeboks, tying the laces in place by bending at the waist instead of sitting down. It stretched her back and leg muscles more that way. The stretch felt good in her legs.

Straightening up, she took the revolver from the top shelf of the locker and flipped open the magnum's cylinder to check it before placing the gun in its holster. She noticed that the belt felt snugger than usual. Was her period coming early? Pulling on her sleeveless white cotton blouse and grabbing her jacket, she felt the intermittent vibration of her cell phone.

It had been clipped to her belt in the locker and had gone off while she and Frank had been giving the samples. Hart flipped it open and saw that it was the number for headquarters along with a low battery warning. Lt. Card's office extension followed. She took a deep breath and closed the locker door.

Hart left the dressing room and approached the stern-looking nurse, who was hunched over the desk talking on the phone. The nurse's back was to Hart, and she could hear that the woman was very agitated at whomever she was talking with.

"Well, it'll be up to the lab to do the analysis," the nurse was saying. "If they need it in such a hurry they'll have to call the lab and tell them to rush. We just guarantee the integrity of the samples." The woman listened for a few moments more and then said, "Well, okay, I'll put a note on it. What's the name again?" Her latex-covered fingers sorted through a metallic basket that held several opaque plastic jars with labels affixed to each. "Okay, I have it here. I'll put the note on it, but tell them to make sure and call the lab, and tell them that it's needed before three o'clock then."

The nurse hung up the phone, then jotted something down on one of those sticky message papers and sealed it on one of the urine samples with a block of Scotch tape. She straightened up and regarded Hart with an exasperated smile.

"These damn people want everything in a hurry," the nurse muttered.

"Hi," Hart said. "I'm waiting for my partner, but I have to call in. My cell's out. Is there a phone around here I could use?"

"Sure, honey, you can use this one," the nurse said, indicating the one on the desk. Hart eyed the receiver, which was only inches away from the basket of urine samples, and smiled. Seeming to sense Hart's reticence, the nurse tore open a towelette and wiped off the instrument before handing it to her.

"Everybody's so worried about pathogens now days," the nurse said with a smile.

Brushing her hair back, Hart took the phone, vowing to wash her hands at the first opportunity, and dialed the number.

"This is Olivia Hart," she said to the secretary who answered. "I got beeped by the lieutenant."

She was put on hold for only a moment when a harsh voice came on the line.

"Hart, I called you three times. Where the hell you at?"

"We were told to report in for a urinalysis first thing this morning, sir," Hart said. She could picture Card leaning over the phone having one of what Ryan called the lieutenant's "Dexpepsia attacks." Card was thin and had a florid complexion. The stereotypical type A personality, he kept a steady supply of Tagamet antacid in his upper desk drawer.

"Oh," Card said. "Right. Well, how soon can you get out of there?"

"I expect we'll be finishing up shortly, sir," Hart said. "Is there something wrong?"

"No," Card said. "We're, ah, holding a crime scene for you two. It's at the Riptide Motel. Death investigation." He gave her the address. "Get over there ASAP. And make sure that Leal is the primary investigator on this one, understand? Leal's the primary."

"Yes, sir," Hart said. Her tone was uncertain.

She heard the lieutenant sigh, then he said, "Another thing. You two are to report in here at HQ no later than fifteen-thirty hours. And make sure you're not late. Chief Burton'll be here. Understand?"

"Yes, sir," Hart said, wondering what all this meant. "Can you tell me what this is regarding?"

"It'll be explained to you when you get here," he said. Then added, "It's nothing to worry about. You got that college kid, Tims, with you?"

"He's in the waiting room."

"Good, good," Card said. "Comes with a very high scholastic record from Western. That's a good law enforcement school."

I know, Hart thought. I went there. "Is there anything else, sir?"

"No, just remember to report here by fifteen-thirty."

When Hart hung up the phone she realized that the nurse

had been staring at her. She handed the receiver back to the woman, then she heard Leal's voice.

"I finally figured out what I was doing wrong," he yelled. "I just pretended I was bringing Ryan some coffee, and it was Card's cup."

Hart smiled. The nurse came around the table to inspect Leal's bottle and slap the seal on it. While she was doing that Hart glanced down at the message slip that she'd seen the nurse scribbling on before. It read: *Hart, Olivia—Lab, there's a rush job on this one.*

Why the hell would they want a quick analysis of my urine? Hart wondered. Do they suspect me of something? She drew in a deep breath as Leal brushed by her.

"I'll be out in a flash," he said, snapping the elastic band that held the locker key on his wrist.

"Okay," she said. "We've got a DOA waiting for us."

3
FAMILIAR FACES

Leal glanced in the rearview mirror and caught a glimpse of Alfred Tims, who was straddling the back of the front seat, his eyes glancing down at Hart as she leaned back to stretch in the front passenger seat. He seemed to have set aside his smart phone for the moment.

The geek's checking out Ollie's tits, Leal thought. He may be a nerd, but at least he's a red-blooded, heterosexual nerd.

He cast a quick glance at Hart himself as she leaned back, the solid muscles of her deltoids and triceps standing out in chiseled relief. Her breasts looked nice, too, straining at the fabric as she stretched. The cooler temperature must have been affecting her too, because her nipples were jutting out against the front of her blouse and for a moment Leal thought about what it'd be like to check them out in the flesh. But he knew that he had about as much of a chance as Tims of seeing more of them.

"So, Al," Leal said, "what made you decide to go into police work?"

The gangling college boy turned his head toward Leal and smiled. "I want to join the FBI," Tims said. "But they don't do internships."

"You want to be a Fed, eh?"

"Yeah," Tims answered. "I figure it's the best way to stay outta jail." Leal saw the simpering grin fill the rearview mirror again. It was almost as if the kid's face crunched together in the middle, making it look more like a grimace than a smile.

"Jail?" Hart asked. "Planning on committing a crime?"

"I'm a hacker," Tims said. "Figured that I might as well join the FBI so I wouldn't get in trouble for all the systems I break into. Get paid for it too."

He laughed, setting Leal's teeth on edge. It sounded like the grating of a rusty pump handle. Leal glanced at Ollie, who didn't seem to mind the sound.

"So what dorm did you stay in when you went to Western?" Tims asked Hart.

"I stayed in Washington," she said. "How about you?"

"Henninger my first three years," Tims said. Leal saw the kid's eyes were still peering downward behind the thick frame of his glasses.

"You want to sit back in the seat, Al?" Leal said. "I gotta see in the mirror."

"Maybe I could just tell you who was coming," Tims said, and honked his laugh once more. Leal shot him a mean look in the rearview mirror, and the geek sat back.

"Put on your seatbelt, too," Leal said, then asked Hart, "Know anything about this one?"

"No," she said. "Just that they're holding it for us at the Riptide Motel."

She looked preoccupied. He hoped she wasn't worried about anything. She'd seemed okay until they'd left the piss-test place. Could she actually be doing 'roids?

"I didn't even know that place was ours," Leal said. "Thought it was in Alsip."

"Me either, but I guess they never incorporated into the city limits," Hart said. "And they want you to be the primary."

"Huh? Why's that?"

"I'm not sure," she said. "That's just what the lieutenant told me."

"Fuck him," Leal said, then regretted it a second later, realizing that they were so used to being by themselves that he had forgotten about the extra pair of ears. Tims's thumbs were working overtime on his smart phone.

"Ah, exactly what are you doing there, Al?" Leal asked.

"Well, I'm tweeting now. Telling people I'm at a homicide scene, just like CSI."

"I'd appreciate it if you would curtail that until I've had a chance to look over what you've written," Leal said. "There are certain things we may not want broadcast."

Tims looked at him with a goofy expression.

"So no more tweeting," Leal said, pointing to the smart phone. "Got it?"

Tims stared at him a few moments more, then nodded. "But I gotta write a paper about my experiences riding along with you guys."

"Well, I hope you're not going to quote me on what I just said," Leal said, with what he hoped was an ingratiating smile.

"What was that?" Tims asked with a big grin. "I didn't hear you after you said, 'Fuck him.' " He punctuated his statement with the laugh again, and Leal's smile faded.

Just what I need, he thought. This little idiot tweeting that over the Internet.

As they approached the entrance to the motel, two marked county squads had the entrance way blocked off. The uniform officers glanced at the unmarked and motioned for them to halt.

"Leal, Investigations South," he said, holding up his badge. "Where's it at?"

"Around the back, Sarge," the patrolman said. "Room thirteen."

"You getting names and plate numbers of everybody that's here?" Leal asked.

"Yeah," the patrolman answered. "But with the turnover in this place, anybody who mighta' been around here last night is probably long gone. Christ, we've already had to turn away half a dozen people who wanted to stop in and grab a quickie."

Leal frowned and drove into the lot. The Riptide was a two-story dark brick structure shaped like an L. The office sat in the front of the lot, with the rooms sitting back-to-back along the side. A gap large enough to accommodate pedestrian traffic, but not an auto, divided the front set of rooms from those facing away from the office side. The purple colored *VACANCY* sign in the window of the office was still lit. On the roof of the building two larger neon signs advertised *4-HOUR-NAP RATES* and *WATER BEDS AVAILABLE*. Leal pulled down to the end of the parking lot and swung around the corner. Two more marked units were parked there, as well as an unmarked and the evidence technician's blue van.

"Looks like the Body Snatcher's here," Leal said.

Hart nodded.

"Who's that?" Tims asked.

"Henry Morgan, one of our evidence techs," Leal said, pulling up behind the unmarked and shifting into park. "Real thorough guy. He sorta steals the scene from you, hence his nickname. Get it?"

Tims just nodded his head, scribbling with his tongue protruding from between his teeth as his thumbs went to work on the iPad again.

As they got out, Leal said to him, "Okay, Al, there's some ground rules here. First, don't touch anything. Second, don't drop anything. And third," he paused to sigh, "you'll have to wait out here in the parking lot."

Tims's face fell, but he made no protest.

"Okay," he said. He leaned back against the car fender and watched as Leal and Hart walked down the sidewalk together, each snapping on a pair of latex gloves from small pouches on their respective belts. "Hey, can I get some gloves like that?" he called after them.

"Sure, Al," said Leal over his shoulder. "A buck a pack in the motel office, but you'll have to buy one for each finger. They're called Trojans."

Hart shot him a sideways smile.

Tom Ryan was standing just outside the door of room thirteen, a smoldering cigarette in his hand. Another uniformed copper stood beside him with a metallic clipboard. Ryan glanced over his shoulder at them, then turned around with a grin. He was a thin man in his late thirties, with a large bushy mustache and oval glasses. His sport jacket seemed to be too large for him.

He stared at Hart's breasts and raised his eyebrows. "Well, is it getting colder out, or are you just glad to see me?" he said, the grin growing broader under the heavy mustache.

"What are you talking about?" Hart asked.

"Just admiring your headlights."

Hart frowned. "Give it a rest, Ryan. I forgot to take my ass-hole tolerance medication this morning."

"What we got?" Leal asked.

"Come on," Ryan said, taking another drag on his cigarette. "Log these two in, Bret. Frank Leal and Olivia Hart. That's H-A-R-T, not like the organ." Ryan smirked and then added, "She's the one with the prominent nipples." The patrol officer scribbled their names on the crime scene log sheet. "Welcome to lucky thirteen."

But as Ryan stepped into the room, a heavy-set black man, who was hunched over with a huge digital camera, said, "Don't you even think about coming in here with that square and contaminating my crime scene." The man wore a black sport shirt, a black White Sox baseball cap, and blue jeans. His hands were glossy looking under the latex gloves, and he had a large quantity of wooden pencils in his shirt pocket. His badge and weapon were clipped on his belt, along with various other knives, screwdrivers, and tools.

Ryan paused, took one more drag, then tossed the cigarette out the door.

"Satisfied, your highness?" he mumbled.

The black guy continued to adjust the lens on his camera, saying nothing.

"Henry, how you doing?" Leal said.

"Frank. Ollie," Morgan said, nodding with each name.

"The room was rented last night by this dude," Ryan said. "Used the name Robert Woods. California D.L. Lindsey's up front there going through the registration cards with the owner. The night clerk don't start till eight, and her phone's off the hook." He pointed to the corpse. "This guy looks familiar doesn't he? Like an old movie star or something."

Leal moved with slow deliberation toward the corpse. The man was on the floor beside the bed, lying on his left side, his face discolored on the bottom, his cheek in a rigid fold against a fallen pillow, sealing his face in a frozen wink. He was nude except for some boxer shorts that were pulled up to just under a now rigid dollop of fat on his buttocks. A dense scarlet discoloration had settled along the lower portion of the torso.

"Looks like just another stiff to me," Leal said. "Whatta ya got so far, Henry?"

The Body Snatcher had lowered his camera and exhaled.

"My best guestimate is twelve hours, or so," he said. "That'd put it somewhere in the late evening last night. Hard to tell without a liver temp, and I ain't about to do that. Lividity settled here," he ran his gloved fingers along the man's darkened left side. "He's stiff, too. Got some darkening here," he pointed to the neck, "and his eyes are splotchy and all busted up inside,

31

which makes me think maybe he was choked to death." He pointed to the lips, which were also discolored.

"So we're talking homicide here?" Leal asked.

The Body Snatcher nodded.

Leal took out his notebook. He'd leave the official crime scene sketch to Henry, but he always drew a rudimentary one for his own notes. Hart had her book out too, scribbling down her observations.

"After I get all my shots," Morgan said, "I'll start vacuuming and sprinkling. I want to take them sheets too. And tell the meat wagon goons not to tilt him getting him into the body bag so he don't void. I don't want to have to go through a lot of shit later."

"Okay," Leal said. "The ME coming out?"

"Ain't you done heard?" Morgan said. "*Quincy* got cancelled a long, long time ago. Only shows up on old cable reruns now, and he was the only ME ever come out to crime scenes. Even the CSI guys and girls know better than to ask for him."

Leal nodded with a smile, then turned to Ryan.

"Did anybody remember what kind of car he drove?" he asked. Ryan shook his head.

"Just that it was gone," he said. "The maid found the body at ten-thirty. Checkout time. The *DO NOT DISTURB* sign was hung on the door, so she didn't try to go in before that."

"Where's she at? We'd better talk to her," Leal said.

"In the office," Ryan answered.

"I'll go, Frank," Hart said, stripping off her latex gloves and compressing them into a little ball. "You might as well stay here since you'll be the primary."

"Whoa, iron maiden," Ryan said grinning. "How did you decide that?"

"I didn't," Hart said. "The lieutenant did." She pressed the balled-up gloves into Ryan's hand, turned, and left the room.

"Christ, what's eating her?" asked Ryan, looking around and catching a baleful stare from the Body Snatcher, then sticking the gloves in his pocket. "She on the rag, or something?"

"Why don't you ask her?" Leal said. He knew better than to try and defend Ollie in front of the other guys. She was adept at fighting her own battles, especially with someone like Ryan, whom she usually just ignored.

"Maybe I will," Ryan said. "Christ, I'll bet she's got nipples you could hang a coat on, huh, Frankie?"

Leal was just about to answer that he wouldn't know when he heard someone say his name, and Alfred Tims appeared in the doorway. The patrol officer blocked Tims's entry into the room, but the intern's face crunched up again as he tried to get a look at the body.

"Hey, Frank," Tims said, holding up his hand. "Look what I found. Is this important?"

"Who the hell is that?" Morgan said, staring at Tims, who tried to squeeze past the uniformed officer. Morgan let out a sound like a car alarm going off, which stopped Tims in his tracks. "Get the hell outta here. Don't even think about coming into my crime scene."

Leal moved forward and ushered Tims away from the door. "Al, I know you don't mean any harm, but you'll have to wait over by the cars until we're finished processing. I'll walk you through everything later, okay?"

Tims pushed his glasses back up on his nose and nodded. Then he opened his hand and held out a shell casing. The hollow end had been flattened. "This is what I found over there," he said, pointing a few feet away. Tims held up his phone and snapped a picture.

"You best be deleting that, Mr. Geek," Morgan said.

Tims grinned.

Leal picked the casing up and looked at it. A .380. He

33

dropped it into a small manila envelope. "Show me." He motioned for Ryan to follow him. "And delete that last photo, Al. Now."

Tims played with his smart phone as they walked over to the unmarked and pointed. Leal began circling the area and found another shell, then another. In all, six more casings were found. Some had been run over, but others still seemed in good shape.

"I guess nobody did a grid search of the lot, huh?" Leal said to Ryan.

The other man shrugged. "Hadn't gotten to it yet."

"Tell Henry that I want him to get some shots of these," Leal said and turned to the intern. "Good job, Al, but next time, don't pick anything up until we've had a chance to look at it first, all right?"

"Yeah, sorry," Tims said. "I thought it being kinda crushed made it okay to pick up." He bumped his glasses up again, then glanced around with a squinting look. "Where's Ollie?"

"She's up front talking to a witness," Leal said.

"Oh," Tims said. He kicked his feet, then said, "Maybe I'll go up there then."

"You delete that photo?" Leal asked.

Tims nodded as he walked off in the direction of the office. Morgan came up and studied the scattered casings.

"Who, or should I say what, is that?" he said nodding his head toward the departing Tims.

"Some intern that's riding with us," Leal answered. "Ryan saddled us with him."

Morgan shook his head.

"Looks like one of them weird motherfuckers from that old *Revenge of the Nerds* movie," he said. He focused the camera for the shot. "Or a fugitive from the geek squad. But looks can be deceiving, I guess, since he was the one found the shell casings. Guess I shoulda used a wider circle for my search radius.

Specially if I'd known you were bringing some fugitive from the geek squad."

"Hey, the orders came down from upstairs," Ryan said. "I had no choice in the matter. But just for the record, there's no way I think that kid has any business even thinking about becoming a police officer."

Morgan snapped a picture. "Ain't that what you always say about us minorities?"

He snapped a second picture and looked up at Leal with a grin. Leal grinned back.

The processing of the room took another hour. Morgan made a thorough examination of the sheets, finding what appeared to be pubic hairs. He vacuumed carefully with his small machine. The black light examination also showed the presence of semen stains.

"Wonder if the poor motherfucker got his rocks off before he died," he said.

"Looks like somebody did," Leal said. "Of course, that's depending on how many times a day they change the sheets."

When Morgan began checking for prints he found only smooth counters everywhere. "Seems like this place has been wiped clean, Frank."

Leal nodded. He was concerned that the victim's clothes, watch, and shoes were in the room, but his wallet and car keys were missing. The corpse also had an expensive-looking ring on its left hand.

"Wait a minute," Morgan said. He took his brush and powder into the bathroom and began dusting. The doorjamb was clean also, but when he got to the toilet seat, it was down.

"Maybe, just maybe . . ." Morgan said, letting his voice trail off. He kneeled next to the commode and feathered the brush over the surface. Dark lines began to appear. He looked up at

Leal and grinned. "Guess he had a lady with him."

The only other item of interest that turned up was a circular plastic cover of some sort. Leal at first thought that the Body Snatcher had dropped the lens cover for his camera, but Henry scolded him for even thinking such a thing. He bagged it and put it with the other recoveries in an open cardboard box. Then Leal helped Henry load the box and the rest of the items he'd designated into the van. They wrapped the body and assisted the two paramedics from the private ambulance service in placing it in the black body bag for transportation to the morgue. Leal and Henry made plans to meet later and shook hands. It was the first time they'd had their latex gloves off since they'd gone in the room. Leal went down to the office to see how Hart was doing.

"This ain't gonna be in the papers, is it?" the owner asked. "I got enough problems attracting a decent clientele." He was a short Italian guy with thinning gray hair and a huge belly. Dark hair sprouted through the open collar of his polo shirt.

He paced back and forth in the small aisle of the motel office. Beyond the immediate reception area, which was encased in Plexiglas, Leal could see what must have been the man's living quarters. Hart sat at a small, folding table, across from a young girl who was obviously the maid. She was in her early twenties and dressed in a short-sleeve sweatshirt and jeans. Albert Tims stood across from them, leaning against the wall.

"I'm afraid that's not up to us," Hart told him. "The initial police reports are a matter of public record." Leal glanced over her shoulder at the notes she'd made from her interview with the maid.

"How often do you change the sheets, Mr. Devroni?" Leal asked.

"Oh, please," the proprietor said, looking offended. "We

change every time somebody checks out. Right, Anna?"

The maid, a pretty, dark-haired young girl, nodded.

"We got our own washers here," Devroni continued.

"This is Anna Rutkowsky," Hart said. "From Poland. She found the body about ten-thirty. She knocked and when no one answered, she used the pass-key to go in. She saw the man lying on the floor and ran over here."

"Did you touch anything in the room, Anna?" Leal asked.

He figured Hart had already asked that, but they always overlapped on their questions, making sure that people's answers were the same in each case.

"I open door and see him on floor," Anna said. "I say, 'Hello, sir, you have to leave now.' I think he drunk, but he so funny looking. I touch him, to wake him up, but then I feel he is hard." She brought her hands up to her face and began sobbing.

"We'd just gotten over this crying before you walked in," Hart said, the irritation noticeable in her voice, and Leal wondered if she was mad at him, or at the maid for starting to cry again.

"You find the registration card?" he asked.

"Yeah," she said. She pulled a three-by-five index card with a license plate scribbled on the front. "It's a rental. I already called it in."

Leal noted that the information on the card listed a California address and phone number for Robert Woods.

"The address and phone number are phonies too," she said.

"The D.L. number was either mis-copied or fraudulent. It comes back invalid."

Leal noticed an undercurrent of tension in her tone. "We need anything else here?" he asked.

She shook her head. "Ryan and Lindsey took the night clerk's home address and left to interview her."

"I can't believe that Ryan showed up at one of our crime scenes and did some work," Leal said with a grin.

Hart smiled a lips-only smile. Leal wondered what was wrong with her. Maybe Ryan was right. It could be that time of the month. "We'd better do a check of the Dumpsters too."

"Yeah, but we'll have to make it quick," she said, glancing at her watch. "I forgot to mention that I've got to see the lieutenant before fifteen-thirty."

4
A SLIGHT INTEGRITY
PROBLEM

As Leal drove the car through the escalating traffic of the Eisenhower, no one spoke much. Ollie just sat and stared out the window, the space between her brows creased. Tims seemed to have abandoned his surreptitious glance over the front seat at Hart's décolletage in favor of his prolific scribblings. Leal wondered what was bothering Ollie. Even as they exited the expressway and coasted through an unusual series of green lights on the way in to headquarters Hart was still silent.

Maybe she's pissed that I asked her to do the Dumpster dive, he thought. That had yielded a set of lights, the kind used for videotaping or something. Those, along with the lens cap in the room, made Leal suspect that they could be related to the crime.

The base of operations for the County Sheriff's Police was located in an area that had transformed from Chicago's West Side into an equally crowded suburban sprawl. Located behind a massive Commonwealth Edison plant, the headquarters was in an almost quaint-looking red brick building composed of three connected sections: the academy, the headquarters, and the administration.

Leal drove around the lot twice searching for a parking place, then did what he always did: parked in the Fourth District courthouse lot. They got out and began walking toward the three buildings, the two outer wings fanning outward from the center section that was their destination. Leal was having trouble keeping up with Hart's brisk pace. Tims, who was jogging along behind them with his perpetual squint, asked what was next.

"What's the hurry?" he asked.

"We have to go in and sit on our asses for an hour while we wait to talk to the boss," Leal said. Once again, he regretted it a moment later as he noticed Tims furiously typing into his smart phone with his thumbs.

"Tweeting again, Al?" Leal asked.

The intern grunted.

"Well," Leal said, "we've got to report in."

"Maybe I'll just go home then," Tims said. "I got something to do tonight."

"Yeah," Leal said. "Go out and enjoy your Friday night. You're only young once."

"We won't do much more today anyway except log and tag our evidence," Hart said. "The first step will be to get the victim ID'd." She stopped and held her hand out toward the intern. "Anyway, it was nice meeting you, Al. Good luck."

Tims ducked his head as he shook hands with Hart. "See you Monday, I guess," he said over his shoulder as he walked away.

"I wonder why he didn't shake hands with me?" Leal said, staring after him. He shook his head. "That's one weird dude."

"Oh, Frank," Hart said. "He's not so bad. He's just a kid."

"He's not that young," Leal said. He was about to tell her that "the kid" had been looking at her tits, but he remembered her distracted mood and decided not to mention it. "Card say what this was all about?"

Hart shook her head. "But I did overhear the nurse at the clinic tag my urine sample for a rush analysis."

"Your sample?" Leal said, perplexed. "What about mine?"

"I don't know."

"Ah, well, it's probably nothing to worry about," Leal said. "Right?"

"I hope not," Hart answered. They walked along the sidewalk

toward the two-story red brick building with the four white pillars in front.

The headquarters section of the County Sheriff's Police was in the center building, flanked on one side by the crime lab and on the other by the police academy. Lieutenant Card's office was on the second floor. Leal opened the door for Hart, and they both went to the winding stairwell just to the right of the doors. When they got upstairs, they saw Ryan ambling about in the hall.

"What the hell you doing here?" Leal asked. "I thought you were out interviewing that night clerk for us."

"Relax, Frank, would ya," Ryan said. He paused to stick an unlit cigarette between his lips. "I got called back in. But we talked to the gal from the motel. Lindsey's typing up the supplemental for you as we speak."

"What's Card want with us?" Leal asked.

"I don't know," Ryan said with a shrug. "I gotta hunch it's about a transfer though."

"What?" Leal said. "Whose?"

Ryan shrugged again. "Beats me, but my squeeze tells me they been pulling a lot of personnel files recently."

Ryan's girlfriend, who worked in personnel, kept him pretty well filled in on any pending developments. It was one of the ways that Ryan was able to land, cat-like, on his feet, whenever any shake-up came down. Michael Shay, who'd beaten the perennial Democratic machine candidate who had ruled the office for over twenty years, had spent the previous year-and-a-half since his election sticking his own patronage agents in every section of the Sheriff's Department. Leal had thought that Howard Lindsey, one of Shay's fair-haired boys, would be the only "political appointee" to the Investigations South Division. He'd even tolerated Lindsey's inept attempts at being a detective, figuring that he'd eventually pick up some tricks. But Leal had also figured that he and Ollie were safe from Shay's axe because they were both classified as "minorities."

"I didn't request a transfer, did you?" Leal asked Hart.

She shook her head.

"Maybe it'll just be a temporary assignment, like the Robertsville detail," Ryan said. Hart had spent the better part of a year working in uniform on that one.

"Christ, I hope not," Leal said. "I hope you at least fight for us. You're in charge of the section."

"Don't I always." Ryan took the cigarette from between his lips, looked at it, sighed and slipped it back into his pack. "Let's go see Lt. Dexpepsia."

Lieutenant Dexter Card was a pale, almost anorexic-looking man in his late forties. He kept his dark hair combed straight back from his face, which made his head seem larger than it was. This, in turn, called more attention to his slender neck. The veins in his neck stood out as he sat behind his large gunmetal gray desk and addressed the three of them.

"All right," Card said. "This is not the way I intended on doing this, but since you're all here, I might as well make it short and sweet." He paused to run his tongue over his upper teeth. When he spoke again, his lower lip draped down like a curtain, revealing an uneven row of dentition. "There's going to be some more transfers within this section. Hart, you're to report to Chief Burton's office for reassignment. Leal, you'll be getting your new partner on Monday."

"When do I report?" Hart asked.

"Now," Card said.

After glancing at Ryan, Leal said, "Wait a minute." Card's head turned toward him, his lips drawing together. "We just started a new homicide investigation, Lieutenant."

"I'm aware of that," Card said. "That's why you were

designated as the primary."

Leal leaned forward, shaking his head before he spoke.

"This is not going to help the investigation, taking one of the officers who investigated the scene off the case, Lieu. I mean, how the hell do you expect us to clear it if you take one of us out just as we're building momentum?"

"Leal," Card said, his lips quivering, "did you hear what I just said?" He paused for effect. "This is a decision from upstairs. You get that?"

"I got it, sir," Leal said. "But for the record, I disagree with it totally."

"Oh, you do," Card said, his large head rocking. "Well, maybe I should look into getting somebody else transferred outta here too, if you don't like the way things are being run here."

Leal was about to say that he'd worn a uniform before, and could do it again, but didn't. He remembered that his clout, Captain Sean O'Herlieghy, was still out recovering from a heart attack. The veins in Card's neck seemed to pulse and his face looked mottled. He turned to Ollie.

"Hart, report to Chief Burton now. Ryan, personnel is holding two files. Go get them and bring them back here. Leal, plant yourself in that chair." He pointed toward the chair in front of the big desk. The chair that was reserved for ass-chewings. Hart and Ryan turned to leave. Leal sighed, massaging his temples as he went to the hotseat. But as he sat down, he saw the lieutenant's commemorative mug, thought of this morning's urinalysis, and smiled to himself.

In the hallway outside Hart watched as Ryan pulled out his pack and shook out a new cigarette. Having to be close to someone smoking made her throat tighten and she widened the distance between them as they walked. The hallway was deserted and she knew Ryan would have no compunction about lighting up even though it technically wasn't allowed.

"Look, Ollie," Ryan said, pausing to cup his hand in front of the flickering lighter. "I feel bad about this. I want you to know that I had nothing to do with it."

Yeah, right, she thought. They moved toward the stairway. "You know why the Chief wants to see me?"

"Uh-uh," Ryan said. "Like I told you, this whole thing was a big surprise to me. I'll see if I can talk to Card when he gets over this latest Dexpepsia attack. It didn't help that Frank got him all pissed off, though."

"Yeah, I know," Hart said. "But that's Frank." The smoke was getting to her now, stinging her eyes. "Why the hell are you smoking inside? You ever hear about the Clean Air Act?"

Ryan shrugged. "Nobody gives a shit."

"I do."

Ryan shrugged again and took another drag. "You know, I just can't figure out what they're thinking." The smoke drifted from his lips with each word. "I mean, you and Frank have one of the highest clearance records in the section."

A lot of good that did me, she thought, pausing at the stairs where Ryan had to go down to the first floor. He held out his hand and Hart shook it.

"You and Frank are the best," Ryan said, descending the winding staircase. "I mean that. I'll bring that to Card's attention."

Hart watched him, the smoke rising upward like a translucent shroud, then continued down the hallway. Sometimes he even came close to being a decent guy, she thought. But then her mind moved forward to the present situation. She had only met the Chief once before when he'd presented her a commendation. He was an ex–Chicago cop who'd been Shay's partner when they'd both been on the city, and had the reputation for being a take-charge kind of guy. Other than that, she didn't know much about him. Hart opened the office door and saw a stunning-looking black girl sitting behind a walnut desk talking on the phone. The girl had a medium complexion and high cheekbones, which were accentuated by her flawless makeup. She smiled up at Hart as she covered the receiver of the phone. "You're Olivia Hart?" the secretary asked. Ollie nodded.

The secretary purred into the receiver, then pressed the button to disconnect the call. Hart noticed that the woman's fingernails had been painted with some exotic design.

"You can go right in, Olivia. The Chief's expecting you." As Hart opened the door to the inner office, she saw Chief Jack Burton sitting behind a formidable oak desk. Several chairs had been positioned in front, and the walls were decorated with various framed degrees, certificates, and photographs. On the back wall a large, recessed window, which had heavy curtains pulled to each side, provided a view of the pleasant wooded area behind the facility.

Another man sat to the left of the desk. His head lolled back in laughter as the Chief seemed to be in the process of delivering the punch line of a dirty joke. Hart moved forward and both men stood up. Burton, who was a handsome man, extended a huge hand across his desk and smiled with a practiced ease. He had sandy-colored hair that was thick and wavy. His eyes were light blue, almost pale looking. As Hart reached forward to grasp his hand, she realized that the Chief's hair was way too thick to be natural.

"Detective Hart," Chief Burton said. He indicated the chair in front of the desk, and then slipped into his own seat. "A pleasure to meet you. Do you know Captain Florian from I.A.D.?"

Hart glanced at the other man and smiled as she nodded an acknowledgment. She knew Florian by name only, as head of the Internal Affairs Division. Up close, she saw that he was in his early fifties with a large handlebar mustache and heavily oiled dark hair. The waxed ends of his mustache, as well as his reputation for ruthlessness, had earned him the covert nickname of Snidely Whiplash among the rank and file. Florian's lips drew back into a smile. The man had small teeth that slanted inward, which, coupled with his expansive mustache, gave him a somewhat sly and sinister look.

Oh, my God, Hart thought. That mustache . . . Doesn't he know they're not even in style anymore.

"Would you like some coffee?" Burton asked, grabbing the phone. "How do you like it?"

"Black is fine, sir," Hart said.

"Janetta," Burton said into the phone. "Bring us three coffees, one black, one cream and sugar, and my usual. Please." His voice had a big, brassy sound to it. He hung up the phone and looked at Hart.

"You're probably wondering what's going on, aren't you?" he said. "Let me begin by telling you that I'm familiar with your record. It's exemplary." His big forefinger tapped a manila file on the desk in front of him. "We called you up here for a very important assignment, Olivia."

The Chief paused when the door opened and Janetta brought in a tray with three steaming mugs on it. She handed one to Hart, saying, "Black, right?" Hart nodded. The secretary gave the second cup to Florian, then went around the desk and set the third mug in front of the Chief. Their hands brushed against each other as she set it down and Hart wondered exactly what his "usual" was.

Hart sipped the hot brew from her mug. It tasted like some flavored brand.

"As I was saying," Burton continued after Janetta had closed the door behind her. "You've been selected for a very special assignment. Are you familiar with directive sixteen eighty-four?"

Hart shook her head.

Burton laughed.

"Sorry, you get behind a desk and you forget that all these directives are just so much mumbo-jumbo to someone who works the street all the time," he said, grabbing a sheet of paper from the manila file on the desk and handing it to her.

Hart read that as of February 14th all search warrants, arrest warrants, and special operations were to be carried out by the Tactical Division. It went on to say that no member of Vice, Narcotics (MEG), or Fugitive Warrants was to execute a search/arrest warrant without the specific approval of the Commander of the Patrol Division.

Hart looked up from the paper to see that both men were watching her. She handed the form back to the Chief.

"Let me show you another bit of information," Burton said, handing a second sheet across the desk. "This one shows the amounts of moneys recovered in narcotic raids for the past three years, in a month-by-month breakdown."

Hart glanced at the columns of figures, trying to make sense of them.

"As you can obviously see," Burton continued, "there's been a drastic drop-off of recovered funds in the past several months. I don't have to tell you how important these recoveries are to our war-on-drugs effort. We thought we could address the problem by having the Tactical Unit conduct all the raids in tandem with the MEG units. I've even been reviewing and directing the sequence in which warrants are to be executed." He paused and licked his lips, his expression somber. "But, frankly, this hasn't corrected the problem."

"In other words," Captain Florian interjected, "somewhere within the group, we have a slight integrity problem."

Oh no, Hart thought. Are they going to reassign me to I.A.D.?

"That's where you come in, Detective Hart," the Chief said.

"You're being assigned to the Tactical Unit. We have to have a man on the inside." He smiled, then added, "Detective Hart, you are that person. We've gone over your background carefully, and we have complete confidence that you're the best choice for an assignment like this."

Hart felt a bit of relief at not being directly assigned to Internal Affairs, but Tactical? It was like being drafted into the Marines.

"All of my people are too well known," Florian said. "And if we put in a man from another agency –"

"Horseshit!" Burton said. "Pardon my French, but, dammit, we've got to clean our own ranks on this one." He stared directly at Hart. "We feel that putting in a female will arouse less suspicion than a male. It's a decision that seems to fit with the sheriff's commitment to promoting women and minorities within the department."

"You'll report directly to the Chief." Florian grinned. "I know this has kind of hit you with a lot all at once, but you can understand our need for absolute secrecy. So, I won't be meeting with you again until the proper time. It'll be less suspicious that way."

"We really need to get the goods on these," Burton paused, glancing down at the desk, "bad cops." He looked up at Hart and smiled. "You're to keep your eyes and ears open. When we got something solid enough to move on, we'll take 'em down." His lower lip jutted out for emphasis. "And it goes without saying that both Sheriff Shay and myself will be very appreciative of your efforts in this assignment."

"I'll do my best, sir," Hart said, realizing that refusal was not among her options, and feeling a creeping dread beginning to collect inside her gut.

"Good, good," Burton said. He handed her a sealed envelope. "This contains your transfer orders. Take the weekend off and report Monday morning to the FBI Training Center at the Great Lakes Naval Base. You'll have to complete the week-long SWAT school before you can be assigned to the raid team."

"It's a pretty rigorous school," Florian said. "But we're familiar with your physical fitness, bodybuilding background so we figured it wouldn't be a problem for someone like you."

Hart suddenly realized why the clinic had received the rush order for her urine specimen. They were doing a last minute check on her before ordering her to do this assignment.

"There's also a purchase order for all your gear in there," the Chief said, indicating the envelope. "As well as a description of the course and a list of what equipment you'll need. You can draw your own squad out of the motor pool, and just submit the standard vouchers for any hotel bill while you're up at the school."

"Unless you want to try and drive it every day," Florian said. He smiled his unctuous smile again. "But that'd be pretty hard considering it's way the hell up there in Lake County."

Hart smiled at him. Like I have much of a choice about that either, she thought.

"Do you have any questions, Detective?" the Chief said, leaning back in his chair.

Sensing that she was being dismissed, Hart said that she didn't and stood up. The Chief shifted to his feet and stuck his big hand across the desk, telling her good luck as they shook. "I'll expect to hear a good report of your performance in the school. I'll also expect biweekly reports on your progress once you've gotten established. You can turn them in to my secretary."

She turned and saw Captain Florian holding up his index finger.

"One more thing, Hart," he said. "You are to consider this your preeminent assignment. If any word of this leaks out, the entire operation could be jeopardized. Therefore, this is a direct order. You are to tell no one of this assignment, understand? No one," he repeated. "Not your mother, your father your partner, your lover . . . if we find out that you have . . ." He left the sentence incomplete. "Have I made myself clear?"

"I understand, sir," Hart said. She turned to leave and closed the door behind her. In the outer office, she saw that Janetta was applying some clear gloss to her sculptured nails.

The secretary looked up at Hart and smiled. Ollie smiled back, but as she left she felt very much alone.

5
CONVERSATIONS PAST AND PRESENT

When Leal got home, the first thing he did was go around to each room and turn on a light. Doing that made the place feel warm and welcome, even if there was nobody else there.

It was one of those big frame houses with two stories on the far southwest side that he and Claire had moved into right after they'd gotten married. Plenty of rooms upstairs for the kids. When things had gone sour with his marriage, he'd moved out to a small apartment, leaving the house for his family. Then Claire had called him with the news that he could move back—because she was taking the promotion/transfer to L.A. that she'd always wanted. The kids, she'd said, had decided to go with her.

To minimize any residual bitterness and hard feelings, for the sake of his kids, Leal didn't object to them going out of state. As long as he'd be able to see them periodically. It was a fight he knew he couldn't win. Not with his job, his hours, his never being home. So he moved back into that big empty house with so many memories.

He walked to the answering machine, stripping off his sport coat, and saw the blinking red light. He pressed the button and listened, hoping in his heart that it would be Sharon, but knowing in his gut that it wouldn't be.

"Hello, Frank, it's Ollie," the recording played. "Give me a call when you get home, or beep me on the cell if I don't answer, okay. I've got to do some shopping and go to the gym. Bye."

Leal sighed and glanced at his watch. It was eight forty-five. He went to the kitchen to rummage through his refrigerator, finding the cold remnants of a bucket of fried chicken that he'd purchased a few days earlier. He was beginning to get that same tightening feeling in his gut. The one that always came after the initial investigative work was done on an unsolved homicide. The pressure building up as you knew you were running a catch-up race against time and a killer who was already several laps ahead. You could only hope that he'd stumble, or drop something, and give you a chance to catch him. But at least this case wasn't a "heater"—some politically heavy or famous victim that the press would latch onto. It seemed routine at this point. Nothing more to do until they could get the victim ID'd.

Grabbing a can of Old Style to go with the bucket, he moved to the TV tray in the living room and set the food down. It was an expansive room with a large screen television, three modernistic lamps, and a thin blue carpet. The furniture consisted of two lounge chairs, a sofa, and several wooden coffee tables. Newspapers, magazines, and unopened clusters of mail were stacked in various-sized piles on the tables. Leal made a futile search for the TV remote, before giving up and walking over to switch on the set. He popped open the can of beer as he went to the phone.

Punching in Hart's number, he let it ring five times before hanging up on her answering machine. He was set to punch in her cell phone number when his own went off. Must be her, he thought, as he pressed the button and looked at the number. It was an unfamiliar one, so he let it go to voice mail, then checked it. An automated voice asked if he'd accept a collect call from the Riverdale Police Department. Leal's brow furrowed, wondering what the hell this was all about. Unable to remember anyone, he pressed redial and waited. The phone rang twice and was answered by a dispatcher, and then, after he explained who he was and why he was calling, he was put on hold and transferred. It was picked up by someone with a black-sounding voice.

"Yeah, you tried to call me?" Leal asked.

"Leal?" the voice said. "It's Roxie, man. How you doin'?"

Roxie? Leal smirked.

"Better than you, apparently," Leal took a swig of the beer. "I'm home with a drink watching TV, and you're callin' me from the shitter."

"Yeah, man," Roxie said, punctuating his sentence with his ingratiating little laugh. Leal could almost see the sad, droopy eyes.

"What do you need, Roxter?" Leal asked. He stretched and walked over to the TV tray as he listened to Roxter's rapid-fire explanation.

"Leal, look, they gots me locked up in jail, man. Fucking bullshit burglary to auto, man." Roxter paused. "I mean, how do you do burglary to an auto, man? It don't make fucking sense, do it?"

"Yeah, it does," Leal said. "Anything else?"

"Well, you know," Roxter continued. "They sayin' I had some motherfucking rock on me, but, man . . ." He let the sentence trail off.

Roxter J. Roberts was one of Leal's older snitches who'd come across with some pretty good tips on drugs, weapons, and stolen property, when he was pushed a little. But Leal hadn't heard from him recently and let him know it.

"Look, man," Roxter said. "I'm sorry 'bout that, but I been kinda busy, you know?"

"Yeah, I been pretty busy myself," Leal said. "So I'm just gonna sit down and watch some TV and contemplate how little you've given me lately."

"Look, Frank, I told you I was sorry about that, man," Roxter said, his voice taking on a pleading tone. "I been trying to keep myself out of trouble, man. I got me a new baby."

Roxter, who was now about thirty, had at least half a dozen kids, all with different mothers.

"So what you're telling me is that you want me to help you out," Leal said. "But what am I gonna get in return? From a guy who never calls me." Leal made it a point never to call any of his informants snitches to their faces.

"Look, Leal, man," Roxter pleaded. "You know I can't do no mo' time, man. Not with a new baby, man. That's what fucked me up the last time."

And the time before that, and the one before that, Leal thought. "Okay, Roxie, I'll see what I can do," Leal said. "But you're gonna owe me big time on this, understand. None of this bullshit about not calling me, or not showing up for a meet when you're supposed to. Got it?"

"Course I do," Roxter said, sounding almost hurt. "Ah, you coming by tonight, then?"

"Uh-uh," Leal said, knowing the bond for the felony would have to be set by a judge. "I'll see you at the bond hearing tomorrow morning. If I can't make it I'll send my partner. But the message is the same. You better get me something big time, or I'll let you swing."

"I'm your man," Roxter said. "See you tomorrow then, and thanks."

Leal hung up, thinking that maybe Roxter could help clear up something in his overflowing case load. Now that he was losing Ollie again, things would really grind to a halt. He drank some more of the beer and dialed Hart's cell phone. It rang about seven times before going to voice mail. After hanging up he cleared a place on the sofa so he could sit down, and began to eat some of the cold chicken.

It had been three months now since he and Sharon Devain

had broken up. He thought of her profusion of blond hair and the wicked way she'd sometimes pull it back into a ponytail right before they'd have sex. The way she'd come in, slipping off her jacket and shoes, all the while telling him about the day she'd had in court. Lawyers and cops, he thought. Never a good combination. Even though Sharon was a state's attorney. And a damned good one at that. He thought about the times they'd made love in her apartment, even when she'd been on call for felony review, and how she'd answer the phone when they were in bed together and she was straddling him.

But he'd come into the relationship with extra baggage. Two pre-teen daughters from his previous marriage. Even though they lived in California with their mother, his ex, and her new husband, he got to see the kids twice a year for protracted stays during the summer and at Christmas. His daughters hadn't hit it off that well with Sharon, even though they'd tried to do all the fun things like going to the zoo and Great America. The relationship between them had always seemed strained. And it didn't help that the girls idolized Ollie.

She was all they talked about. They called her "awesome." And Hart, who had been kind enough to babysit a few times the previous summer, liked the girls too. But that was before she got busy with her new boyfriend. Last Christmas the task of entertaining the girls, and Sharon, was Leal's alone.

He'd done his best, taking two weeks off to spend with them. All of them. But Sharon told him that she'd already made reservations at a ski lodge in Wisconsin for the week after Christmas. There was no way he could take the girls up there, so he told her to go without him. It wasn't till later that he found out she went with Steve Megally, one of the district supervisors in the state's attorney's office.

It was cold and snowy when she'd told him it was over for them, but she hoped they could "part as friends." Almost a fucking cliché, he thought, as he replayed the conversation over and over again in his mind. He'd already seen the girls off at the airport, and when he came home that time after the bitter conversation, the house had been dark and empty too.

The phone rang, snapping him out of his reverie. He reached over and picked it up.

"Frank, it's me," Hart said. "What happened with you and Card?"

"Oh, he chewed my ass a little bit," Leal said. "Did his usual huffing and puffing, but you know him. Just a big fucking bag of wind. It don't mean nothing anyway."

"That's good," she said. Leal could hear the underlying concern in her voice. "I was a little worried about you."

"I'm okay. What happened with you? Where you going to be reassigned?"

Hart paused before she answered, then said, "You'll never guess. They're putting me on Tactical. The Raid Team. I've got to go to SWAT school all next week up at Great Lakes. That's why I've been out shopping all afternoon. There was a ton of stuff I had to get. And then I had to get my legs workout in or Rory would have killed me."

"Sounds like fun," Leal said. "The shopping I mean. The Raid Team's pretty heavy duty. I used to do a lot of raids when I was with MEG, but I guess Tactical's doing them all now."

"Yeah," Hart said.

"Did the Chief say why they were transferring you?"

She paused again before answering. "I gathered it was a politically correct move on their part. He did say that it'll help me out when promotion time comes."

Leal let out a slow breath. He was sorry as hell to lose Ollie but didn't want to stand in her way either.

"Look, I'm gonna go see Sean this week," Leal said. "He's still got lots of clout in the department. I'll see if he can pull some strings to get you back in Investigations. If you want."

"Oh, Frank, that's so nice of you," she said. "But let me do this a while. If I hate it, I'll come running, okay?"

"Yeah. Sure."

"So, what did you do on the homicide investigation?" she asked.

"Not much. I started the report. Like you said, those California IDs were phonies, and someone used an American Express card with the name Richard Phipps to rent the car. The card's not reported lost or stolen so the credit card company won't release any information without a court order. Ryan's taking care of that for me."

"No kidding?" Hart said. "He's actually doing some work?"

Leal laughed, in spite of his dour mood. "He must have felt guilty about what happened to you."

"Not a chance," Hart said. "That creep doesn't have enough sensitivity to feel guilty about anything except missing the chance to load his pockets with pretzels before the last call at the bar."

Leal chuckled, then said, "I did manage to put out a type three if the vehicle's recovered. Other than that, we'll just have to wait till the autopsy tomorrow morning, then see if we can ID him through the prints. And hopefully we'll find out something on this credit card owner."

"Frank," she said slowly. "I've got the weekend off. The school starts Monday."

"Oh yeah. Right. I forgot."

"So do you think you could do me a big favor?" she asked.

"Name it," he said.

"I'm going to stay up there in North Chicago all week, and I was wondering if you'd come over and feed Rocky and take my mail in." Rocky was Hart's cat. A huge black, half-Persian, half-alley that they'd rescued from one of their many crime scene investigations. "I'd have Rick do it," she added, "but he's on afternoons this week, and he likes to go visit his brother in the mornings."

"Sure, Ollie. No problem. I'll even scoop out the litter box for you."

"Wow, that's above and beyond." She giggled. "Look, Frank, I really appreciate it. I'll give you the key at the gym tomorrow, okay?"

"Say, I was going to ask you something," Leal said. "I've got that autopsy in the morning, and one of my snitches got arrested. I need to see that he gets an I-Bond. Think you could handle it for me in Markham if I'm not back?"

"Sure," she said. "Who is it?"

"Roxter Roberts."

"Oh, I remember him," she said. "He's the one that always leers at my breasts."

"No, that's Ryan," Leal joked. Hart laughed too. He thought how much he liked the sound of her laugh. "So I'll call you from the morgue if I can't get back in time then?"

"Sure," Hart said. "I'll put all the cat food on the kitchen counter, okay? And don't forget to stop by the gym and get the key, even if you don't have time to work out."

"I will, Ollie, and don't worry about anything. I'd wish you good luck at the school, but I know you'll do great anyway." He paused, then added, "And let me know if you want me to talk to Sean about getting you transferred back, okay?"

"Okay, Frank," she said. There was a catch in her voice that made him think she was holding something back. "I'll think about it. But whatever happens, just remember we'll always be friends." He could hear Rocky's plaintive meowing coming over the phone.

"Yeah," Leal said, looking around the empty house and wondering if maybe he should get himself a cat. "Friends."

6
UNKIND CUTS

Whenever Leal had an autopsy to attend, he always made sure that he got there early with coffee and donuts. He pulled up in the visitor's lot on the east side of the building at seven-thirty and saw a few cars. None looked to be an unmarked squad. Good, he'd beaten the crowd: The first step in being the initial autopsy of the day. Considering it was Saturday morning, the day after Friday night, this was a prudent move. Balancing the coffee cups in one bag and the donuts in another, he went over to the front door and pressed the bell under the hand-printed card that read: *Press For Service.* A bent-over old man in a white shirt and gray pants came ambling down the hall. When he saw Leal his face crinkled into a creased smile. He opened the door and said, "Morning, Frank. Where's your pretty partner?"

"She's getting transferred, Gordon," Leal said holding out the bag of donuts and reaching into the other bag to snare his own cup of black coffee. Gordon grinned as he held up the bag and gazed inside. He'd been at the morgue for as long as Leal could remember, and the old man's penchant for apple-cinnamon donuts was well known. That's why Leal always made the stop at Dunkin' Donuts on his way in.

Gordon turned and led Leal to the Investigators' Office. It was a large room with numerous cluttered desks. Even at seven-thirty the three people who'd manned the night shift were all talking on the phones and scribbling notes on their pads.

"Busy night?" Leal asked as Gordon motioned him to sit at

59

one of the unoccupied desks.

Gordon took one of the apple-cinnamon donuts and bit into it before answering. When he did speak, he opened his mouth wide so Leal could see the chunks of partially chewed food.

"Sunrise bodies," the old man said. "You know how it goes. When the sun pops up, so do the dead bodies." He chuckled and took another large bite out of the donut. "What case you here on?"

"A guy named Robert Woods," Leal said, reading off the M.E. number. "Gotta go to court this morning too."

Gordon nodded as he placed the last part of the donut in his mouth and withdrew a second one. Leal sipped his coffee. Gordon told him to wait there and the old man hobbled off. One of the women on the phone said, "Are they sure he was stabbed and shot?" Then added, "Oh, well, I'm going to note it as a possible exit wound then." Leal drank some more of his coffee and reviewed all the things he had to do that morning. He took out his notebook and read over the list that he'd written out at the breakfast table. At least he could scratch off the first two items: get coffee and buy donuts.

Gordon came back and motioned to Leal, small crumbs from the partially consumed donut dropping to the floor.

"You're set," Gordon said. "Want to wait in the lounge?"

"Sure," said Leal. He followed the old man to the elevator, which popped open as soon as he touched the button. They entered the car and went down to the basement.

"So where'd this one get dumped?" Gordon asked. The doors slid open and they walked to the small lounge area. It was a long room full of vending machines, Formica tables, and chairs. The rear wall had been decorated with an extended mural of a lake replete with trees, blue sky, and majestic looking birds. Just to the right of the entrance was a huge metal gate. It was composed of heavy looking bars and had an old-fashioned slot for a skeleton key. A gold plaque was mounted on it denoting it as the old front gate to the old morgue, 1928–1984. Gordon always talked fondly of the old morgue that had been on Polk Street behind the county hospital. "You could smell it four blocks away," was his favorite reminiscence.

Leal sat at one of the tables and finished the remainder of his coffee. Gordon took out his last donut and removed his cup.

"This should be just about drinkable now," he said.

"You don't like it hot?" Leal asked.

The old man shook his head as he took a careful sip. "Don't want to melt the Polident," he said, showing his porcelain-perfect smile. Leal didn't want to tell him that he had gooey-looking clumps of dough stuck along the plastic gumline.

Twenty minutes later Leal stood shivering in the coolness of the autopsy room. The odor was overpowering, as it always was, but he continued breathing through his nose knowing that in a couple minutes he wouldn't notice it anymore. Three nude bodies lay on separate steel gurneys. One was an older white female, the second a young black teenager, and the third was the man from the Riptide Motel. The door swung open and an attendant in medical scrubs strolled in and said hello to Leal. Dr. Gleason, a pretty woman in her late thirties with auburn hair, came in a moment later.

"Hello, Officer," she said. "Looks like you're up first, huh?"

"Looks like," Leal said, grinning and wondering how she kept the smile on her face knowing that she'd have to come in and sift through dead bodies all day long.

The doctor held out her latex hand, palm up, and raised her eyebrows. "So who has first honors?"

"Him," Leal said, pointing to the Riptide Motel stiff.

Gleason walked over to the gurney and pushed it to the corner by the counter full of instruments. "Hmmm," she said, gazing at the corpse, then turning on her tape recorder. "He looks like somebody, doesn't he? Like some old movie star, or something?"

Leal shrugged.

"Tell me about the case, Detective." She turned to the attendant. "Gavin, we'll be doing this one first. Can you prep him, please?"

The attendant nodded.

Leal gave her a cursory rundown: the body in the sleazy motel; the fact that the room was locked; the darkened area around the neck and the blood splotches in the eyes. When Gavin had finished positioning the gurney by the sink, Dr. Gleason ran her fingers over the body as he talked, nodding as he said certain things. When he finished, she looked up at him and smiled. "We might as well start," she said, pulling open the eyelids of the dead man. "Yes, I do see definite pinpoint hematoma in the sclera." Her fingers went to his neck. After looking and probing she asked, "Could this have been an autoerotic death? This looks like it was made by some sort of constricting ligature."

"Not likely on the autoerotic," Leal said. "There was definitely someone with him in the room. He was in his underwear, and there were no signs of any suspended nooses."

"Oh, darn," Dr. Gleason said, looking up with a smile. "So much for the easy write-off, then, eh? Suggestive of sexual-asphyxia, but if there was a partner that's rare in males. More common in females. But I'd say it looks like asphyxiation due to strangulation, but we'll have to check further, of course."

Leal was thinking that Dr. Gleason was pretty and her smile seemed to light up the dreary, cold room. She went to her recorder and spoke softly into it as she walked around the body, describing the corpse. After setting it down, she picked up a clipboard with a pre-printed diagram of a human body on it.

She continued to walk around the gurney and made some more notes. "Would you flip him, please?"

Gavin walked over to the gurney and pushed the end up against the metal counter, adjusting it so that it canted downward toward the large metal sink. His dark hands were covered with blue latex gloves. He grabbed the corpse by the arm and leg and in one deft movement, flipped the body face-down onto the metal table. It made a clunking sound on the stainless steel, like a big, hard rubber mannequin being knocked around. Gavin swung the gurney to the side as Dr. Gleason examined the corpse's posterior and made more notes. They took measurements, then Gavin flipped the body over on its back again and put the specially cut wooden block under the corpse's head. After hooking up the plastic hose to the faucet, Gavin set the hose at the top of the table so that the water began a gentle cascade down the tilted steel top and drained into the sink. Dr. Gleason moved away from the body with her clipboard and tape recorder as Gavin pulled the surgical mask over his broad features and plugged in the saw. He set the saw down well away from the water and picked up a large scalpel. After lifting the body enough to make a T-shaped cut on the back of the corpse's head, he began to peel away the skin from the scalp, slicing the white membrane underneath.

Dr. Gleason came over and examined the membrane, then spoke into her recorder. "No signs of subdural hemorrhaging," she said. "So we know he wasn't konked over the head."

Leal nodded and stepped back farther. Gavin was pulling the skin away from the facial bones now. Soon he'd be using the saw, and Leal knew from past experience not to stand too close. Even Dr. Gleason moved back as Gavin turned on the saw and began making the oval-shaped cut in the back to the skull. The blade kept binding, making a grinding sound. When Gavin finished with the skull, he pulled skin back over the corpse's face again, then used the scalpel to make the long Y-cuts on the torso's chest and abdomen. After stripping away that skin, he used the saw again. On the ribs this time. Popping open the chest cavity, he picked up the hose and rinsed off the circular blade, dabbing at it with a sponge. Dr. Gleason went over and began removing the organs. Leal winced as the brain was removed with the accompanying suction-breaking pop.

After weighing it, Dr. Gleason set it aside and began examining the other organs. Gavin would occasionally kink the hose and use it to remove some blood from the body cavity.

"I don't see anything abnormal in here," Dr. Gleason said, holding up a deflated dark tan lung. "Except that he was a smoker." She set the organ on the counter. "You smoke, Detective?"

"Not any more," Leal said, remembering how Sharon's continued smoking had been one of the many sources of their arguments during the penultimate stage of their relationship. "Seen the consequences in too many of these."

Dr. Gleason smiled at his remark as she began withdrawing blood from various organs using large syringes.

She cut loose the heart and held it up.

"This could be something," she said pointing to a darkened area. "It's possible that he may have had a coronary spasm, but that could have been brought on by the asphyxiation." She set the heart aside and started on the stomach. "Any idea what he had for his last meal?"

"Not yet," Leal said, watching her peel back the layers of the organ. The door opened and Henry Morgan walked in carrying several sets of fingerprint cards and an ink pad.

"Henry," Leal said. "Didn't know you'd be here so soon."

"Figured I'd come in and get them prints as soon as the doc was done," Morgan said. "Those IDs were bogus, right?"

"Yeah."

Morgan nodded his head. "Oh, no prints on them lights you found in the Dumpster either. Wiped totally clean."

"Figures," Leal said. "I had a hunch they'd be tied in some way, especially with that lens cap being in the room."

Dr. Gleason was already dropping the stomach on the counter and checking the intestines. Gavin suctioned out more blood. "It won't be long now, fellows," she said. "I'm almost done."

Morgan nodded. Leal glanced at his watch and tried to estimate how much time he had before the bond hearings started at Markham.

"As long as you're here, Henry, I'm going to run down to the lounge and make a couple of calls, okay?" Leal said. "Unless you're gonna need some help straightening out those fingers."

Morgan shook his head. "My main man there will help me," he said bobbling his head toward Gavin, who was already looping the coarse plastic wire through the eye of the fish-hook-shaped needle.

"I hope you're not talking about this one, brother," Gavin said, smiling for the first time that morning as he nodded toward the corpse.

Leal pulled up to the Markham branch of the county courthouse at twenty minutes after ten. The deputy in the lockup had assured him that they wouldn't be getting around to the felony bond hearings until at least ten-thirty, so that gave him plenty of time to grab the state's attorney and make his arrangements. He walked up the long, pebbled series of stairs toward the glass-covered entrance, watching his reflection as he approached. After badgering his way through the gate guards, he went down to the basement and looked in the bond hearing room.

It was chock-full of people, but the judge was absent from the bench. Leal walked up the side aisle and asked one of the clerks who the judge was.

"Judge Bell," the girl said.

That was bad news for Leal, because Judge Norresa Bell was notorious for her eccentricities. She might give an Individual Recognizance Bond to a brutal thug, then turn around and send a drunk down to the county jail. She was well-known to be "anti-police," having once said that she'd never once met a cop who didn't aggravate her, and she and Leal had locked horns before on various cases.

He frowned and asked who the state's attorney was. The clerk pointed to a slender young woman with curly brown hair. "Laurie," she said.

Leal went over and flipped out his badge case. The state's attorney looked up and smiled.

"Could I talk to you in the hallway for a minute?" Leal said.

"Sure," Laurie said. They went through the doors and Leal introduced himself.

"I've got sort of a problem," he said, smiling. "One of my snitches is locked up on a felony beef. PCS and burglary to auto. I was hoping to get him an I-Bond without having to go all the way down to twenty-sixth street." He was referring to the practice of issuing Individual Recognizance Bonds to all non-violent arrestees at the main jail facility to alleviate overcrowding. "You see, I'm working on a homicide case and I'm kinda pressed for time."

"What's his name?" Laurie asked. She was a rather pretty girl, Leal noticed.

"Roxter Roberts," Leal said. "And I'm not on Judge Bell's favorite person list."

"Who is?" Laurie said with a laugh. "She was just yelling at me a little while ago. Luckily she always calls a fifteen minute recess midway through so she can water her plants."

She smiled again, canting her head as she looked at him.

"You're Sharon's friend, aren't you?"

Leal was taken aback by the question. He murmured a yes, somewhat irritated that that was how he was defined by this woman: "Sharon's friend." Would that mean that he was now her "Ex-friend?"

"We met at the state's attorney's Christmas party last December, remember?" she said.

Leal squinted and said that he did, letting a slight smile creep over his lips. He'd tried so hard to suppress all his memories of that bitter month.

"How's she doing?" Laurie asked. "She's still down at twenty-sixth street, right?"

"I think so. We're not seeing each other anymore."

"Oh," Laurie said, drawing her lips into an O-shape. She looked down at her legal pad, then smoothed some of the curly hair away from the side of her face.

"Maybe the best thing would be to try to find another judge to sign an I-Bond, but I don't think anyone else is here since it's Saturday."

"You got any rapport with Lady Bell?" Leal asked.

"Hardly," Laurie laughed. "Wait a minute, I think I did see Judge McGuffy up by the law library earlier. Just a minute." She went back into the courtroom, then came back out carrying her notebook and the file on Roxter Roberts. "Maybe we can catch him upstairs and he'll sign it." She snickered as they walked up the stairs. Leaning close to him she said, "He's like that old commercial—Give it to him. He'll sign anything." Leal smiled back, once again appreciating the perfect symmetry of her teeth. They took the escalator up to the second floor and went to the law library. It was locked. Laurie turned and walked down the hallway toward the rows of unoccupied courtrooms. She leaned against one of them, raising both hands up against the glass.

"I can't tell, but his chambers are right back there," she said. Just then the hallway door opened and a heavy-set, gray-haired man in a plaid sport jacket and dark slacks stepped out. His head did a quick jerk as he noticed them, then a practiced grin spread over his face. His nose was large, with a latticework of red veins winding over the bulbous end.

"Hello, Judge," Laurie said.

"Miss Pescnik," the judge said. He nodded an acknowledgment to Leal.

"Judge we have a slight problem," Laurie said. "This officer's working a homicide case and needs an I-Bond for one of his informants."

Judge McGuffy raised his eyebrows.

"Isn't Judge Bell on call this morning?" he asked.

"Umm, she's on recess," Laurie said. "We were just trying to expedite."

McGuffy let out a heavy snort of a laugh that let Leal know that the man's breakfast had come in a bottle. He reached out and took the I-Bond from Laurie's outstretched hand.

"What's the offense? Anything violent?" he asked.

"No, your honor. PCS," she said.

The judge shook his head. "I assume Gerstien is satisfied?"

"Yes, sir," Laurie said. "Do you want me to read the one-oh-one?"

"Say no more, my dear," he said, scribbling his name across the bottom of the I-Bond. "Say no more." He finished with a flourish and showed them the practiced grin again, then ambled off in the direction of the down escalator.

"Thank you, your honor," Leal said. The rotund man waved his hand without turning around. As he and Laurie walked over to the elevator, Leal thanked her and asked if it was going to cause any problems being off the court record.

"None for me," she said. "And certainly not for him. Once you get to be a judge you can pretty much do as you please."

7
REPETITIONS AND VIDEOS

Hart hung suspended in space, gripping the horizontal bar at the widest possible length to do the lat workout. The muscles from her shoulder to spine flexed on each side as she began each rep, then froze into a solid bas-relief as she held the movement at the apex with the back of her neck against the bar. She lowered herself down slowly, feeling the pull on her lats, her forearms and delts aching. In the mirror she saw Rory Chalma standing behind her, ready to grab her feet at the crucial second, should she need it. "Twenty-eight," he counted out loud as she did another pull-up.

"Twenty-nine. Come on, Ollie. Strict form."

"Okay," Hart grunted, her voice raspy from the effort as she tried to raise herself again, but stalled midway up.

Chalma grabbed her crisscrossed white gym shoes and lifted ever so slightly. The huge muscles of his arms and chest rippled and bulged despite the paucity of his actual effort. "Okay, thirty," Chalma said as Ollie's neck met the bar. "Come on, strict form. Squeeze them."

He readied for another assist, but Hart kicked her feet loose as she lowered herself and then dropped to the floor.

"What'd you stop for?" he asked. "You did thirty-five with no problem the day before yesterday." Chalma put his hands on his hips and cocked his head to one side as he spoke. They were almost the same height, with Hart being taller.

Chalma had short blond hair that had thinned at the crown

and temples, forming a V-shaped wedge in the front.

Hart raised her arms and flattened her hands against the wall to stretch. She had on a one-piece black nylon exercise outfit that was composed of a snug halter-top, cut low in the front and back, and mid-length shorts. Her blond hair had been put up in the familiar French braid that she always wore during her workouts. The gym itself was an expansive building with parallel rows of weights, racks of dumbbells, and various machines. Each wall was covered with large plate mirrors, and the paint pattern was red, black, and gray. On the far right side a medium-sized room had been set up as an aerobics area, but a heavy bag and speed bag hung in one corner. Chalma had maintained this equipment as a favor to Leal, who had been a fine amateur boxer and still enjoyed doing boxing-style workouts. For a long time Rory had called that section of the gym "Frank's corner," because Leal had been the only one who still used the bags. But with the popularity of the Boxing for Women videos and the like, the section was now often filled up with more than a dozen women clad in leotards and bag gloves, doing a dance-like series of punches, bobbing, and weaving. Today was no exception, as at least thirteen or fourteen women bounced around, smacking at the air, the focus mitts, and the two bags as the video droned on a portable television that had been set up on a chair in front of the mats.

"Well," Chalma continued. "Nothing to say for yourself?"

"Rory, I'm taking a light one today, okay?" Hart said.

Chalma backed off and raised his eyebrows. Hart continued to stretch and saw him looking at her.

Christ, she thought, it was still months away from contest time. So what if I let my weight creep up a bit from one-hundred-forty-five? Well, maybe a hundred-and-fifty.

She looked in the mirror. The extra pounds gave her a heavily muscled look, but without the striations and definition that weeks of strict dieting would bring out.

"Sometimes I wonder about your dedication," Chalma said.

"I'm here, aren't I?" She finished stretching and turned around to face him.

"You finish number six in your first Olympia, then the next year you don't even break the top twelve," he said. "We've got to start concentrating on one of the interim titles. And I do mean concentrating. You look terrible. You've got to bulk up."

Hart blew out a long breath. "Rory, I'm doing the best I can."

"I know what it is," he said. "It's that new boyfriend of yours. He's doing nothing for you except dragging you down. When are you gonna realize that?"

"Rick is not dragging me down. And I don't appreciate your bringing him into this." She nodded toward Rory's live-in lover who was across the gym doing flys and out of earshot. "How would you like it if I got on you because of Don?"

Chalma frowned.

"Well, look, Ms. International is coming up," he said. "Why don't you at least let me put you on a quick cycle and see if it helps?"

Hart stared at him, then bent forward, putting her hands on her knees.

"No way," she said.

"Why? Just look at the gains that Marsha's been making." He pointed across the gym to an immensely muscled woman who was doing poses in front of one of the plate mirrors. Her huge arms and thighs bulged in almost ludicrous symmetry.

"Yeah," Hart said. "Just look at her, not to mention what her liver's probably like. And besides, I can't afford to come up positive on a urine test."

"I told you I can get you something that will mask it. We could even use HGH," he said. "They say that it won't even show up on most tests."

"Human growth hormone," Hart said. "Right. Just what I need. You know, I just had to do a urinalysis for work yesterday."

"I told you, we can mask it."

"What's this 'we' shit? Whose job and career is on the line?"

Chalma clucked. "So you want Marsha to pass you up? Is that it?"

Hart took a deep breath before she spoke, then straightened to her full height.

"Rory, I've got too much going on in my life for this kind of bullshit," she said in a husky whisper. "Now lay off with the steroid crap, or else. And you can tell Ms. Anabolic there that if I catch her shooting up in the locker room again, she won't have to worry about passing me because I'll bust her ass and see that she spends six months in county."

Chalma dropped his hands from his hips and pursed his lips. After a moment of silence he asked, "Are we going to finish lats, or what?"

Hart sighed and moved to the rowing machine.

"Ollie," Leal called as he walked in. He was dressed in a sport shirt and slacks, his badge and gun fastened on his belt. Hart straightened up as Frank walked over and shook hands with Chalma.

"So you get your buddy Roxter all taken care of?" she asked. "I didn't get any calls."

"Yeah," Leal said. "Hopefully he'll get me something decent before the prelim, or I'll let him hang."

"Come by for your workout, Frank?" Chalma asked.

"I'm kinda pressed for time, Rory," Leal said, glancing over at the women doing the boxing aerobics. He smiled at Hart. "I just stopped by to get Ollie's key. I hope you've stocked up on cat food and kitty litter."

"Key?" Chalma interjected. "Now don't tell me that you two

are finally setting up house together?" He was always assuming that, despite her relationship with Rick, Hart and Leal were lovers.

Leal started to say something, but Hart cut him off. "No, I'm going out of town for a week," she said.

"Out of town?" Chalma said. "Where? When? Why?"

"Didn't she tell you?" Leal said. "She's going to SWAT school."

Hart shot a look of daggers at Leal, then turned to Chalma, who had adopted his arms akimbo stance again.

"I was going to tell you that I'd be gone next week," she said. "It's only for a week."

"And what about your training schedule?" Chalma asked.

"It's a pretty rough school," Leal said, sensing that he'd mentioned something that Ollie hadn't wanted Rory to know yet.

"I'll just have to take along some dumbbells and my home gym," Hart said. "It's up by Great Lakes, so they'll probably have a gym up there I can use. Anyway, it's not like I have a lot of choice about it."

"That's not what bothers me," Chalma said. "Why didn't you tell me this earlier?"

"Because you've been acting so . . . bitchy," Hart said.

Leal could tell she regretted the adjective the moment after she said it. She had always cautioned Frank against making any derogatory inference to Rory's homosexuality and now she was doing it.

"Sorry, Rory," she said. "I'm having a real rough couple of days."

"Looks like my corner's real busy, eh?" Leal said, trying to change the subject while nodding at the group following the Boxing for Women video.

"At least some people are serious about their training," Rory said before turning and walking away.

"How was the autopsy?" Hart asked. She'd assumed her position at a new machine, gripping the handles of the V-shaped wedge and lowering herself to a sitting position on the floor with her feet braced in perpendicular fashion against the vertical edge of the stacked weight plates.

"Pretty much as we expected," Leal said. "We'll get the subpoenas for the credit card info on the guy who rented the car. Maybe even have him ID'd through fingerprints." He watched as Hart began pulling the handle back toward her chest, the muscles of her arms and shoulders seeming ready to pop through her skin.

"Anything on the latent that," she paused as she tensed up at the apex, "Morgan found on the toilet seat?"

"He told me he'd run it through AFIS," Leal said. Watching Hart's bare arms and back was getting to him. He realized that he was thinking of her more and more in sexual terms, and not as his partner. But then again, she wasn't his partner anymore. "So, Ollie, can I buy you lunch?" he said.

She smiled as she lowered the stack of chrome plates down to the brace.

"Thanks, but I'm going to meet Rick," she said. "Besides, you have a homicide to investigate, right?"

"Ah, there's not much pressure finding out who did some middle-aged nobody in a sleaze-bag motel," Leal said. "Probably some hooker he tried to stiff."

The weights clacked down on the resting bar and Hart stood up, wiping off her face with the terry cloth band she wore on her right wrist. Leal couldn't help but admire the fine bone structure, the high cheekbones of her face. She was one gal that sure looked sexy when she sweated.

"Just let me run and get the key, okay?" she said and trotted across the floor. Almost all the male eyes in the place were glued to her tight buttocks and long, sinewy legs. But on this Saturday morning, with the gym almost evenly divided between relative novices and serious lifters, no one dared offer even a whistle due to Hart's reputation as the preeminent professional bodybuilder who trained there.

Chalma came up to Leal and said, "I'm really getting worried about her, Frank. She doesn't seem as focused as she usually is. Is there something going on I should know about?"

"Oh, I wouldn't worry about her, Rory," Leal answered, looking at the group of women throwing synchronized jabs and hooks. One of them was at the speed bag trying unsuccessfully to master the striking rhythm. "If there's one thing I know about our Ollie, it's that she's a survivor."

Taji pounded the speed bag with such rapidity that it looked like a dark blur bouncing in front of his face, and the noise even drowned out the percussive beat of the rap music that blared from a boom box at the other end of the large, dingy looking gym. The sweat poured off his wiry muscles and made splotches on the worn floorboards. He wore no shirt, only long black sweatpants. His feet were bare. In prison, when he'd competed in the boxing tournament, he'd always entered the heavyweight division even though his weight would have allowed him to compete as a light heavy or cruiserweight. He had always been blessed with an almost preternatural quickness, which he had used in the ring against the bigger men to out-box and set them up. He had won the tournament three years in a row. The three years he'd spent incarcerated on the delivery-of-controlled-substance charge. And now, he knew there was no way he was going back.

The gym occupied the expansive lower floor of a huge two-story building in Cicero Heights. Its previous owner, Anthony "Big Mo" Morrison was in the county jail on Drug and

Conspiracy to Commit Murder charges and had signed over control of the gym to the General of the Black Soul Gangstas, Otha Spears. Otha, who always had his computer expert and ace accountants looking for "investments," accepted the "gift" from Morrison in exchange for the drug dealer's protection behind the walls. It was all done as a legitimate transaction, although no actual money had changed hands, except on paper. Morrison claimed to have sold the property to raise money for his defense fund, but he actually had his attorney move some of the vast supplies of cash from one of his many safety deposit boxes to a special account, and knew that he didn't have to worry about one of the Souls or their rival gangbangers inside messing with him. The agreement had also included another little matter: an incarcerated cop named Lance Harmon who had been in Morrison's pocket on the outside, when he'd been king shit of the drug dealers in Cicero Heights. Harmon was sitting in the isolation ward facing charges for a murder that he'd done for Morrison.

Big Mo saw him as the ultimate liability: the guy who'd eventually plead out to a lesser offense and testify for the state.

Otha had promised that the Harmon matter would be taken care of, even if he had to send his number one enforcer/ bodyguard Oman Taji into the jail to do it. But Taji had no intentions of going back into stir, even for a short time. That was why he was so worried that that bitch Chocolate had gotten away from him. She had the video equipment and the tape of them in the room. If she dumped the car or something and somebody found that fucking tape . . . it was just like she was holding his balls in her motherfucking hand. He'd checked her crib and all the usual places she hung out, but the ho had up and vanished. It was unreal.

He finished punching the speed bag and went to the heavy bag. Circling it, he pounded out a series of hooks and crosses until he was winded. Too much fucking rock, he thought. Yet he seemed unable to totally give that up either. He knew it was poison and it was dragging him down, but, Christ, it was the only way he could relax lately with so much on his mind. As long as Otha didn't find out. The sweat stung where his chest was cut from the pipe. That reminded him of his other problem. He didn't want Otha to know about that either, but how was he gonna hide it? He sat on the floor beside the swinging bag and pulled off his gloves. Then over the din he heard someone calling his name.

"Taji," one of the brothers by the front door called again. "Phone, man."

Taji got to his feet, his sweaty back leaving a dribbling wet spot on the wall. He walked over to the front desk and grabbed the phone from the dude's hand.

"Yeah," he said.

"Hey, baby," a woman's voice said.

His brow creased. "Chocolate?" he said.

"You got it, baby."

"Where you at, sweetcakes?" Taji said, trying to cover his anxiety with charm. It didn't work.

"I'm where you can't get at me," Chocolate said, "with our little videotape. You know, you look so good in living color doing that dude."

"Come on, baby. Don't do me like that. Tell me where you is at and I'll come by. We can talk."

"About what?"

"About getting high, baby," Taji said. "And have a good old time. What you think?"

"I think I tell you where I'm at before I get the money for this motherfucking videotape I got, you'd be most inhospitable."

He blew his breath out of his nostrils, scowling, but trying his best to keep the malice he was feeling out of his voice. "What you talkin' about, baby?"

"You forgettin' you took those shots at us, motherfucker?" Chocolate said. "Cause I ain't. I ain't."

"Aw, baby, that wasn't me."

"Fuck you, motherfucker," she said, her voice venomous. "Who the fuck was it then?"

All he could think to do was keep breathing and listening.

"I'll be callin' you back," she said. "With instructions on how you can buy this motherfucking tape back from me, so right now you best be figuring out how you gonna ask yo' boss for a hundred thousand dollars."

"Hey, that's crazy, woman," Taji said, his voice starting to sound nervous. "I can't come up with that much."

"You best, *sweetcakes*," she said mimicking his previous tone. "Cause if you don't," her voice rose to a harsh crescendo, "I'll mail the motherfucking thing to the man."

She hung up before he could say anything more. The dude guarding the front door looked at him as he slammed the phone down so hard it made a ringing sound.

That bitch! That motherfuckin' ho! She knew she had him by the johnson, sure as if she was holding a straight razor over him. He wondered if that other bitch, Janice, was in on it too. Visions of the two of them dancing and laughing flashed through his mind. He breathed a heavy sigh. There was nothing to do but play along, until he could find out where she was at. He had to be cool till he got his hands on her . . . Then he'd make her tell him where that tape was. He could do that. That was the one thing he was sure of.

8
RICK'S PLACE

Hart still had her hair in the French braid, having decided not to wash it until later on that night. Too many showers through the course of the day, one when she got up, another after her workout, then still another if she and Rick were going out . . . caused excessive dryness, especially for her hair.

She used cocoa butter to keep her skin moist, and used Quick Tan for contests, rather than sunning herself the natural way. Cooking herself, she thought. Drying her skin out even more. She had, however, applied her makeup and mascara, then given it one last check before going into the restaurant and taking their usual table. She glanced out the window at the bright sunshine and wondered if the nice weather would hold out for the school next week. She'd read the course description and it sounded like a lot of outside stuff. Morning runs and outdoor ranges. Sort of like the way Leal had talked about his army training.

Deep down the ambivalence about this whole assignment began to bubble in her stomach. She hadn't asked for it. She'd been happy in Investigations. And Frank was such a great partner. She thought about all that they'd been through together. How he'd taught her so much and always respected her as a person. Poor thing, she thought. He'd seemed so lost since he and Sharon had broken up. It was too bad, too, because they'd seemed like such a nice couple. Maybe he'd find somebody else soon.

Her reverie was broken as she saw the marked county unit pull up and park. Rick Harmon got out and gazed around the parking lot before he began his long-legged stroll toward the doors.

God, he's handsome, she thought. Tall, with broad shoulders and an athlete's body. Blond hair cut short and dark sunglasses covering his blue eyes. But perhaps the feature that fascinated her the most about him was his nice teeth.

Plus the dimples that graced each of his cheeks when he smiled at her.

He came to the table, after having taken the sunglasses off and looking around the restaurant. It wasn't because he didn't know where Hart would be, but rather because as a Field Training Officer he was conscious to do everything by the book. They'd met when they'd both been assigned to the Robertsville Detail. The Sheriff's police had taken over the policing duties of the impoverished south suburb when the new mayor had fired the entire police department. It had taken the better part of a year to recruit, hire, and train the new police officers, and little by little, the county units had been cut back. But several officers had remained in Robertsville to act as FTOs. Rick had been one of them.

"Hi," he said as he sat down, taking the seat in the booth that would allow him to have a clear view of the door and cash register.

"Hi," said Hart, still thinking how good he looked in his uniform. "So how's your day going?"

"Oh, not bad," he said. "I managed to get up early and go for my run, then I shot over to visit Lance."

"How's he doing?"

Rick sighed. "Not good. He's still in the isolation wing and his attorney's still negotiating with the prosecutor. In the meantime, Special Prosecutions seems like they're serving a search warrant for something every other day. The IRS froze all his assets. I can't even drive the Corvette any more."

Hart said nothing but squeezed his hand in commiseration.

"I just wish it would be . . . over with, I guess," he said. "But then sometimes I don't know if I'm ready to face what that might bring." He stopped as the waitress came by with two glasses of water and menus, then flipped open her pad.

"Coffee?" she asked.

"Yeah, I'll have some," Rick said.

Hart nodded also and the waitress left.

"Sorry I couldn't make it last night," he said. "We got tied up on a shooting and a cocaine bust."

"Wow, how much you get?"

"A bag of about thirty rocks," Rick said. "The bad part was that it was a juvenile. The gangbangers are having the little shorties make all their runs for them. That way, if they get caught, they don't do any bad time."

"I don't suppose the Audy Home will take 'em either?" Hart said.

"Hardly," he said. "They won't take any juvie unless it's a crime of violence. Drugs, stolen cars, aggravated assaults . . . we just release 'em back to mommie so she can turn them loose and we can pick them up the next time." He laughed. "If I wasn't so glad to see you I'd almost be pissed off. So how'd your day go yesterday? I did try to call but you were out."

She admired his perfect smile once again before she answered.

"I got transferred," she said. "You'll never guess where I'm going."

"Transferred?" Rick said, his brow furrowing. "I thought you liked Investigations."

"I do. It wasn't my idea."

"Christ," he said, pausing as the waitress set the cups down in front of them. "Is this to make way for another one of Shay's cronies?"

"You ready, or you need a few minutes, or you just gonna get your usual?" the waitress asked.

Hart ordered her customary tuna sandwich on whole wheat and a salad, while Rick got his broiled chicken luncheon special. He tore open a packet of cream and dumped it into his coffee.

"Actually," Hart said, taking a sip from her cup, "I think it's another stab at their ever-going campaign to appear politically correct."

"Huh?"

"The Chief feels that it's high time there was a woman on the Raid Team," she said. She watched his reaction as she told him. He froze in mid-movement, his coffee cup held in both hands at chin level.

"You're kidding, right?" he said.

"Un-uh," she said.

"Jesus H. Christ," he said, setting his cup down without taking a drink. "I've had my application in for Tactical for months, and they give it to you. And you don't even want it."

"They said it would be a great opportunity," Hart said, somewhat stung by his response. "Look good on the next promotional exam."

"Oh, I'm sure it will," Rick said. "And don't get me wrong, I know you'll be a great asset to the team. It's just that they seem to make their decisions based on . . ."

"On me being a woman?" she asked.

"Yeah," he nodded. "Like you said, crazy reasons . . . political correctness. Whatever happened to putting the most qualified man in the position?"

"Maybe they're looking for the most qualified *person*," Hart said. She hadn't anticipated this reaction from him.

"Look," he said, letting out a slow breath. "I didn't mean to imply that you're not qualified. It's just that I spent three years in the Marines in Iraq. Advanced recon was my middle name. I'm a natural for the kind of stuff they do in Tactical. And I was really hoping to get it. Besides, you're a great detective. I'm sure Frank's gonna miss you."

"He offered to go to Captain O'Herlieghy to try and get me transferred back."

"Oh, what'd you tell him?"

"I told him that I wanted to try this new assignment," she said. That was all she dared tell him. "It sounds kinda neat, and I'm sure I'll get a lot of training and experience that I wouldn't be getting otherwise."

They stared at each other over the steam rising from their coffees, then Rick smiled. "That's what I love about you so much. You always look on the bright side of things. That and you put up with me."

Hart smiled too. It was encouraging to hear him use the word "love." Maybe he meant it like she hoped he did.

"I was out shopping yesterday, picking up all the uniforms and things," she said. "They fit horribly, so I spent half the night tailoring them."

The waitress brought their food and set the plates down on the table. After she left Hart picked up her sandwich and took a small bite. Harmon was already spreading the butter on his baked potato.

"So are you going to come over after you get off?" she asked.

"Well, I don't know," he said. From his tone it was clear he was teasing. "You want me to?"

"Would I have asked if I didn't?" she shot back. "Besides, this might be your last chance." She waited for him to look up at her before she added, "At least for a few days anyway. I'm going up to Great Lakes for a week's worth of SWAT school."

"Well, just remember a good Marine always finds a way to

improvise and overcome," he said. "And I will come over on one condition."

"What's that?" she asked.

He glanced around before leaning toward her and whispering, "That you show me how you look in and out of your new uniform." His gaze settled on her breasts.

Hart saw where he was looking and smiled. "Maybe we can do some . . . advanced recon. If you're up to it, that is."

"In that case, maybe we better meet at my place," he said, grinning back at her. "I've got some very special equipment we can use."

Leal walked up the escalator to the second floor of the Markham Sixth District Court Building. It had been one of Shay's few good ideas, moving the Investigations units out to the actual districts they worked in rather than keeping everything centered way up in the Maywood headquarters. It saved him a lot of driving time and allowed him to be close to the office if he was called out. One good idea floating in a sea of bad ones, he thought. Maybe the next election would change things for the better. He thought about Hart as he rounded the corner and went into the sheriff's police office. It was the closest thing to a station that they had. His home away from home. He was sure going to miss Ollie, and wondered if Sean O'Herlieghy could do anything. But should he even ask him?

Hart had seemed ambivalent about that. Maybe she wanted out of the pressure cooker. But Tactical wasn't any picnic either. Those poor bastards were doing round-the-clock drug raids, plus surveillance duties, and any special operations call-outs that came along. She'd get tired of that real quick. Maybe she wouldn't even get through the school, he mused.

No, she'd make it. He knew she would. She was the best cop he knew.

Inside the office area Leal spotted Ryan leaning against the wall, a carton of milk in one hand and an unlit cigarette in the other. Those clean-air act restrictions were killing the poor bastard. When Ryan saw Leal he grinned.

"You ain't gonna believe what I'm gonna tell you," Ryan said, his mustache curling over his teeth in what passed for a smile. "You just ain't gonna fucking believe it."

"Lemme guess," said Leal strolling by him and pointing at the milk carton. "You're going on a health kick?"

"Naw," Ryan said. "Just hot pipes." He touched the carton against his stomach. Then he took a deep breath and began whistling, his gaze following Leal as his cheeks puffed out the tune.

Leal looked at him.

"What the fuck you doing?" he asked.

Ryan paused, put the cigarette in his mouth for a second, squinted, then took the cigarette in his hand and continued whistling.

"Will you cut it out with the fucking whistling," Leal said.

"It's a clue," Ryan said. "Listen." He whistled the tune one more time. It had a nagging familiarity about it, but Leal couldn't place it.

"What theme song is that?" Ryan asked.

Leal shook his head. "Maybe if it sounded like a song I'd be able to tell you."

Ryan smirked as he sipped the milk from the carton. The center of his mustache was white. "Want me to whistle it again?"

"Please, spare me," said Leal. "If you're finished playing name that tune, just tell me what it is you're talking about."

"*Rick's Place*," Ryan said. "Remember that old TV show?"

Leal considered this for a moment, then realized that the tune Ryan had been whistling was actually a poorly done rendition of the show's theme song.

"We got a homicide to investigate and you're wasting my time talking about old TV shows?" Leal said.

Ryan's mouth snaked into his rakish grin again.

"You're not listening to me, Frankie boy," he said. "Who starred in *Rick's Place*?"

Leal shook his head again. "I don't remember. The show's been off for years. It was on when I was in high school, for Christ's sake."

"Well, you might say that Dick Forest, the star," Ryan said, emphasizing the name, "has made one final performance for us." He paused again. "As the victim in our little Riptide Motel murder."

"That was him?"

Ryan's lip curled up into a patronizing smile. "In the dead flesh. I told you he looked like somebody, didn't I?"

Oh shit, thought Leal. Now the little routine homicide that nobody cared about was about to become "a heater."

9
PARTNERS

Rick's Place had been a television parody of the movie *Casablanca*. Set in Morocco before the American involvement in World War II, it had Dick Forest in the Bogart role, only playing it as a small screen, watered-down version. Forest played Rick, the suave bar owner who was an American spy working to smuggle refugees and Jews out of German-dominated Europe. The rest of the cast included the bumbling Nazis, who were played as either buffoons or secretly sympathetic, the crooked French police chief whom Rick kept in line with his fixed gambling, and the black piano player who lapsed into "As Time Goes By," which had been jazzed up and modified into the show's theme song.

It lasted five seasons before getting canceled and making Dick Forest a celebrity-on-hiatus. He made the rounds on various talk and game shows until *Rick's Place* was sold to syndication. It still ran on some of the nostalgia-based cable channels. Forest, whose real name turned out to be Richard Phipps, had played several smaller roles in some made-for-TV movies, but, his agent had told Leal, he was currently starring in a play at the Shady Lane Theater in Evergreen Park, Illinois. The agent's phone number had been supplied by the LAPD, whom Ryan had contacted shortly after discovering the identity of their corpse.

"The agent says he was also renting a condo on Lake Shore

Drive, courtesy of the theater company," Leal said, hanging up the phone.

"Were there any keys recovered in his property?" Ryan asked.

"No," Leal said shaking his head as he glanced through his original notes. "I suppose management can let us in. I have the address."

Ryan glanced at his watch. "Let's find out what time the next show is scheduled for," he said. "We can go interview the cast and crew so they can tell the stand-in it's his turn in the barrel."

"I think they're called understudies," Leal said. "And I'm sure he's already been filling in. The star's already missed a bunch of shows. We'd better get a move on before the news media gets wind of this and the shit hits the fan."

"Yeah, right," Ryan said. "And maybe we can get one of them nice young actresses to give us head too."

"You got a one-track mind," Leal said. "Say, this thing is gonna turn into a heater real fast. What do you say we try and get Ollie back to help us?" Leal knew that Ryan, who made it a point to always kiss the ass of the boss closest to him, would be in a better position to work on this than he was.

"Yeah," Ryan said. "I'll see what I can do."

Since the next performance of *Send Me a Tenor* at Shady Lane wasn't scheduled until eight, Ryan told the production manager, Chaz Winters, that they needed to get the cast and crew in as soon as possible for interviews. Winters, a rather thick-looking man in his late forties with a bad toupee, was visibly shaken by the news his star was dead. He seemed to wilt as he picked up the phone.

"You have no idea how much of a blow this is," Winters said. His voice was a few octaves above tenor, and his hands moved with fluttering gestures. Ryan glanced at Leal when Winters's back was turned and mouthed the word, "Fag." He then raised his eyebrows and pursed his lips as the production manager began dialing the phone. Leal thought about how much Ryan's antics bothered him and how much he missed working with Ollie.

"Mr. Winters," Leal said. "We'd prefer it if you didn't tell each person why they're to report here. Just say that it's an emergency and that they're to get here as soon as possible."

"Certainly," Winters said, shaking his head. "I mean, Mr. Forest had missed a few rehearsals, but we were a bit used to that. Stars, after all, can be temperamental at times, right? This is just terrible."

"If possible we'd also like to interview each member separately as they arrive," Leal added. "Is there a room we could use?"

"You can use my office," Winters said.

The office, with its bright theatrical posters and lavish furnishings, was hardly suited for interviews, and they yielded very little in the way of information about the murdered star. All of the cast members were local actors doing stage work and the occasional commercial, hoping to get that big break that would send them on their way to bright lights and stardom.

The break for the detectives came when Ryan asked one of the women if Forest had been seeing anybody connected with the show. The girl, who was named Marcia Paxton, looked down quickly and the detectives picked up on something.

"I'm not sure," she said. She was a tall and leggy redhead with her thick hair pulled back away from her face.

"Marcia, a man's dead and we're in charge of finding out who did it," Leal said. "If there's something you can tell us that might help, please don't hold anything back."

The girl looked down again, then swallowed before she answered.

"Well, when Mr. Forest got here everybody was kind of excited, you know," she said, clenching her hands together. "He was the first real big star that a lot of us had worked with, so we were always anxious to spend a lot of time with him."

Leal nodded.

"Then he asked me and Bill, he's the guy that used to play the police inspector, if we'd like to stop by his apartment after one of the performances." She stopped and looked at her hands again. "Well, we went, and Mr. Forest kinda got me a little bit drunk. I normally don't drink too much, but it was sort of like a special occasion and all." She paused and looked at Ryan. "Will I get in trouble if I tell you all of it?"

Ryan smiled and patted her arm.

"It's best if you do tell us everything," he said.

"Well," she continued, "we were up in his apartment and he started getting kind of weird, you know, like he wanted us all to get into bed together. Bill was kind of wasted too, and the next thing I know we were taking off our clothes. They . . . we did a couple lines of coke." She bit the corner of her mouth. "Mr. Forest had this camera all set up and wanted to record us, but Bill got a little bit nervous and couldn't . . . Mr. Forest took me aside and began putting these handcuffs and things on me, saying it would all be okay, but I got scared." She swallowed. "But what really got me nervous was when he put this noose over my head. It was like a silk cord, or something, and he was tucking something under it so it wouldn't bruise my neck. I started screaming for him to stop, and he just kept trying to reassure me, saying that it wouldn't hurt and it would make me come real good. He said that I could do it to him then, if I didn't want him to do it to me. I told him yeah, just to get loose, then grabbed my clothes and got the hell out of there."

"When was this?" Leal asked.

"About two weeks ago," she said. "Mr. Forest had just been

91

here about three weeks."

"What happened to Bill?" Ryan asked.

"He got a bigger part in a play downtown, at the Organic," she said.

"The Organic?" Ryan asked, wrinkling his forehead.

"The Organic Theater on Clark," she said. "Chaz can give you the address."

"Did you speak to Bill later about the incident?" Leal asked.

Marcia shook her head.

"He's kinda kinky too, but I never knew till I told my girlfriend about it," she said. "But Bill belongs to some kind of swinger's club that uses this computer bulletin board to set up meetings."

"You have Bill's phone number by any chance?" Leal asked.

"I also want to make sure I get your home number too," Ryan said. "I may need to get with you again."

Leal noticed the sly wink. Yeah, he thought. We got a pending heater and he's got a one-track mind.

After gathering the pertinent information on William Autumn, as he called himself, Leal and Ryan grabbed a quick dinner and ran a criminal history check on Autumn's real name, William H. Sax. He had been arrested for solicitation numerous times and had several drug arrests. It also kicked back a warrant for Failure to Appear on a DUI charge out of Cicero Heights. It was encroaching on late afternoon/early evening when they drove past Sax's apartment in Alsip to scope the place out. Ryan went about a block past the building before dialing his number on the cell phone. He answered on the first ring.

"May I speak to Dick?" Ryan said, mimicking a southern drawl.

"Wrong number," the voice said, and hung up.

"Looks like Mr. Autumn is at home," Ryan said grinning.

"Now the only question is will he let us in?" Leal grinned.

"The way I figure it," Ryan said, "this guy Autumn's the coke connection for the theater. You know how those fuckers can smell out one another. So Forest approaches him about some dope and maybe a broad and when they try to put the moves on Missy Scarlet, old Bill realizes that Dick Forest is really the king of kink. When they bomb out with her, he lines something else up and Forest ends up dead. What do you think?"

"Sounds good, but it's still too early to formulate any solid theories," Leal said. He knew it was one of Ryan's flaws as an investigator to come up with theories and motivations too early in the case and then try to make all the subsequent evidence fit. It narrowed your perception and tended to affect all subsequent information. What they needed to do was backtrack through Forest's last known activities. Find out who he was with, what they had done. What was the reason for the sleazy motel or the rental car, not to mention the fake name? Questions he would have to find the answers to before he started to formulate any theories. He wouldn't have had to tell Hart those things, but Ryan wasn't half the detective she was. But still, in spite of everything, he was almost beginning to enjoy working with Ryan. There was a certain adrenaline high that came with working a big case, a heater, which this one would surely become. And having a partner made things move a little bit smoother. But he knew that wouldn't last. And he also knew that if they picked up a suspect, he'd miss Ollie's sure-fire hand at interviewing. She seemed to have a knack for knowing just what tactic to use to break down a suspect and they worked great in tandem.

Ryan's cell phone went off. He looked at the number and told Leal it was headquarters.

"Yeah, this is Sergeant Ryan. What ya got?" He listened for a moment, then covered the mouthpiece as he turned to Leal.

"The rental car's been recovered, Chicago P.D. They saw the type three and are awaiting instructions."

"Tell 'em to send a hook and to get a hold of—" he started to say, but Ryan handed him the phone and took out his pack of cigarettes.

"You tell 'em," Ryan said, shaking one out of the pack. "It's your fucking case."

Leal identified himself to the dispatcher and listened to her description of the recovered vehicle. He let out a low whistle. "Have it towed to headquarters. Then beep an E.T., preferably Henry Morgan, to go over the car with a fine-tooth comb. It's related to the Riptide Motel case, and it's turned out to be a heater. He'll understand. Be sure you tell Morgan that, okay?"

Leal terminated the call and turned to Ryan. "The car had bullet holes in the back window, blood all over the front seat and passenger door."

"Hmmm, the plot thickens." Ryan took a long drag on the cigarette.

"What do you say we pick Mr. Autumn up and put him on ice for a while. Maybe it'll loosen him up a little."

"Yeah, but I'd hate for him to miss his performance," Ryan said, grinning as he exhaled a cloudy breath.

The apartment building was located in the middle of a street full of two- and three-story brownstones. Sax's place was listed as 3NE, in a building with six units. Leal and Ryan decided to call for a backup after riding down the alley that ran behind the buildings. It opened on either end to a perpendicular street. The closest county unit was thirty minutes away, so they called Alsip P.D. and requested one of their marked units to assist them.

"We're picking up a guy on a warrant," Ryan told the dispatcher. "But he's also a suspect in a homicide investigation."

"Why did you tell them that?" Leal asked after Ryan had ended the call.

"Why not?" Ryan said, shaking out another cigarette. "Gets results that way." He lit up the square as Leal rolled down the window.

Two marked units met them at the corner a few minutes later. After introducing themselves, they decided that Ryan and one of the uniformed officers would go to the front of the apartment building while Leal went around the back. The other marked car would stay in position down the alley in case the suspect fled. Since it was getting dark, Leal figured that it was a passable plan.

"One other thing," he said, glancing at Ryan, "we're picking this guy up on a DUI warrant. We haven't tied him up to the homicide we're working as of yet, so don't mention it, okay?"

The other officers looked at each other and nodded.

They spread out. Leal strolled down the alley noticing that the rear parking lots were all pretty well lighted. And each Dumpster had the numerical address painted in black on the side. It made for easy identification of the building from the rear, something that often tripped up the back-door man. He came to the building just west of Sax's and crouched by the side. It was getting dark, and Ryan had taken the flashlight from the squad. Leal realized he'd forgotten his Mini Mag but figured the ambient lighting was good enough. That was a double-edged sword though. He could probably be seen by anyone looking out his window. Glancing toward the front he saw Ryan and the marked squad pull up.

Ryan rang the doorbell for 3NE several times but there was no answer. He continued to lean on it when a door on the second floor opened and a woman looked out. Seeing the uniformed officer through the glass partition, she ducked back inside her apartment; the safety door buzzed open a moment later. She appeared again in the doorway.

"You guys after somebody?" she asked.

"Just want to talk to the gentleman upstairs," Ryan said with a congenial smile.

"Paul?" the woman asked.

"No," Ryan said. "Bill."

"Oh," she answered. "You know, I think you just missed him. I thought I heard somebody running down the back stairs."

"Coming your way, Frank!" Ryan shouted into his radio.

Leal got the transmission just as he heard the back door of the apartment building bang open. A wiry-looking blond guy ran to a red Trans Am, his hand squirming in his pocket for the keys.

"Hey," Leal said. "I'm a police officer. Hold it a minute." The blond guy stopped and smiled. He seemed to be turning toward Leal, when suddenly he bolted and ran in the other direction. Leal yelled, "Shit," and took off after him. The guy was already a good twenty feet in front of him by the time Leal got his radio up to his mouth and screamed, "Foot pursuit northbound down the alley."

Giving directions as he was running, every other word a gasping sound, Leal managed to stay behind the fleeing suspect. The guy was wearing those gym shoes with the blinking lights on the heels. Each lurching step was punctuated by a red flash. The old TV ad for the shoes flashed in Leal's mind: "If you want to own the night, you got to own the light."

Pretty soon we're gonna own you, asshole, he thought.

As they got near the mouth of the alley, Leal heard the roar of the squad car's engine right behind him. He sidestepped, letting the vehicle pass him. The headlights caught Sax in full gallop. Leal felt a surge of satisfaction as he saw the guy's head swivel backward with a terrified expression stretched over his face.

Soon, asshole, soon, Leal thought as he kept running.

Sax cut to his left, into a parking lot, and ran between two apartment buildings. Leal went after him, damned if he was going to lose the son-of-a-bitch now. His lungs felt like they were on fire, and he cursed himself that he hadn't made more of those early morning runs with Ollie.

He cursed too the bullet that had torn open his chest a few years ago and all the cigarettes he'd smoked before he'd quit after getting shot. While he was doing the internal cursing, he tossed a couple at the fleeing asshole in front of him for good measure.

Just as Leal was beginning to wheeze, Sax caught his foot on an extended gutter and went sprawling. He began to roll to his feet but Leal was on top of him and gave him a hard shove. Sax went down to his hands and knees just as Leal wrenched a section of the rain gutter loose from the side of the building. Swinging it like a baseball bat, Leal smacked Sax across the back, then swung it again across the man's legs and arms. The impact made a loud whacking sound, and Leal knew it probably stung like hell, but wasn't going to leave that much lasting damage.

Leal hit him three more times, managing to say between strokes, "You're . . . under . . . arrest."

"Okay, okay, for Christ's sake," Sax said, curling into a protective ball. "Stop fucking hitting me, will ya? You got no right to beat me."

"You ain't even seen a beating yet, asshole." Leal held the piece of gutter in front of him, then ordered the suspect to roll over and spread his arms out. Sax complied, and Leal kneeled on the man's back and twisted his right arm behind him. He unsnapped his handcuffs and had both the suspect's hands secured by the time a breathless Ryan and the two uniformed coppers found him.

"Christ, where'd you go?" Ryan said, leaning against the side of the building. "Scared the shit outta me."

Leal, who'd recovered enough to be able to speak with only the hint of exhaustion, coughed. The coolness of the April air seemed to have seared his lungs. He spit out some phlegm.

"You piece of shit," he said to Sax, already deciding that he'd be the "bad cop" when the interview began. He pulled the suspect to his feet, trying to make it look as effortless as he could.

"What you guys want with me anyway?" Sax said. "How was I supposed to know who the fuck you were?"

"What'd you think when you saw a police car pull up in front?" Ryan asked, lighting the cigarette that he'd placed between his lips. "We were out selling tickets to the policeman's ball?"

Crazy Bob Lemack heard the broadcast of the foot pursuit over ISPERN. He was not close but never too far to assist a brother officer. By the time he got turned around the follow-up broadcast stated that the suspect was in custody. He nodded with satisfaction and went back to radar patrol, zeroing the beam on an approaching Buick. The digits locked in at sixty-five, which was a full twenty over the posted limit on Harlem Avenue. Pushing up the square-framed glasses on his nose, he let the Buick pass him then swung behind it. The intersection ahead was well lighted and perfect for his purposes. He flipped the toggle switch that activated the emergency lights. The Buick slowed to a stop and pulled over to the right shoulder. Lemack slipped the glove on his left hand and got out of the squad car. There was only one occupant in the Buick.

Better and better, Crazy Bob thought.

Lemack was aware of his big look. His body was block-shaped

with wide shoulders and thick arms. The bullet-proof vest, the square-framed glasses, the shaved head, and the large Fu Manchu mustache fed the image he cultivated. Despite the coolness of the evening temperatures, Lemack wore no jacket; his shirt sleeves were rolled up revealing a tattoo on the outside of each forearm. On the right one was the Marine Corps emblem, under which was lettered in all capitals: *SEMPER FI*. The left had a well-defined picture of the head of a German Shepherd. Under this one was lettered: *BRUTUS*.

"Good evening, sir," Lemack said. "May I see your driver's license and proof of insurance please?"

The driver was a middle-aged white guy, tie loosely knotted around a white shirt. "What are you stopping me for?" He made no motion to produce anything.

Lemack looked down at the man and repeated his request as politely as he had the first time.

"No, not until you tell me what I'm being stopped for." His voice had a petulant sound to it.

"I have you clocked in at twenty over the posted limit," Lemack said.

"What? That's impossible. I know I wasn't speeding. You must have clocked somebody else."

"The man said, he needs to see your license and registration, asshole," a rather high-pitched voice said. The motorist's eyes widened as he looked first at the big copper standing there, then at the officer's left hand, from where the voice had seemed to emanate. The glove had a large pair of eyes painted on it, a waspish nose, and big, cherry-red lips.

Lemack's thumb formed the lower jawbone and his index finger the upper lip. "You hard of hearing or just plain stupid?" the voice said again. It had a Daffy Duck style twang, right down to the lisping sibilance of the "S." Lemack's lips did not move.

The man shifted in his seat, looking up at the officer, then he reached into his pants pocket and quickly withdrew his wallet. He handed up his driver's license.

"I'll need to see your proof of insurance too, sir," Lemack said.

"I don't have it with me," the man said.

"Well, what do you think?" Lemack asked, canting his left hand toward himself.

"This guy's a real smart ass," the glove said. The glove rotated back, the eyes seeming to stare at the motorist again. "He deserves to have the book thrown at him. Take him to the cooler."

"The cooler?" the motorist asked.

"Jail, asshole," the glove said.

Lemack sighed. "I'm afraid my partner's right, sir. For that particular violation, you can't use a bond card. You'd need to post your driver's license or two hundred dollars. For that you'd need to follow me to the nearest police station."

"Just use the license, please," the motorist said, his eyes straying to the large framed Glock in Lemack's holster. The guy seemed nervous to Crazy Bob. In fact, he looked about ready to shit his pants.

"Fine, sir. We'll be right back."

When he returned with the ticket a few minutes later, Lemack instructed the motorist on mailing in the fine.

"What if I want to go to court?" the guy asked.

"That's your right, of course," Lemack said, "but I did give you a pass on the failure to have proof of insurance. Like I said, that's a two hundred dollar bond, and a mandatory court appearance."

"I don't think going to court would be such a good idea, buster," the high-pitched voice of the glove said, canting slightly to give the motorist what could have been interpreted as a malevolent look. "Then we'd have to tell the judge what a jerk you were when we gave you this speeding ticket. And that you had no proof of insurance. The judge ain't gonna like that. Not one bit."

The man swallowed and said, "All right. Thank you, Officer." He flashed Lemack a weak, nervous smile before pulling away.

Crazy Bob smiled back as he watched the car pull away.

"Aww, what's the matter, big guy?" the same high-pitched voice said. "The guy was an asshole. He had it coming."

Lemack looked at his glove, then spoke in his own voice. "Yeah, he did, I guess, but he was still a misguided citizen looking for guidance."

"You're getting to be too much of a fucking liberal," the glove voice said.

Lemack's call-sign came over the radio and when he answered, the dispatcher instructed him to return to base ASAP.

"Oh oh," the glove said, the lips moving with exaggeration. "Now what have you gotten us into?"

Lemack pondered this, then shrugged.

Hart had finished showering and was drying her hair. She'd taken extra time in shaving her legs and underarms then splashed on a hint of perfume behind each ear. Rick had called and was on his way over. She wanted everything to be as perfect as possible tonight. After all, this would be it until she was finished with that damn SWAT school.

The thought of it depressed her. Everyone kept talking about how rough it was going to be, and she was beginning to feel some real dread. She hadn't even wanted to go to it at all, much less have to go through it just so she would fit in with this special assignment. A rat's assignment at that—working with I.A.D. Not something she ever wanted to do. But it was not like she had a lot of choice, and maybe it would help her out when she took the sergeant's test in August. Her last evaluation had been good. An 84, although she felt that she deserved higher. Card was real stingy with the ratings, unless you were "connected." But her clearance rate was one of the highest, and nobody could discount the departmental decorations she'd been awarded. Two medals of valor. Most coppers would kill for that decoration. You couldn't buy those, although Howard Lindsey had gotten one the same time she'd gotten her second one, and all he'd done was get shot in the vest. And Frank, who'd saved her life, had gotten nothing. But she knew that awards meant nothing. The only thing that really counted was the survivor's satisfaction of not getting killed.

She flipped on the TV and caught the tail-end of the ten o'clock news. Rick had told her he was getting off at eleven, and they'd decided that it would be easier for him to come to her place instead of the other way around. She'd laid out a towel for him knowing that he'd want to shower after wearing his vest for an eight-hour shift.

At least he'd better, if he plans on anything happening between us tonight, she thought, giggling to herself.

Thoughts of her and Rick, and the pleasure of being in bed together, his strong hands going at their customary half-speed, as they roamed over her were supplanted when the bright lights of the mini-cam showed the reporter standing outside headquarters. Hart grabbed the remote and turned up the volume. ". . . live here in Markham where Cook County Sheriff's Police are investigating the death of television star Dick Forest. Forest starred in *Rick's Place*, a situation comedy that was popular fifteen years ago. Sources within the police department tell us that Forest's body was found in a room at the Riptide Motel . . ." The picture switched to a black and white publicity still of the actor in the white tuxedo that he'd worn on the series. It then shifted to a picture of the motel.

"Investigators refused to comment on the cause of death, but did state that they had a person of interest in custody at this time." Ryan's face appeared on the screen looking drawn and gaunt under the bright light.

"At this time we are interviewing a person of interest regarding Mr. Forest's demise," Ryan said. "But other than that, we have no further comment." He smiled into the camera.

"We'll be standing by for further developments," the reporter said, his image returning to the screen. "Back to you, Lester."

"Thanks, Ron," the anchor said. He smiled into the camera and said that weather and sports would be corning up next, and a commercial followed.

Hart was glad they'd come up with someone so fast, but wondered just how solid the connection was. Either way, TV reporters spreading the news about a dead celebrity meant one thing: they had a real heater on their hands

Wow, she thought. I hope Frank's got a good partner for all of this.

10
HIGH INTENSITY

The course instructions had specified the Special Weapons and Tactics class would begin at 0700 hours sharp. Attendees were advised to wear BDUs, full duty gear, and bring various other workout clothes. At 0701 hours Monday morning Hart stood at attention in a triple line formation on a grassy field of Great Lakes Naval Base. The orange glow of the sun was suspended over the lake in front of them. The water, visible at a distance only, looked gray and choppy under a thin layer of foggy mist.

"I am Special Agent Deckons," the tall slender man in front of them said. He had light blond hair cropped close to his head, and Hart could tell from his narrow waist that he was fit.

"My partner, and your instructor for the next week, is Special Agent Cook." Deckons held out his hand toward a swarthy guy who appeared to be in his early forties, but equally well conditioned. He also wore the same type of white nylon pants and sweatshirt.

"This is a high intensity course, gentlemen," Deckons continued, then paused and looked at Hart. "And lady." He smiled, showing sculptured teeth that somehow looked as wicked as a picket fence. "We reserve the right to ask you to leave if you can't keep up. Be prepared for a lot of physical activity. SWAT members have to be in tip-top physical shape. As we used to say in the Marine Corps, we can only go as fast as the slowest man." He paused again and stared at Hart a second time. "Excuse me, I meant the slowest person. Now, as stated in your instructional packets, we're going to start things off with a physical fitness test to determine your eligibility. Should you not pass it, you will not be allowed to continue. Anyone wishing to spare himself, or herself, the embarrassment of failing the test can leave now and go back to your individual department. Otherwise, you can stow your weapons and gear in the locker rooms and report back here in five minutes." He pointed to a large brick building to their left. "You may wear gym shoes for this part of the course."

As Hart started to carry her duffel bag toward the women's locker room Agent Cook ran up next to her. "Officer Hart," he said.

She stopped. He smiled before he spoke. It was a gentler smile than Deckons's had been.

"As my partner said, this is a very high intensity course."

"I gathered that," Hart replied.

"Well, we don't want to come on in the wrong light, but we feel that if we make allowances here, we'd be doing a disservice to the other officers." He hesitated and smiled again. "What I mean is, there are no allowances made on the street in an actual situation."

"Agent Cook, are you implying that because I'm a woman I shouldn't be here?"

"Not at all," he said. "I'm merely saying that we don't make special exceptions for anyone of either sex." The corners of his mouth drew down before he spoke again. "You see, that goes for our own female agents too. Unfortunately, we've never had a woman finish this course."

"Well, I guess I'll be the first then, won't I?" Hart said and shoved open the door.

The locker room was large, with rows of full-length metal lockers.

At least I'll have the place to myself, she thought.

105

Hart hung up the extra uniform and placed the bag with her towel, toilet articles, and notebook inside the locker. She put the Sig Sauer 220 that Rick had given her Saturday night on the top shelf. "You can't go to SWAT school with a revolver," she remembered him saying. "They'll laugh you off the range. And this one has night sights."

Nobody was laughing now. Just waiting for her to fall on her face.

She had a lightweight black nylon sleeveless leotard on under her fatigue jacket, just in case she had to strip off the shirt. Under that she had on a brand-new sport's bra that gave her excellent support, and had some gauze tape for her wrists in her lower shirt pocket in case she needed it. Her hair was in her usual workout style, a French braid, which she adjusted and tucked as she checked herself in the mirror before going out.

The remarks of the two instructors had made her feel very uncomfortable. She hadn't even asked to go to this stupid school. It was just the first part of a very stressful assignment. An odyssey, the nature of which she couldn't even share with the people closest to her. *Like I really need some chauvinistic Feds trying to discourage me before I even get started,* she thought, trying to push the negativity out of her mind. But instead, she almost felt like crying.

There's no turning back, she decided. *I can only go forward.*

The entire group of officers showed up on the field outside the main classroom building. Hart took a few moments to study them. There were about twenty-five of them in the class. Some of them were young and trim, but others looked as if they'd been doing most of their patrolling at the donut shop. She was certain she could at least keep up or better their performances.

"Okay, nobody decided to drop yet, huh?" Deckons said. "Well, look around, because unless this is a very unusual group, some of you won't be here tomorrow."

"And some won't be here after this test," Agent Cook chimed in. He pointed to the classroom building, a large metal prefab structure with no windows. "Line up and proceed in there."

The inside of the building was equally Spartan looking. The rooms had been constructed from drywall frames and extended up to about ten or twelve feet. There were no ceiling tiles.

At the front of the room was a large blackboard, a podium with the FBI seal, and an overhead projector. The room was filled with plain folding tables and chairs.

Deckons picked up a long metal instrument, squeezing the tongs together as he spoke.

"These calipers are designed to measure body fat," he said. "This requires several measurements to be taken on various parts of the body. It will necessitate you pulling down your pants so we can take a measurement on your thighs, and also removing your shirts so we can measure your upper arms and abdomens." He turned and looked at Hart.

"We can do you in the other room if you prefer, Officer Hart."

She nodded and Cook stood up. He grabbed a pair of calipers and began walking toward the door.

A couple of the guys let out exaggerated moans as Hart started out of the room. Deckons clapped his hands together.

"Gentlemen, we're all adults here, I hope. I want to caution you as to inappropriate outbursts. They also will get you expelled from this class, along with a letter that you can take back explaining the reason to your commanding officers." Nobody spoke. "Is there anyone here who is not wearing any underwear?" Again, nobody spoke. "Okay, as I said, we're all adults. Drop your pants down to mid-thigh level."

Hart had stopped when she'd heard the groaning. If she expected to get through this course, she realized that the quicker she could be assimilated the better. And after all, she wasn't wearing a thong. She turned to Cook, who was standing next to her and said, "I'll just stay in here, okay?"

His nod was tentative and Hart realized she'd thrown him off his game. Good, let him see how it feels. She undid the belt and then unbuttoned the pants. The long shirttails covered most of her underpants, which were gray Jockeys, and not very revealing in any case. But then again, what did she have to be embarrassed about? She was used to working out in high-cut leotards and posing in the tiniest of bikinis in front of massive crowds for her bodybuilding contests. She did enjoy Cook's reaction as he tried unsuccessfully with the calipers to find some fatty tissue on the thighs. When he straightened up and told her he had to measure her hip at the belt line, she pulled up the shirt leaving her pants down. He again applied the calipers to her sculptured waist and made some notations on a sheet of paper with her name in block letters printed across the top.

"The last one is the upper arm," he said.

Hart pulled up her pants and buttoned them, leaving the shirttails out. She then slipped the heavy fatigue shirt off and placed it on one of the tables. When Cook saw her rippling upper body his jaw dropped.

"Straighten your arm, please," Cook said.

Hart did, causing her triceps to contract raising a large horseshoe ridge of muscle. She heard Cook exhale as he applied the calipers, then made his notations. "Thank you," he said. Hart slipped the fatigue shirt back on and turned to watch the rest of the men being measured. Several of the heavier, out of shape guys blushed as they saw her turn, but so what? She knew they had been watching her.

Completing the measurements took about ten minutes, then Deckons led them into a large gym section. Several heavy mats had been placed on the floor. A bench with a set of weights was at one end, and a chinning bar was fixed to one wall. A Styrofoam "Red Man" suit was stacked in the corner. "The remainder of the test will consist of the maximum number of push-ups, pull-ups, and sit-ups that you can do," Deckons said. "There will be a two minute time limit on the sit-ups. This will be followed by a timed, two-mile run. Each exercise will be demonstrated beforehand. Any questions?"

No one said anything, but several of the guys looked nervous. Deckons spoke as Cook walked over to the bar, stepped on the rung, and grabbed the bar with his palms facing inward. He raised himself up so that his chin was above the bar. After a quick ten pull-ups Cook dropped to the floor.

"We consider eight the minimum for passing," Cook said.

A line formed and Hart went to the end of it. She wanted to check out the competition, so to speak, and see the condition of the others. Some of them looked in pretty good shape. The guys who'd lined up first were the ones who turned in pretty good performances. Several guys did more than fourteen and one guy managed nineteen. One husky man who looked about thirty-five managed two before dropping red-faced to the ground. Then it was Hart's turn. As she stepped to the bar, Deckons said, "For females three is considered passing."

Hart glanced at him as she raised her foot to the rung. What was this asshole's problem? Was he trying to psyche her out before she even started? Before stepping up she'd stripped off the fatigue shirt and let it drop to the floor. She was certain that she heard at least one gasp when they saw the high definition and massive musculature of her upper body. "I thought you said no special treatment for anyone?"

She took a wide grip and began doing pull-ups, raising herself so effortlessly each time that she began to lose count after twenty-five. She did four more, then hung suspended while she asked, "How many is that? I lost track."

"That's twenty-nine," Deckons said, his voice cracking.

Hart murmured a thanks and did one more pull-up. She

knew she could have strained out several more, perhaps ten, but she wanted to pace herself for the unlimited number of push-ups coming up. She dropped to the mat. As she straightened up, she was aware that all of their eyes were on her, and nobody said anything. The rest of the test went much the same way, with Hart out-performing everybody with one-hundred and fourteen sit-ups and onehundred and fifty push-ups. In each case she only did enough to pass her nearest competitors, saving something for the two-mile run. Several of the better conditioned guys had done well over a hundred push-ups, and she knew they might be able to pass her in the run. But it had been worth the extra effort to see the look on Deckons's face when she stood up.

The run was done on a gravel track outside near the range. Twelve times around equaled one mile and by her eighth time around, Hart was already beginning to lap some of the slower runners. The runners divided into two groups, more or less. The fast group and the slow group. Hart was number three in the fast group. But it was taking its toll on her. A couple of those guys ran like gazelles and had longer legs than she did. Plus the strain of the other events had tired her more than she'd figured. This was the first time she'd taken this test, and had misjudged her pacing.

As they neared completion of the twenty-second lap she realized that there was no way she could win, so she settled in behind the two front runners. Two other men pulled ahead of her as she came around for the last lap, and remembering her days in track and field at Western, she gave the kick everything she had. She came in third, but it was a burning, gut-wrenching third. Staggering past Cook and Deckons who shouted out her time, she continued to walk with a shaky-legged strut around the inside of the track, her lungs on fire and the banana, orange juice, and coffee breakfast threatening to come up with every step. She bent over and vomited in the grass, as if performing some ritualistic ceremony. It was standard procedure for someone to puke after a strenuous effort at the gym, and she did so without the least bit of compunction. When she straightened up she saw that some of the heavier guys still hadn't completed a mile and a half. Cook was standing next to her and asked if she was all right.

"I've been better," she said, still nauseous. She leaned over after a few steps and spit.

"You want some water?" Cook asked, handing her a squirt bottle.

She took it without comment and sprayed water over her face and into her mouth. It ran down in rivulets and soaked her black nylon top. Some of the other guys were yelling words of encouragement to the rest of the runners.

"You came in first over all," Cook said. "I thought you should know."

She nodded. If it got them off her back, the extra effort had been worth it, puke or no puke, she thought.

Leal had been told to cooperate with the reporters who had descended on headquarters like a swarm of locusts. He clipped the small mike to his shirt pocket and sat as the technician adjusted the bright, high intensity light of the camcorder on his face. It was his third such interview of the morning, but none of them amounted to much more than a series of no comments or the standard "the matter's still under investigation." When asked about "the suspect" that Sergeant Ryan had mentioned on Saturday, he was forced to reply with the same refrain once more: "The man being held. He was considered a person of interest." Leal hated that term. "He was also wanted on an outstanding warrant."

That prick Ryan had called in sick, just as Leal figured he

would when they blew the interview with Bill Autumn, as he liked to be called. They'd let him sit over two hours while they handled the horde of reporters before starting the interrogation. Not that it made much difference. As soon as they started, even before they'd read Sax the "Miranda" form, he'd clammed up saying that he wanted to call his lawyer.

"Look, we just want to ask you a few questions about your association with Dick Forest," Ryan had said.

"Are you guys gonna let me call my lawyer, or not?" Sax said.

"Like I told you," Ryan said, trying to ingratiate himself to the suspect, "we just want to ask you about Dick. You knew him, right?"

"Fuck you," Sax said. "I ain't saying nothing till I talk to my fucking lawyer. Now, can I call him or not?"

Ryan had looked at Leal, then had turned back to Sax with a smile. The telephone hung on the wall of the interrogation room and as he stood Ryan swept his hand out knocking the phone at Sax's face.

"Of course you can!" Ryan screamed. "There's the fucking phone."

Leal knew it was over when about an hour later Ronald Hollingsworth III arrived. The lawyer, looking dapper in his tailor-made gray suit and carrying a hand-crafted black leather briefcase, asked to speak with "Mr. Sax." How the hell did a second-rate actor afford one of the most expensive attorneys in the Chicago area?

Hollingsworth turned as Leal approached him and smiled.

"You're Frank Leal, aren't you?" the lawyer asked.

"That's right."

"My partner represented the late Marcus LeRigg. I think it was the time you got shot. Do you remember?"

Leal did, most vividly, but all he said was, "That's ancient history now."

"I'm glad you've put all that behind you." The lawyer's nose twitched as he made a sniffling sound. "What's my client being charged with?"

"We're holding him on a warrant," Leal said.

"A warrant?" Hollingsworth asked. "For what?"

"Failure to Appear. DUI," Leal said.

"DUI?" Hollingsworth laughed. "My God, what an idiot. What's the bond?"

"Three thousand D."

"I've a good mind to let him sit," Hollingsworth said as he took out his leather wallet and removed three one-hundred dollar bills.

The thought of the conversation brought a smile to his lips as the reporter went through the interview in the press room. Leal gave the standard answers, finishing up with a request for anyone having any information about Dick Forest's recent stay in Chicago to contact them.

"So you got anything else?" the reporter asked while the cameraman disconnected the camcorder from the tripod and went around for some shots of the reporter facing Leal. It felt good to have the bright light shining on somebody else's face for a change.

"We're waiting on some other leads," Leal said. "We have recovered the car Forest rented."

"Great," the reporter said. "Can I get a shot of it?"

"It's still being processed," Leal lied. He wanted to try to get a jump on the rest of the day and not have to waste time leading some civilians around.

"Well, I'll come back this afternoon if we can get those shots," the reporter said. "Can we see it before the five o'clock?"

"I'll see what I can do."

The reporter fished his card and was explaining when the

intercom light lit up.

"Sergeant Leal?" the feminine voice said. "Report to Lieutenant Card's office immediately."

Leal frowned.

"That connected to the Dick Forest story, Sarge?" the reporter asked.

"Nah," Leal said, grinning. "I'm probably just gonna get my ass chewed out for leaking so much to you guys." He turned and walked out of the press room, leaving them to review their tapes and wind up their cords. Leal walked down the hallway and wondered if Morgan had had any luck getting the latents identified. He'd promised to run the prints from the toilet seat and the car through AFIS. They needed a break on this one real fast. Leal was beginning to feel the twisting in his gut again. In Card's outer office he leaned over Jackie's desk.

"What's this about?" he whispered.

"You wait and see," she said, smiling so that the whiteness of her teeth was in sharp contrast to her dark eyes and coffee-colored skin.

Leal regretted that Joe Smith, one of the black detectives in Investigations South, wasn't working. Jackie had a severe crush on Joe, and Leal could have probably had him call ahead to find out what was what. Straightening up, he took a deep breath and reached for the office door. When he went in Card was shaking a plastic bottle of some kind of stomach medicine. He gestured for Leal to sit in the "hot seat" and took a long swig.

"What's the latest on this cluster fuck?" the lieutenant asked, twisting the cap back on the bottle.

"I'm waiting on info on the latents," Leal said.

"How about that fucker that we had to let go?" Card's color looked florid this morning. "Any indication why the S-G's lawyer would come down and bond out a white shithead like him?"

"I put a surveillance team on him," Leal said. "But so far he's holed up in his apartment."

"Think he's our man?" Card asked.

Leal shrugged. "Too early to tell."

"How about that serial rapist that we were working on before this Dick Forest thing cropped up?" Card asked. "We got anything new on that one?"

"I submitted the M.O. to the FBI so they could do a ViCAP workup," Leal said.

The lieutenant nodded, rolling his tongue over his teeth. "Shit," Card said, looking down at his desk. "I don't have to tell you how much pressure this is putting on the department, and me in particular. We gotta move on this one, Frank."

Surprised that the lieutenant had called him by his first name, Leal decided to chance it.

"Well, Lieu, I could use some help. Did Ryan mention to you that we would like to get Detective Hart back on this one? She was in at the scene, and she'd be a valuable asset to the investigation. Both investigations, actually."

Card shook his head, still staring at the desk top.

"Forget that," he said. "Out of the question. But you are getting some help." He reached forward and pressed the intercom button. "Is he there yet?"

Jackie's voice came on the line saying that he was.

"Well send him in then," Card mumbled. He looked up at Leal and said, "Frank, this is your new partner."

Leal turned and glanced over his shoulder as he stood. A solid-looking man with a shaved head, square-framed glasses, and a rather garish green-plaid sport jacket strolled in, extending his right hand. Leal took it and noticed that the hand felt hard and calloused, like a worn-out catcher's mitt. The guy had an out-of-style mustache that was big enough to house a family of sparrows.

"Frank Leal," he said. "Glad to meet you."

"Robert Lemack," the man with the shaved head said, then with a smile, "but most people just call me Bob."

11
HIS WILL BE DONE

Oman Taji was getting desperate. He'd spent the last four days prowling the streets around Chocolate's pad, but the bitch was nowhere to be found. Janice either. He knew they must be hiding out somewhere, playing with his mind, just waiting to call him back and spring the blackmail trip on him. Amazing when you considered how much both of them liked to get high.

Maybe they in jail, he thought. But that sent a shiver down his spine because he knew they'd trade his black ass in a minute for a pass. So he couldn't afford to sit around waiting for them to contact him. He had to take the offensive. Find them now. Then get that fucking tape. Otherwise it was only a matter of time: He'd be dead meat.

Taji drove his buddy's borrowed Ford Taurus down past the old abandoned Dixie Square, so called because the road on which it had been located was called Dixie Highway. Putting a mall called Dixie in a black community never made much sense to Taji, who figured people would avoid it just on principle. But then again, maybe the area hadn't been black when the mall had first been built. Now it stood like a huge, boarded-up tomb that seemed to store all the lost hope of the impoverished suburb. Funny, with all the buildings and businesses that Otha Spears owned, he always liked to stay in the big apartment building in Harvey. Sort of like that sly rabbit in that old cartoon that Taji remembered from back when he was a kid, liking to stay near the briar patch. And the community had become

Otha's briar patch all right. Taji glanced at the colorful swirl of five-pointed stars, crescent moons, and capital Ss and Gs that had been sprayed all across the walls of what had once been one of the largest JC Penney stores in the south suburban area. Now it was just a shell in some old run-down building surrounded by a no-man's-land parking lot overrun with weeds.

He drove past the mall and turned left down an adjacent side street, then parked his burgundy Escalade, the one that Otha let him drive around in, at the curb in front of the big duplex. Two "shorties" on roller blades raced up and down the sidewalk, each fitted with those headsets and speaker mikes like they wear at McDonald's. To the untrained eye, they just looked like ordinary ten- or eleven-year-olds with Bluetooth, but Taji knew they'd be transmitting his movements as soon as he reached the steps.

The building itself was a huge, two-story white stone structure with a roof like one of them old fashioned castles. Big pillars stood on either side of the door at the top of the massive stone steps. It gave the impression of entering a fucking fortress, but Taji knew this moat was a helluva lot more dangerous than any medieval waters had been. He bounced up the steps, shooting a quick glance at one of the shorties who was talking fast into his mouthpiece. Forming a gun with his thumb and forefinger he pretended to take a shot at the kid before pushing open the solid front door.

Inside the hallway was long and dark. Two men appeared out of doors on either side pointing semi-autos at him with the sideways grip that had become popular with street punks and movie stars.

Taji held up his hands, the left fist held against the curled upright palm of the right, in the hand gesture of the Black Soul Gangstas.

"All souls," one of the gunmen said.

"His will be done," Taji answered.

The guns lowered and one of the men stepped out into the hallway. He was dressed in a black tee shirt and camouflaged pants.

"What you need, brother?" he asked.

"I need to see the Great Leader," Taji answered. "Tell him it's Oman Taji."

The man turned and went back into the room. He picked up a phone and hit two buttons. When he spoke it was in hushed tones. Then he placed the phone down and stepped back into the hallway.

"Raise your arms," he said to Taji.

"What's this shit," Taji complained as he complied. The man's hand ran over the contours of Taji's well-toned body. After the man finished, he straightened up and extended his palm for Taji to go forward. As Taji moved down the hallway, he glanced to his left. The click-clacking of fingers on a keyboard caught his attention. He saw Efron James sitting in his wheelchair in front of a computer monitor. The room was dark, except for the faint glow that shone from the screen.

"Hey, bro," Taji said in a heavy whisper. Efron's narrow face turned. He was skinny and dark-skinned, with wire-rimmed, thick glasses perched on top of the narrow bridge of his nose. The scraggy mustache curled up on each side as he smiled.

"What's up?" Efron's voice sounded like a girl's. "What you doing here?"

"I'm here to see the Great Leader."

Efron nodded. "Otha's plenty pissed off at you, man." He was the only person who could get away with calling Spears by his first name, or addressing him as anything but "Great Leader." Efron had taken a bullet, fired by the Chicago Police, and had won a huge settlement. Under the ruse of being Efron's guardian, Spears said he was investing some of the money from this settlement. Thus he was able to purchase several of the houses and businesses that he used to create his laundering system. And Efron being good with computers, a motherfucking prodigy, allowed Spears to have instant access to all of his business dealings.

"How come?" Taji asked in a hushed tone.

"Your favorite actor friend and mine got picked up," Efron said. "He called me here from jail, man, and Otha had me send Hollingsworth down to spring him."

"Fuck," Taji said under his breath. "I guess I'm gonna be in shit for that, huh?"

"You know it," Efron said, his tinkering little laugh sounding like a fucking rat's feet skittering across a metal roof.

Taji swallowed hard, steeling himself for whatever punishment was to come, and stepped out into the hallway again. If they were going to do him here, there wasn't shit he could do about it. He continued to the next opening and turned to his right. The room he entered was large, the carpeting feeling thicker under his feet, with several big-ass chairs and sofas lined up around the walls.

The plasma screen seemed to take up a quarter of one wall, playing some old Mel Gibson movie.

This is it, Taji thought.

Several planters, with green tendrils dangling, hung suspended from the ceiling at spaced intervals. Otha Spears, clad in a maroon satin bathrobe, sat on a huge sofa at the other end of the room. Five thick gold chains were visible against the dark skin of his chest. The longest one had the ornate gold charm of a crescent moon and a five-pointed star. His head was shaved slick and dark sunglasses covered his eyes. A thin white girl sat naked on the floor by his slippered feet, her face resting against his big thigh. Otha said nothing as Taji entered, but nodded and took a sip from the smoky-colored glass that he was holding.

Taji bowed, keeping his eyes on the seated man. The white girl's eyes opened slightly and Taji saw the eyelids droop back over pinpoint pupils.

"Great Leader." He knew better than to violate the prescribed protocol when he was in the man's own house. Especially when he was asking for help.

Otha raised his glass again and poured some of the amber liquid on the girl's face. She jerked up with a start.

"Get outta here," he said.

It seemed to take a few seconds for the message to register, then she got up on unsteady legs. Taji watched the pale cheeks of her ass as she padded out of the room.

"And put some fucking clothes on, bitch," Spears shouted after her. He set the glass down on the nearby coffee table and stood, extending his hand toward Taji. They did a ritualistic handshake and Otha smiled. Taji admired the man's grill. Big, shimmering teeth, capped with gold, each one the design of a five-pointed star next to a crescent moon.

"My man," Spears said. "Good to see you."

Taji nodded.

Spears walked over and retrieved his drink, then popped open an ornamental gold box on the table for a cigarette. The flame of the lighter danced over the end of the tobacco reflecting in the dark lenses of his glasses. Exhaling smoke, he said, "It's been too long, my brother, since you've been here. I even had a job or two that I had to give to the lesser devoted because you not coming by."

Play the game, Taji thought. "I'm sorry, Great Leader."

The apology dangled while Spears took another long drag on the square. Exhaling the smoke through his nose, he said, "I expect my governors to keep me posted weekly on any new developments, but someone like you, one of my knights . . .

121

when you stray from my side it's cause for worry."

"I've been training real hard for my fights, Great Leader," Taji said.

Spears smiled.

"So why have you chosen today to come home, Taji?" He placed the cigarette between his lips once more and picked up the phone. "Yeah, have Shondra get Doris dressed. She's wandering around naked again." He set the phone down and looked back at Taji. "Take that ho with you when you leave. Put her white ass to work in one of the clubs. I'm getting tired of the bitch anyway. Got the fuckin' nods all the motherfucking time."

Taji licked his lips. He wanted to tell Otha about his request, but knew he had to wait until the proper time.

"I ever tell you about this play?" Spears pointed to the screen.

Taji shook his head.

"It was when I was in the 'ville, taking one of them English lit classes so I could get more good time off my sentence." Spear's face looked dreamy. "Teacher explaining 'bout this cat Hamlet . . . how these motherfuckers kill his father and stole his kingdom. There was this one line that the teacher wrote on the board, 'hoisted with his own petard.' Know what a motherfucking petard is, man?"

Taji shook his head.

"It's a shiv, man." His voice rose. "I heard that, and it was like this message from mighty Allah. That night I took a shank and stuck it in Leroy Kitner and merged the Gangstas and the Black Souls." He removed his sunglasses. His eyes had a wet, glassy look. The man was probably coming down from some kind of high.

"That's why I dig this motherfucking movie so much, man," Spears said, slipping the sunglasses back on. "Now, what you need?" He took a sip of the drink, staring over the rim of the glass, his eyes once more unfathomable.

Spears plopped down on the couch, which was specially designed to be raised slightly higher than any of the other chairs in the room. He pointed to a chair, indicating for Taji to sit.

"Great Leader," Taji said. "I have a problem."

"Begin," Spears said, showing his gleaming teeth, "at the beginning." His expression didn't change as he listened to Taji tell the story.

After he'd finished Spears asked, "This is why Efron had to call the lawyer the other night?"

"Right," Taji said. "This white boy we know got himself arrested. He set me up with the rich TV honkey that croaked." He figured if he made it sound like Efron was tied in too, it wouldn't sound as bad.

Spears considered this. "Be wise to ice that white motherfucker."

Taji shrugged. "I suppose. But he do bring in some business pushing on the side at them theater companies he work at." He hated to let go of the dream of becoming the black prince of porn. "But my main worry those fucking hos Chocolate and Janice."

"I'll put the word out on them," Spears answered. "K.O.S."

"But, Great Leader," Taji said slowly, knowing better than to contradict a Kill on Sight order from Otha, "I need that tape first. If we can just find one of them, I know I can make her talk."

"Of course," Spears said. He stood up and took another cigarette out of the gold case. "And just like my man Hamlet need Horatio . . ." He paused to flick the lighter, "I have need of a strong, loyal friend as well." He patted Taji's shoulder. "A knight to help with his king's enemies. Once this is done, there's no limit to what we can do."

Taji knew there'd be a price, but he didn't mind. He'd killed before for Otha, and if it got him out of this mess with Chocolate it'd be worth it.

"Just tell me who and when," he said.

Spears smiled, letting the smoke seep from between his gold teeth.

"In due time," he said. "In due time we see them hoisted with their own petards." A thin smile crossed his face as he stared off at the wall. Through the window Taji could see him looking at the abandoned shell of the Dixie Square.

"Your will," Taji said, "be done."

12
STANDING INSPECTIONS

Leal had just finished writing out the type three for computer LEADS message requesting any information on the Dick Forest homicide. The receipts they'd found in Forest's rented condo for a set of flood lights and a tripod had been traced to a downtown Best Buy. There was also one for the repair of a DV camcorder. The kind that used videotape but could be transferred to disk. It became a matter of leaning extra hard on the manager to look up the invoices and find the serial numbers for the equipment. With that entered into LEADS, Leal would be alerted if the items were recovered and checked. He'd also be contacted if anyone located either of the two women whose fingerprints had been recovered from the motel room and Forest's auto.

Morgan had done an excellent rush-job getting the prints identified. The one from the toilet seat had come back to a Janice Parker, who had a long sheet for prostitution, theft, and drug arrests. The most recent one, a Disorderly Conduct out of Chicago a year ago, seemed like the best bet for a good photo. Leal had instructed his new partner to go down to CPD and get pictures of Janice and the other possible hooker, Gladis Brown. Brown's thumb print had been found on the trunk release push-button inside the rented car's glove box. While it didn't place her at the crime scene, the way the toilet print did Janice, it was enough to bring her in for questioning. In fact, those were the best leads he had at this time. The fact that Gladis Brown also had numerous arrests for prostitution and drugs led Leal to feel hopeful that she was somehow involved.

But finding them was another matter, and he had just finished making a call to the Chicago P.D. requesting that the two women be listed in the Daily Bulletin as suspects wanted for questioning regarding a homicide. After hanging up the phone he heard a slight snorting sound and became conscious that someone was standing very close behind him. Turning, he saw a large assorted bouquet of flowers—the kind you get at a 7-Eleven or White Hen rather than a floral shop.

Alfred Tims's face, wearing the usual scrunched-up look, hovered over the flowers. He was wearing the same brown corduroy sports coat and rumpled black pants. A tie was loosely secured under an out-of-fashion collar.

"What the hell? Al, what are you doing here?" Leal said.

"It's Monday. I'm supposed to ride with you guys today, remember?" Tims looked around. "Where's Ollie?" He reached up behind his glasses and rubbed a forefinger over his left eye.

"Ollie's not here," Leal said, trying to think of a way to ditch the kid. The last thing he needed working a high-profile homicide case was some geek tagging along driving him nuts. "She's at school this week, then she'll be going to the Raid Team."

Tims seemed to ponder this for a moment and shoved the flowers toward Leal. "I guess these are yours then." He punctuated this with that irritating, honking laugh.

Leal gritted his teeth. "Go find a paper cup and put them in some water." He looked up in time to see a very surprised look-ing Bob Lemack entering the office staring at Tims holding the flowers out toward Leal.

"Am I interrupting something?" Lemack asked slowly with a sly grin. He was holding a brown envelope.

"No," Leal snapped, standing up quickly. He resisted the

impulse of grabbing the flowers and dumping them in the nearest wastebasket. Instead he stepped around Tims and held his hand out toward Lemack. "That them?"

"Right." He handed Leal the envelope.

"Bob, this is Al Tims," he said, thinking Lemack's gruff appearance might frighten the kid off. "He's an intern from Western who's been riding with us."

"Bob Lemack." He grabbed the nerd's outstretched hand. "Glad to meet ya."

"Man, you got a strong grip." Tims shook his hand twice after Lemack released him.

"Got to have a strong grip if you want to handle an eighty-pound dog, son."

"Huh?"

"Dog handling," Lemack said. "I was one in the Marine Corps, and on the police department too." He flexed his big calloused palm. "Even though I'm working Investigations now, I still like to stand ready."

Tims bumped his glasses up higher on his nose as he stared at the bald man's huge hand.

"You look like one of those guys on TV," Tims said. "You know, on the WWF."

"You mean wrestling?" Leal asked.

"Yeah," Tims said. "Or on the *Ultimate Fighter,* or something." He took out his smart phone. "Here, I'll get a picture of one of them for you."

"Al," Leal said, "can it."

"Huh?" Tims said, his face scrunching up again.

"Actually," Lemack said, "I was on TV once. A show called *Amateur Hour.* It was a long time ago."

"Oh yeah?" Tims asked. "What did you do?"

"Ventriloquism." Lemack's lips didn't move. A glove with a face sprung up on his left hand and was doing all the talking now in the high, cartoonish, Daffy Duck tone. "And we were pretty damn good too, buster," the squeaky voice said.

Leal stared at the two of them and then at the gloved hand of his partner. What the hell was that?

Tims emitted the irritating laugh again. He held up his phone and snapped a picture.

Leal rolled his eyes toward the ceiling. How the hell did he get saddled with these two losers in the middle of the biggest heater of his damn career? "If you guys don't mind, we do have a homicide that we're working on here."

Lemack mumbled "Sorry, Sarge," as he stuck the glove back in his pocket. Tims scrunched his face up in a squint, then squatted down by a nearby metal waste container.

"Say, I think I see a big paper cup in here," he said, rummaging through the can.

Leal rolled his eyes again and blew out a slow breath. I wonder what Ollie's doing right now, he thought.

On the drive back to the hotel all Hart could think about was soaking in a nice hot bath. The rest of the day had been hectic: more running, followed by classroom instruction in tactics on room searches, followed by another run and range practice. Despite being in good shape, she did notice that her marksman skills degraded significantly after the quick sprints the instructors had them do before firing.

Deckons and Cook had seemed less hostile toward her after the physical fitness test. In fact, they seemed less intense toward the whole class. Several of the out-of-shape officers had failed to return after the shower break that followed the test. The class had shrunk to well below twenty. Most of the ones who stayed seemed to have little trouble with the physical part of the training that followed. And none of them seemed overly concerned with the fact that she was a woman. They seemed more intent on just getting through the damn class.

Hart found a parking spot that was near the back stairway and picked up her bags. She knew she'd have to let the barrel of the .45 soak for a while because she'd fired so many rounds.

Even though she hadn't fired the weapon before, she'd still done reasonably well. She was somewhat familiar with automatics thanks to Frank's insistence that, as his partner, she should know how to fire and re-load his Beretta 9mm. But, according to Deckons, it was not as good as she could have performed. She realized that it had been a mistake not taking the .45 to the range and practicing with it before the class, but then again, everything about this assignment was turning into a mistake. Plus, she and Rick had had other things on their minds when he brought the gun over last Saturday.

Wearily, she pulled open the glass doors and moved toward the stairwell, not wanting to waste the time walking to the front elevators. Her room was on the third floor, and the bed looked very inviting as she opened the door. She didn't even want to think about the bruises on her shins and legs. Glancing at herself in the full length mirror, she saw the crusty dirt stains on the fatigue pants. Her boots, too, were a mess.

Deckons and Cook had made it very clear that everyone would be expected to "stand inspection" each morning before their run. She sat in one of the chairs by the table and unlaced her boots, then pulled them off along with her socks.

Working her bare feet into the dense carpeting felt refreshing. A stress reliever. Standing, she undid her pistol belt, then took out the big automatic. After spreading newspaper on the table, she grabbed her gun cleaning kit and took out the Hoppe's cleaning solution and several patches.

Rick had shown her how to disassemble the weapon, but she still had trouble. Finally Hart got it and moved the slide forward and took out the spring and barrel. She did a quick brush job on the gun and then packed some solvent-soaked patches down the barrel.

"You soak, while I soak," she said aloud, then remembered the boots. The bath would have to wait. She spread some newspapers on the floor and scraped the dirt and mud off the corrugated soles. By the time she'd finished shining the boots to a dark luster her fingers were black as well. Standing, she stretched and then unbuttoned the fatigue shirt and pants. Her undershirt was streaked with sweat stains too, and she took everything off and stuck it in a plastic laundry bag. At some point she knew she'd have to wash the clothes, but tonight all she could think about was taking a bath and resting. Naked, she walked into the bathroom and pulled the shower curtain out of the tub. She was adjusting the water to the right temperature when she heard the knock on the door. Wrapping herself in a towel, she moved to the peep hole and looked out. Rick stood in the hallway holding a bouquet. Hart immediately opened the door and stood back. Rick's grin was both spontaneous and lascivious.

"Well, this isn't quite the reception I was expecting, but I'm not one to complain," he said, moving forward to embrace her.

Hart pushed him away.

"Rick, no," she said. "Not till I bathe."

"You can bathe later," he said. "In fact I'll scrub your back if you want." He leaned forward and kissed her softly on the lips.

"I'm totally filthy," she said. "And the only thing I've been looking forward to all day is a hot bath."

"Well, far be it from me to stand in the way of a lady and her bath," he said with a grin, stepping back. "Since it's my night off, I decided to come up and see if you needed some company. I got your message, by the way. That's how I knew what room you'd be in."

"How do you know I wasn't expecting someone else?" she

said coyly as she stepped into the bathroom and partially closed the door. She checked the temperature of the rapidly rising water, then shut off the faucet. Going back into the room, she took the flowers from Rick and placed them in a plastic glass.

"Well, if anyone else shows up I'll just tell him that I'm carrying a gun," he said, moving toward the table with the disassembled weapon. "Oh, the Sig. How'd you like it? Any problems taking it apart?"

"Are you kidding," Hart said. "A piece of cake. And thanks for the flowers. They're lovely."

She closed the bathroom door, dropped the towel, and stepped into the tub. She'd just settled back into the hot water when the door creaked open. Rick stood there, completely nude, his penis already semi-engorged, smiling that nice, irresistible smile with his perfect teeth.

"So . . . want your back scrubbed?" he asked.

After they'd piled into the unmarked and started for the expressway, Leal remembered that he had to stop by Hart's place to take in the mail and feed Rocky. He made an abrupt exit at 147th Street, which caused Lemack to look at him.

"I thought we were going downtown to talk to the CPD vice guys and that electronics store manager?" he said.

In the rearview mirror Leal caught a glimpse of Tims, who was virtually hanging over the back seat. The same, perpetually scrunched-up expression seemingly frozen on his face as he looked from Lemack to Leal.

"We are, but I've got to stop by my ex-partner's place and feed her cat," Leal said. "I should've done it earlier, but I forgot."

Lemack nodded.

"This Ollie's cat?" Tims asked.

"Yeah," Leal said.

Tims's thumbs immediately went to work typing something

into his smart phone.

"My Brutus used to love cats," Lemack said, leaning against the door so that he faced both Leal and Tims. "I remember when we were partnered up, I took him over to the ex's to see the kids. My little daughter had a kitten and came running out to show me. Well, you know how them cats'll spit and hiss . . . It saw Brutus running up towards it and it got so scared it was almost petrified, but he just up and about licked it to death." He paused to laugh. "What a dog," he said, shaking his head. "Best damn pooch this department ever had. Could he track? Like he was following a map. And building searches . . . I can't even begin to tell you how many burglars we caught together."

No, but I'm sure you'll get around to it, Leal thought.

Tims looked up from his phone. "You still got him?"

Lemack shook his head. He seemed ready to say more when Leal made an abrupt stop as somebody pulled out in front of their car.

"We should've given that guy a ticket," Lemack said. "And I'll bet you woulda too, if you still had your ticket book," the gloved hand added in the forced-falsetto voice.

Once again, Tims thought the routine was the greatest thing since flash drives. He snapped another phone pic.

"She just lives down the road a bit," Leal said, turning onto Pulaski and trying to ignore the face on the glove.

"That's pretty neat," Tims said, pointing to Lemack's gloved hand. He punctuated his comment with another of his grating hee-haw laughs that set Leal's teeth on edge. "What was your dog's name again?"

Leal wanted to kill him.

"Brutus," Lemack said. "After the play. You know, *Julius Caesar* by Shakespeare? I used to quote it every time I fed him. Et too, Brutus? Get it? Et—ate?" He let out a hearty laugh. Tims laughed too.

"I thought Brutus was the glove's name," Tims said.

"No," Lemack said, raising his gloved left hand and stroking it with his right. "This is Oscar."

Leal, on the other hand, just gripped the steering wheel tighter and continued to drive.

13
VICE CONTROL

The whole floor of VCD, Vice Control Division, on Maxwell was divided up into small cubicles by portable drywall sections. Leal made a quick stop at one of their empty phones to call the Best Buy manager who was supposed to be getting him those serial numbers for Dick Forest's missing camcorder. The manager, a young guy named Pat, had seemed anxious to help.

"I'm in the Loop," Leal told him. "I could stop by when we're done here, but I don't know how much longer it'll take. What time do you close?"

"We're closing at eight tonight, sir," Pat said. "But I only have a few more invoice lists to check. I could fax the numbers to you tonight."

"That'd be great," Leal said. He gave him the department's fax number and told him that he'd send somebody down tomorrow to pick up the actual copies. After he'd hung up, he called the department and told the dispatch center to be alert for the fax. He also instructed them to enter the serial number of the camcorder into LEADS as soon as they got it, along with an attachment to contact him immediately if anyone had any information. "Make sure you put in that it's in reference to an ongoing homicide investigation."

The dispatcher replied with a bored-sounding, "Okay," which infuriated Leal. Didn't she know the pressure he was under? The raucous laughter from Lemack and Tims, who seemed to be getting along better than Bert and Ernie, snapped him out of it.

All right, he thought, since they enjoy each other's company so god-damned much, I'll send the two of them down to the Best Buy store tomorrow.

He paused to blow out a slow breath. No sense letting the pressure get to him. Right now he was doing all that he could with the case, and he might as well take advantage of this part of it. One of the few advantages of working a heater was that the brass was willing to give you just about anything you wanted in the beginning: Unlimited overtime, extra personnel, surveillance teams . . . but the honeymoon wouldn't last forever. Soon they'd want something solid, or the rug would be pulled out from under him. His rumination reminded him to check in with the team watching Sax. He called their cellular phone number and identified himself.

"Nothing yet, Sarge," the officer told him. "We followed him to that place on Clark Street where they're doing that play. Want us to keep on him?"

"Yeah," said Leal. "Sooner or later something's got to give. See if he meets up with anybody and get whatever plates you can."

"Want us to pinch him if he does something wrong?"

Leal considered this for a moment, then said, "Use your own discretion, but I'd like to have something decent in the way of an arrest. In other words, if he's just pissing on the sidewalk let it slide."

"Gotcha," the surveillance officer said. "We'll keep you posted."

Leal thanked him and hung up. He looked around for Lemack and Tims, then followed the sound of Tims's grating laugher to one of the cubicles. The two of them were sitting across from a vice cop. Both of them were doubled over with laughter. What the hell, Leal thought. They're supposed to be trying to get information on two hookers, not trading punchlines.

"Oh, Lord," Lemack said. "I ain't heard one that good since my days at Camp Pendleton." He took off his glasses and wiped at his eyes.

"Did you get a chance to show him the pictures?" Leal asked, sounding more sarcastic than he intended. To cover, he extended his hand toward the fortyish white guy sitting behind the big wooden desk, and said, "Frank Leal."

The man had closely cropped dark hair and wire-framed glasses. He grabbed Leal's hand in a surprisingly strong grip.

"Todd McKnight," the man said. "I was telling your partners here that the officer who actually made the arrest on this one," he pointed to the picture of Janice, "is due in any minute now. He'd be able to tell you more about it."

"You got any last known address for her?" Leal asked.

"Sure," McKnight said. "Just let me call for the booking information we got." He picked up the phone and spoke to someone for several minutes. When he hung up he turned to Leal and said, "She'll bring it up."

"Thanks," Leal said.

"So what kind of case you working on this?" McKnight asked.

"A homicide. That former TV star."

"Dick Forest?" McKnight asked.

Leal nodded.

"No shit?

"I used to love that show of his. What the hell was it called?"

"*Rick's Place*," Leal said.

"Yeah, right. Sorta like a small screen *Casablanca*," McKnight said.

"But without the class," Leal added. "Apparently this guy Forest had a few secret kinks in him."

"Yeah, ain't that the truth," McKnight said. "A guy with all his money messing with a couple of low-class hookers. Don't make sense. But then again, not much does anymore, right? Hey, there's my partner now."

Leal looked around to see a slightly built blond man walk in. He appeared to be in his early thirties.

"Ain't he got a great face for a vice cop?" McKnight asked.

"Why, whatcha got in mind, big boy?" the blond cop asked in an exaggerated effeminate tone. A smile quickly flashed across his handsome, baby-faced features.

McKnight introduced his partner as Rex Peters.

"He's got a great name for a vice cop, too," he added.

"These guys are county mounties and are asking about one of your old flames." He showed Peters the picture of Janice.

Just then, a female officer, a pretty black girl walked in, handed McKnight a stack of papers, and said, "Here's those reports and booking info you wanted, Sarge." McKnight thanked her, and she eyed Leal and the rest of the unfamiliar faces before leaving. Peters reviewed the report and nodded his head slowly.

"She looks familiar, but I can't be sure," he said. "You know how it is. . . . After a while they all sort of blend together. She hangs with this one, huh?" he asked holding up a mug shot of a black girl.

Leal nodded.

Peters scratched his upper lip, then shook his head.

"Doesn't ring a bell, but the address she gave is unusual. Pretty far out. Cicero Heights. Say, I used to know a guy out there you might talk too. Lance Harmon. He seemed to have a handle on everything that was going on out there."

"Yeah, too good a handle," Leal said. "He's in county now on a murder charge."

"No shit, who'd he kill?" Peters asked.

"He did a hit for a drug lord out there," Leal said.

"Oh yeah, I think I heard something about that," McKnight answered. "Didn't know it was him though. Well, I guess you won't be talking to him then."

"I guess not," Leal answered, silently wondering if he was ever going to get the break he needed in this case. That's it, he thought. I'm going to call Sean when we get back and ask him to pull whatever strings he can to get Ollie back for me.

Chocolate leaned over the pay phone by the 7-Eleven on the southeast side of 14th Street in Cicero Heights. She knew she was taking a chance calling from this phone in an area that was primarily Latino, but she felt she had a better chance of not getting picked up by any S-Gs on this turf and she didn't have no money for no disposable cell phone.

Her sister had a place Taji didn't know about that was sandwiched between the borderline of the Soul Gangstas and the Latin Conquistadores.

The area was composed of a bleak stretch of industrial buildings, many of which were closed down hulks, pockmarked by broken windows and extensively painted with gang graffiti. Her hands shook as she dialed the gym and asked for Taji.

She only had three of the Tylenol #4s left, and knew that she'd be coming down really hard tomorrow. But she had to keep things cool. Keep herself under control. Leastways until she got the money from him. And she was going to up the price too, since seeing on the news that the dead john was actually some motherfucking TV star. Then she'd be set.

"He ain't here," a voice on the phone said. "Who this?"

"Tell him it's Chocolate," she spat back angrily. "And tell him to put his motherfuckin' ass on the phone now."

"I told you, he ain't here," the voice replied. Then added, "You wanna leave yo' number?"

She knew she couldn't afford to do that, so she tried to turn on what little charm she could manage. "When he be back, sugar?" she asked.

"Don't know."

"Well, you tell him that Chocolate called, you hear," she said, mustering bravado even though her stomach was on the verge of being seized with the dry heaves again. "Tell him I'll be callin' him back tomorrow at noon about that tape. And he better be there." Then she hung up.

She doubled over as another wave of nausea swept over her. She clenched her fists, saying to herself over and over again that she could deal with it. Keep it under control.

At least until she got that payoff. Otherwise she'd end up like poor Janice.

14
INCREASING THE PUCKER FACTOR

Any thoughts that the second day would be easier than the first were dashed as Special Agents Deckons and Cook extended the mid-morning run by one more mile. Ordinarily the three-mile distance wouldn't really have bothered Hart, but doing her amorous activities with Rick, "all night long," as the saying goes, seemed to have sapped some of her strength. Leal always used to imitate Burgess Meredith playing Rocky's trainer when he'd slowly fold himself into their squad car and say in a rasping tone, "Ohhh, women weaken legs," after which he'd always add, "You drive." Today she wished it could be that easy for her.

And neither Deckons nor Cook were burdened with the full SWAT regalia: flak vest, pistol belt, weapon, canteen, gas mask, and rifle. Everybody had to carry a rifle. Luckily, they'd assigned Hart an M16, which was fairly light compared to the wooden-stocked shotguns, although one of the compact MP5s would have been preferable. But the two FBI agents had made it clear that everyone would be expected to run with a shotgun at some point during the training. Cook turned and ran backwards as he shouted to pick up the pace. "Pick it up. There's a storm coming," he yelled. "You're running like a bunch of sissies."

Hart wondered if that was directed at her. She decided to block out the pain and creeping exhaustion by focusing on something else. Something pleasant. Like the time she'd spent with Rick last night. After making love he'd held her and massaged her sore and aching parts. Then they'd watched TV until she fell asleep in his arms. That morning they'd eaten an early breakfast in the hotel restaurant and he told her that he'd come back tonight.

"You should have just brought some clothes," she'd said. "You could just wait in my room, or go to that big discount mall up this way."

"I got too many things to do," he'd said hesitantly, looking down at his plate. "I gotta visit Lance today. He's expecting me. I did put in for a personal day on Friday, though, so we can celebrate."

She'd only nodded. The subject of Rick's brother wasn't something that they spent a lot of time discussing. Hart made it a point to listen and offer encouraging nods whenever Rick talked about it, but she seldom offered any advice. Rick had been on the verge of resigning after his brother had been indicted, but Frank had talked him out of it.

Her thoughts turned to Leal, and she wondered how he was doing with the Dick Forest case. There had to be some real heavy pressure to clear such a heater. She didn't envy Frank's task and suddenly running in the warm sunshine didn't seem such a bad tradeoff for that gut-wrenching feeling that always accompanied a high-profile homicide. Hopefully, the press wouldn't nag Leal too badly and let him do his job.

Her reverie broke as the group slowed to a halt. Cook and Deckons told everybody to drop for push-ups. They did this several times during the runs, and each time you had to place your rifle over the tops of your hands so the weapons didn't touch the ground. Neither of the two agents did push-ups with the group. They merely stood by and yelled. That, in conjunction with their light running attire, told Hart they were using an old instructor's ploy: work the class hard, and do less, so you magically never appear to be tired. They were using every psychological trick in the book, and then some, to mess with the group's minds. After twenty repetitions the two agents told everybody to stand and put on their protective masks. One guy laid his rifle on the ground while he was securing his mask and Cook ran over and snatched it.

"One man messes up, everybody suffers," he yelled. "Drop for ten more."

The class dropped for ten more push-ups. When everyone had recovered, Deckons showed them how to hold their weapons between their thighs while they slipped on their masks.

"That way, you won't be fumbling around for it in case you can't see," he said. "Now, we got a quarter mile left. Let's go."

"And we're gonna check for filters when we finish up," Cook called out as they began a slow formation-run. They kept the pace slower than the previous jaunt. Every breath was a struggle, never quite full enough, and the stifling effect of the tight rubber-plastic over their faces increased the stress.

"We have no way of actually bringing the 'pucker-factor' up to real life and death levels," Deckons had said that first afternoon. "But what we will try and do is wear you down physically and mentally, then put you in different situations."

This must be one of those times, Hart thought as she heard each breath rasp out through the mask's filter. It was like running with a plastic garbage bag over her face. She was surprised at the discomfort and incipient panic that she felt from just mild exertion. Finally they came up toward the field next to the range where their runs began and ended. The class started to slow up, but Cook turned sideways and motioned them to continue onto the range. Three by four silhouette targets had been set up on the twenty-five-yard line.

"Put on your earmuffs and fire on the whistle at those targets with your handguns," he yelled as he and Deckons continued to usher everyone into the proper places on the firing line. When everyone was assembled down the line, Cook blew his coach's whistle and quickly covered his ears with his hands. Deckons did the same. After everyone in the group had expended all the bullets in their magazines, Cook blew the whistle again.

"Now strip off your masks," Deckons yelled, walking up and down the line behind them. "Do you see now why you never want to put gas into a building unless you absolutely have to?"

I do, thought Hart as she pulled the mask up over her head, making sure the straps didn't catch on her hair. Oh, G, do I ever. The cool air hitting her sweat-drenched face revived her somewhat.

"Clear and holster all weapons," Cook called out. When this was done he told them to go down range and look at their targets. As the line advanced, Hart saw that her hits were all over the paper. Only one of the nine bullets she'd fired was even remotely close to the kill-zone.

"You use a scatter-gun for that one, Hart?" Deckons said, walking up behind her.

"Looks like it, doesn't it?" she said, trying to muster a smile. She'd be damned if she was going to let him think the mind games were getting to her.

Deckons continued down the line punctuating his walk with more derisive comments as he went.

Mr. Personality, Hart thought as she watched him walk away. But at least I am learning something.

15
LONE WOLF

The steady rain splattered the windshield of Leal's unmarked as he parked in front of the house and made a run for the front steps. He punched the bell several times anxiously as he flattened against the wall. The inner door opened and he saw Sean O'Herlieghy, dressed in a loose-fitting flannel shirt and blue jeans.

"You look all wet, officer," O'Herlieghy said with a grin. Leal noticed Sean wasn't wearing his toupee and his cheeks sagged slightly, indicating sudden weight loss.

"Thanks," Leal said, stepping inside and shaking his wet hands.

"Let me get you a towel, Frank," O'Herlieghy said. Leal followed him into the living room. "You're all dressed up. You look nice for a change."

"Yeah," Leal said. "I was down at the Grand Jury."

"What, were you up there seeing that pretty little state's attorney of yours?" O'Herlieghy called out from farther back in the house.

"No, getting a subpoena," Leal said. He heard Sean grunt.

The room looked garish, with multicolored wallpaper and several out-of-place chairs. A sound system was set into the wall in a wooden entertainment center. Leal stood there, still dripping slightly, when O'Herlieghy returned and handed him a blue towel.

"Appreciate it." Leal wiped his face. "Where's Bambi?"

"Where she's always at, doing what she does best," O'Herlieghy said with a sigh. "Shopping till she drops."

Leal continued to dry his face, glad for the respite of not having to comment on Sean's new, much-younger wife, who seemed intent on gathering as many material possessions as she could.

"She decorated this place," O'Herlieghy said, holding his arms up. "What do you think? Pretty good job, huh?"

Leal nodded and handed the towel back to his mentor. O'Herlieghy had worked with Leal's father when they'd both been on the job. Leal's father had long since retired, but the somewhat younger O'Herlieghy had become Leal's clout and protector when he came on the department and moved up through the ranks. Now Captain O'Herlieghy was on medical leave, recuperating from a heart attack that had, to his ultimate humiliation, occurred several months back on his wedding night.

"You want some herbal tea?" O'Herlieghy asked. "I can put the pot on."

Leal shook his head. "Like I told you, I'm on my way in to work."

O'Herlieghy nodded and dropped the towel onto the floor beside the coffee table.

"So how you been feeling?" Leal asked. "You been keeping up with the treadmill?"

"It's been barely keeping up with me," O'Herlieghy laughed. "How 'bout you, Frank? You look like you put on a couple of pounds. That bodybuilding partner of yours ain't keeping you in shape?"

"Ollie got transferred."

"Oh? I didn't hear nothing about it, but then again, they're hardly gonna call me every time one of the commanders gets a hair caught in his ass. So what else is new?"

Leal swallowed, wanting to bring the topic of Hart's transfer up again, but unsure how to do it. He hadn't expected that O'Herlieghy would drop the matter so quickly.

"So how you doing, Sean?" Leal asked. "You're looking stronger."

"I'm feeling great," O'Herlieghy said. "Even Bambi and I been getting along better since I been on this home-rehabilitation. That gal really knows how to take care of me, if you know what I mean."

Leal nodded, hoping she wasn't trying to prod Sean into another heart attack.

"Well, don't try to do too much too fast, now," Leal said.

"Oh, nah," O'Herlieghy answered with a shake of his head. Without the toupee that he'd started wearing after his divorce and quick remarriage, his face and head looked softer and somehow more vulnerable. "I been learning all sorts of ways to relax now that I never even knew about. You got a minute?" O'Herlieghy said, leaning forward to push a DVD into the sound system. "Listen to this and tell me what you think it is."

Leal listened as the recording played a series of eerie howling sounds. First one far off, then another that seemed closer. The howls doubled and tripled. Sean leaned back in the chair, his head resting against the soft cushion, his eyes closed.

"Know what it is?" O'Herlieghy's voice was a whisper.

Leal shook his head.

"Wolf calls," O'Herlieghy said. "A whole sixty minutes of them. You'd be surprised all the different variations you can hear in them if you listen close."

"I'll bet," Leal said. O'Herlieghy's head was still back, his eyes closed. The howling continued.

"I do this several times a day," O'Herlieghy said. "Usually after my time on the treadmill. Lets me think. Been thinking a lot lately, Frank."

"That's good." Leal didn't know what else to say.

"Been thinking that you only go around once in this life," O'Herlieghy continued. "You ever think about that?"

"All the time."

O'Herlieghy's eyes opened and he smiled at Leal. "I know what you're thinking. Crazy old fart, right? When I was your age I never took time to stop and smell the roses either. The price of being on the job. But let me tell you, a heart attack does something to you. Makes you reassess a lot of things. A lotta things."

"Meaning?"

"You know, Frank, I got twenty-eight years on as of last month," O'Herlieghy said. "Makes you think, you know."

Leal saw where Sean was heading and asked the question. "You're not considering retirement, are you?" Just the question alone was a shock to him. He'd taken Sean's recent absence in stride, but always figured his mentor would return. But shit, retirement . . .

O'Herlieghy took a deep breath and nodded.

"I got two more months coming on medical," he said. "Then I could come back for a few months on light duty, use up all my time due and sick leave, and make it through the rest of the year, so I'd have twenty-nine."

"And then pull the pin?" Leal asked, thinking of how much he depended on Sean, just knowing that he was around. Without him, it would sure be different.

"I'll tell you, after the heart attack, then going back in for the bypass, all I kept thinking about looking through my window and seeing all that snow was how warm it must be in someplace like Florida or Arizona."

"Wouldn't you be bored?"

O'Herlieghy shrugged. "Like I told you, Bambi and me been getting along better."

He let the end of the sentence hang there and Leal recalled

147

how Bambi's main concern seemed to be that she wasn't going to get to go to Disney World on her honeymoon because Sean had ended up in the hospital. But he just grinned and said, "It'd be hard getting by without you."

"Oh, hell, well it wouldn't be for a few months yet," O'Herlieghy said. "The better part of a year or more. So what was so important that you needed to talk about today?"

"I don't want to bother you, Sean," Leal said, getting to his feet. "I gotta get into work anyway. It was great to see you."

"Sit down," O'Herlieghy said in mock anger. "You wanted something, otherwise you wouldn't have called out of the clear blue and asked if you could stop by. Now spill it."

Leal slumped back into his chair, and took a deep breath. "Actually, I wanted to talk to you about Ollie's transfer."

"I shoulda guessed," O'Herlieghy said. "Are you fucking her, or what?"

Leal didn't answer.

"What about Sharon? You still seeing her?"

"No on both," Leal said. "But this transfer thing popped up right in the middle of a couple of crucial investigations. We been working that serial rapist who keeps masquerading as a cop, and then we caught that Dick Forest homicide."

"Dick Forest." O'Herlieghy grinned. "I used to love that show, especially that Jew they had playing the Nazi colonel. That musta really burned the Krauts' asses. Maybe some crazy skinhead did it for revenge." He laughed, then asked, "So, did Hart get tired of Investigations?"

"Hardly," Leal said. "She didn't ask for the transfer, and we were doing real well on our clearance rate, then boom, she gets called into Card's office and she's out."

"Where to?"

"She's been transferred to the Raid Team," Leal said. "She's up attending SWAT school now."

"She should do well at that," O'Herlieghy said with a chuckle. "I always thought she looked more like a guy anyway. But, then again, I never saw her outta uniform." He flashed a lascivious smile at Leal.

"That ass-kisser Ryan's still sucking Card's dick so he's still second whip," Leal continued. "The prick's been calling in sick just about every other day. Then when I ask for some help, they give me this nut case who talks about dogs all the fucking time and wears this hand puppet."

"Hand puppet?" O'Herlieghy laughed. "Sounds like things are going to hell in a handbasket around there. I might not be able to retire if things are that messed up."

Leal thought that sounded hopeful.

"All right," O'Herlieghy said. "I'll make a couple of phone calls, see what I can do. What's your new partner's name?"

"Bob Lemack. I really appreciate it, Sean," Leal said, standing.

O'Herlieghy stood too and smacked Leal's shoulder.

"I'll call you later, after I find out something," Sean said. "Just don't expect miracles though. Okay? And you're sure Hart wants to be back in Investigations too, right?"

"Absolutely," Leal said.

O'Herlieghy nodded and gave him a solid wink. "All right, I'll see what I can do."

Leal smiled and thanked him again. In the background he heard the plaintive howl of a lone wolf.

The day actually was beginning to look halfway decent as Leal pulled up into the Sixth District courthouse parking lot. At least the rain had stopped. He slipped on his sport jacket and made the long walk up the pebbled sidewalks. People were congregating in front of the big building waiting for associates, conferring on their problems, waiting for their lawyers, or trying to figure a damn good excuse before they went inside to face the music. A deputy presided over several prisoners doing "community service" by going around picking up all the scraps of paper in front of the courthouse. Leal nodded to the deputy as he pushed through the revolving doors and turned to his right. The guy at the employee entrance smiled.

"How's it going, Sarge?" the guard asked.

"I hope to find that out," Leal said with a grin. He turned right and walked down the narrow hallway in silence. Ryan was standing there holding a carton of milk. When he saw Leal he immediately began whistling the theme for *Rick's Place,* and Leal frowned. "Why don't you come help me solve the thing instead of just whistling about it?"

This brought a big grin from Ryan, who fell into step beside him.

"Don't be so grumpy," Ryan said. "You got a whole lot of messages in there, and I'm sure your two partners will be raring to go."

"Partners. Fuck you."

The secretary held out her hand and gave him half a dozen pink message slips and a sheet of white computer paper. Leal asked her for the surveillance logs on Sax and she dug into a pile of papers on her desk and then said, "They must be in your box already."

"I'd like to dig into her box," Ryan whispered. "How's the case coming?"

"Which one?" Leal asked.

"Which one you think?" Ryan started whistling the theme song again.

Leal held up his hand. "Please. I went down to the Grand Jury to get some subpoenas this morning for medical records on our suspect whores and also on the unlisted phone number that Sax called that night we brought him in. The surveillance team's still following our actor buddy. Hopefully, they'll catch him fucking up on something, and we'll have some leverage to put the squeeze on him." He blew out an exasperated breath. "As far as I know, nobody's picked up those two hookers yet, and I called around to all the area hospitals inquiring about anybody with gunshot wounds, since there was blood in the car. Nothing remotely possible there. Something's gotta break sooner or later."

"Let's hope for sooner," Ryan said. "The old man's really feeling the pressure on this one."

"Want me to tell him about pressure?" Leal felt a twinge in his gut.

Ryan just slapped his shoulder and shuffled off. "It could be worse. I gotta go in for a lower G.I. Friday."

"Oh?" Leal asked, searching for the surveillance logs in his mail drawer. "What's wrong?"

"Passing blood," Ryan said. "Every time I take a shit it looks like an abortion."

Leal suddenly felt sorry for him. "Sorry to hear that."

"Hear what?" Bob Lemack asked. He was wearing his usual tight-fitting plaid sport jacket and slacks, but he wore a black baseball cap with a K-9 patch on the front.

"Bad pipes," Ryan said. "What's with the hat?"

"Oh, this," Lemack said, taking the hat off. "Just don't like being under-arms and not having my head covered," he said with a grin. "A carryover from the Corps." Suddenly the gloved hand sprung up and the red lips said in the strained-falsetto voice, "Can it, dickhead. You're not in the Marines anymore."

"Hey, Semper fi," Lemack said, thrusting his lower lip out toward the gloved-face. "Once a Marine, always a Marine."

"Or, as they say," the glove answered back, "once a jarhead, always a jarhead."

Ryan roared with laughter, but Leal just shook his head and

went through the message slips.

"Talking to Oscar again?"

Leal looked up and saw Alfred Tims walking down the hallway. Tims had on a tan jacket with a blue and white striped shirt. The flap of the plastic pen holder with the half-dozen or so assorted pens was folded over his pocket. Leal wondered why he even carried them. Every time he wanted to make notes he did so on his smart phone or iPad. The kid's Adam's apple seemed to jut out an inch over the knotted, needle-like necktie. As soon as Leal looked up Tims snapped a picture with his phone.

Christ, thought Leal. This place is turning into the gathering point for the Idiot's Convention.

"Knock off the god-damn pictures," Leal said, cognizant of the anger that had crept into his tone.

After a moment of uneasy silence Lemack raised his gloved hand. "Hi, Al," letting "Oscar" do the talking.

Tims squatted so his face was level with the glove.

"We going to go look for any perpetrators tonight?" he asked. His upper lip curled over his teeth as he squinted at Oscar. He held his phone out from his face and snapped another picture, then looked at it and smiled. Lemack laughed.

"I thought I told you to knock off the fucking pictures," Leal said, then a moment later regretted it. Tims looked like someone had stepped on his iPad.

Lemack looked down at Oscar and said, "The Sarge is getting pissed. You'd better cool it for a while."

"Okay," Oscar answered. Lemack lowered his hand.

Leal rolled his eyes. *Why me?* "If you two guys are finished fucking around, I need you to run down to that Best Buy and get those serial numbers on that video equipment." He watched the two solemn expressions. "Then go to CPD and pick up some more of those vice arrest reports. And on the way back stop by the FBI office in Orland Park and pick up a ViCAP report for me."

"What, we got a profile of the suspect already?" Lemack asked.

"Un-uh," Leal said. "It's for that serial rapist that keeps masquerading as a cop. That's also one of our open cases. The FBI took a bunch of info sheets on the five previous rapes and is trying to come up with something."

"Oh, boy, the FBI," Oscar said in alto-voice.

"I told you I'm not in the fucking mood," Leal said. "And tomorrow either lose that mustache, or tighten it up so it conforms with regulations. We're not in the Navy SEALs here."

"Oh, sure, Sarge," he said, peeling the glove off his hand and jamming it into his pocket. He ran his fingers over his hairy upper lip. "Sorry. I guess sometimes I don't know when to quit." He turned to Tims. "Come on, Al, let's make like a tree and get outta here."

"Huh?" Tims said, squinting again behind the thick lenses. "Like a tree?"

"Didn't you ever see the *Back to the Future* movies?" Lemack asked. He began giving the intern a detailed description of the old movie series, lapsing into a hackneyed imitation of the various actors by reciting various lines from the movies. This further irritated Leal. They turned and began walking away. Leal stood there, watching their departure, then shifted a look of irritation toward Ryan, who was leaning against the wall grinning.

"I guess I'll make like a tree, too," Ryan said.

Leal gave him the finger.

"Sergeant Leal," the secretary called. "You have a call holding on line one."

He went to his desk and picked up the receiver.

"Leal. Investigations."

"Yes, Sergeant, this is Linda LeVeille, Forest Preserve Police," a female voice said. "Did you get my message?"

"I just got in," Leal said. "What was it regarding?"

"Your type three on Janice Parker," she said.

"What? You got her?" Leal asked. He felt the excitement building up.

"In a manner of speaking," she said. "I'm investigating her homicide."

16
WELCOME TO THE PRESSURE COOKER

Linda LeVeille turned out to be tall, slender, and in her early thirties. Her dark hair was cut short and styled in a fashionable, but very utilitarian, way. She was wearing a dark brown skirt and a sleeveless white blouse. Her brown pumps made her eyes almost even with his. They were brown eyes, very dark, almost obsidian-like.

Ojos negros, Leal thought.

Her grip was firm as they shook hands, and she ushered him into her office and handed him the file on the Janice Parker homicide. The brown jacket matching her skirt was draped over the back of her chair. The office area was large with several desks pushed together in the center of the room. Two other male investigators sat near the far wall speaking on the phones, oblivious to anyone else's entry. Leal sat in a padded metal chair next to the desk and went through the file. It was meticulous and thorough. The narrative summarized the discovery by hikers Saturday of a female Caucasian found lying about twenty feet from the road in some high weeds near the forest preserve area at 131st and Central. The body was clad in a pink halter top and blue jeans. The subsequent autopsy revealed that the cause of death was homicide from a gunshot wound to the back of the head, not fired at close range. The recovered projectile was a .380 caliber. The victim had small fragments of glass in her hair.

"Looks like you've got all the bases covered on the crime

scene," Leal said. "We recovered an auto that was involved. Has a couple of bullet holes in it. Looks like they went in through the back window. Some blood, too."

"So it's likely that she was shot in that vehicle then?" Linda said. "Do you know the blood type?"

Leal nodded, reaching over to page through his report packet on the crime scene photos to get to the toxicology report. "Looks like type A."

"That matches," Linda LeVeille said.

"And this is interesting," he said, referring back to her report. "The scrapes and stains on her back and halter top. Indicates that she was dragged feet-first. Probably already dead."

"That's what I figured. Very little blood at the site," she said. "So why is it interesting?"

"It indicates that she was shot and died someplace else," Leal said. "And if she was dragged from the car rather than just dumped on the shoulder, it tells us something about the person who did the dumping."

She nodded.

"Look at the photo of the body here," he said, pointing to an 8 × 10 color glossy. "Somebody took the time to smooth down her blouse after it got all pulled up around her neck."

"In other words," Linda said, "covering her breasts?"

Leal nodded. "And look at the way the hands were folded together on top of the abdomen. Like an undertaker would do."

"Assuming some other person didn't do that after she was dumped," Linda said.

"Good point, but how many people are going to go messing with a bloody dead body off in the weeds?" Leal said. "Plus, the prints we got off the car matched up with another hooker. A Gladis Brown. Janice's prints were on the toilet seat at my crime scene."

"So it's your theory that the two women left your crime scene in the recovered vehicle and were shot at?" Linda said, talking slowly and gesturing with her hands as she spoke. "By a third party."

"Right," Leal said. "We found several spent cartridges at the scene. Three-eighties. Once we establish who that person was, we'll have both cases solved."

"So the two cases *are* connected then," Linda said. It was more of a statement than a question. Leal sensed that she seemed tentative in the conversation. "Where was your crime scene?"

Leal reached into his briefcase and pulled out the Dick Forest case file. It was already several inches thick, with case reports, witness statements, surveillance logs, and notes. "The Riptide Motel," he said. "Ever hear of Dick Forest?"

"The old TV star who was murdered?" Linda asked. Then her eyes widened. "You don't mean . . ."

Leal grinned. "Welcome to the pressure cooker."

He handed her his case file so she could peruse it and sat back in the chair, catching a glimpse of the framed pictures on the front of her desk. Two small boys grinned up at the camera. They looked to be in the five-to-eight age-range. He waited while she finished looking at his file.

"Would you mind if I made a copy of your original case report?" she asked, looking up. "It reads so well. I'd like to go over it in more depth."

"Copy the whole file if you want. I'd like one of yours too."

"Great, I'll be right back," Linda said, getting up with the two files.

"Take your time," he said, taking out his cell phone. "I want to touch base with my partner."

He called the office and asked if Lemack and Tims had returned yet.

"Not yet," the secretary told him.

"Okay, tell him to beep my cell as soon as he gets there." He sat back and finished his coffee and got up to get a second cup. When he'd settled down in the chair again, Linda came rushing back holding the files and the copies against her breasts like a school girl carrying a bunch of books. She laid his original case file in front of him, along with a copy of her reports, then sat down in her chair, smoothing her skirt as she did so. She smiled at him.

"So were you able to get a current address on Janice Parker?" Linda asked. "When I checked out her last known one on the computer, the landlady said she hadn't lived there in quite some time. She also mentioned that your guys had already been by there too."

"I wish we could have found something more current for her," Leal said. "The one we had for Gladis Brown didn't pan out either. I went for a court order to check out Gladis's mother's house. Medicaid records. My partner's picking up some old vice arrest reports on both girls. Hopefully we'll be able to assemble something from them. If possible, I'd like to check it out tonight. Want to come along if we get something?"

Her lower lip drew down at the sides.

"I'd have to see if I could get a sitter," she said. Then added with a quick smile, "The joys of single-parenthood."

Leal nodded. That must mean she's divorced, he thought. He glanced down and made sure she wasn't wearing any rings.

"Yeah, it sure ain't easy," he said. "Let me give you my card. I'll jot my home and cell numbers on the back. If you get a break and want to come along, just call. In the meantime, I think it'd be great if we could work together on this. Obviously the cases are intertwined, and I'd appreciate your input."

"Wow, that's a refreshing change from what I'm used to around here," she said, lowering her voice. Neither of the two male detectives gave any indication that they'd heard or cared about her comment. She glanced at her watch.

"Oh, great," she said. "I've got to pick my oldest up from school and my youngest at the day care."

Leal nodded and started to get up. "Well, I gotta get going myself. I'm taking care of my partner's cat while she's away at school."

"You have children, Sergeant?" Linda asked.

"Yeah," Leal said. "Two girls. My ex has custody. She lives in L.A."

"Oh, God," Linda said. "I'll bet that's rough."

Leal nodded again and said, "Yeah, sometimes."

They started for the hallway. As they neared the door Linda stopped and held out her hand and said that it had been nice meeting him. Leal shook it and reached for the doorknob, but she laid a hand on his arm.

"I really appreciate your offer of working together," she said. "I just got promoted to Investigations last month and this is my first homicide. I think they just gave it to me so they could all gloat when I fell on my face."

"Well, we'll just have to make sure that doesn't happen," Leal said with a grin, hoping he sounded more confident than he felt.

Hart had never rappelled before and found that the hardest part for her was the initial step where you had to lean out and position your body perpendicular to the wall. The fact that this particular wall, which was part of a rappelling tower on the naval base, was six stories high, only added to the anxiety of that initial step. But once she was past that, she loved it. The feeling as she glided down the wall, stopping to catch herself as she measured her bouncing leaps, was indescribable.

A few of the guys had even balked at leaning out over the smaller walls. Especially Dave Maxwell. It had seemed incongruous to Hart. The guy was in pretty good shape, well-muscled with a Marine tattoo.

"Pull me back up! Pull me back up!" he'd yelled as he started to assume his leaning position on the starter wall. Deckons, in a surprising display of compassion, had talked to the guy, reassuring him that if he started to fall the belay-man down below would tighten the rope and stop his descent. They'd only been about thirty feet high at the time. Maxwell had tried it and, after mastering the shorter walls, had started right before Hart to do his final descent from the last, and highest, structure. They were the last two of the group to go.

She glided down beside him, noticing that they were at the same level now, even though he'd started down before she had.

"Dave," she asked, pausing beside him, "you okay?" His face was white.

He grunted, his breathing rapid.

Oh my God, she thought. He's lost it.

"Dave, we're halfway down now," Hart said, trying to calm him. "Come on. Glide with me on three and in a few more stops we'll be on solid ground."

Maxwell turned his face toward her. It was covered with sweat.

"Can't make it." He glanced down then looked back toward the wall, closing his eyes. "I got to have them pull me back up."

"Dave," she said, "it's a piece of cake now. All we have to do is glide down. Pull the rope tight with your right hand when you want to stop. Just like we did before, remember?"

"This is so high." His voice cracked.

"Hey," somebody called out from below. "You two making a date up there, or what?"

Hart's mind raced. How she could keep Maxwell from panicking and finish his descent? More catcalls from below. Deckons had told them that everyone had to master the rappelling before they'd be allowed to get out of class that day.

"You did the rappels on the other tower, right?" Hart asked, still balanced perpendicular to the wall. Maxwell's hands seemed frozen in their positions on his line. The cords in his neck stood out like taut cables.

"What's going on down there?" Deckons called from above.

Great, Hart thought. We're getting it from both ends.

"Nothing," she yelled, then turned back to Maxwell. "Come on, Dave, I know you can do it." She ran through her memory trying to think about what she knew about him. Then she saw the tattoo peeking out from under his rolled-up shirtsleeve. "You're a Marine, right?"

"Was," he muttered. "A long time ago."

"Then I *know* you can do it," she said. "My brother was in the Corps and he told me that there's no such thing as an ex-Marine. Let's go down together on three, okay?" Walking over toward him, she let go of the rope with her left hand, her guiding hand, and touched his arm. It felt as solid as stone. "It'll be okay, I promise. If a girl can do it, a gyrene sure can, right?"

Her touch seemed to jolt him and for a second she thought he was going to fall. His face, still white and dripping with moisture, rotated toward her.

"You promise you'll be right beside me?" His voice sounded timid.

"Sure I will," Hart said. "Right beside you."

"But what'll the rest of the guys think about me?"

"We'll just tell them that we were talking about going out to dinner after work," she said with her most beguiling smile. "Now, you ready?" She squeezed his arm and took hold on her rope again. "On three, right?"

He nodded. She counted and at three they both zipped down several more feet.

"That was good," she said. "Now one more and we'll be

down around the same height as the small tower we did before."

Hart was exaggerating, but knew she had to get him to continue to move.

"Ready?" she asked.

Maxwell nodded and they descended in another leap. The ground looked closer now. "One more and we'll be so close we could jump down."

She pushed out with her legs and seconds later Maxwell did the same. This time they were almost to the bottom. Hart felt a surge of relief when they touched down.

"You okay?" Cook, who had been belaying Hart's line, asked.

"Sure," she said. "Never better."

"What the hell was going on up there?" Cook asked.

Maxwell gave her a quick look.

"We were just admiring the fine view of the lake from up there," Hart said. "You should try it sometime, Special Agent." She heaved a sigh. "I was just telling Dave that some lucky girl's probably getting a nice yacht ride out there, and I'm stuck here playing Rambo." She disconnected her D-ring and stepped away from the line.

"You got better muscles than Stallone," one of the other guys said. "Especially your pecs." A splattering of laughter spread through the group.

Hart looked at him and nodded. "Gee, thanks."

Deckons came zooming down the rope with the aplomb of a master rappeller. He turned and glanced at Maxwell then at Hart.

"What the hell took you two so long up there?" he asked.

"Just two friends out for an afternoon rappel," Hart said, reaching over to squeeze Maxwell's arm again. The tension in his muscles had almost dissipated. "And Dave, being the gentleman that he is, was kind enough to wait for me on the way down so we could descend together. We planned it that way.

Wasn't that nice of him?"

She smiled and slipped off her harness. The rest of the group was milling about and Cook said that two people had to go up to the top and wind up the ropes.

"Hart and Maxwell," Deckons said. "Since they seem to enjoy each other's company so much." His eyes narrowed as he watched Hart's reactions.

"Sure," Hart said. "Come on, Dave."

"Come on, Dave," someone mimicked as they walked toward the rear stairs of the structure. Maxwell had recovered some of his composure and shot a smile back toward the group, accompanied by the finger.

"At least I'll be able to take the stairs down this time," he whispered. "Thanks, Hart." His voice had taken on almost a stuttering quality. "I never would've made it down from up there without you."

She tapped his arm. "Sure you would've."

He shook his head. "And thanks for not saying anything in front of everybody."

"No problem," she said smiling. "My old partner taught me that we have to depend on each other sometimes. I'm sure you'll have the chance to return the favor, so we'll just keep it our secret, okay?"

Maxwell grinned and nodded. But Hart's quick glance over her shoulder told her that Deckons's shrewd gaze was still following them.

17
TIMELY LECTURES

Leal came in early on Wednesday afternoon to check his messages and see if there'd been any mailed responses to his subpoena inquiries. Any thoughts of making some progress with the investigation last night had evaporated after he returned from his meeting with Linda LeVeille. Despite speaking with several people in the records section of the Department of Public Health, and even faxing them a copy of the subpoena for the Medicaid records he wanted, he'd received no reply yet. He knew they wouldn't be working after hours to look anything up for him.

They didn't feel any pressure to help him solve the case and would probably prefer it if Ms. Brown remained lost in the system.

He began to feel that things might be looking up when he discovered a large manila envelope from Ameritech Security in his mailbox. He was set to open it when the secretary paged him, telling him that he had a call on hold. He reached for the phone and punched the blinking extension. "Leal, Investigations," he said.

"Christ, that almost sounds like some private detective agency or something." It was Sean O'Herlieghy. "Can't you at least say Sergeant Leal, County Sheriff's Police Investigations?"

"If I did, they'd hang up before I got it all out," Leal said. "How you doing?"

"Not good, Frank."

"Nothing medical, is it?"

"Oh, no, no," O'Herlieghy said. "I just wanted to call you and let you know I nosed around a little about your ex-partner."

"And?"

"And," he cleared his throat, "don't hold your breath waiting for her to get transferred back."

"They say why?"

"Nah, wouldn't say shit. And I want you to know that I made more than just a couple of calls, too. Got the impression that it was orders from upstairs," O'Herlieghy said. "And you ain't gonna believe what else."

"What?"

"Debbie's getting married." Debbie was Sean's youngest daughter.

"That's great." Or was it, Leal wondered. "When's the wedding?"

"They set it for next month," O'Herlieghy said. "I can't fuckin' believe it."

"Well, kids grow up faster nowadays," Leal said.

"No, that ain't it," O'Herlieghy said, some irritation creeping into his voice. "She called me today to tell me, and asked if I wanted to give her away. Christ, my own little baby asking if I wanted to be the one giving her away at her own wedding . . ."

Leal, sensing there was more to come, said nothing.

"So I says sure, I wanna do it. Then she drops the bomb on me, telling me how it would be better if I came alone, so as not to upset her mother. Can you imagine that?"

Leal managed a commiserating grunt.

"So what am I supposed to do, Frank? Not take Bambi, or miss my baby daughter's wedding?"

Leal did not want to even try to offer any advice in a situation like this. He searched for something noncommittal to say and came up with, "Have you talked to Bambi about it?"

"Are you nuts?" O'Herlieghy shot back. "Things were tough enough between them when I was in the hospital, when they ran into each other during visiting hours. It was like the Cold War, Part Two."

"I wish I knew what to tell you, buddy," Leal offered. "Let me think on it and I'll get back to you. Oh, by the way, did you check on that other matter I asked you about?"

"Yeah," O'Herlieghy said. "Your buddy Lemack has nineteen years and eight months on the job. Spent most of it in patrol, received good evaluations all the way along. Got a bunch of commendations for being a brave son-of-a-bitch. Marine Corps vet, chosen for K-9 officer six years ago, and stayed in that position until a year-and-a-half ago. Then he got into some shit. They took his dog away from him, and he was put back in regular patrol."

"Any idea what happened?" Leal asked.

"As a matter of fact, I do," O'Herlieghy said with a chuckle. "He was always in good with the old Chief, then with Shay getting in, and things getting changed around, he stepped on his dick, big time."

"How?"

"He got called to search the house of some big-wig politician who was asshole-buddies with Chief Burton," O'Herlieghy said. He chuckled again. "I guess this politician had a poodle who was in season, or something, and Lemack's dog must have smelled it and commenced to pissing and shitting all over the living room. The politician went after the dog with a stick or something and Lemack tossed him up against the wall. Told him that nobody was going to hit his dog, and he was gonna arrest him if he tried it again." O'Herlieghy laughed.

"And I take it that it didn't have a happy ending?" Leal asked.

"You got that right. The next thing Lemack knew he was relieved of duty and they took his dog away from him. Caught a suspension, too."

"They took his dog?"

"Right," O'Herlieghy said. "The animals are property of the county, so . . ."

"Man, that's low, taking a man's dog," Leal said.

"I heard that he took it pretty hard," O'Herlieghy said. "But I talked to a couple of his old area commanders. Everybody says that the guy was a sharp cop, once upon a time, but he's been acting a little weird lately. Earned him the nickname Crazy Bob."

"Crazy Bob?"

"Yeah, I'll let you figure that one out," O'Herlieghy said. "Probably a little bit too inexperienced for Investigations, too."

"That's what's got me wondering how the hell he got assigned here," Leal said.

"Oh, that's easy. He's still got a Chinaman," O'Herlieghy said. "He used to be in your favorite lieutenant's squad. Word is that he helped cover for Card on more than one occasion back when him and Dex was on the street together. Now I think Card's just trying to return the favor. Lemack probably always wanted to be a dick so he called in a marker. Let him coast out his twenty in plainclothes."

Christ, another fair-haired boy, Leal thought. Except this one's bald. That's all I need working a heater like this.

"So whaddya think, Frank?"

"I guess I'll have to make do the best I can," Leal said. "At least maybe he'll be good backup."

"Well, yeah," O'Herlieghy said. "But I was talking about the wedding. You think I should go, or what?"

"Sean, I wish I knew the magic answer to tell you on that one, but I don't," Leal said. "I appreciate you making those calls for me."

"Don't mention it." The dejection was heavy in his voice. "At least I felt like I was worth something for a while."

Leal could sense that if he didn't end this conversation soon, it was going to turn into a *Dr. Phil* call.

"Look, Sean, I gotta another call coming in," Leal lied. "I gotta go, okay?"

"Okay, Frank. See you later maybe."

Leal hung up the phone just as Lemack and Tims walked in side-by-side.

"Hi, Sarge," Lemack said. "In early, huh?"

Leal nodded.

"What we gonna do today?" Tims asked, taking one of the ballpoint pens out of his plastic pocket holder and scrunching up his face. He bumped his glasses up on his nose with the back of his hand and Leal wondered if the masking tape on the center of the frame would hold up.

"We're gonna do the same thing we do every day, Al," Lemack said in a serious voice. "We're going to go out and provoke crime." He grinned like a clown.

Crazy Bob, Leal thought. It fits him like a glove.

It was after lunch and Deckons's voice had a monotonous tone to it, seeming to never vary in inflection or purpose. Hart's thoughts turned to Rick and how moody and distant he'd seemed last night in the hotel. Finally he'd confided to her that he was concerned about his brother. She listened as he related his visit to the jail and how worried he was about the way things would turn out. Ollie listened to him, and held him, and that seemed to help a little. But she still had the feeling that he was holding something back. This bothered her because she knew how much Rick had always looked up to his older brother. It made her feel only slightly better when he told her that his requested personal day for Friday had been approved, so they could celebrate her graduation that night.

The mention of her name snapped her out of her reverie. She looked up and saw that Deckons was staring at her.

"I'm sorry," she said. "I didn't quite hear what you said."

Everybody seemed to be watching her. Deckons licked his lips before speaking.

"I was talking about the difference between cover and concealment," he said. "Why don't you explain the difference for us, Officer Hart."

"Cover," Ollie said, "would be something that protects you from ballistic fire, like a concrete wall, while concealment would be something that conceals you from view, but wouldn't necessarily provide protection. Some thick bushes, for instance."

"All right," he said. "I'll accept that. So you're saying that the two terms aren't interchangeable then?"

"I suppose, technically, you could say that cover could also be concealment," she said, "but concealment isn't always cover."

Deckons beamed.

"That's exactly right," he said. "Which brings us to our next topic: Raids. There are basically two purposes for a raid. To recover property, like drugs or evidence, or to recover a person, as in an arrest. But the essential aspects are still the same." He drew a square shape on the blackboard with his chalk. "Suppose that this is the house you want to hit. What's the most important thing to remember in effecting a successful raid?"

A couple of guys called out different answers like planning, firepower, and sufficient personnel.

"All those things are important, but," Deckons said, pausing to print *SURPRISE* and *SPEED* on the board. "Remember that on a raid you're going into the proverbial lion's den. The other guy's backyard to pick a fight. You lose either one of these," he tapped the chalk on the board next to the two words, "you increase the chances that you're going to lose everything, including your life."

18
You Never Know

Leal was even more discouraged after reading through the surveillance logs on Sax. The actor hadn't done anything out of the ordinary, according to the men assigned to follow him, and their boredom was showing in the narratives. "Subject went for his *usual* cup of coffee at the Dunkin' Donuts, his *usual* stop, on his *usual* way to the theater for the *usual* afternoon rehearsal."

Assholes, thought Leal. I give them an important assignment on one of the biggest murder cases going, and they're making stupid jokes on surveillance. He knew he could beef them to their supervisor, but he didn't want to get them in trouble. Sax was the only lead he had, albeit a weak one, but he couldn't afford not to exploit it. As long as the brass was giving him leeway by okaying the surveillance, he'd keep using it. But, he knew that the honeymoon wouldn't last forever. Hopefully the two-bit actor would slip up and then Leal would have some leverage. Sax knew more than he was saying. After all, he wasn't saying shit. Leal glanced at his watch. Quarter to eight.

He'd sent Lemack and Tims down to the Department of Public Health and the Hall of Records to get those addresses for Gladis Brown, and they still weren't back. What the hell could be taking them so long?

Crazy Bob, he thought. And his partner the Boy Geek. Almost sounded like Batman and Robin. No, this was more like one of those animated movies where the characters looked too weird to be real. Plus, he forgot to include fucking Oscar.

Leal blew out a slow breath. He'd hoped to get the information soon enough to call Linda LeVeille and ask if she wanted to check out the addresses with them. It was her case too. But, being honest with himself, that was only part of the reason he wanted to call her.

Sighing, he tapped the printout from Ameritech Security identifying the unlisted phone number that Sax had called that night from the slammer. Efron James. Leal had run a Soundex on the name through SOS/LEADS/NCIC but couldn't come up with a match to that address. Hopefully, the information from the County Assessor's Office would show who owned the property at that address. This James character could be renting there or something and have a driver's license under another name. Damn, he missed Hart. After having been a dispatcher, she knew all the ins and outs of finding things on the computer. He only knew enough to putter around and get himself in trouble. And now he cursed himself for relying so much on her and never taking the time to learn how to find things for himself.

"Another damn miscalculation," Leal muttered out loud.

"Talking to yourself, Frank," a voice said. "That ain't good."

Leal looked up to see Joe Smith, the black detective who worked the night shift.

"Joe, how you doing?" The men shook hands.

"Be doing a lot better if you do me a little favor," Smith said.

Leal nodded. "Shoot."

"I'm hoping I won't have to," Smith said, with a wide grin. He was dark-skinned and kept his hair cropped short. "That's why I want you to come along."

"Where we going?" Leal asked.

"Gonna meet one of my informants in Cicero Heights," Smith said. "At the White Castle. Like to take along some backup in case I have to squeeze this motherfucker a little."

"Sure," Leal said, standing and slipping on his sport coat.

"What kind of case you working?"

"Drive-by," Smith said. "Come on, I'll fill you in."

Smith's informant, a guy called JJ for Johnny Johnson, was working off a bullshit felony shoplifting beef. Or hoped to, at any rate.

Smith had told him to produce on this drive-by shooting or face the judge by himself. And since JJ's record was anything but the best, he knew he needed Smith's help.

"He called me to set up the meet," Smith said. "I just don't like to go to these things alone. Promised Helena I wouldn't."

"How's the baby doing?" Leal asked.

"That little guy's finally sleeping at night now," Smith said with a grin. "And I end up getting stuck on nights."

"Make sure you spend some quality time with him," Leal said. "I sure wish I'd done more of that with my kids. When I had them."

Smith blew out a breath and nodded.

Traffic was pretty light and a misty rain had begun to fall. Smith had commandeered an old, purple Cadillac Seville with tinted windows and a Continental-kit on the trunk from the seized-vehicle pound. He always said it made him feel like he was stylin' whenever he took it for a covert surveillance or met with an informant. They entered the expressway and shot past a big truck spewing up a heavy torrent of water from the slick roadway. The headlights flashed over the transient tire impressions on the dark asphalt as the wipers clicked back-and-forth clearing the windshield.

"So what you been working on?" Smith asked.

"That Dick Forest murder," Leal said. "That old TV actor they found at the Riptide Motel."

"Shit, that place nothing but trouble," Smith said.

"I sure miss not having Ollie with me on this one," Leal said. "She's up at Great Lakes for SWAT school."

"SWAT school? I heard that's one rough time," Smith said. "But she's one tough lady. So who you partnered-up with now?"

"Bob Lemack."

"Crazy Bob? You're shittin' me, right?"

"Huh-uh," Leal said. "Why, you know him?"

"Man, we had the same court call when I was in uniform. That cat's far out." His belly shook from a deep laugh. "One time we was up before old Judge Topper. You remember him— the old drunk. Well, this attorney shows up and they want a trial on this speeding ticket. It was one of the ones where old Bob had used his hand puppet. He called it Oscar or something." Smith laughed again. They came to their exit, and he slowed the Caddie for the long curve of the ramp. "You ever seen him do that?"

"Oh yeah," said Leal.

"So anyway, they get up there and the attorney asks Bob, 'Where's your partner?' And Crazy Bob says, 'He's in the car.' So the judge, who's half in the bag anyway, cause he just came back from lunch, says, 'Oh, is there another officer that's gonna testify? Tell him to come up.' And Crazy Bob says, 'No, he has trouble getting around by himself.' And old Judge Topper was so messed up that he didn't even say nothing."

"Yeah, that's my new partner, all right," Leal said. "I sent him and this intern I'm stuck with down to get a simple set of names and addresses, and I still haven't heard from them."

Smith clucked. "He still got that awesome Fu Manchu?"

"Yeah, but I told him to get rid of it," Leal said. "Ever hear of a guy named Efron James?"

"Yeah. Where you know him from?"

"One of my suspects called a number that comes back to him at an address in Harvey, but I can't match up his name with that address to get a Soundex."

"Shit, Efron's the right-hand man of Otha Spears."

173

"Otha Spears? The Soul Gangstas?"

Smith nodded. "Yep. Efron's been running with them since he was a kid. Leastwise, he was. Got himself shot in Chicago by a copper and won some big settlement against the city. He's in a wheelchair now. But he's still a hardcore gangbanger."

"That'd make sense because Roland Hollingsworth the third came to post the guy's bond," Leal said.

"Yep," Smith added. "That's Spears's attorney. Otha keeps him on retainer."

"I wonder if the house is in Otha's name then?" Leal said.

"What's the address?"

Leal told him.

"Yeah, that's the headquarters," Smith said. "Otha's been stayin' up in there directing all the dope and shit in the south suburbs. I think he ordered this drive-by I'm working on."

Well, at least the evening wasn't a complete loss for the heater after all, Leal thought. He'd learned some information about the case. Now he had to figure out how a white boy like Sax was connected to the Black Soul Gangstas. And how this factored into the Dick Forest case. If it did. More than likely the gang was Sax's source of dope. He'd have to let the surveillance team know that. It would be ideal to catch Sax making a buy. Smith swung the Cadillac into the White Castle, backed into a parking spot, then cut off the lights.

"Want me in back?" Leal asked.

"Yeah, that'd be best, I guess," Smith said. "That way nobody'll see two brothers sitting in the same car with a Latino." He punctuated it with a quick laugh, and Leal knew he was right. In these parts, when you saw "mixed company" in a car, it usually meant that the people in the mixed group were coppers.

"You want anything?" Smith asked, hopping out of the car.

Leal shook his head. He already felt like he'd gained ten

pounds since last week, and knew that he didn't have Ollie to keep him on the good nutrition kick. It seemed like an eternity since he'd last run or worked out, and that bothered him. Even though things had been slow lately, he knew that sooner or later he'd end up dancing with one of these motherfuckers who didn't want to come along peacefully. You needed to maintain your stamina for occasions such as that. But when Smith returned a few minutes later with a bag full of sliders, fries, and a Coke, Leal began to get hungry.

"Maybe I will get something after all," he said, sliding across toward the back door.

"Here," Smith said, handing two boxed hamburgers and a greasy paper package of fries over the seat. "I figured that once you smelled that smell . . ."

"Thanks," Leal said. "I don't suppose you got an extra drink too, did you?"

"Man, do a bear shit in woods?" Smith handed him a small pop with a straw.

"Joe, you think of everything, don't you?"

"That's why I'm a detective," Smith said, grinning.

They finished eating and were working on their drinks when Smith grumbled, "Let's give it a few more minutes."

"He got a cell phone you could call him?" Leal asked, remembering that he'd have to call his buddy Roxie to see if he'd come up with anything useful.

"It's his mother's house," Smith said. "The fucker's twenty-eight-years old, and he's still sponging off his mama." He snorted, then said, "This looks like him now."

Leal looked across the parking lot and saw a thin black man in a dark jacket, his collar turned up against the rain, walking along. The man's head bobbling around under the brim of a dark baseball cap. Smith tapped the horn and the man's gaze centered on the car and he smiled. He walked to the front passenger side door, opened it, and flopped inside. "What's happening?" the man said.

"What's happening is we been sitting here for fucking thirty minutes," Smith said.

"Sorry, bro, but I couldn't catch no ride." He flipped down his collar and said, "It's rainin' out, man."

"No shit," Smith said. "Now what you got for me that got me outta warm bed with my woman?"

"You got a square, man?"

"Un-uh," Smith said. "We don't use 'em."

"Who's your friend?" the informant asked. "I'm JJ," he said over his shoulder toward Leal.

"He's my partner," Smith said, irritation creeping into his voice. "Now is you through playing games?"

"Shit, bro, just trying to be sociable."

Smith blew his breath out of his nostrils. The only other sound was the intermittent scrape of the windshield wipers across the glass.

"I guess you want to know 'bout that drive-by, right?" JJ said.

Smith nodded.

"It was a cat named Marcellus. I can't remember his last name, but on the street they call him Raw Dog," Johnson said. "See, he be dealing along that no man's land between 15th and East End, where them motherfucking spics used to hang." He cast a quick glance at Leal, then continued. "Otha been taking over since Big Mo been inside. Otha was lining up with Morrison against LeRigg 'fore they got did. They was gonna just gobble up this whole southern area, all the way south from 42nd Street in the city."

The comments had piqued Leal's interest. He'd stalked LeRigg and Morrison when he'd worked narcotics, and he'd been shot during a drug buy with LeRigg. The escalating turf war between the two men had ended with LeRigg dead and

Morrison in jail, awaiting trial for the dirty deed.

"What's Efron James been up to lately?" Smith asked, cocking his head in Leal's direction.

"Efron?" JJ said. "He a crip, man. You know, in a wheelchair. But he real good with computers though."

"Ever heard of a dude named, what's he called?" Smith said, looking toward Leal.

"Bill Sax," Frank said. "Called himself Bill S sometimes."

"Bill S, Bill S," JJ whispered to himself, as if running a mental review. Or perhaps debating whether or not he should fake knowing the name just to try and impress them.

"He's a white guy," Leal said.

"Un-uh," JJ said. "I ain't never heard of him."

"So you're saying this dude Marcellus did the drive-by?" Smith asked. "What for?"

"Shit, man, retaliation, what else?" JJ said. "Them S-Gs been creatin' all kinds of fussin', anybody even breathes wrong on their turf. They gettin' everybody in line behind Otha. Word is that he be gettin' his shit real cheap from some dudes on the coast. Anybody wanna do anything 'round here now, they gotta go through him." He pointed toward the bag. "Any more fries in there?"

"Here," Leal said, handing his half-eaten portion across the seat. JJ nodded an appreciative thanks and began stuffing the greasy potatoes in his mouth.

"You got to come up with more than that," Smith said. "What you told me ain't shit."

"What ain't?" Johnson said, opening his mouth and spewing small chunks of half-chewed fries as he spoke.

Smith badgered him for a few more minutes, and JJ was able to come up with a last name, approximate age, and address for Marcellus. "Take me for a ride and I'll show you where he hang at," Johnson said. "Long as you promise not to arrest him when

I'm in the car. But, then again, I doubt he gonna be out in this shit." He waved his hand at the rain-spattered windshield.

"Okay," Smith said, starting the engine.

Leal felt inconspicuous in the back with the tinted windows obscuring anyone inside from view. Johnson gave Smith directions and they rode down several side streets. As they passed a large wooden-frame house Johnson ducked down in the seat and said, "That's it." Smith made a mental note of it and sped down the block. He made a right turn, then went back toward the main drag.

"You gonna give me a ride to my house, ain't ya?" JJ said, leaning back in the seat. "Not right in front, but close, so I don't get wet."

Smith nodded.

"And you gonna tighten me up on that little shoplifting beef so I don't get violated on my probation, right, bro?"

"If what you told me checks out," Smith said, "I'll see what I can do. But in the meantime, you keep working this for me. No favors unless I can close the case."

Johnson sighed.

"Come on, man," he whined.

"Come on, shit," Smith said. "You didn't tell me nothing I didn't already fuckin' know."

"Oh, yeah?" Johnson said. "Well, I got somethin' you ain't heard, I'll bet. And you can take this one to the bank, bro." He pointed toward the curb. "Down by that alley's good. I don't want anybody seein' me gettin' outta this ride."

Smith veered toward the curb and slowed to a stop. "So what you got to tell me?"

"Word is that Otha's pissed off at that dude Marcellus, man. Big time," Johnson said. "I heard tell that when he sent one of his Harvey boys over to collect from Marcellus in Cicero Heights last week, there was a little dispute over how the cash profits was a little light." He paused and ducked his chin for emphasis as he looked up at Smith. "When Otha's boy said something about it, Marcellus pimp-slapped him in front of everybody and told him to get the fuck out."

"So what you sayin'? Our boy gonna get whacked, or something?" Smith asked.

"Could be," JJ said with a smile. "Could be. If I was you I'd watch Marcellus *real* close. He got some bad-ass dude named Taji as a new enforcer." He nodded and slipped out of the car. Smith pulled down the block then drove back toward the area from which they'd just come.

"I want to make sure I got that address right," he said.

"Okay," Leal said. "Sounds like you got something to work with. Got any witnesses on that shooting?"

"Yeah, the victim's girlfriend. Hopefully she be able to pick Marcellus out of a photo line-up and I can get a warrant for his young ass."

"What about that other thing? That guy Taji?"

"That's something I can pass along to intelligence, I guess," Smith said. "Be nice if we could get some surveillance on this cat Marcellus to catch him whacking somebody. You think they'd okay a surveillance? And if they did, for how long?"

Leal thought about his own use of the team and hoped he wouldn't lose it anytime soon.

"Wouldn't hurt to request it, Joe," Leal said. "You never know."

19
ALMOST

"So then we finally get back to Markham," Leal said, "and I ask if anybody's seen my partner." Linda LeVeille took a sip of her coffee, staring at him over the rim of the cup. Her dark eyes seemed to hang on his every word. "So somebody says, 'Crazy Bob, yeah, he's down in the basement.' " Leal paused. "And I'm thinking what the hell is he doing in the basement, so I rush down there and find him and this intern cleaning the car."

"Cleaning the car?" Linda said, smiling.

"Yeah," Leal said, grinning back. "So I ask him where the hell he's been and what the hell he's doing, and he gets this real stupid look on his face and begins to tell me this story about how they're coming back from downtown, and they see this dog running around on the expressway. The damn thing is darting in and out of traffic and cars are just missing it, so Lemack decides to try and catch it. Well he pulls over and him and the intern are trying to grab it when the dog gets clipped. Lemack wraps it in his sport coat and rushes it, lights and sirens, to that emergency vet care in Crestwood."

He paused again, trying to read Linda LeVeille's reaction to the story. She had an amused expression, and her face crinkled when she heard about the dog.

"How bad was it hurt?" she asked.

Leal smiled and held up his index finger. He decided that he'd made the right move asking her to have lunch with him, ostensibly to discuss the cases. She looked quite nice, her makeup subdued in hues of dark brown, and she wore a sleeveless print blouse and a tight black skirt.

"Then Tims, that's the intern," Leal said. "He looks just like one of those guys from that old *Revenge of the Nerds* movie." Linda giggled out loud. "He holds up Bob's sport jacket, and it's covered with blood. But Lemack has this big grin on his face as he tells me that it looks like the dog's gonna be okay."

"Well, at least it had a happy ending," Linda said. "You going to write him up?"

"Well, I chewed him out a little," Leal said. "But it's hard to be pissed off at the guy. Besides, I'm an animal lover myself. Who knows, I might've done the same thing." He smiled. When the waitress came to refill their cups, Linda shook her head and covered hers. The waitress sorted through her apron pocket and laid the check face-down on the table. Leal reached forward and took it.

"So anyway," he said. "The good news is I got the addresses for Gladis Brown from Public Aid."

"Great, did you check any of them out?" Linda asked.

"I had only a few minutes to go through them, but it looks like she may be at a place in Harvey that's probably her mother's or something. Apparently her kid stays there. At least I'm assuming it's her kid from the dates of birth on the Medicaid card," he said. He took a sip of his coffee, then added, "I was going to go over them closer, but we got called to help interview employees on that hotel robbery last night."

"Oh yeah, I heard about that," she said. "Quite a few of those getting hit lately."

"Yeah. Sounds like the same guys. They've been hitting places just like a commando team," he said. "This time a surveillance camera caught them on tape."

"Great. Whose case is that one?"

"Who's sitting here?" Leal said with an exaggerated grin.

"Oh no," she said. "Really?"

"Actually, Ryan's supposed to be handling those, but he was off sick last night. I'll just have to do an initial write-up and he'll take over."

"That's nice," she said. "That way we can concentrate on this one, right?"

Ah, back to business so soon, Leal thought.

"Yeah, the way I see it Gladis is the key to the whole thing," he said. "Your case and mine. Obviously Dick Forest was in the motel room with the two hookers and someone else. When we find Gladis, she'll be able to tell us who, and that's most likely the guy who killed both victims."

"You seem pretty sure," she said.

"It's gotta be," he said. "What other explanation is there?"

"I mean that this other person is a man," she said smiling.

Leal took a breath and smiled. Hints of feminine militancy?

"I'm betting it is," he said. "But we won't know for sure until we collar Gladis. After we write up this thing from last night, we're going cruising around with some of the vice guys, trying to scarf her up. Want to come along?"

"I can't tonight," she said. "It's my last night with the kids before their father takes them for the weekend."

"Oh," Leal said. "I could always call you if we find her . . ." He let the proposition drift off.

"Okay," she said, reaching in her purse and taking out one of her cards. She clicked the end of the ballpoint pen and wrote two phone numbers on the back of the card in neat script.

"The one with the C is my cell. The other one's my home number." She smiled. "You know, I could go along tomorrow."

"Great," Leal said. "If we find her tonight I'll call you and let you know. If not, I'd like a woman's touch when we go to talk to mama."

"Sounds like a date," she said with a laugh. "Almost."

Leal was in good spirits after his lunch with Linda. He spent most of the ride into the office not thinking about the case but wondering about the various nuances that had sprung up during their conversation.

She mentioned that her kids would be gone for the weekend, and she did give him her home phone number. And that reference about their planned trip to Gladis's mother's house on Friday being almost like a date. What was she implying with that?

When he pulled into the expansive parking lot he felt great. Refreshed. Optimistic. The feeling lasted until he got inside and was told by the secretary that Lt. Card was looking for him.

He went down the hallway toward Card's office and saw Ryan leaning against the wall drinking milk from a carton.

"Thanks for covering for me on that hotel thing last night," Ryan said.

"No problem," Leal said. "How you doing?"

Ryan cocked his head to one side in a quick grimace.

"Got to go in for that fucking rectal exam tomorrow afternoon," he said. "They're doing a lower G.I. Nothing to eat after two o'clock today, then I gotta start drinking this stuff that makes you shit all day."

"Sounds like fun," Leal said. "I hope everything comes out all right."

Ryan frowned. "Yeah, thanks."

The lieutenant's secretary whispered into the phone as she saw Leal approaching and told him to go right in as he stepped into the room. He pulled open the door and saw Card shaking one of his Mylanta bottles. The lieutenant motioned for him to sit down in the chair in front of the desk. The hot seat.

Leal waited for Card to take a long drink of the stomach

medicine before saying, "What's up, Lieu?"

Card recapped the bottle and wiped at his mouth with the back of his hand. A chalky residue still dotted his upper lip.

"What's the story on that thing last night?" Card asked.

"Those motel bandits hit a Budgetel on Cicero Avenue," Leal said. "Just like the last two times. Went in right after the night girl and was alone. Wore masks and jumped the counter. Tied the clerk up and hit the safe. We got 'em on video."

"Any leads?"

Leal sighed and shook his head.

"I'm writing it up now," he said. "Figure I'll get a summary done for our beat-sheets today."

"Yeah, get that out to the area commanders ASAP," Card said. He took a sudden deep breath and froze for a second, then rubbed his abdomen. "How we doing on that other case, Frank? The Dick Forest cluster-fuck?"

"Well," Leal sighed. "I have located the hooker whose print we found at the crime scene," he said with a weak smile. "Only problem is, she's dead. The tree police are working that one 'cause she was dumped in the Preserve, but I'm sure she was shot at the motel."

"Marvelous," Card said. "So this might turn into a double homicide? Got any other good news?"

"We're looking for the other broad," Leal said. "She had to witness the killings. I think she drove off with the murdered one and dumped the body. The killer wants her too, judging from the way the car was shot up."

"I don't have to remind you that they're leaning all over me on this one, do I?" Card rubbed his stomach a little more, then said, "What about that surveillance team on that actor guy? I got a call about that this morning. We getting anywhere with that, or we spinning our wheels?"

Leal felt the sweat trickle down from his armpit. "Yeah, well,

I mean, we haven't gotten anything solid yet, but that's my best lead right now."

Card sighed.

"Frank, I got a bunch of pricks breathing down my neck about the cost of going round the clock on that guy," he said. "Christ, it's been what? Almost a week now?"

"Almost," Leal said. His mind raced. "But, Lieu, like I told you, that's the best lead we got. In fact, Joe Smith and I talked to one of his informants last night about this Sax guy. Something's gonna break soon with him, I just know it."

"Oh yeah," Card said. "Well, that's kinda funny since Smith requested a surveillance on one of his suspects. It's tied up with the Soul Gangstas, and I don't have to tell you how much weight that carries with the Chief. He's taking anything with them real personal."

"Yeah," Leal said. "I know." He thought for a moment. "Lieu, you can't cut the surveillance on Sax. Not now. I'm getting close to a break."

"I don't know," Card said, massaging his temples. "It don't seem like you're making a lot of progress . . ."

"You got to give it a chance."

"Look, Leal, I'm the guy who's responsible for the cost over-runs." Card's hand slammed down on the desktop. "And it seems like all we're getting outta this is a lot of overtime and no fucking results."

Then you should have made sure I had Ollie with me and not some inexperienced goofball who's one step away from the rubber-gun squad, Leal thought. But what he said was, "If you can just give me a little longer, Lieu. . . ." He let the sentence trail off. God, he hated having to kiss ass, but he was dealing with the ultimate bean counter.

Card blew out a long breath.

"All right, I'll see what I can do," he said. "But, Christ, get

185

something soon or the gravy train's gonna grind to a quick halt. Make sure I got summaries on my desk before quitting time."

He was reaching for the bottle of Mylanta again as Leal stood to leave.

"That time was faster," Special Agent Cook said, hitting the stop watch. "You managed to trim twenty seconds off the A-team's time."

Hart was on the B-Team, which meant nothing more than they weren't the first group that had to endure this tedium. After splitting the class into two parts, the instructors had one of them do simulated drug raids while the other practiced night-firing on the adjacent range. She'd done well in the night-firing exercises with the gun Rick had loaned her. The Sig Sauer had tritium night-sights that glowed in the dark, providing her with a perfect sight-picture. Deckons, who'd run the range portion, had seemed impressed by her close shot-pattern, and she was beginning to feel real comfortable with this gun.

I'll have to see if Rick wants to part with that baby, she thought, wondering what he was doing, then being snapped back to the present when Cook shouted that they had to run another simulated raid. The announcement was met with groans from the rest of the guys, but, hell, everyone was tired, having continued with the rigors of the raid practicing and the night-firing after they'd eaten dinner.

"Come on, people," Cook called out. "Let's go."

The group assembled, chambering more of the paintballs in their weapons and adjusting the Plexiglas goggles that they were required to wear for eye protection. They had to assemble about twenty yards away and run up to the door of the house. One of the problems was that the goggles tended to steam up somewhat, obscuring their vision. Several times people had tripped over the furniture in the semi-lit house. The door, which had been specially fortified with one of several braces, had to be knocked down. Then a systematic search of every room had to be conducted, and the "dope" had to be found. The clock kept running until all of the rooms were secured and the simulated narcotics, usually stashed in the bathroom, were located.

"On a real drug raid, the goodies won't be so easy to locate," Cook said as B-Team lined up. "That's why it's important to try and figure out as much about the interior as possible. Remember, plan for everything, including the unexpected."

"Yeah, yeah, yeah," one of the guys muttered. Hart was up for point this time, with Dave Maxwell and another big guy manning the ram.

"Okay, ready, set . . . GO!" Cook yelled. "Come on people, the clock's ticking! That dope's gonna get flushed."

Maxwell and the other man stumbled getting set up in front of the door with the ram. They raised it in unison and let the big flat end slam into the door. The wood buckled but held.

"Must be a high brace," Maxwell said, and, swearing, they swung the ram lower this time to strike the bottom quarter panels. This time the door popped downward with a sudden snap. The two men dropped the ram and flattened against the walls allowing the rest of the raid team to enter. Hart ran into the first room. It was large and had a worn-out old sofa and a couple of dilapidated chairs positioned in various places.

"Police! Search warrant!" she yelled, her paint gun out in front of her at the ready. She advanced toward the hallway, the same way she had during the ten previous raids, only this time Deckons stepped out of one of the rooms.

Hart felt a sting as something punched her on the right side of her face. Crouching, she felt something hit her side, then another paintball whizzed by her and the man behind her grunted. Deckons continued to fire, his weapon some sort of paintball machine gun. He stepped over Hart and shot three more men when Ollie reached up, firing her own weapon, and sent a red splatter between Deckons's shoulder blades. Her face still stung, as if someone had smacked her. She shook her head trying to clear it and then she hear Cook's whistle.

"Okay, cease fire, everyone," Cook said, walking through the door. "As you see, this time we threw you a curve ball." He paused as he saw that Hart was standing with her hand on her cheek. "Are you all right?" he asked.

She nodded, but Dave Maxwell came over and shone his flashlight on her face.

"Looks like that damn paintball didn't rupture on contact," he said.

"Sometimes they can get hard if they're too old," Deckons said.

"It did feel like somebody hit me with a marble," Hart said. She wished she had a mirror so she could see how bad it was.

"Christ, man," Maxwell said. "Why the hell didn't you check them before you fired?"

"Sorry, Hart," Deckons said. "I assure you that it wasn't intentional. But we do try to keep these training sessions as realistic as we can. Put some ice on that and it'll help keep the swelling down," he added almost as an afterthought.

"This time we wanted to instill in you that despite all the pressure to make a fast entry and recover whatever drugs you can," Cook said, "you can't do so at the expense of safety and planning."

"Some lesson," Maxwell said. "At the expense of one of us getting hurt."

"Just think if it had been the real thing," Deckons countered. "And, I'd like to point out, if it had been, the wound that Officer Hart had sustained would have incapacitated her, so she couldn't have returned fire. That means that probably more of you would have been casualties."

"Yeah, but this is just training," Maxwell shot back.

"Training, mister, is where you want to make your mistakes," Deckons said. "Now go take five and have A-Team assemble out front. Each group will run three more raids."

They staggered out of the house and went to sit in the grassy area about twenty yards from the house. Hart felt like the side of her face was on fire. She touched it gingerly, wishing she had a mirror. It felt puffy. Oh, God, she thought. Tomorrow it'll all be over. Across the yard the other group was in a huddle getting briefed by Cook, who was explaining the scenario to them.

"Look," someone whispered. They followed his finger and saw Deckons loading more paintballs into his machine gun as he crept around the back of the house.

"That son-of-a-bitch is gonna ambush A-Team this time," Maxwell said. "Come on." He got to his feet.

"Where you going?" another of the group asked.

"If he can sneak in the back way, so can we," Maxwell said. "Let's get him."

"But we're not part of the scenario," Hart said. "Won't they be upset?"

"They told us to expect the unexpected, didn't they?" Maxwell said, his big grin showing white in the ambient lighting. "Murph, go over and mingle with one of the A-Team guys and tell him what's going on and that we'll be coming in the back door."

Murphy got up and grinned just as broadly as Maxwell, then shuffled off toward the other team.

Hart stood up.

"Dave, you don't have to do this just because I got hurt," she said. "It's not that big of a deal."

"I'm just showing initiative," he said. "Come on. Nice and quiet now, B-Team." The rest of the group members were already on their feet and began a silent approach toward the house. Hart slipped on her goggles and went with them, bringing up the rear. They flattened against the side wall and Maxwell took a quick peek around the corner.

"The back door's here," he whispered. "Get ready to move when you hear Cook's whistle."

Everyone nodded. The whistle sounded and Maxwell tore around the corner, the others in B-Team following. The big man gripped the door, which was unsecured, and threw it open. At the front of the house they heard the sounds of the ram smacking against the wood of the front door. "Police! Search warrant!" somebody called from up front. As if on cue Deckons stepped from a small closet and began to raise his paint machine gun. His back was pelted with at least half-a-dozen red splotches. As he turned, Maxwell's wide shoulder slammed into Deckons's mid-section, and the thin FBI agent went flying into the living room area.

"This one's secure," Maxwell shouted. "Get the dope."

The combined raid team circled the rooms, shaking because they were laughing so hard. Several came over to look down at the captive Deckons, whom Maxwell was holding face-down against the coarse fabric of the dirt-covered rug.

"Maybe we should interrogate this suspect here," one of the guys said.

"Or just execute him," someone else joked.

Cook came rushing over and told them to get off Deckons. "This is not part of the scenario," he said.

"Oh yeah?" Maxwell said, getting up and making it look like he was helping Deckons to his feet, while yanking his arm. "You been harping at us all week to use our heads. Well, we figured a little rear-guard action was necessary." He punctuated his sentence with a wide grin.

"You okay, Don?" Cook asked.

Deckons nodded his head, then said, "Yeah."

"Okay, I can see that we're just about ready for the showers tonight," Cook said. "So we'll call it a night. Now don't forget that tomorrow, after our morning run and PT, we'll have the final phase of our classroom lectures, followed by a written exam. So I suggest that you review your notes tonight."

A few more groans emanated from the group. But Cook continued. "Also, our graduation ceremony will be at 1400 hours, and, as I said, if you have departmental people or family that wish to attend, they will be welcome." Some hoots began and Cook quickly added, "Several Chiefs of Police have already said that they will be there."

"That's all for tonight, then," Deckons said. "Turn in your paint guns here, and we'll see you in the morning."

He still looked shaken. Maxwell had given him a hell of a hit, slamming into him like a defensive lineman. The two agents turned and began collecting the weapons. Hart turned in hers and caught up to the lumbering figure of Maxwell who was several feet ahead of her.

"Dave," she said.

He turned and said, "How's your face?"

"I'll live," Hart answered. "You really didn't have to body-slam Deckons that way, though."

"The bastard had it coming," Maxwell said. He heaved a sigh, then laughed. "That was the only fun I've had in this whole damn class."

"Well, cheer up," she said. "It's almost over now."

"Yeah," he said. "Almost."

20
TOP COPS

When Hart woke up at six Friday morning she knew it was going to be more than just a bad hair day. The whole right side of her face was not only puffy and swollen, but a bright scarlet spot splashed over her cheekbone as well. The ragged edges of the bruise seemed outlined in purple, and a good portion of the color was centered under her eye. The injury was aggravated by her fitful night's sleep, no doubt. She'd held some ice against her face as she sat reviewing her notes before bedtime. But the blinking message-light on her phone had disturbed her concentration. It was a notification to call the Chief's office tomorrow (Friday) morning. Hart wondered if that meant someone was coming up for the graduation.

She'd tried Rick as soon as she'd gotten back to the room, and he'd called her about ten minutes later. Not wanting him to worry, she didn't tell him about her injury. It was minor anyway, and hardly worth mentioning. But she knew he'd worry and she wanted him to concentrate on the street dangers, not be concerned about her. When he mentioned that his personal day for Friday night had been approved, she felt ecstatic.

"I could drive up there for the graduation ceremony, if you want," he'd said.

"That would be nice," she'd said, hoping he didn't hear the ambivalence in her voice. If the Chief or some of his cronies were to come up for the ceremony also, it might be awkward if they saw Rick there. Not that their romance was any secret.

Frank knew about it, as well as a few others, but still, with this I.A.D. assignment looming on the horizon maybe it would be better not to advertise that she had a relationship with another county copper. She certainly didn't feel like being grilled about that.

"I was gonna visit Lance," Rick said, his voice trailing off. "I've been worried about him."

"Oh, then visit your brother," Hart answered. That would solve her dilemma. "We'll celebrate by ourselves tomorrow night."

"You're sure it's okay?" he asked.

"Of course I'm sure," she said, already hating the nature of this assignment for causing her to be manipulative with someone she cared so much about.

After her shower, Hart put her hair up in the usual French braid and began applying some heavy-duty foundation over the bruise. The magnifying mirror made the swollen area look even more distorted, but at least she was able to cover the discoloration. Even so, she knew it would wear off rather quickly. Hopefully it would get her through the graduation ceremony. At seven she went down to the hotel restaurant and had a quick breakfast of scrambled eggs on whole wheat and orange juice.

No more restaurant eating she thought as she gobbled it down. Rory would be so upset if he knew she'd gone off her diet.

At eight sharp she was lined up in formation for their final inspection. Both Deckons and Cook stared at her cheek as they walked by, but neither said anything. They got into formation for their early morning run and went for a quick-paced three-and-a-half miles. When they finished Hart noticed that Deckons had dropped out before completing the distance. She wasn't the only one who was hurting. Afterward, the instructors told them to take their time showering and to be at the classroom by nine-thirty. Then Cook came running up next to Hart.

"Hi, how's your face?" he said.

"Oh, it's fine," she said.

"Good, I took the liberty of calling the Sheriff's Department, and they're sending somebody out for the ceremony."

Hart nodded. "How's your partner?"

Cook's mouth twisted. "He's a little bit under the weather this morning. By the way, I'm supposed to tell you that you have to call the Chief's office first thing this morning," he said. "You can use the phone in the office." He pointed toward the classroom building.

Hart thanked him and walked over to make the call. It was answered by the Chief's secretary, who seemed almost cordial after Hart identified herself.

"Oh, Olivia, hi. It's Janetta," the secretary said. "How you doing up there?"

"Getting by," Hart said. "It's almost over."

"Yeah, I'll bet you'll be glad, huh?"

"Uh-huh," Hart said, but she was wondering why this girl, whom she barely knew, was being so friendly.

"I was told to call first chance I had." Hart let the sentence sound open-ended.

"Oh, right," Janetta said. "Chief Burton wants you to report here as soon as you're finished with the class. Before five. Before four-thirty, if possible."

"All right," Hart said. "I thought he'd be coming up for the graduation ceremony?"

"I think he's sending somebody," Janetta said. "But I'm not sure who. So, anyway, good luck and we'll see you before five."

We'll see you before five, Hart thought as she walked over to the women's locker room to shower. Just like she was invited over for cocktails or something. Didn't they realize how grueling this damn class had been? How hard it had been on her taking this class on such short notice? Canceling all her personal plans . . . Her body was bruised and sore, not mention how her face looked. And the Chief wasn't even going to come to the graduation: *I think he's sending somebody.*

Thanks a lot.

The final classroom lecture was a review of all the lessons, and the test that followed was multiple choice. Hart took her time and read over each question. After the test they did a quick critique of the class and the instructors. Hart gave them high marks, because she really had learned a lot. Upon reflecting, now that it was over with, she was able to look back with a feeling of accomplishment and wonder. She noticed that Dave Maxwell had taken almost as much time on the critique as she had on the test. The section reserved for remarks and comments was filled up on the big man's sheet. After the exam they were given an hour for lunch. Hart and the others were told to report back to the auditorium on the Naval base for the graduation ceremony. At one o'clock sharp they walked in and saw Deckons and Cook standing there in blue suits. Cook was posting a sheet on the bulletin board with the scores on the test. Hart meandered over and was surprised when she saw that her name was first. Behind it was a 100%. The next highest number was a 94. She'd figured that she'd done well, but had never expected to come out on top.

A couple of the guys congratulated her on getting the best score. Officials from the various departments were starting to arrive and Cook told them to be seated in the auditorium. It was a rather large, theater-like room with comfortable seats and a stage.

The two FBI men glanced at each other, then Cook nodded and Deckons walked over to Hart. "How's your face?" he asked.

"Oh, I'm fine," she said, trying to smile. She was scanning

the audience trying to see who was there from the Sheriff's Department.

"Ah, I just wanted to tell you that I'm sorry you got hurt last night," Deckons said. "It was an accident."

"That's okay," Hart said. "I'm sure you didn't mean it."

"You did very well in the class," Deckons continued. "And you really weren't the first woman to make it through. We just said that to add more pressure." He shrugged. "Sometimes we have to find out what buttons to push to simulate the stress of an actual situation, and we end up pushing a lot more than we need to. You did do better than any of our previous females though."

"Thanks." Hart smiled. "I learned a lot."

"Well, I also wanted to tell you that you won both the physical fitness award and the top classroom honors," Deckons said. "We'll make the formal presentation on the stage after the commencement address. The speaker is our regional supervisor. He's in charge of our SWAT team."

"Thank you," was all Hart could think of to say.

The physical fitness award was a big gold-plated medallion on a red, white, and blue ribbon not unlike one of the bodybuilding awards that Hart had gotten in some of her various competitions. The scholastic award was a wooden plaque with two gold books and a lighted lamp on it. A smooth strip of gold on which was lettered, TOP ACADEMIC HONORS, was set along the bottom with room for her name underneath. The county official proved to be one of the undersheriffs Hart had never met before. He spent most of the time congregating with the chiefs and big-wigs from the other departments. He congratulated her in a perfunctory kind of way, then, after glancing at his watch, said he had to get going.

It was close to three and Hart was dreading the long drive

back to the city, fighting the incipient rush-hour traffic to get to Maywood before five. She was fingering the medallion around her neck when Dave Maxwell came up to her.

"Ollie, congratulations," he said, holding out his big hand. "You did real good."

Hart shook it and thanked him.

"Um," he said, "a bunch of us are gonna hit the strip to do a little celebrating, and we were wondering if you might like to come along. Figure that the traffic's gonna be murder till after six anyway."

Hart was surprised that they'd asked her, but as a non-drinker she knew that these guys would be trying to drink each other under the table. Not her scene trying to deal with a group of guys who'd probably be drunk and all hands in no time flat. But what surprised her the most was how tempted she was. Going through this class she'd developed a real affinity for the rest of the guys, Maxwell and Murphy and a few more, and found herself delighted to know that it was mutual.

She knew it was a bonding that so often occurs in situations where people work together under such stress. Sort of like what she had with Frank. Still, she had that appointment to keep—a reminder of the true nature of this assignment, which made things even more troubling. This had been just the first step in a long, difficult, solitary journey. She hoped that she would be able to weed out whatever bad apples there were, if any, in her new team. At least before the inevitable bonding took place with the new group.

"I'd love to, Dave," she said. "But I have orders to report to my Chief before five." She smiled. "Looks like I'll be fighting some of that traffic. But I've really enjoyed being in this class with you."

"Same here," he said. "You know, I learned a lot this past week."

197

"Yeah, me too."

"Sorta like we been through something together," he said. "Kind of like the Marines." He smiled. "And I'd have never made it down that wall if it wasn't for you."

He extended his hand again and she shook it.

"Well, if you're ever up around Des Plaines, look me up," he said.

"I'll be sure to do that. And good luck on your SWAT team."

He pointed to her medallion. "Congratulations again." His grin looked forced as he began to walk away, then he paused and turned. "You were the best out of all of us, you know."

It was all working out better than Leal had figured. The surveillance guys were still on the job following Sax, waiting for him to make a false move. Now if this visit with Gladis Brown's mother turned up something positive, they'd have reason to celebrate. And Linda LeVeille had managed to persuade her ex to pick up the kids early so she could accompany them. Leal glanced in the rearview mirror and saw Linda half-turned against the rear door and Alfred Tims leaning toward her from the other side. The intern was typing furiously on his iPad as he asked Linda questions about the Forest Preserve Police Department.

Tims squinted as he leered over the top of the iPad, and Leal chuckled to himself. A nerd of the heterosexual variety, he imagined some foreign doctor saying with a German accent as he examined the kid. Linda dressed more conservatively than Hart did. But then again, Ollie was used to dressing in those skimpy outfits to show off her body. Not to be boastful or anything, but just because it seemed natural to her. Linda wore a light blue blouse and a longish print skirt of a darker shade. Her weapon, he imagined, must be in her purse. Hart had almost always worn hers on her belt in a pancake holster, like most male cops. But then again she looked like an athlete. Plus she usually wore jeans every chance she got when they were working. Leal found himself wondering what Linda LeVeille would look like in jeans. And without them.

Crazy Bob, who'd been riding in the front passenger seat, said, "So you mentioned you got kids, Linda? Ever thought of getting 'em a dog?" He'd taken Leal's directive about the mustache to heart and was now clean-shaven.

"Actually, no," Linda said. "With my schedule it would be rather difficult. My children are still pretty young to have a pet anyway."

"Yeah," Crazy Bob said, nodding his head. "Having a dog's a lot of responsibility. I gotta try and find a home for that one we saved last night, if she pulls through. Maybe we can stop by and check on her, huh, Frank?"

"It'd be better to call," Leal said, glancing in the mirror again and catching a quick, commiserating wink from Linda. "We may not have time."

"Good point," Crazy Bob said, taking out his cell.

"The place should be right up here," Leal said. "What I'd like is to have just Linda and me go in. If all of us pile out, it'll look too much like the stormtroopers have arrived. Besides, I'm hoping that Linda can kind of talk to her woman to woman."

"Sounds good to me, partner," Crazy Bob said. Leal almost cringed as he thought about that last word.

They rode down Dixie Highway past the abandoned mall. The crisscrossed steel girders that had marked the entrance to the main parking area were covered with a dark patina of rust. Beyond it, the massive brick structures sat behind a sporadic barrier of waist-high weeds, the large picture windows now covered with weather-beaten plywood. The only bright spot was that they'd constructed the new Harvey Police Building on the far corner of the lot.

"Ever been in there?" Crazy Bob asked, pointing toward the mall.

Leal shook his head.

"I can remember when they first built it," Crazy Bob said. "Used to be a real nice place. I worked there when I was in high school. They had these big, circular columns of glycerin that dripped from the ceiling in some kind of art display. Looked like regular glass columns from a distance, but when you got up close, you could toss pennies through them."

"Looks like it's seen better days," Leal said.

"They filmed *The Blues Brothers* inside of it," Crazy Bob said. "You know, the old movie with Belushi and Ackroyd. That scene where they get chased through the mall."

"What's the old movie about?" Tims asked.

"Heroes and villains," Crazy Bob said. "Two guys out to do the right thing. Sorta like the Sarge and me."

"That was this place?" Linda asked. "I remember seeing the movie on TV, but never knew it was filmed around here."

"Yeah, at one time they were even talking about making this a permanent sound stage," Crazy Bob said. "Too bad that never materialized. God knows this area could use something besides pushers and gangbangers. Something for all the good people trapped here."

They passed a large group of nomadic-looking youths meandering down the sidewalk, their hats all cocked to the same side.

Leal turned left and went into a residential subdivision.

Some of the houses seemed well kept up, with trimmed lawns and high fences. Others were boarded up, covered with the ubiquitous graffiti that depicted the crescent moon and five pointed star. Groups of mean-eyed young blacks eyed them as suspiciously as if they had been driving a marked squad.

"Kind of makes you feel like we're the vanguard of some occupation force, doesn't it?" Crazy Bob said.

Leal drove on toward the next block. A group of younger children ran and played in front of a section of apartment buildings.

"This is it," Leal said. "Second floor, east end. Bob, why don't you stay down here and keep an eye on Al." Crazy Bob nodded. Tims continued to type away in his iPad. Linda and Leal went to the front doors of the apartment building and looked on the register beside a row of buttons.

Slips of paper with the occupants' names, handwritten in blue ink, were beside each one. The mail boxes, all looking as though they'd been pried open more than once, were located under the buzzers. Leal pressed the button beside the name Brown.

A moment later a distorted female voice asked who it was.

"Police department, Mrs. Brown," Leal said. "We'd like to talk to you please."

" 'Bout what?"

"Your daughter Gladis."

Silence, then the speaker said, "Come on up." The solid-looking white door buzzed and Leal pushed it open. He and Linda stepped into the darkened hallway and went up the stairs. The carpeting over the steps had worn away in spots and the whole structure seemed to creak as they ascended. At apartment 2E Leal stopped, removed his badge case, and flipped it open before knocking.

The door was opened by an attractive, medium-built black woman who appeared to be in her mid-to-late thirties.

The woman wore a green uniform dress and had her hair pulled back in a bun. She was very dark and her loam-colored eyes were piercing.

"What you want?" she asked, squinting as she looked at Leal's ID.

201

"We'd like to talk to you about your daughter Gladis," Linda said.

The woman's gaze shifted to her. "What she done now?" Then, stepping back from the door, said, "Come on in."

They went inside. The apartment had a large living room with a set of sliding glass doors that opened out onto a balcony. The doors were open, letting a cool breeze filter in, rustling some long gossamer curtains. Beyond the living room Leal could see a kitchen area and adjacent bedrooms. The walls were beige and showed traces of dirty smudges: A child's small handprints. But the rooms looked clean and fairly well kept up. He smiled and let Linda take the lead, just like he would have done had he been with Ollie.

"Is Gladis staying here, Mrs. Brown?" Linda asked.

"No, she ain't. Can you tell me what this is about?" The woman's tone was hostile and defensive.

"Ma'am, we have reason to believe that your daughter may be in danger," Leal said. Better that he break the bad news and keep Linda available for commiseration. "We think she was a witness to a crime, and we want to talk to her." He smiled again. "Let me emphasize that we only want to *talk* to her, not arrest her. She's not in any trouble that we know of with the law."

Mrs. Brown scoffed in derision.

"But we are concerned for her safety," Linda added.

Mrs. Brown let out a long slow breath, her head nodding and her eyes focused on a picture that sat across the room on a television set.

"If you all knew what I been through with that girl," she said. "The times I tried to get her straight." She shook her head. "She ain't been staying here for long time. I wouldn't allow it. You see, I got her little boy." She nodded toward the picture again and Leal glanced at it. He saw three figures: a younger, prettier Mrs. Brown, Gladis, obviously fixed up and looking better than the mug shot he'd seen of her, and a small boy with a huge grin. The boy was a shade lighter than either of the women, but shared their general features. Three generations summed up in a single picture, Leal thought.

"Nice looking kid," he said.

"Thank you," Mrs. Brown said. "She was staying here for a while, till I wouldn't put up with her doing that dope all the time. Not with the little one livin' here. Told her to clean herself up or get out. She left, then would come back a couple times a month to get her check. Pretend that she was gonna get cleaned up, but then as soon as the check got here she'd be running down the stairs and out to buy her dope." She paused and looked at them. "What she mixed up in now?"

"We think she may have witnessed a murder," Leal said.

"My Lord," said Mrs. Brown. "It get worse and worse."

"Ma'am, like I told you," Leal continued in a soft tone, "the people who did this know what she saw. It's important that we find her before they do."

Mrs. Brown nodded.

"I understand, but I ain't seen her," she said. "She call here a few days ago to make sure little Dewayne okay, but that's all."

"Can you think of anywhere she might go?" Linda asked. "Friends, relatives . . ."

"I don't know none of her friends," Mrs. Brown said with a trace of indignation. "All the rest of her people, they know what she been doin'. You can only be ripped off so many times . . ."

"When she called you, did she say where she was at?" Leal asked.

"No," she said, shaking her head. "But I know it wasn't around here. The phone clicked off, you know, the operator cuttin' in sayin' her time was up."

"A pay phone?" Leal said.

Mrs. Brown nodded.

"Does she have a cell?" Leal asked.

Mrs. Brown shook her head. "If she do, I don't know it."

They asked a few more routine questions, getting nowhere.

Leal stretched. "Ma'am, would you mind if I used your washroom?"

"It's down there," Mrs. Brown said. Linda began asking more questions about Gladis and the two women seemed to be engaged in a conversation when Leal moved down the hall to the bathroom. After closing the door he turned on the tap and then opened the medicine cabinet. Two toothbrushes, one the small type that would be used by a child. The usual assortment of medications, aspirin, toothpaste, ointments, and mouthwash were on the shelves. Leal saw a package of disposable razors with several missing. In the narrow closet he found an assortment of towels, matching the two hung over the shower curtain rod. He also found a box of Kotex, partially full. He opened the top of the hamper and fingered through the clothes looking for telltale signs that two adult women might be sharing the residence but found clothes that appeared to belong only to Mrs. Brown and her grandson. He closed the lid and washed his hands, after flushing the toilet. As he walked out he listened for any other sounds but heard only the murmur of the two women's voices.

When he re-entered the living room Linda stood up. She extended her hand to Mrs. Brown, who took it.

"We're going to give you a card with a number on it that you can reach us at," Linda said. "Would you call us if you hear from Gladis?"

The woman nodded.

"I hope you do catch her," Mrs. Brown said. "Maybe put her in jail for a while so she can get herself straightened out." Leal started to hand her one of his cards, then scribbled his cell number on it.

"This is my cell phone number, Mrs. Brown," he said. "If she does call and you want to get ahold of us after hours, just beep me. What's your number here? So I'll know it if you call," he added, almost as an afterthought.

She recited her number, and he wrote it in his notebook.

After receiving more of Mrs. Brown's reassurances that she would call if she heard from Gladis, they left and walked down the stairs. Leal raised his eyebrows at Linda and she smiled.

"What do you think?" he asked as they stepped outside.

"I think she'll call," Linda said. "How about you?"

"I hope," he said. "No signs in the bathroom that there was more than one adult woman living there."

"I figured that," Linda said. "Oh my God, look." She pointed out toward the car, which was surrounded by a large group of kids. The screams of youthful laughter seemed to reverberate through the crowd like an electrical current. Looming above them, the slick head of Crazy Bob carried on a conversation with his hand puppet. The gloved hand rotated toward the group of kids and seemed to nod in sympathy, as if imparting that they were all in the presence of a bald-headed idiot.

The glove made some sort of comment and the kids roared with laughter. Crazy Bob's face twisted into a ludicrous frown.

As Leal and Linda approached, the glove said in its forced falsetto, "Oops, there's the boss. Gotta go, kids."

The group of youngsters all implored him to stay, and Crazy Bob made several bows and waves to them as Leal got into the car. He started it and shifted into gear, somewhat amazed as he began to pull off at all of the cries of "Good-bye, police" coming from the group of children.

21
GANGSTAS

"So how'd it go?" Crazy Bob asked as they drove down the street.

"Struck out as far as finding her," Leal said. "But we might have developed a rapport with the mother. If Gladis does call there, the old lady will call us. Maybe."

"That's good," Crazy Bob said. "I kind of questioned the kids. Ah," he held up the glove as he stripped it off, "me and Oscar. Showed the picture to 'em. Some of them knew her, but they said she ain't been around here in a while."

Leal raised his eyebrows, impressed and pleased that his partner had shown some initiative. He caught a quick glance of Linda smiling at him in the rearview mirror.

"Well, we'll still have to go for some Grand Jury subpoenas Monday for the old lady's phone records," Leal said. "She admitted that Gladis has called her, but said that it's always been from pay phones. There's a chance she's lying, and she knows where her daughter is. There's also a chance that if Gladis did call from a pay phone that the mother called her back at that number, unless she wanted the operator breaking in every minute asking for more money."

"I get you," Crazy Bob said. "If we get the mother's MUDS records and find the number for a pay phone that keeps cropping up . . ."

"Right," said Leal. "I'm sure if she does know where Gladis is at, she'll be sure and call her after our little visit today too."

"It would give us some place solid to look," Linda added. Leal glanced in the mirror again, and this time saw Tims leering down over the top of his iPad at Linda's crossed legs. A boob man and a leg man. Who'd a thunk it?

"Al," Leal said. The intern's head snapped around. "Remember, not a word of this to anybody, understand?"

"Roger Willco, Sarge," Tims said.

"Where the hell did you learn that?" Leal asked.

"Oh, I taught it to him," Crazy Bob said. "Just an old expression from the Corps. And I already stressed to Al about the confidential nature of this one."

Leal shook his head. "I mean it, Al. No tweeting about this or anything, understand?"

"Affirmative," Tims said. He glanced at Crazy Bob again.

"Another expression from the Corps?" Leal asked.

Crazy Bob nodded.

Leal took a deep breath. "We're talking a major investigation. We can't afford any slip-ups." Tims's mouth drew down at the corners and he looked like a Sad Sack cartoon. Leal felt bad for belaboring the point. "Look, when we crack this one, the paper you'll be able to write for your professor will knock his socks off."

"You think so?" Tims said.

"Make sure I get a copy of it," Linda said, smiling.

Tims got a simpering expression on his face. "Cool."

"You know, Al," Crazy Bob said, "in civilian law enforcement we say ten-four. You might want to put that in the paper, too."

"Ten-four." Tims's face scrunched into his regular hackneyed smile, his tongue pinched between his teeth, as Leal saw him typing on his iPad again.

Shit, I'm going to have to get a look at what he's writing soon, Leal thought. And the way he tweets, this could be all over the Internet in no time. What if some smart defense attorney was able to subpoena the notes and impeach him because Tims had documented some legal slip-up?

"Attention area units district four," the ISPERN radio crackled. "Officer needs assistance Shell gas station at 167th and Cicero. Any unit in the area, respond."

"Shit, that's right down the street," Crazy Bob said, shooting a quick look at Leal, who was already flipping the toggle switch to activate their elliptical red light. Crazy Bob snatched the light off the floor and jammed it onto the magnetized plate on the dashboard. Leal hit the horn, then flicked the second toggle switch, which was a siren, and shot around a slow-moving car in front of them. But everything was slow-moving compared to them now. Tims squinted over the seat at the dashboard and the intern's eyes widened as he saw the speedometer.

"Gosh," he said. "I've never gone this fast before."

"A brother officer needs help," Crazy Bob said. He was gripping the dashboard so hard his knuckles were turning white. Leal swung around another car.

"How's come you don't put it on the roof?" Tims asked.

"What?" Leal grunted.

"The light," Tims answered. "The guy on *CSI New York* always used to put his on the roof."

"He didn't have to worry about the fucking wind ripping the sucker off of the roof either," Leal growled.

"Maybe it's the guy on *CSI Miami*," Tims said.

They could see the shape of the Shell sign a half a block away now. Leal zigzagged around a raised cement medium and went the remaining quarter block in the wrong lanes. There were two cars in the gas station lot. One was a dark blue Buick Electra and the other was the familiar white Chevy with the State Police insignia on the side. They could see a uniformed trooper wrestling with a wiry black man. A heavy-set black female was pulling at the trooper's arm and screaming. Their squad skidded to a halt and Leal and Crazy Bob were out of the car and running toward the figures. Linda was scrambling out also.

"He okay! He okay," the woman screamed. "He just need his medication."

Leal tried pushing her away, but she gripped the trooper's right arm harder. Afraid she'd be able to grab the officer's gun, Leal said, "Bob, take her," then yelled, "Police. Stop resisting."

Not that Leal thought that his announcement would do much good, but he'd learned a long time ago you always identify yourself loudly as one of the good guys, especially if you were working in plain clothes.

"S-G! S-G!" the black man screamed. "I'm a gangsta! I'm a gangsta!"

Crazy Bob managed to pull the woman's hands away and held her arms behind her back. Leal reached around behind the screaming black man and tried to encircle the man's neck with his arm.

"Gangsta! I'm a gangsta you white motherfuckers!" the man screamed. From his actions and strength, Leal figured that the guy was flipping out on drugs. PCP probably. He worked his hand under the man's chin and started to peel his head back.

"Don't you be chokin' him!" the woman screamed. "He got a plate in his head!"

Suddenly the man shoved the trooper away and wiggled his head and shoulders with a deft, almost unnatural quickness. The move threw Leal off-balance and then somehow Leal's left index finger was caught between the man's frothing jaws. Screaming in pain, he tried to pull his finger loose, but the man grabbed Leal's left hand in both of his and bit down harder.

"He's got my finger," Leal yelled.

Crazy Bob released the woman with a quick shove toward the cars and grabbed the man's face. Pressing his thumbs into the frothy jaws he twisted upward and back. The man emitted a hissing growl, but Crazy Bob continued to twist at the man's face. Leal felt the pressure on his finger slacken and he ripped it loose. He shook it once, then smashed his right hand into the side of the asshole's head.

"Watch it, Bob. The fucker must be on tac," Leal said.

"Don't you hit him!" the woman screamed, lurching at Leal and trying to scratch his face. Leal slung his now bloody left hand at her, splattering her with crimson. She paused for a second and Linda hit her with a dose of pepper spray. The woman screamed, then began gagging and gulping for breath. Linda turned the canister toward the black man and sprayed him in the eyes too. He grunted and spit at her. The trooper brought his ASP baton down with terrific force on the man's right shoulder.

With a snarl, the man jumped forward, the frothy jaws now blood-red. The trooper sidestepped and smacked the ASP at the flailing arms.

"He's on PCP," Leal yelled, wondering whose blood it was he saw on the man's face. His or mine, he wondered, incipient panic sweeping through him as he worried about microbes seeping into his body as the bloods mixed.

The man stumbled, now looking blinded by the Cap-Stun spray. He walked around in a little circle, ropes of snot dangling from his flared nostrils, pawing at the air like a groping animal, then fell to his knees. The trooper and Crazy Bob moved forward and forced the man the rest of the way to the ground, then snapped handcuffs over his wrists. Crazy Bob went to the woman and began instructing her on how to get her breathing back under control. Leal, holding his left hand upward to staunch the flow of blood, walked to the mini-mart section of the gas station.

"Where's your bathroom?" Leal yelled at the clerk behind the counter.

"Employees only," the clerk said. He was a dark, Third World type, and his speech was heavy with some sort of foreign accent.

"Police," Leal growled. "Where's your fucking bathroom?" He was still holding his hand.

"Get out! Get out!" the clerk shouted. "You are getting blood all over my floor."

Leal strode over to the refrigerated coolers and pulled open the glass door. He grabbed a can of 7Up from the shelf and turned toward the door.

"Wait," the clerk shouted. "You must pay for that."

"Blow it out your ass," Leal said as he shoved open the door and went outside. He popped the tab on the can and poured the foaming liquid over his cut finger. The lot was filling up with a sea of oscillating red and blue lights. Linda appeared at his side, her hands on his arm.

"Oh, Frank, are you all right?" she asked.

"Yeah," he said as he continued to empty the can. "Go in and give that piece of shit behind the counter whatever he wants for this can, would you, before he beefs me, saying that I stole it."

Some paramedics had also appeared and were strapping the thrashing figure of the doped-up asshole onto a wooden backboard. Crazy Bob and Tims walked over to Leal, who had emptied the can of pop and was now just holding his hand down and letting it bleed. Tims raised his phone to take a picture but before Leal could yell at him Crazy Bob put a hand on Tims's arm and shook his head. Tims lowered the phone.

"You okay, partner?" Crazy Bob asked.

Leal just nodded and then said, "Thanks for getting him off me."

"No problem," Crazy Bob said, slapping Leal on the back. "Used an old dog-stripping technique on him. You see, when a dog bites down on something you have to use your thumbs to push their lips back over their teeth then work their jaws apart. They gotta let go or they'll start gagging. Works on humans too."

"I'm glad it worked on that asshole," Leal said, thinking if he elevated his hand it would stop bleeding faster, but then it would stain his sport jacket even worse than it was already. He decided to let the finger continue to bleed.

"You said he was on crack?" Tims asked.

"Tac," Leal said. "That's the black street name for PCP."

"In the old days we used to call it angel dust," Crazy Bob offered. "It's an animal tranquilizer. Used for horses. They don't use it on dogs."

Doesn't he ever stop thinking about dogs? Leal wondered.

"Frank, let's go over and let the paramedics take a look at your hand," Linda said.

"Did you pay the asshole behind the counter?" Leal asked.

"Yes, now come on," she said.

"Search that car real good, Bob," Leal said.

Crazy Bob made a circle with his thumb and forefinger and started over toward the blue Buick. Leal and Linda walked over to the ambulance and Leal, after telling them that he was a cop, showed the paramedic his bloody finger.

"Looks pretty bad," the paramedic said. She was a pretty girl with brown hair pulled back in a pony tail. She gripped his swollen finger in her latex gloved hands and began wrapping some gauze around it. "You're going to need some stitches," she said.

"Make sure you take me to the same hospital as that asshole," Leal said, nodding toward the screaming black man who was now being strapped to a gurney. He was still screaming about being a gangster.

"Pay dirt," Crazy Bob said, coming up next to Leal holding a plastic baggie full of a chalky white powder in his hand. "It was under the front seat."

Leal gripped Bob's hand and moved it toward his own face, smelling the plastic baggie. Just like dog piss, he thought.

"It's tac," he said. "PCP."

"Don't you have to taste it to be sure?" Tims asked. "I seen McGarrett do that on *Hawaii Five-O.*"

"They only do that in the movies and on TV, Al," Crazy Bob said. "You wouldn't want the Sarge to taste it and get all messed up like that guy, would you?"

Tims's grating laugh made Leal want to put his fingers in his ears, except one of them was now swathed in bandages.

"Frank," Linda said. "I'd better do a report on this since I sprayed them."

"Right," Leal said. "Bob, give the dope to the trooper and sign battery/resisting complaints. Put it all on his court date, okay. Tell him to subpoena us if he needs us. We haven't got time to mess with this."

"Gotcha, Sarge," Crazy Bob said. He turned and began walking back toward the Buick and heard the asshole screaming for his glasses.

"At least he's stopped saying he was a gangsta," the forced falsetto voice said.

Crazy Bob slapped at his pocket. He looked down and saw a pair of new wraparound sunglasses—the expensive designer kind that cost well into the double digits, lying on the ground next to the door. Crazy Bob looked to the trooper, then back to the sunglasses.

The asshole screamed again, something about the lights hurting his eyes.

"Gimme my fucking glasses, motherfuckers," the man yelled.

Crazy Bob raised his foot and brought the sole of his shoe down on top of the fancy plastic frames, which popped and snapped as he twisted his foot, bearing down with his full weight.

"My, my, my," the falsetto voice seemed to say from his pants pocket. "Those were Oakleys, too. That was very clumsy of you."

"Yep," Crazy Bob said in his regular voice. "It sure was."

Hart was worn to a frazzle by the time she pulled into the Maywood headquarters parking lot. It was four-thirty. She'd made good time until she got to the outskirts of the Loop. Then she got caught up in a long line of cars all squeezing into one lane due to an accident. She'd tried to call HQ to tell them she was caught up in traffic, only to find that she'd forgotten to charge her cell and the battery was dead. To make matters worse, she'd given in to her hunger pains and stopped for a vanilla yogurt shake just before getting onto the expressway. Feeling guilty about blowing her diet and wondering what Rory would say if he knew, she'd opened the car door in an effort to hurry and mashed the paper cup against her fatigue jacket. She threw the remnants of the shake away and stripped off the shirt. She'd worn a black sleeveless tee shirt under it, as she had most days, and decided that it looked all right to report in. Anyway, all of the rest of her clothes were locked in a suitcase in her trunk, and she didn't want to waste time before she got to Maywood by looking for another shirt. She figured that she'd arrive in plenty of time to change before seeing the Chief.

But that had been before the accident and the god-awful traffic that seemed to move at a snail's pace. Finally, when she made the turn into headquarters, she didn't even care how she looked. With her badge clipped to her belt, and her big Sig Sauer .45 in a black nylon holster, she made her way through the parking lot in the black tee shirt, her camouflaged pants, and her polished, bloused boots. She wished she had taken the time to clean up, but then thought to hell with it. They were the ones who'd assigned her to go through this. They were the ones who told her to report in before five. So they could take her as is. And if they didn't like it . . .

Oh, God, she suddenly thought. This is the Chief I'm meeting, not just some run-of-the-mill higher-up. Glancing at her watch she saw it was now four-forty. No time to go back and rummage through her suitcase now. Not unless she wanted to be late. Maybe he'd be in a hurry to get out of there and wouldn't really notice.

The Chief's secretary looked up from her desk and smiled as Hart approached.

"Hi, Olivia," she said. "I'll tell the Chief you're here."

Hart flashed a quick smile and went to sit down in one of the gray metal chairs. Janetta picked up the phone and murmured softly into the receiver, then put it down.

"You can go right in," she said and smiled. But as Hart stood up she noticed that the other woman was scrutinizing her. Almost as if she was sizing her up.

When Hart pulled open the door she saw Chief Burton sitting behind his desk with his hands clasped behind his head. There were two chairs in front of the desk and one of them was occupied by Captain Florian. They both grinned and nodded as she walked across the thick carpet.

"Glad you could make it," the Chief said, glancing at his watch.

Hart couldn't tell if he was being sarcastic or not, so she said, "Sorry, Chief. Traffic was murder. I left right after the graduation. Didn't even have time to change." She held up her arms in a palms-outward gesture. She noticed both of them staring and figured that they were staring at the size of her arms, which most people did the first time they saw them. Or were they star-

215

ing at some other part of her? She folded her arms across her breasts anyway and wished she'd worn the fatigue jacket, stain and all.

"So you got through it all right. No problems?" the Chief said. It was a statement phrased like a question.

"Yes, sir," she said. Doesn't he know how well I did? Or maybe he doesn't care.

The Chief sighed.

"Good, but as you know, that was just the *first step.*" He emphasized the last two words. Hart watched him, trying to read what he was leading up to.

Chief Burton's eyebrows flickered.

"What happened to your face?" he asked.

"A training accident, sir," Hart said. Thanks for noticing so quickly.

"Well," Burton said, taking a deep breath, "you remember Captain Florian from I.A.D." He held his hand palm-up toward the other man. Hart nodded and smiled and saw the corners of Florian's handlebar mustache lift.

"Officer Hart, have you discussed the nature of this assignment with anybody?" Florian asked. His voice was flat and without emotion, yet at the same time, almost congenial sounding.

"No, sir," Hart said.

"You're certain?" Burton asked.

"Yes, sir."

The Chief inhaled through his nostrils, staring at her as he did so, then said, "Do you know Captain Sean O'Herlieghy?"

"Why, yes I do," Hart said. "I was invited to his wedding last summer."

Chief Burton nodded. "Did you discuss or mention to Captain O'Herlieghy about your transfer from Investigations?"

"No, I didn't."

"Then why," Florian asked, "do you think he's been asking a lot of questions about why you were transferred, and if it was possible for you to get re-assigned back to Investigations?"

They were double-teaming her. Just like she'd done with Frank when they had an unsuspecting suspect in the interview room. Frank, she thought. And Sean . . .

"I'm not sure, sir," Hart said. "Captain O'Herlieghy is good friends with my ex-partner, and perhaps he mentioned that I'd been transferred."

"That would be Sergeant Francisco Leal?" Florian asked.

"That's right," Hart said.

"How well do you know Leal?" he said.

"We've worked together for a while." She was afraid if she used the word "friends" that they'd interpret it as "lovers."

"Do you see each other socially?" Florian again.

"We're not dating, if that's what you're implying," Hart said. Who the hell did they think they were, anyway?

Chief Burton took another deep breath.

"Officer Hart, we already stressed to you the sensitivity and importance of this assignment," he said. "Fortunately, word of O'Herlieghy's inquiries got back to me, and I was able to put a squelch on them. But I'm rather upset that this has happened at all."

Hart decided to let him get it all out before offering any defense.

"So let me spell it out for you, okay?" He centered his dark stare on her face. "We're working under a time constraint here. I've got only a limited time to clean this mess up or I'll end up looking like an idiot, and that's *not* going to happen. You were hand-picked for this assignment, and as we've already told you, there will be great rewards for you when it's over. But in the meantime, I don't want you to discuss this with anyone. Understand? Nobody. Not your parents, your priest, your ex-

217

partner, your boyfriend, or your lover." His voice had escalated in forcefulness as he spoke. "Am I making myself perfectly clear?"

"Yes, sir," she said, thinking it was very clear he was an asshole.

"Now, you've been assigned to the red team under Lieutenant Doscolvich," he said. "Your cell number has already been placed in with the rest of the Special Response Team members. If there's a call-out, you'll get an alert beep. The number will be followed by a 9911. That's the code for the SWAT team."

"Here's a list of the other team members," Florian said, handing her a folder. "Study it and keep your eyes on them."

"As I told you," the Chief said. "We have a real problem. A bad apple. Maybe more than one. Otherwise that much dope and money wouldn't be disappearing like it has been."

"A bad cop's a bane on us all," Florian added.

"Now, Lt. Doscolvich has been told that you've been assigned to his team," the Chief said. "He'll be contacting you regarding your hours. But he is unaware of the true nature of your assignment. As far as he's concerned, it was just another politically correct move on the part of this administration. The only people who are to know otherwise are the three of us in this room. Understood?"

"Yes, sir," Hart said. *Or should I say, perfectly clear, asshole?*

"You should have ample opportunity to view them in action," Florian said.

"That's correct," Burton added. "There's a standing directive that I'm to be notified of all prospective raids, and this week there's going to be a shitload of them. Looks like one or two a day."

"Something should break soon, Officer Hart," Florian said.

"You're to report to Captain Florian every day, or as needed," the Chief said.

Florian handed her a card. "This is my private cell phone number. Call it and punch in the number you're calling from and your star number after it so I'll know it's you calling."

Hart held the card in her hand.

"You might just want to write the number down so no one knows that it's my pager number," Florian said with a superior-looking grin.

Hart nodded. She felt drained, her armpits sticky.

"Anything else?" Chief Burton asked, turning his head toward the other man.

Florian shook his head.

"Good," Burton said, standing up and extending his hand across the desktop. Hart rose and shook hands with the Chief, then with Florian.

"We'll be looking forward to working with you," Florian said.

"And to wrapping this up quickly," the Chief added.

After answering in the affirmative, Hart smiled, turned, and walked out the door. She felt like she'd been through another wringer and couldn't wait to get the hell out of there.

22
ABSOLUTELY NECESSARY

Although Leal was in another area of the hospital emergency room, away from the main sections, he could still hear the asshole screaming. The combination of the PCP and the pepper spray must not be agreeing with him, Leal thought. But the image gave him little pleasure as it momentarily took his mind off his throbbing finger. He was lying on a gurney, which the nurse had elevated for him, and his forearm was elevated to help stop whatever bleeding there still was. A silver-colored tray sat next to him with an assortment of scissor-like clamps. His sport jacket and shirt, both stained with blood, had been placed in a paper bag at his request.

Straining his ears he heard the yelling: "I'm a gangsta! I'm a gangsta!" over and over again. He was glad that he'd told Crazy Bob to hand over the drug arrest to the trooper. Now the state police would have to babysit the prick until he came down. The white, floor-length curtain parted, and the emergency room doctor came in. He was in his thirties with dark hair. His face and hands were chubby and soft. His gray lab coat swirled around an oversized gut.

"Sorry that you had to wait, Mr. Leal," he said, glancing at the chart to check for Frank's last name. "I had to attend to your friend for a moment."

"He ain't my friend," Leal said. "You do a drug screen on him yet?"

The doctor looked up, almost surprised at Leal's question,

then said, "Yes, as a matter of fact."

"Well, off the record, doctor, can you tell me if he's on PCP?"

"I'm really not supposed to."

"Look, doc, I've been sitting here worrying because this son-of-a-bitch bit me and drew blood," Leal said. "I told the nurse before, I'd appreciate knowing if we're dealing with a stone junkie here who's mainlining, or what."

The doctor heaved a sigh, then told Leal to wait for a moment and slipped through the curtain. He came back a few minutes later.

"Okay, I checked his chart," he said. "Off the record I can tell you that the urine screen does show phencyclidine, PCP, is present in his system. No indication of any other drugs, and there's no track marks that we can see. Of course if you want that information officially, you'll have to subpoena it." He glanced at Leal's chart again. "You said that he bit you?" He moved forward and looked at Leal's left index finger. After going to the sink and slipping on a fresh pair of latex gloves, the doctor unwrapped and cut his way through the gauze that the paramedic had put on. Then he removed the blood soaked bandages as if he were peeling back the layers of an onion.

"Yes, you're going to need stitches here," the doctor said. "When was your last tetanus?"

"I don't remember."

"I'll order another for you. You've had your hepatitis B series?"

"Yeah."

"And the follow-up blood test to make sure it took?"

"I haven't had that," Leal said. "Didn't know I needed it."

"Well, chances are you don't," the doctor said. "But it's always best to be certain, right?"

"I guess so," Leal said.

The doctor went to a medicine cabinet and unlocked it with a small key. He removed a blue canvas bag, which when

221

unzipped, revealed several hook-shaped needles of various sizes and some spools of black-colored thread. He set the kit down and picked up the clipboard with Leal's chart.

"So do I need to be concerned about AIDS?" Leal asked.

"Well, any time there's a break in the skin there's a risk of pathogenic contamination," the doctor said. "But everything we know of to this day, all the research, indicates that the HIV virus is not transmitted by saliva. Was there any blood to blood contact between you two?"

"Hard to say," Leal said. "After I got my finger out of his mouth, I noticed that his lips and chin were all bloody, but whether it was his or mine, I don't know."

"He does have a slight laceration on the inside of his mouth," the doctor said, scribbling on his clipboard. "It appears to be from blunt trauma."

Not so blunt, Leal thought, remembering the right he'd planted on the asshole's jaw.

"I think that happened after I'd gotten loose," he said.

"Well, I would think that you're probably pretty safe, then," the doctor said. He looked up from his clipboard and added, "We can give you a test for HIV if you wish, but there are several things to consider."

Leal waited for him to continue. The doctor set the clipboard down on the tray and moved a step closer to Leal. As he spoke, his eyes drifted around the cubicle as if he was reticent to make and hold eye contact.

"Okay, worst-case scenario," he said. "The guy is HIV positive. Even with that supposition there's only a minuscule chance that you're in danger of being infected. The AIDS virus is very fragile and doesn't live long outside the body. In order to be transmitted, it requires mucous membrane contact and has to be carried by some viscous bodily fluid, like blood or semen.

"Saliva, as I mentioned, is not thought to be thick and viscous enough for transmittal. And even if he were HIV positive, and even if you were to be tested today, you'd most probably come up negative. The virus wouldn't show up in an infected person's system for about six months or so." He looked back at Leal and forced a smile. "There's another thing to consider. If you were to be tested today, and for some reason you came up positive, then you'd have a hell of a time trying to convince workman's comp to pick up the bills for your future treatment. Whereas, if you were tested in six months, and showed up positive at that time, then you could point back to this incident as a source of infection and they'd have to cover you. However, for the sake of argument, let's just say you picked up the virus last winter cheating on your significant other. Then that would give workman's comp an out not to cover the medical bills for you."

"That ain't too likely, doc," Leal said. "I ain't been laid in so long, I forgot who's supposed to get on top."

The doctor chuckled. Leal thought that it sounded like the same kind of nervous, uncertain, embarrassed laugh of a tenth-grade schoolboy standing in front of an older, tougher classmate who'd just told a dirty joke.

"So I assume that you're going to wait on the test then?" the doctor asked. "As I said, it's not absolutely necessary that you have it today."

"How about you sneak in a blood test on him for me?" Leal asked. "As a personal favor. I'd appreciate it."

"I'll see what I can do. In the meantime, the nurse is going to come in with your shots," he said. "One tetanus and some Novocain to numb that finger before the stitches."

Leal's cell phone went off and he reached down with his right thumb and pressed the acknowledge-button. The number was unfamiliar, but Ollie's star number was at the end, so he knew it was from her.

"Ah, cell phone usage in here is a no-no," the doctor said.

"Have you got a phone I could use?" Leal asked. "This is important."

"Sure," the doctor said. "We can plug one in here for you."

Hart had found the first unattended, un-tapped line in the building after leaving the Chief's office and immediately beeped Leal. She knew that he had to be behind O'Herlieghy's poking around about her transfer, and she was furious. Why couldn't he know enough to just stay out of things and not meddle? Christ, this damn thing was hard enough, getting through that damn class, and then getting called on the carpet by the old man . . . When the phone rang she grabbed it on the first ring and answered it with a harsh hello.

"Ollie, it's Frank," the voice said.

"Frank," she said. "Did you send Sean nosing around about my transfer?"

"Uh . . . I guess I did mention it to him. Why?"

"Why?" she repeated. "I just came from the Chief's office, that's why. Frank, didn't I ask you to stay out of it?"

"Well, I—"

"Didn't I? Look, I need to make this clear between us. I don't want you to be interfering in this transfer, okay?"

"Ah . . . sure," Leal said. Then added, "Sorry, I didn't mean to make any trouble for you."

"Trouble?" she said. "That's putting it mildly. I just finished up that damn SWAT class, after working my ass off, and then I had to come in here and explain why I was so unhappy about the damn transfer."

"Well, I thought that it wasn't something that you requested, Ollie."

"I need this new assignment, Frank. It's very important to me. Career-wise," she added. "I need to start making some moves that will benefit me."

"Yeah. Well, other than that, how'd the class go?"

Hart sighed, then said, "It went all right. It was hard. Glad it's over." I'll be glad when this whole thing is over, she thought.

"Well, I took your mail in and fed Rocky before I came in today."

"Oh, yeah. Thanks for taking care of him," she said. In the background she heard a STAT page for doctor-somebody and asked, "Where are you?"

"I'm in the E.R. at South Suburban," Leal said. "We helped out some trooper on an officer needs assistance call and the prick bit me. The asshole, not the trooper," he added with a laugh.

"Oh, my God," she said. "Are you all right?"

"Yeah, I just gotta get a couple of stitches is all."

"I'm sorry you got hurt." He's in the hospital, and all I've been doing is being a bitch, she thought.

"Well, you shoulda seen the other guy," Leal said.

"Frank, I'm sorry I got on you about Sean, but—"

"Hey," he said, cutting her off. "Don't worry about it. I'm the one who should be apologizing. I should've kept my big nose out of it. I just thought . . ."

"I know. I miss you too, but this is something I have to do, okay? Something I really want."

"Yeah. I realize that now. And I'm sure you'll do great."

"Are you going by the gym tomorrow?" she asked.

"I could. What time?"

"In the morning sometime? Before noon?"

"I'll do my best," Leal said.

"Okay, I'll see you then," Hart said. "And don't forget we have court Monday."

"Shit, yeah, I forgot about that. Thanks. And good luck with the SWAT stuff."

"Thanks, Frank. I'm excited about it."

They said good-bye, with another promise to see each other at the gym the next day. When Hart hung up the phone her words of assurance felt hollow.

God, she hated this new assignment, and most of all, she hated that it was necessary for her to lie to everyone she cared about.

23
A BEEP IN THE NIGHT

Leal flipped on a few more lights to make the place look lived in and picked up the remote to turn the TV on. He went into the kitchen and opened the refrigerator, checking to see what he had in the way of food. Damn little, he decided, and settled for a quick drink instead. He realized that he'd forgotten to go to the store like he'd planned, and so he grabbed a half-full carton of orange juice and popped open the spout.

His left index finger had been bandaged and was practically useless, so he had a hard time twisting the top off the vodka bottle. After pouring a shot glass full of the crystal-clear liquid, he dumped it into a glass, added orange juice, and went back to the living room.

"Too damn late to eat anyway," he muttered as he glanced at the digital clock in the VCR and saw that it was already after nine. For the life of him he couldn't understand why a simple procedure like some stitches and a few shots took three times as long as it should have just because they were in a hospital emergency room. He took a sip of the drink and felt the alcohol burn its way down his throat, until it hit his stomach and radiated warmth from there. After settling in on the couch he adjusted the volume for the TV and stretched out his long legs on the cushions.

The only thing on network TV that he hadn't seen was a preachy show about a heroic group of lawyers fighting injustice. What a load of horseshit, he thought. This one infuriated him after about ten minutes, so he picked up the remote and flipped through the rest of the channels.

Not much else on, he thought. Just a news show that they referred to as a magazine, for some reason, and a show about some super cop CSIs.

Lawyers and CSIs, he thought. Put them together and watch them solve all the world's problems. He smirked. Tims was probably out there somewhere watching and tweeting.

He clicked the remote again, settling on a boxing match being telecast in Spanish. Both fighters were lightweights, and tough *hombres*. The punches were zinging in, first from one guy then the other. He was enjoying it, and starting to get a little bit of his appetite back when his cell phone went off. At first he ignored it, then, thinking that it might be Ollie, he set the half-finished drink down, got up, and checked it. It was the number for headquarters. He hit the redial and identified himself when the dispatcher answered. He was put on hold for a few moments, then a different voice came back on the line.

"Sergeant Leal?" the voice said. He recognized it as one of the female dispatchers.

"You got him. What?"

"We're holding a rape for you at Palos Hospital, Sergeant," the dispatcher said.

"Huh?" Leal replied. "You must be mistaken. I'm off duty now."

"Well, I'm sorry but the call-out sheet lists you as available," she said. "We've been kind of busy and the other detectives are out on another one of those motel robberies. We called Sergeant Ryan and he said to contact you."

Ryan, that son-of-a-bitch.

"Oh, he did, did he?" Leal growled. Then he stopped himself. There was no sense taking his anger out on the poor dispatcher. "Where the hell's he at? Why can't he take it?"

"We called him at home," she said. "He's sick."

Sick, my ass, Leal thought. The prick's on call and he's probably drunk. But then he remembered that Ryan had been scheduled for that rectal exam. Maybe he really was sick after all.

"So you're going to respond then, Sergeant?" the dispatcher asked. But it was more like a statement. "Sergeant Ryan mentioned something about you being familiar with the case. It sounds like that guy who masquerades as a cop."

"Yeah, that is mine," Leal said. He heaved a sigh.

"Should we beep Detective Lemack also?" the dispatcher asked.

"No," Leal said. "No, he's had a rough day. I'll take care of it."

"Okay, thanks, Sergeant," she said. "I'll tell the officer standing by at the E.R. that you'll be en route then."

Leal hung up and thought for a second. He stepped over to the living room and picked up the drink. After carrying it to the sink, he poured it out, watching the flash of orange circle down the drain. He went into the bathroom and stripped off his tee shirt, wiping his armpits with a wet washcloth and then drying off. He made a quick swipe with some deodorant under each arm, gave his teeth a quick cursory brush, and then went into the bedroom for some fresh clothes.

It was an important case and he couldn't afford not to give it all the attention he could muster. He needed a partner. Still, talking to these female victims was always difficult, especially for a male officer. Adding Crazy Bob to the mix would change it from difficult to impossible.

Instead, he thought for a moment, then went to the phone. He knew who he could call.

Hart rotated her face so that the swollen part wasn't pressing against Rick's bare shoulder. In doing so she felt their sticky skins peel away from each other, before pressing close again. It felt so good just to lie there next to him, in her bed, Rocky curled up on the far corner sleeping, the television flickering almost silently with some old black-and-white movie.

They'd opted for a quiet evening at her place instead of the dinner and dancing that they'd planned earlier in the week. Hart hadn't anticipated feeling as beat-up and sore as she did, and when Rick offered to give her a massage she jumped at the chance. He had great hands. So strong, yet gentle.

Now, basking in the soft, post-coital glow, she felt so relaxed it almost seemed delicious. It was nice, having completed that rough and tumble SWAT class, having come through at the top of the class, and then having a Friday night to spend with Rick. Despite the true nature of her assignment, and the unenviable task that lay ahead, it was kind of nice to be free from the constant, hovering pressure of Investigations. The worry that her cell would go off at some inopportune time, like when she was with Rick, and it would be Frank, calling her to tell her that they had to go to some crime scene. The freedom from being on call was nice, and tonight at least, she was going to relish it. Then the damn message feature buzzing on her cell went off.

"Ohhh," Rick moaned. "Do you have to answer it?"

"I'd better," she sighed, wondering maybe if it was Frank and that he was hurt again, or shot or something. She turned and separated herself from Rick's warmth, then swung her legs over the side. The movement was enough to send the cat lurching off the bed with a thump.

She wondered if Rick was watching her as she padded nude over to the dresser and picked up the cell phone, the muscles of her legs rippling with each step. A glance in the mirror told her that he was, and she surreptitiously checked her reflection as she looked at the displayed number. Her body looked trim and toned, but a little too smooth for bodybuilding standards. But after a week of going off her regular diet and eating restaurant food, what did she expect? Rory would blow a gasket when he saw her tomorrow, but so what? It's not like she had a choice.

The number was unfamiliar, but the final four digits, a 9911, were like a star number. Then it came back to her. The Special Response Team signal.

Oh, God, she thought. I hope this isn't what I think it might be.

Her fingers trembled at the thought of having to get dressed, leave Rick, and go out onto the night on some sort of call-out. The freedom from Investigations that she'd been musing about a few moments ago now seemed a cruel irony. A deep male voice answered after the first ring. "Doscolvich."

"Yes," Ollie said. "This is Officer Olivia Hart. Did you page me?"

"Yes I did," the deep voice said. "I'm Lieutenant John Doscolvich, and you're my new SWAT team member, right?"

"Right, I just finished the school today." Maybe she could lie and tell him that she'd had a little bit too much to drink or something, if he wanted her to respond to a call-out tonight. But then, what if he found out later that she didn't drink?

"Yeah, I know," Doscolvich said. "I'm sorry to be bothering you so late, but I wanted to tell you about our weekly Saturday briefing. It's at 1000 hours at Markham, but I'd like you to report in at about nine so we can get all your equipment squared away."

Hart felt a surge of relief. As if concurring, Rocky rubbed himself against her bare calves.

As long as I don't have to report in this minute, she thought. "Yes, sir," she said.

"We have a briefing every Saturday," Doscolvich continued. "From now on your RDOs will be Sunday and Monday, and

231

we do training every Wednesday. Now I know that you just finished the school and were figuring on having the weekend off, but it don't work that way. We've got a raid tomorrow night."

"Okay, Lieutenant," she said.

"Well, I'll see you at nine then," he said. After a pause he added, "Sorry to bother you like this at home, but you're used to it from being in Investigations, right?"

"Yes," Hart said. Obviously he's familiar with my personnel file, she thought. She'd never met Doscolvich, but he had the reputation of being a consummate professional. After hanging up she asked Rick if he wanted anything to drink.

"The only thing I want is for you to come back here," he said, smiling. "Who was it on the phone?"

"Oh, just the SWAT lieutenant telling me that I've got to report in for a meeting tomorrow morning," she said walking over and then getting in beside him.

"How do you feel about this new assignment with the SWAT team?" he asked.

"It's okay," she said. "Why?"

"Just wondered if you were happy with it," he said. "It came up so suddenly. You didn't request it, right?"

"No, I didn't." She leaned forward and kissed him as she lifted the sheet and slid under it.

"So did you miss me?" she asked, changing the subject as she curled up next to him again.

"Yeah, I did." He gave her forehead a tentative kiss.

Hart's hand was stretched out on Rick's chest, rubbing it. It was as if she could feel a slight tension there in his muscles. His breathing was quick and shallow. And when they'd made love he had seemed detached. Distant. Almost as if he was pre-occupied with something else. Or somebody? she wondered.

"Is everything okay?" she asked.

"Yeah, sure." But a few seconds later he said, "Well, there is something that I wanted to talk to you about. I guess I'm lousy at keeping secrets."

"Secrets?" she said, rolling away from him and getting up on one elbow so she could look at his face. Oh, God, here it comes she thought. It's been fun, babe, but now . . .

"Like I told you I went to see Lance today," Rick said. She waited for him to continue. "His attorney's discussing a deal. A plea bargain."

"Well, that's good isn't it?" She knew that they had Rick's brother on a solid murder-one. The Feds had recorded him discussing the plans to carry out the hit for a local drug dealer.

"Yeah," Rick said. "Being an ex-cop, he's a dead man if he ends up going to Stateville. His only chance is to plead out and see if they'll cut some kind of deal to let him serve it in the federal pen."

"Mmm-hmm," Hart said. She had no idea where this was going.

"Well, that's up in Minnesota," Rick said. She waited. He continued.

"I been toying around with the idea of going up that way," he said. "I mean if he gets placed there."

"That'd be nice," she said. "How long of a drive is it?"

"Six, seven hours, I guess."

"I suppose we could go up for a long weekend sometime," she said.

"Well, that's not quite what I had in mind."

She looked at him.

"I'm going up there Wednesday to test for Minneapolis P.D." His lips drew into a thin line after he said it. Hart felt stunned. Like someone had punched her in the gut. "I thought maybe you'd like to come too."

"I've got to work," was all she could get out.

233

"No, I mean come up there and test for that department," Rick said. "They've got an ongoing testing program, so you just have to call up there and make an appointment. Then you go up and take the physical agility, written, and psychological all at once." He paused and searched her face, looking for a reaction.

"You mean change departments?" she said.

"Yeah, right. I know you wouldn't have any problems passing the written or physical parts, and with your experience, they'd probably want to scarf you up. Well, what do you think?" He punctuated his last sentence with a tentative smile.

"I'm not sure what to think," she said. "This is all so sudden."

"Well, the plea bargain hasn't been formalized yet, and then it'd still be a while away. But I figured that we'd better get moving on this transfer thing if we wanted to get settled in up there."

"If *we* wanted? It sounds like something that you want."

"Well, I was hoping that you'd want it too."

"Oh, Rick, this is so abrupt," she said, feeling as if he'd just loaded a huge weight onto her shoulders. "I'll have eight years on counting my dispatch time. Do you think I can throw all that away? Do you have any idea how long it took me, how hard it was to work my way up, being a woman?"

"I know it was hard," he said. "But I don't want to lose you." He encircled her back and pulled her towards him. She resisted slightly at first, then slid next to him, feeling the heat and texture of his skin against hers.

It wasn't fair, she thought. After putting up with all the shit for so many years, the things she had to do, being a woman, to earn the respect of her partners and bosses, to give it all up now and begin again at the bottom on another department . . . Didn't he realize all she'd gone through? But then there was Rick. She didn't want to lose him either. He was such a sweetheart, and she loved him so much. Why should she have to choose? It wasn't fair. It just wasn't fair. She felt the uncontrollable rush of the tears and tried to hold them back as they welled up in her eyes and ran down her face. Rick noticed them too, as they splashed onto his chest.

He drew her close and said, "I'm sorry. We're supposed to be celebrating, aren't we?"

She made no reply.

"Look, just think about it, okay," he said, his big hands gliding softly over her back and shoulders. "That's all I'm asking right now. Just think about it."

Hart wondered at that moment how she was going to be able to think about anything else.

It was Leal's second trip to an emergency room that day, he reflected, as he walked in Palos Community Hospital. This one was different from South Suburban, where he'd received his stitches. Less crowded, less busy. A newer coat of paint on the walls. Numerous people sat in various padded chairs with plastic molding over the metallic arms, watching a TV that had been attached to some sort of metal frame hanging from the ceiling. The ten o'clock news was on, and several anchors and a weatherman joked about the overnight lows. He glanced around and saw a set of glass windows, behind which sat a woman at a computer monitor. Leal strode over and flashed his badge.

Leaning over, he asked, "You got a rape victim here?"

"Yes," the woman said. "Go through those doors." She pointed to a set of collapsible electronic doors. They whooshed open, sliding into the walls, as she pressed a button. Leal went through them and held up his badge when he got to the other side. Nurses and technicians rushed past him. To his right, down a hallway, he could see several long, ceiling-to-floor white curtains. An unoccupied gurney had been pushed against the wall in front of him. He saw an arrow with the word *LOUNGE*

printed underneath it. Strolling over he found a small breakroom next to another carpeted room with several cushiony
chairs.

A pretty blond nurse was pouring herself a cup of steaming
coffee from a pot next to an electric coffeemaker. She looked at
him, holding up the pot.

"Want some?" she asked.

"If you've got another cup," Leal smiled.

She indicated a metal cabinet set off to the side and said, "In
there."

Leal opened it and saw several stacks of Styrofoam cups in
elongated plastic tubing. He grabbed a cup from the torn end
of the plastic and held it toward the nurse.

"You need cream or sugar?" she asked, pouring some of the
hot, dark liquid into his cup. Leal shook his head.

"I'm looking for one of my officers," he said as she poured.
"I'm an investigator. Here on a rape."

The nurse nodded and told him to follow her. She led him
back down the hallway past the abandoned gurney to a larger
room with a nurse's station in the center. A uniformed officer
was standing off to one side, writing his police report.

"What you got?" Leal said, walking up next to him and holding his badge in one hand and the coffee in the other.

The patrolman turned. He was a slender black guy in his
mid-twenties. He flipped open his notepad and licked his lips.
Leal took his first sip of the scalding coffee.

"Aggravated Criminal Sexual Assault. Looks like it's that
same guy we had the notification about on our beat-sheets,
Sarge," he said. "Female, white, driving home alone on 127th.
She'd just come from shopping. This was at approximately 2015
hours. She turned right onto Rt. 83, and then saw this car
behind her with this flashing red light on the dashboard. She
pulled over and the guy came up to her car showing some sort

of badge. He IDs himself as a cop and asks for her driver's license. She gives it to him and then he tells her to pull up off the road a ways so they're out of traffic. She does and he pulls his car up behind hers, but without the light. Then when he comes back up to her car, he pulls out a piece and orders her to slide over on the seat.

"She does and he gets in, still holding the gun on her. He takes out some handcuffs and cuffs her behind her back. He then pulls the victim's car further off the road into the bushes and commits the rape." The young officer stopped and closed his notebook. "That's pretty much all the preliminary info I got, except for a description of the asshole, which I already put out over ISPERN," he said. "Male, white, thirty to thirty-five, five-ten to six feet, one-seventy to one-eighty. Brown hair and mustache, sunglasses, wearing a dark blue jacket and dark pants."

Leal nodded and said, "They do a rape kit?"

"They're doing that now," the officer said.

"Good, I'm waiting on my female partner," Leal said. "I'd like you to take charge of the kit until the ETs get here. Make sure you tell them to keep it refrigerated." The patrolman nodded. "Where's her car at?"

"It's out in the lot," the patrolman said. "She drove here after she managed to get loose."

"What'd he use to secure her?" Leal asked.

"After the rape," the patrolman said, "he secured her with some flex cuffs. She was able to work her hands loose and then drove right here."

"Sounds like our boy, all right," Leal said. "Maybe the ETs will find something when they go over the car?"

"They're on the way," the patrolman said.

"Speaking of being on the way, I'm going out and see if my partner's here yet," Leal said, sipping the coffee again. It was

237

almost drinkable now. "Where's the victim at?"

"She's in there," the patrolman said, pointing to one of the curtained rooms. "Got an advocate with her. Name's Janet, last name unknown. She wouldn't give it to me."

"Yeah," Leal said. "They never do."

The rape advocates were female volunteers who responded to sexual crimes to comfort the victim and lead them through the hard parts. They seldom gave their last names, but Leal felt that their intentions were admirable, even if they did get in the way of the police investigation sometimes.

"There she is now," the patrolman said.

Leal turned and saw a middle-aged woman walking toward them. She looked like a typical suburban housewife, dressed in jeans and a tan sweater.

"Hi, I'm Janet, from the South Suburban Crisis Center," the woman said. She wore large oval-shaped glasses, and her hair was pulled back from her face revealing a mouth that was bracketed by stern-looking lines.

Leal nodded to her. "Frank Leal, Sheriff's Police. How's she doing?"

Janet blew out a brusque-sounding puff of air. "As well as can be expected. Are you the investigator we've been waiting for?"

Her tone irritated Leal. He grinned and said, "None other than. Why, have you heard of me?"

"No," Janet said, shaking her head and drawing the corners of her mouth down slightly. "I just assumed that they'd send out a female officer. That's usually standard procedure, isn't it?"

"If one's available," Leal said. "As a matter of fact, I'm waiting on my female partner now."

The doors from the outer waiting room area slid open, and Linda LeVeille came walking in, glancing from side to side. Then she saw Leal and smiled. She walked over to them and said, "Sorry it took me so long. I had to change."

She was wearing tight jeans, a lavender sweater, and black pumps. The sweater had been pulled down over her side to cover her gun.

Leal raised his eyebrows and said, "Well, it was worth the wait."

24
AS TIME GOES BY

Leal stood just outside the curtain so he could listen as Linda interviewed the rape victim, asking her all the sordid details of the incident: What the suspect had said, how he had touched her, where he had touched her . . . It was always better to have a woman asking those kind of questions, Leal thought as he eavesdropped. That's why it had been standard procedure for him to let Hart conduct the interviews on female victims. It also gave him the opportunity to stand to the side, in semi-detachment, and listen. But he and Hart had worked together so long that they were almost always on the same wavelength. Seldom would she miss a question that he would have asked. Linda was good too, but she hadn't asked enough about the actual act. It was seamy, but it had to be gone over for the sake of a thorough investigation. Leal knocked on the wall and peeped inside the curtain after Linda said, "Yes." He asked to speak to her a moment, then down the hall in hushed tones he suggested a few more additional questions.

"Oh, right," Linda said. "Thanks. It's been a while since I've handled one of these." She went back inside. Leal resumed his position and took copious notes. Or tried to, feeling the twinge of shooting pain in his bandaged finger. After Linda came out she inhaled and showed him a grim smile.

"You need anything else?" she asked.

"Just tell her we'll be in touch," Leal said, handing over one of his cards. "Thanks."

As they walked out to the parking lot Leal asked if she had time for a cup of coffee or something to compare notes. "After listening to that I need a drink," Linda said.

Leal glanced at her and said, "I know a place close. We can get something to eat there too, if you want."

"Sounds great," Linda said. "I'll follow you."

Leal got in his dark-colored unmarked squad and pulled near the main exit road from the parking lot. Linda's black Jeep Cherokee swung in behind him, and she flashed her lights. He noticed that it appeared to be her personal car. He picked up his mike and ran her plate. Finding out that she lived in Oak Lawn, he then drove to a small bar called The Candlelights, which was on Cicero Avenue, near to the address he'd gotten back from her license plate. When he pulled into the lot she pulled up right next to him and rolled down her window.

"My house is only a few blocks from here," Linda said. "Would you mind following me home so I can drop this off? I like it to look like somebody's home at night. Then we can come back in your car."

"Sure," Leal said.

He followed her down a few side-streets and she wheeled the Cherokee into the driveway of a white, ranch-style house. It had a large tree in the front yard and an attached garage. The drapes were drawn across the front picture window, but a light was on behind it. Linda locked her car and stuck the keys into her purse as she walked back toward the unmarked. She got in the passenger side and smiled.

"Convenient that the place you thought of was so close," she said.

"How 'bout that," Leal said, wondering if she knew he'd run her plate for that purpose.

They went back to The Candlelights, and the hostess seated them in a booth away from the noise of the main bar area. A

241

waitress took their order and brought their drinks. Leal had a screwdriver and Linda a glass of white wine.

"This is on me," Leal said. "For you helping me out tonight."

"Thank you," Linda said. She raised the glass to her lips and took a delicate sip. "But I was glad to help out. Your regular partner couldn't come?"

"Actually, my regular partner's Crazy Bob," Leal said. "And I'm sure you can see why I didn't want him there."

Linda smiled. "Him and Oscar?"

"My ex-partner was real good at talking to people, and every time we had a case like this I'd always let her do the interview."

"Her? Your ex-partner was a woman?"

"Yeah," Leal said. "Olivia Hart."

"Don't know her," Linda said. "Say, how's your finger?"

"Cutting down on my typing by half," Leal said with a grin, holding up his two index fingers. Linda laughed.

"You don't type?" she asked, taking another sip of her wine.

"I just hunt and peck. Ollie did most of our typing."

"Well, I can type up a transcript on the interview if you want. On my computer."

"That'd be great," Leal said. "But I wouldn't want to put you out. You've really been a big help already, just by coming out and doing the interview."

"It's no bother," Linda said. She took another sip of the wine and looked at him over the rim of the glass. Then asked, "You miss her, don't you?"

"Who?"

"Your ex-partner."

"Yeah, I guess I do," Leal said. "How'd you know?"

"You talk about her a lot."

He raised his own glass and sipped. "We made a good team."

Linda eyed him over the rim of her glass. "Did you two see each other?"

"You mean date?"

She nodded.

"Un-uh. Not that I wasn't attracted to her. It was just that we sort of became . . . I don't know, friends. Buddies. Does that make sense?"

Linda nodded again.

"It was almost like we didn't want to cross a certain line, because we knew that it would change things between us."

She canted her head and smiled. "How so?"

"It was like we wanted to maintain our friendship without," he paused to find the right word, "complicating things."

"So you think that it would?" Linda said. "Complicate things?"

"Well, they say you should never get involved with someone you work with," Leal said. He added, "I mean someone like a permanent partner. Same department. Besides, we were both involved in other relationships at the time."

"How about now?" she asked. "Are you . . . involved?"

"No," Leal said. "You?"

She shook her head. "It's hard to concentrate on a relationship when you've got two kids to raise. I seem like I'm running all the time, between them and work. This is the first Friday night that I've been out in I don't know how long." She sipped her wine again, finishing the last bit of the amber liquid. Leal's drink was still half-full.

"Usually I'm at home watching TV," she said.

Leal grinned.

"Sounds like me," he said.

"Wouldn't it be nice if the real crimes were solved so easily?" Linda said.

Leal nodded, then asked, "You want a refill?"

When Leal had pulled up beside her Cherokee a little while

243

later, it seemed perfectly natural when she invited him in. They walked up to the front door, standing close, but not touching as she unlocked the door and opened it.

"The kids are with their father this weekend," she said, breathing an exaggerated sigh of relief. "I was looking forward to getting some work done, but now it seems kind of empty."

Leal smiled. "Sometimes you don't miss 'em till they're gone," he said.

She took his jacket and laid it across a chair. The living room had a long couch along one wall and she told Leal to sit there. Disappearing into the kitchen, she appeared a moment later with two glasses of orange juice.

"This is all I've got," she said. "I haven't had a chance to get to the store."

Leal smiled. "I was just thinking the same thing before I got beeped," he said.

Linda flipped on the TV and they watched the end of some talk show. She pressed the remote until the black-and-white images of Humphrey Bogart and Ingrid Bergman appeared on the screen. They were gathered around a piano and Bogie was telling Dooley Wilson that he told him never to play that song.

"*Casablanca*," Leal said. "One of my all-time favorite movies."

"Mine too," Linda said, and started to hum "As Time Goes By." "Those were really movies in those days, weren't they?"

"Yeah," said Leal. "And there'll never be another Bogie. Almost makes me sorry I quit smoking, sweetheart."

Linda asked Leal if he was hungry and he shook his head.

"It wouldn't be any trouble to fix you something," she said.

"No thanks," he said. "But there is one thing."

"What's that?" she asked, smiling as she looked across at him.

Leal stood up and asked her where the bathroom was.

244

"It's down there," she said with a giggle. "Here, I'll show you, but *I* get to go first." A quick smile traced over her lips. She rose and he watched her hips move under the tight fabric of the jeans. She walked down a hallway to the room on the left. Turning, she smiled again as she leaned around the half-closed door. Leal stopped and began looking around. Lots of pictures on the walls. Farther down he could see other rooms off on both sides. A large rattan chair sat in one of them. He speculated which would be the bedroom.

Her bedroom, he thought, and wondered if he was going to get to see it.

He decided that no matter how much he wanted to, it was best not to push things. This was her turf. He was the outsider. The roaming lion. And, after all, she was a cop too.

He heard the sound of the commode flushing, and the door opened, after the gurgle of tap water in the sink. She stepped out and asked him if he wanted something more to drink.

"Well, just some ice water would be fine," he said. Then added, "Or some more orange juice if you got it."

He went into the bathroom and urinated, raising the seat, and concentrating the stream in the middle of the bowl to minimize the splashing. He even remembered to lower both seats when he'd finished. When he stepped out she called from the kitchen.

"Here's your OJ."

He moved down the hallway again, eyes straying only for an instant toward the bedrooms in the other direction. In the kitchen she had spread some pictures on the table. "Come here and look at these," she said.

"These are my sisters." She pointed to one of the photos. It showed three girls of varying ages, Linda being in the middle. The same smile, imbued with youthful innocence, grinned up at him from the matte finish. "This one lives in L.A.," she said, pointing a long fingernail at the girl on the right. "And this one lives up in Wilmette."

"And who's this?" Leal asked, pointing to the girl in the middle.

"That's me, silly," she said, giving his arm a mild slap. "Don't tell me I've changed that much."

"Oh, you're a lot prettier now," he said, taking a sip of his juice.

She flipped through several more photos, showing him pictures of her kids, then set them down in a stack.

"You're really a different kind of guy for a cop, Frank."

"Oh? Is that good or bad?"

"Good, of course. I mean, you seem to take the fact that I'm a woman as no big deal. The guys in my department either treat me like a baby sister, or try to hit on me all the time. And when I don't go out with them, they say I'm a lesbo." She lowered her voice as she finished the last part of the sentence. Leal grinned.

"Like I told you, I've worked with a female partner before," he said. "In fact, she was one of the best I've ever worked with."

"Best what? Woman or cop?"

"The best period. She saved my life."

"Wow, you must have really been close then. I'll bet it was hard to split, huh?"

"Yeah," he sighed.

"So, tell me again why you two never . . ." she left the sentence unfinished. He detected a slight slurring in her words.

Leal smiled and shook his head.

"Well, like I told you, we didn't have that type of relationship," he said. "It was something we both thought about from time to time, but it was almost as if we were afraid to get involved that way, because we didn't want to lose what we had."

"What makes you think you would have lost it?"

He considered her question for a moment. "We worked

together every day," he said. "We made a good team, but . . . I guess it's hard to explain."

"So what you're saying is that if two people go to bed, then they're not going to be effective working together?"

He exhaled before answering.

"Not necessarily," he said. "It just wouldn't have worked for us."

"Us?"

"For Ollie and me."

"What about someone that you wouldn't necessarily work with on a regular basis?" she asked. She turned toward him and tossed her head, letting her hair bounce softly across her forehead in ragged bangs. Before he could answer, she leaned forward and kissed him. It was a soft kiss. Almost gentle. Then she looked up at him, canting her head as the dark eyes appraised his face. He started to speak, but she put a finger to his lips, then took the glass from his hand and set it on the table. He moved forward so he could embrace her, and they kissed again, only this time it was more urgent. Their mouths stayed together, tongues intertwining, as he pulled her close to him.

They stayed that way for a few minutes, until, conscious of the large windows, she led him into the hallway and leaned against the corner near the bathroom. He embraced her again, their mouths hungrily seeking each other.

Tangled against the wall, Leal's hands explored her back, crept over her waist and hips, and centered on her breasts feeling the growing hardness in his groin. Her hands began to explore his body also, through his hair, down his back.

As Leal's hands moved under her sweater, her hands were pulling at his belt, then unfastening his pants. As the zipper went down, so did his pants, the heaviness of the Beretta causing a resounding thump as it struck the carpeting.

Leal's fingers found the fastener for her belt and then undid her jeans. After easing them over the oval of her hips, the weight of her holstered pistol caused the jeans to drop, making another muffled thump as it struck the carpeting.

He pulled at the nylon panties, easing them downward as she held him in her hands.

Pausing, he leaned back to slip off his shirt, then eased her hands above her head to take off her sweater. Moments later they were skin to skin, still leaning against the wall, exploring each other. As he was about to enter her she whispered.

"You do have a safety on that thing, don't you?"

"If you mean my Beretta, yeah. If you mean my other gun, no."

"Maybe we'd be more comfortable in the bedroom," she said, her voice still a whisper even though there was no one else around. Pausing, they both stooped and picked up their sagging pants, making controlled steps. Linda managed to pull her legs out of the fabric as she walked, leaving a trail of pants, underwear, and bra in her wake. Leal, struggling to refasten his pants while he slipped his undershirt off, knew that he'd have to sit down to untie his shoes, and began to curse himself for not investing in a pair of tasseled loafers.

Pausing at the doorway, Linda half-turned and smiled at him. As he sat on the edge of the bed and started to untie his shoes, she pulled back the covers and stretched out next to him.

"It's too bad you didn't wear loafers," she said. "But don't worry, I'll wait."

25
ONE ASTERISK

It was easy finding a parking spot, for a change, in the huge lot at the Markham courthouse. The day had turned out bright and sunny. It was so warm that all Hart needed was a light jacket over a pink silk blouse and blue jeans. She parked her unmarked there and walked with solemn resignation past the small crowd waiting just inside the glass doors. Losers, all of them, Hart thought. Who else would be down here on such a fine Saturday morning? But, then again, if only losers come here on a day like this, what am I doing here?

She showed her badge and ID to the lone deputy manning the entrance checkpoint, and went through the employee's gate, bypassing the metal detector. After going up the escalator, Hart went into the washroom and touched up her makeup and hair. Her cheek was still a little swollen, but she'd loaded on the makeup to cover the colorful bruise. With her hair pulled in the usual French braid, since she planned on going right to the gym from here, it made the swollen cheek stand out a bit more. Plus, her eyes still looked puffy from all the silent crying she'd done after Rick had fallen asleep. It was still hard to imagine what life was going to be like if he left. Or maybe how it would be if she went with him. . . . But did she really want to leave?

Put it out of your mind, she told herself. Just like working out. Think only about the immediate problem, and get through that. Like doing a set that she dreaded. Squats. God, she hated squats. And the throwing up afterward. Tucking everything back into her purse, she glanced at her watch. Eight-fifty-five. She was a few minutes early. Better than being late.

Hart had never met Lieutenant Doscolvich, but she'd seen him in the hallways of the sheriff's section of the building a few times. He was an enormous man. His dark hair and mustache gave his face a foreboding look, but he always seemed to smile as they passed in the hall. She wondered if he knew who she was. Pausing at the door, which was open, Hart tapped her knuckles and spoke his name.

Doscolvich was seated behind a big metal desk scribbling some notes on a sheet of paper. Outlined boxes and arrows were all around the notes. He stood up and smiled, extending his huge hand across the desk. She noticed immediately that he'd shaved off his mustache, but he still looked just as foreboding. As Hart shook the hand, she was reminded of when she was a little girl and how it had felt when her father would grab her hand and her brother's as they crossed the street. She noticed that his beard was so heavy it almost gave his cheeks a bluish cast.

"You must be Hart," Doscolvich said, sitting down. He leaned back in his chair, and Hart sat in the chair in front of the desk. The top of it was well organized, with a pen and pencil set, emblazoned with the Marine Corps emblem in the center, and neat stacks of papers and binders at the far corner. Several framed photos behind Doscolvich showed him with members of the Special Response Team, as well as framed certificates and degrees. In between them was an 8 × 10 picture of a black shield that had a symbol, a large *1** printed on it in gold.

"So," Doscolvich said, pulling open a desk drawer and handing her a radio with a long cord wrapped around it. He was wearing his BDUs, and a pin with the same design as the poster was attached to his collar next to his lieutenant's bar. "Here's your radio and ear plug. The plug's specially made. It screws into the jack so you won't accidentally catch it on something and pull it out. The ear piece and throat-mike are there too." He smiled again. "I guess I forgot to tell you, I expect everyone to attend the briefing in uniform. Builds esprit de corps."

"Oh, I'm sorry," Hart said. "I was planning to get some personal things done after the meeting. I can rush home and change if you want."

Doscolvich shook his head. "Just remember it next time. What happened to your face?"

Hart wondered if he meant her swollen eyes, but then realized that he was talking about the bruise on her still-swollen cheek. Was it showing through already?

"A training accident," she said. "It's nothing, really."

Doscolvich nodded. "I spoke with Agents Deckons and Cook. They both gave you high marks for the school."

"I did learn a lot."

"Well, my basic philosophy is that we get the job done as safely and expediently as possible," Doscolvich said. "I don't believe in multiple entries, unless there are very special circumstances. That breeds a cross-fire situation. The type of situations we go into are always dangerous. You may have to shoot very quickly."

Hart nodded.

"By the way," Doscolvich said with a grin. "I read your personnel file, including the officer-involved shooting part. I was glad that you're not afraid to drop a cap on somebody . . ." He paused. "Until I found out that the person you shot was a police lieutenant. And that he was your boss . . ."

Hart wondered for a moment if she should add that when she shot Lt. Paul Brice he'd been about to kill Leal. Then she heard Doscolvich's low chuckle.

"Anyway, I'm a big believer in planning and training. But other than that, we're pretty informal. Come on." Doscolvich stood up. It seemed like a wall rising up in front of her. "I'll introduce you to the guys."

They walked down the hallway toward the large briefing room. Doscolvich expressed concern about her last name, which he said sounded too much like Art, one of the guy's names.

"We use first names or nicknames," he said. "This not only makes it clearer for us, but more confusing for anybody listening on a scanner, like some reporter. The last thing the guys need if we have to tactically neutralize somebody—that's our euphemism for killing the bastard—is to have some fucking reporter calling up to speak to officer so-and-so because he caught his name on the scanner. So what's your first name again?"

"Olivia."

Doscolvich grimaced. "You got any nicknames?"

"My friends call me Ollie."

"Ollie," he said, beaming with approval. "I like that." They entered the briefing room, and Hart saw that all the rest of the team had assembled around the long table. Each was dressed in his BDUs, and cups of coffee and cans of pop sat next to yellow legal-sized pads. The introductions were brief, but Hart tried to size each man up, and put a face with the list of names she'd been given by Florian.

The second in command was Sergeant William "Buzz" Turner, a stocky, middle-aged guy who looked like a young Richard Widmark with a blond flat-top. He smelled like cigarettes, Hart noticed. The two snipers, Mike Jahn and Dick Plutarch, were both white guys in their early thirties. Jahn seemed indifferent to her, shaking hands politely. He had an Irishman's fair skin, brownish hair, and blue eyes. Plutarch was older and more of an extrovert. He wore a baseball cap with a cross-hair sight on it, and what Hart could see of his black hair was dusted with gray. She was willing to bet that there was none on top under the hat. "Anybody gives you any trouble on an operation, babe," he told her as they shook hands, "just yell, 'Dick 'em,' over the radio and I'll take my shot." He dropped his extended thumb on top of his pointing index finger.

"That's good to know," said Hart.

Jimmy Gonzales was a tall Hispanic, with dark features and eyes. His mustache seemed to droop on each side of his mouth, but he looked to be in pretty good shape. He said his nickname was Lobo.

"That means wolf in Spanish," Marcus Jones said. "And he is one, too." Jones was a big, muscular black guy whose shaven head glistened under the lights as if it had been polished. His sleeves were rolled up over heavily muscled arms.

"How would you know that? You bilingual?" a slender white guy with light blue eyes said. He moved forward and held out his hand. "I'm PJ Terwiliger," he said. "PJ for Peter Joseph." When he smiled Hart noticed that he had nice teeth.

"Lincoln Johnson at your service, ma'am," the second black guy said. He was light-skinned and small-boned. Almost dainty looking, but his grip was strong. "And you can call me Linc."

"Edward Presley, ma'am," said the barrel-chested redhead. He looked to be as big as Marcus, but much of his bulk seemed to be settled around his middle. His hair was combed back in a pompadour, and his sideburns were long. Hart wondered how he got away with it until he said, "I'm Elvis, to all who know and love me."

"And not too tenderly either," said a smaller man. He had brownish-blond hair the same color as Rick's, Hart thought. A pair of gold, wire-rimmed glasses sat on his nose. "I'm Tom Campbell. TC whether you love me or not."

"We all love him," another white guy said. He was tall and rangy, with corded forearms. Hart also noticed a wedding ring on his left hand. He looked like somebody's postcard picture of a dad. "I'm Arthur Newman. Art. Glad to meet you."

"Thank you," Hart said. Oh, God, I hope it isn't him, she thought. What about his wife and kids?

"We call him Fred MacMurray," said a tall, broad-shouldered guy with light blue eyes and jet black hair. The unusual coloring made his handsome face appear striking. He was impeccably dressed, his uniform having that tailored appearance, and from the looks of him, he worked out a lot. His waist was slim and firm, and tapered outward showing good lat development. The sleeves of his shirt were rolled up to the elbow, and his forearms seemed packed with writhing muscles. "I'm Jack Stone, aka Blackjack." He smiled as he held out his hand. He had nice teeth too, Hart noticed. Very nice.

"Ramon Garcia," the last man said. "Ray on the radio."

He was shorter than Blackjack, but just as wide, making it apparent that both men were into weight lifting. Hart noticed that each man was wearing the same pin on his collar. The one that Doscolvich had hanging in his office. A numerical one, followed by an asterisk. Gold symbols on a black background. She told them to call her Ollie and was going to ask about the pins when Doscolvich bellowed for everyone to sit down because there were a lot of things to go over. Hart sat by the corner near the lieutenant.

"Somebody wanna get those lights," Doscolvich said as he activated a laptop connected to an overhead projector. The rooms darkened and the projector clicked. A black-and-white mug shot filled the screen. The man pictured was sullen and black, his somewhat corpulent face reflecting a look of pure hatred.

"This is Otha Spears, gentlemen," Doscolvich said. "For those of you who don't know, he's the head of the Black Soul Gangstas."

"Shit, I thought it was Marcus trying to be cool," somebody said.

"Yeah, same haircut," another voice chimed in.

"Fuck you guys." Marcus grinned.

"Knock it off," Doscolvich said. The room quieted instantly. "He's our primary target for this next week. We're gonna be hitting one or two houses a day, from the looks of it. They been saving up all these search warrants so we can make Otha's life as miserable as possible." He clicked the mouse and a black-and-white picture of a two-flat with a crenelated roof appeared. "This is Otha's main crib in Harvey," Doscolvich said. "It's rumored that he keeps his dope somewhere in there, probably on the second floor. The place is well fortified, with shorties out in front acting as look-outs. They're in radio contact with somebody inside." The machine flipped again and the picture of an eleven-year-old youth on rollerblades, wearing a headset with a microphone resting just in front of his mouth, appeared.

"You telling us we gonna hit that place?" Marcus asked.

"Maybe someday," Doscolvich said. "If we do, it'll take a real good scouting plan. This is the one we're hitting tonight."

Another picture snapped onto the screen. It showed a large, wooden-frame house. Doscolvich pressed through several more shots showing the house from various sides, as he read the address. Then he reversed the slides and went back to the beginning. He held up a pen-like pointer that sent a red laser-dot of light onto the screen.

"This is where they're supposedly stashing the dope," he said, holding the light on the upper floor. "They sell it here." The light went to the front door. "And there's a room down in the basement." The red dot reappeared on the side where a set of stairs descended. "We got a surveillance team on it now, just waiting for the shipment to arrive."

"They got the warrant?" Blackjack asked.

"Yep. It's been in the works for a while," Doscolvich said. "They were doing a Bollinger. Stopped two shitheads that came outta there yesterday with some crack. They flipped, and the warrant was already being assembled. But we want to wait for tonight, so we'll get a big load."

"In other words, wait till it's all cut, cooked, and halfway sold, so we get to take the bread," Linc said.

"Hit the asshole where it hurts," Jahn said.

The lights flashed back on, and they saw Doscolvich standing by the switch.

"That's right," he said. "Now I don't have to tell you that the Chief's taken a personal interest in this one. And he's expecting results."

"Yeah? He gonna join us tonight?" Blackjack asked, causing a few scattered laughs.

"No, he ain't," Doscolvich growled. "And he ain't supposed to either. It's not in his job description. It's in ours. And as the boss, he has a right to think that we can do our job without whining like a bunch of pussies."

Several of the guys suppressed giggles and snorts as Doscolvich, who must have realized what he'd said, began to turn red.

Hart smirked. If they thought something like that would bother her they had a lot to learn. Of course, the Lieutenant might be worrying about a sexual harassment charge.

"All right," Doscolvich said after the snickering had stopped. His face was still dark with the look of embarrassment and residual anger. "Break into two teams. I want full scouting on this one. Routes, alternate routes, diagrammed out. Risk assessments and entry plans. We meet back here at twenty-hundred hours."

The men started to get up and Doscolvich said, "TC and Blackjack. You guys stay here and go over entry techniques with

Ollie. Teach her everything she'll need to know to go in with the entry team tonight." He turned and strode out the door. "Twenty hundred."

With some muttering and a lot of laughs, the rest of the team meandered out of the briefing room. TC and Blackjack came over to Hart.

"You just got out of SWAT school, right?" Blackjack said.

"Right," Hart answered.

"Well, basically everything's the same, but it's a lot different doing it for real. So I guess it wouldn't hurt to go over a few drills. Plus, you'll have to know what Big John's shouting on the radio."

"One thing I would like to know is what that pin is?" Hart said, pointing to his collar.

"Oh, it's a one, and an asterisk," Blackjack said, smiling. "Get it? One-ass-to-risk?"

"Big John gives them out to the guys on the team once you've, excuse the expression, popped your cherry." His light blue eyes seemed to study her for a reaction as he spoke. She kept her face neutral.

"You'll earn one if you stick with the team," TC added. "You just gotta kinda prove yourself in Big John's eyes."

Hart nodded.

"Big John. Is that what we're supposed to call him?" Hart asked. "On the radio?"

"What else?" Blackjack said with a grin.

26
SQUEEZING

Leal pounded out a one-handed rhythm on the speed bag as a couple of the women who were doing the boxing aerobic workout followed the video's choreographed series of jabs, hooks, and crosses. Leal devoted most of his attention to the bag, but noticed out of the corner of his eye that a few of them were watching him. He finished with a flurry, still using only his right hand, as his timer bell rang. Then he glanced at his watch and rested for one minute.

Eleven o'clock and still no Ollie, he thought, wondering if she was still mad at him. It had been kind of intrusive asking Sean to nose around without telling her, but what the hell? He thought that she would be in favor of it. Could he help it if he'd misread the situation? Maybe he'd misread more than that. Maybe Hart wanted to get away from him. Had he done something to piss her off? He saw Rory going over to check the parking lot, then amble over towards the boxing room.

"She did say she was coming today, didn't she, Frank?" Chalma asked.

"When I talked to her she did," Leal said. "But, Rory, remember, she's been through a rough week. Maybe she's going to take a day off or something."

Chalma's lips pursed into a haughty pout. "Well, if that's her attitude, she might as well hang it up now," he said. "We've got to get on track for that Ms. International contest."

Leal smiled and tugged at his glove, setting the watch down

258

and moving to the heavy bag. He set the dial on his timer for three more minutes and began jabbing and hooking the suspended heavy bag, barely touching the surface in deference to his injured finger. The boxing video played on in the background, and he let himself sink into an almost automatic punching sequence as he thought about last night, and how special it had been.

Linda had turned out to be a somewhat tentative lover, which surprised him after the way she'd embraced him in the hallway. But her apprehension seemed to vanish, and they'd ended up making love, off and on, the whole night. But, oddly enough, today he felt refreshed, not exhausted.

This morning she'd awakened him with a kiss and told him that she'd made him pancakes. It had been strange waking up in a different bed, a different house, but her kitchen was bright and sunny as they ate the flapjacks. He'd told her that he had several things to get done, as did she, and they made an agreement to meet later on that night and cruise some of the areas to look for Gladis.

As he thought about the case, the tension in his chest and gut returned, and he began to feel winded. He'd have to check with the surveillance team on Sax, too. No telling how much longer Card was going to let him keep them in place. Something had to break soon. Otherwise . . . he felt the case slipping away. All the principal leads seemed elusive.

The timer bell rang, and Leal sat down on the mat in disgust, wiping his cheek on the sleeve of his sweatshirt. Shitty workout, shitty leads, half-assed investigation. What do they all add up to on one of the biggest "heaters" that I've ever handled? He wondered. If he blew this one he would always go down in the record books as the guy who let Dick Forest's killer get away.

"You look down in the dumps," a voice said. Seconds later he recognized it as Hart's. "How's your finger?"

"Hi," he said, looking up at her. "It's okay. I was wondering if you were gonna show." His eyes narrowed. "What happened?"

"Oh, this?" she said, her fingers tracing over her swollen cheek. "It's nothing."

Leal wondered if someone had clipped her. But Hart looked like she'd been crying too. He was going to inquire further, then thought better of it. If she wanted to tell him she would. He got to his feet. "Rory's been looking for you," he said.

"Yeah, I had to go over some entry techniques with some of the guys so I'm set for tonight."

Jesus, he thought. She really is into that SWAT shit.

"You're taking it easy today, aren't you?" she said.

"Just finishing up," Leal said. "We're gonna hit some of the spots tonight looking for that hooker."

"Neat. How's the investigation going?"

Leal held up his gloved hand and turned it thumbs-down. "Something better break soon."

"Well maybe Monday you can tell me all about it," she said.

"Monday?"

"You didn't forget that we have court, did you?" she asked. "That subpoena on that motion to suppress on the Lloyd Petitia case."

"Oh, shit," he said. He was about to say something more when he caught some movement out of the corner of his eye.

"And just where have you been?" Rory said, moving toward them at a fast clip, holding his watch out for her to see. "I thought you said you'd be here by ten?"

"I did say that," Hart said with an exasperated resignation. "But I was delayed, Rory, okay?"

Chalma stood there, arms akimbo, giving her one of his petulant stares. "What happened to your face?"

Leal, deciding to try and break the tension, said, "Well, she's SWAT now. They live to get busted up."

Hart shot him a sharp glance.

"I'm not in the mood, guys," she said, and snatched her gym bag and started toward the women's locker room. Rory fell into step beside her, trying to keep pace with her longer legs.

"Did you go off your diet?" he said. "You look like you've gained five pounds. Do you know how long it is before the contest?"

Leal thought that Chalma was going to follow her right in the ladies' room, but he stopped short as Hart went in and slammed the door.

Chalma scratched his head and walked over to Leal. "Frank, maybe you can talk some sense into her."

"I wouldn't want to try, the way I been hitting 'em, Rory," Leal said. "I got to boogie anyway, so it'll be up to you."

Hart struggled to feel the pump, but it just wouldn't come. She curled the bar up one more time, tensing her biceps as they rested against the flat portion of the preacher's bench. Chalma urged her on, his face only inches from hers, the tips of his index fingers pushing up on the bar. At the peak she tensed again, and this time the rush of pain seemed to radiate through her arms.

"You feeling it? Good," Chalma said. "Give me another one. Squeeze it."

Hart grunted and tried to lift the bar. It stalled halfway up, and she exhaled several short, rasping breaths. Chalma again pushed up on the bar ever-so-slightly. At the apex she gritted her teeth through another searing-tense, as the pump shot simultaneous feelings of intense pain and pleasure through her. She lowered the bar and Chalma guided it onto the steel holders.

"Good girl," he said, patting her on the head. Hart smiled weakly, trying to get her breathing under control, the sweat roll-

261

ing off her face, neck, and arms.

"I've got to rest," Hart said.

"Rest?" Chalma said. "Do you know how much time we've got before you really have to start dieting seriously? And you've definitely lost mass. Don't try telling me otherwise."

"Maybe," Hart said. "But I've also got to work tonight." He took a deep breath and squatted down in front of her.

"Have you thought any more about what we were talking about?" he said.

She looked at him. "I think we've had this conversation before, Rory."

He sighed and pursed his lips.

"Look, I can practically guarantee that this HGH won't show up on any test you might be worried about." He shook his head, looking her over, and added, "You really need to bulk up."

"And what is that shit going to do to my liver?" she said. "Or my ovaries? I have no desire to turn into another freak around here."

"Marsha is not a freak," he said.

"Yeah, right," she said, standing up from the bench. "I'll do flys, and then I'm outta here."

"Suit yourself," he said, standing also. "Hit the sauna for a while to sweat off some water-weight, though. And take a long hard look in the mirror before you decide."

Hart shot him an angry look, then raised her hands to her face as she felt the tears rush up. Chalma did a double take, moved toward her, putting a hand on her shoulder. "Ollie?"

She shook off his hand as she pressed the towel against her face. He managed to get her to sit down. Everyone in the gym was looking at them. He knelt in front of her and whispered.

"Ollie, I'm sorry," he said. "I didn't mean that the way it sounded."

Drying her face she looked at him, her cheeks still infused with red.

"Rory, I've just got so much going on right now, I can't handle any more," she said. "I feel that I'm caught in a vise and it just keeps on squeezing and squeezing."

Chalma licked his lips, as if trying to think of what to say.

"Maybe just get some rest in the sauna, then," he said. "Okay? We won't talk about the other matter anymore."

"Promise?" she asked.

"Promise," he said. "Boy Scout's honor."

"You were never a Boy Scout in your life," she said, a faint smile etching its way over her lips.

"Are you kidding? I've been one ever since puberty." His grin was rakish. "Hit the showers, Sweets. You're done for today."

She smiled, feeling the bone-weary fatigue seeping through her, and knowing that she still had to get past tonight's raid before she'd truly be done.

27
SATURDAY NIGHT FEVER

"All right, listen up," Big John Doscolvich said, his deep resonant voice reverberating in the briefing room. He was wearing his camouflaged BDUs, as were all the other members of the team. Each of them, Hart noticed, had their *1** pins fastened to their collars. "Mike and Dick are rear containment. TC and Linc are front. I'll do the breach, then Buzz, Marcus, and Elvis will do the first floor." He pointed to each man as he spoke. A large diagram of the house, displaying each level in an overview drawing, sat on an easel behind him.

"Lobo, Blackjack, and Ollie do the upstairs. PJ, Art, and Ray, you hit the basement. Secure the rooms, put all occupants on the floor, and cuff them. Once everything's secured, the case officers will come in and handle the search with the K-9 officers. Sergeant Berry will be in charge of that phase."

Zackary Berry, a lean-looking black man, with a processed set of Jheri curls and a pencil-thin mustache, stood up and smiled. He was wearing a large, gray raid jacket over his lavender shirt.

"One thing," Berry said, pointing to the *POLICE* emblazoned in large white letters on the breast pocket and back of the jacket. Berry turned around. "Please note: One brother," he pointed to his chest, "one badge. Po-lice. Do not shoot." He grinned, then sat back down.

"In other words," Doscolvich said, "familiarize yourselves with the members of Sergeant Berry's group. We don't want any friendly fire incidents." He paused before continuing. "Now the surveillance team has been sitting on this house all day long. They reported seeing two male blacks carry in two blue nylon duffel-like bags about three hours ago. That, we believe is the dope. People been going in and outta the place ever since. Intel says that the dope's kept upstairs, they sell it on the first level, then have an optional smoking room in the basement." He pointed a small flashlight toward the chart, and a red sniper-dot appeared on the section of the diagram marked basement. "Note the side entrance. I'm gonna have uniformed officers assisting with the outer perimeter at these points." The red dot flicked over the chart. "Our job is going to be to hit the place hard and move fast. I want to get to the bathrooms upstairs and downstairs real fast to prevent them from flushing the dope. Just leave any money where it's at until the search team can come through and get it." His big head rotated around the room, looking at each person. "Marcus, what's your assignment?"

"First floor," he said, chewing on some bubble gum.

Hart froze, hoping that he wouldn't call on her and grill her about where she was supposed to be.

But he did.

"Who are you going in with, Ollie?" he asked.

She inhaled, her mind a numb blank. She'd just heard him give out the instruction a moment before. Her mouth twisted open, but no sound came out.

Doscolvich frowned. "Okay, people, one more time, out loud. Repeat after me." He went through the sequence again, with all the team members repeating it after him, like some sort of religious mantra. Hart could feel herself blushing.

When they'd finished, Doscolvich said, "Oh yeah, another thing. We'll come in from this street here, so we'll deploy to driver's side when we exit the van." He drew an oblong block representing the surveillance van on the chart. The red dot traced the route they would take to the front door.

"Any questions?" he asked, looking around the room once more. His look was solemn. "All right, let's move out."

Leal turned the car down the block of the boulevard and slowly cruised past a group of women leaning against the urban terrain. Each wore some exaggerated outfit, emphasizing breasts and legs, with the maximum amount allowable showing. A few stepped forward as the car approached, only to be warned off by some of the more experienced girls. A dark blue Escalade with tinted windows had just pulled away from the group with a start as Leal had come down the block.

"Should we stop and talk to some of them?" Linda asked. "Ask them if they've seen Gladis?"

"Probably wouldn't tell us if they had," Leal said. "Our best bet is to pick a bunch up in a sweep, if we don't see her. Maybe we can lean on them that way."

Linda smiled.

"You ever work vice?" she asked.

"MEG," he said. "Why?"

"I was just wondering," she said. "You'd have a hard time convincing one of these *ladies* that you were so hard up you needed to pay for it."

He grinned.

"So . . . did I tell you how much I enjoyed last night?" she asked, her fingers walking over the seat to brush his leg.

Leal smiled. "Me too."

The radio squawked out, "Frank, you there?" on one of the chatter-bands. It was Ryan. Leal grabbed the mike and replied.

"Seen anything?" Ryan asked.

"Un-uh," Leal answered. "You?"

"Nah. What you say we send the paddy wagon through and

do a sweep," Ryan said. "Otherwise we'll be out here all night with nothing to show for it. Unless you're enjoying yourselves more than we are."

Leal knew that Ryan's remark was meant as a dig because he had told Lemack and Tims to ride with Ryan, while he took Linda in his car. Ryan's mustache had snaked up in a salacious grin as Leal had made the assignments.

"Might as well call in the troops," Leal said. "We'll grab some coffee and meet you at the staging area."

"You gonna eat too?" Ryan's voice said. His tone implied that he wasn't talking about food.

Leal just re-hung the mike in its holder and spun down the block.

"Is he always that obnoxious?" Linda asked.

"He's usually worse," said Leal. He pulled into the drive-thru of a Dunkin' Donuts. "But he knows I need all the help I can get tonight trying to close this one." He paused at the window and ordered two coffees, one black and one with cream. A heavy-set blond woman dressed in a dusty white apron took their orders without comment.

"I'm surprised he volunteered to help us tonight," she said, reaching for her purse. "Let me pay for this one, okay?"

"After that great breakfast you made me this morning?" Leal said. "Not a chance." He handed the clerk a five and waited for his change.

"I really enjoyed being with you," Linda said, leaning across the seat, her lips close to his ear.

"Same here." Leal smiled as her fingers wound around his chin and she tipped his face toward her and kissed him.

"Then let's do it again, after we finish tonight, okay?" she asked in a husky voice. "My ex will have my kids till tomorrow afternoon."

"Sounds good to me," Leal said, wondering how, if things

kept progressing this way, her kids would react to him. Would they resent him the same way his girls had acted toward Sharon?

When he turned, Leal saw the clerk holding the change from the five in an extended hand. "The coffee going to be hot enough for you two?" the woman asked.

Leal shoved the money in his jacket pocket and drove forward. "Everybody thinks they're a comedian tonight."

Taji wheeled the Escalade over toward another group of hos and lowered the electric window. Several of them rushed to the side of the car, calling him Sugar and letting their breasts spill forward out of their tight halter tops.

"I'm looking for my favorite lady," Taji said. "She go by the name of Chocolate. You seen her?"

"No, baby, but why settle for second best when you can have me," one heavy-breasted black whore said, peeling her tittie out of its cloth prison and displaying her dark nipple for him.

"Wanna try vanilla, baby?" a thin white girl with a fucked-up face said. Her titties were smaller than the black ho and Taji could tell she was pushing underneath them to crowd the skin upward. His cell phone rang and he pressed the button to roll up the window, crowding the hos out of the door frame. He flipped the phone open with a low sounding, "Yeah."

"Taji?" A squeaky little girl's kind of voice. Only this wasn't no girl. It was Efron James.

"Yeah, bro, what's up?" Taji said. "You got something fo' me?"

"Otha want to see you Monday," Efron said. "Got a little job for you."

"Uh-huh," Taji said. He knew what that meant. "What about Chocolate?"

"What about her?" Efron said, chuckling. "She bound to turn up sooner or later, bro. Just be cool, like they used to say."

"You be cool, man. That bitch holding my motherfucking balls in her fucking hand."

Efron laughed. The high-pitched giggle reminded Taji of a woman. Good thing little Efron was never on the inside.

"Relax," Efron said. "I told you we got the word out on her. And you know she gonna be callin' the gym to put the squeeze on you some mo'. Otha got caller-ID on the phone, so as soon as she do call again, we'll get a fix on where she at."

"Yeah?" Taji said. The little fucker was just being too damn smart. "What if she call from an unlisted number?"

"No problemo, brotherman," Efron said. "They don't call me the king of cyberspace fo' nuthin. Wherever she at, I'll find her. Listed or unlisted."

Taji exhaled through his nostrils.

"What time Monday do he want to see me?" he asked.

"Oh, come by 'bout six," Efron said. "And in the meantime, chill out." He hung up in a flurry of high-pitched laughter.

Chill out. Who is that little bitch to tell me that? Taji snapped the phone shut and dropped it back down on the seat and thought how he really wouldn't mind dropping that little crippled smart-ass motherfucker someday.

They sat facing each other along the bench-like seats that ran parallel to the walls of the van. Helmets on, microphones in place. A large metal battering ram rested on the floor between Doscolvich's legs making crunching, metallic scraping noises with each sway of the truck's suspension.

Hart felt tense, not knowing what to expect, and wondering what was going to happen in addition to the raid. Maybe she'd have an easy go of it, spot somebody pocketing something, and be able to report it to Florian. Maybe then her life would get back to normal. It just seemed like lately everything was getting turned on its head. Her job, her bodybuilding training, her

269

relationship with Rick . . . Rick. She thought about their last night together.

All good things, she thought, as she checked her equipment again, then adjusted the body-bunker shield that she had been assigned to carry with her on the raid. Since her group would have to ascend the stairwell, one of them would have to lug the shield along, in case someone at the top of the stairway reached around and opened fire. The body bunker weighed about twenty-five pounds, which can seem like an anvil when moving fast. But when Big John had said that one of them had to carry it, Hart volunteered. She'd handled one during the training, and no one on the team doubted her strength. Not after someone had brought in a copy of a *Muscular Development* magazine with a feature article about Hart with color photos of her in several muscle poses, doing various exercises while well-pumped.

The van hit a bump and jostled them. Elvis let out a loud howl. Sort of a protracted "Woooooweee!" The others smiled and laughed as the big hillbilly yelled, "Damn, I loooove this job."

"Hillrat, you do that inside that house and somebody gonna shit their drawers for sure," Marcus said, grinning.

"Well, damn man, that's the idea ain't it?" Elvis bellowed. Marcus raised his hand and Elvis slapped the palm in a high-five gesture.

Blackjack, who was seated next to Hart, whispered, "Just the usual pre-raid jitters. We all feel it every time. They just don't want to admit it."

Hart smiled and nodded. Doscolvich said, "Which side we deploying on?"

"Driver's side," came the unified response.

"Okay," Doscolvich said as the driver made a thumping sound on the wall of the truck, indicating that they would be there in about thirty seconds. The van slowed to a stop and Big John grabbed the ram as Buzz popped open the rear doors. They filed out like paratroopers going out of a plane: in formation, single file, each man knowing his exact place in the line-up.

Doscolvich was already running up toward the porch. Hart could see Marcus running past him. He moved with the grace of a natural athlete, taking the steps of the porch in one stride, stopping his momentum against the front of the house with his left hand, while ripping back the screen door with his right. Doscolvich ascended the steps in two over-sized strides, planted his feet, and swung the battering ram high to his rear.

"Police! Search warrant!" he yelled out.

Hart saw the ram swing forward three seconds later, and the door seemed to fly inward, then spring back as it bounced off the inside wall. Doscolvich let the ram continue inside the house and then stepped back. Buzz, Marcus, and Elvis were already inside, guns drawn.

"Police! Search warrant!" they yelled.

Lobo and Blackjack were at the stairway as Hart ran between them.

"Keep that shield up, Ollie," she heard Big John's voice say over her radio earphones. She elevated the body bunker and continued up the stairs as fast as she could, the Sig Sauer in her right hand ready to fire. She took the stairs two at a time, wondering with each step if she was going to see a hand with a gun curl around the top corner and start firing. Or would she just see the flame of the exploding rounds, she thought a millisecond later, as she crested the top and went to her left. Lobo was right behind her, going straight, shining his flashlight on the darkened room before him. She reached the bathroom and saw that it was clear. No flushing tonight, boys, she thought.

"Upstairs toilet secure," she barked into her radio.

"Downstairs secure," she heard someone say over the radio. "Two suspects."

"Lobo?" she heard Blackjack say.

"It's cool, Blackjack," came the reply.

"Basement has several," someone shouted.

Then she heard yelling coming from the next room. "ON THE FLOOR! ON THE FLOOR! NOW! POLICE!"

She saw Lobo move quickly into the adjacent room and then with a flickering of motion, she saw a woman flung to the floor, face first. Lobo stooped over her back as Blackjack shoved another female, face-first, down on the carpet. "Two females up here, Big John," Lobo said.

Hart set the bunker down and went forward, pistol still extended, and stood watch while they handcuffed the two women.

"Basement secure," the radio crackled. "Three in custody."

"Ollie, search 'em," Blackjack said, standing up.

Hart nodded and holstered her weapon. She had on thin leather gloves that would give her hand a modicum of protection should she feel anything sharp or pointed.

"You got any needles on you?" Hart asked, feeling along the woman's heavy pant-legs.

"No," the woman grunted.

"How about you?" Hart asked the second woman.

"I ain't got nothing in there but me," the woman said. "But you is welcome to check. I just don't appreciate being thrown down on the floor like that. That ain't even no way to treat a lady."

"Sorry, babe," Blackjack said with a grin. "But I thought you were a man."

The women and the four stoned-out junkies from the basement were taken out first. The two suspects from the first floor, the ones that the surveillance team had seen entering with the blue duffel bags earlier, were left face down on the living room rug while the K-9s did their search. The preliminary walk-through by Doscolvich and Buzz had turned up nothing out of the ordinary. Or the unordinary. No bags of dope sitting out, no stacks of money. The kitchen did have a large flat pan, a couple cartons of baking soda, and a huge supply of plastic bags of various sizes. After the dogs failed to find anything substantial, Zack Berry and his men began to tear the place apart. But it was a dispirited search, each knowing that if the dogs had failed to alert on anything except the baking pan, there was probably nothing to find. Sixty minutes went by before Berry, his face shiny with sweat, came back in the living room and shook his head at Doscolvich, who was standing off to the side with Marcus, Lobo, and Hart. Berry heaved a heavy sigh.

"Didn't find no shit, did you, motherfucker?" one of the men on the floor said, rolling his head to the side to smile up at Berry.

Marcus moved over and gave the prone man a light kick on the shoulder.

"Shut the fuck up," Marcus said.

"Hey, *brother*," the man said. "Ain't no need to get physical."

Marcus stepped around and squatted down next to the man's head. He grabbed a handful of the slick processed hair and pulled, causing the prisoner's head to wrench back. The whites of the man's eyes seemed ready to pop out of their sockets.

"You ain't my brother, motherfucker," Marcus growled. "You the one selling poison to my real bros. He's my brother," Marcus said, pointing to Doscolvich, "and him," pointing to Lobo. "But you just a piece of dog shit that got stuck to the bottom of my boot tonight." He punctuated his last sentence by slamming the man's face back down onto the rug.

"Marcus, chill out," Doscolvich said.

As Marcus stood the man on the floor said, "Shit, man. You ain't nothing, motherfucker. Just some white man's boy." Marcus started for the prone figure, but Doscolvich shot forward to block him and shoved him back.

"Easy!" Big John shouted.

Marcus took two steps back, looked at the big lieutenant, the handcuffed prisoner, then stepped over and kicked the toe of his boot through the screen of a large plasma screen television sitting a few feet away.

"Jesus motherfucking Christ!" Zack Berry shouted. "What you go and do that for, man?"

Marcus shot an icy stare at him.

Berry smirked.

"Shit, I had my eye on that TV, too," Berry said. "Wanted to see if I could put a round right through the center without it shattering."

Marcus stared at him for a moment longer, then his chest shook with a heavy chuckle. He held out his palm and Berry slapped it with his.

"My motherfuckin' plasma," the other man on the floor moaned.

"You wanna tell us where your stash is so no more of your shit gets damaged?" Zack Berry said, stooping next to the second man.

"I ain't saying shit till I talk to my lawyer," the man answered. "And he gonna pay for that TV, too."

"Fuck you, man," Marcus said.

"Let's take these guys down for a warrant check," Doscolvich shouted. "Put 'em in a marked squad and get 'em outta here."

Hart looked over as several of the uniformed coppers came in and picked up the two prisoners to escort them out.

"Shit," Hart heard Doscolvich mutter as the two men were hustled past them. "The only thing they didn't do was bake us a cake."

The debriefing was mercifully short. Doscolvich had a "private" session with Marcus, which could be heard halfway down the hall. Marcus came out of the room sullen and downcast, his heavy lips drawn into a tight line. Doscolvich looked flushed, too, splashes of red still evident on his high cheekbones. But the big man was complimentary on their overall performance. He let each member go through his own critiques, then said, "Okay, we struck out again as far as finding the proceeds, but the raid itself went down pretty damn good. Take off, and I'll see you all here Tuesday at fourteen hundred."

Hart felt a wave of relief. Two days off, even though she had court on Monday, that would give her time to catch her breath. Provided that she could quit worrying about everything and get a handle on her life. She felt a hand touch her shoulder.

"Ollie," Blackjack said. "All of us are going over to the Black Knight to get a drink. Want to come? It's sort of like tradition after a raid."

"I don't know," she said.

"Aww, come on," Plutarch said. "It's tradition, especially after losing your cherry, so to speak." He grinned at her. "Oh, you did good, by the way."

Hart stared at him for a moment, her expression neutral, then she said, "Gee, thanks, *Dick.*"

Elvis, who had been standing nearby, howled with laughter. "That's right, Ollie," he said. "Dick old Plutarch before he dicks you."

Hart was supposed to meet Rick at midnight, and it was already close to eleven-thirty. But, on the other hand, she thought, perhaps it would help to ingratiate her into the group if she at least made an appearance there. The Black Knight was a cops' bar, so she wouldn't feel too out of place. She had told Rick that she'd beep him after the raid was finished anyway.

"Maybe I will stop for one," she said, punching in Rick's number on her cell. "But I'm supposed to meet somebody so I can't stay long."

"Great," Blackjack said. "We always just go in our BDU pants. No need to be formal at that place."

"It helps Blackjack look more macho if he decides to hit on one of the waitresses," Buzz said.

The group rocked with laughter as they began stowing their gear, helmets, vests, and tactical holsters in their ditty bags. Hart listened to several rings before he answered.

"Hi. How'd it go?"

"Great," she said. "Except we didn't find anything." She heard a beep on the line. "Where you at?"

"I'm at the station in Robertsville," he said. "Waiting on Felony Review to call back. We got a guy for PSMV and he had a couple of rocks on him."

"Great."

"Say, I don't know what time I'll get done. Like I said, I'm still waiting on the state's attorney to call back, and I haven't even started my report."

She waited for him to continue. "So?" she asked.

He took a deep breath. "It's just that maybe it'd be better if you didn't plan on me coming over after work. I don't know what time I'll be finishing up, and you're probably tired, right?"

On the contrary, she thought. I'm wired. But she said, "Whatever you want. A bunch of us were talking about hitting the bar for a post-raid celebration anyway."

"Oh, you going?"

"I may."

"Well, I guess I'll see you tomorrow then, okay?"

"Yeah, right," she said. "Good luck with the felony."

"Thanks, I'll call you after the bond hearing," he said.

She ended the call and locked her phone, wondering if he was already trying to exclude her from his life. She didn't doubt that he had a felony, but if the positions were reversed, wouldn't

shouldn't have said that, Frank."

"Yeah, yeah, I know. It'll come back to haunt me," he said. Then he grinned. "But it might have been worth it. Anyway, that son-of-a-bitch McGuffy couldn't make a decent decision to save his life."

Hart smiled. They rode the escalator down.

"Got time for lunch?" she asked. "You can catch me up on all the stuff I've been missing."

"You haven't been missing much," he said. "But the lunch sounds good."

They went in separate cars to a restaurant on 189th street. Leal ordered a hamburger and fries and Hart a salad. The waitress poured two cups of steaming coffee for them. They both drank it black.

"So how's things going?" he asked her, holding the cup under his nose to test the aroma before taking a sip.

"Personally or professionally?" she said, wishing that she could open up and tell him everything that was bothering her. She had always confided in Frank, but this time she knew she had to be discreet.

"Well, both," he said.

"Professionally, great." She took a small sip and set her cup back down on the saucer. "I did my first raid Saturday night, and it went just like clockwork."

"Nothing like just finishing the school and putting you to work, huh?" He paused. "I used to go on raids when I was in Narcotics."

"I know, but this was just incredible," she said. "It was just like a military operation that you see in the movies or on TV. Everybody had a specific assignment, and we just took the place down one, two, three."

"Sounds like you're really getting into that stuff."

"Zack Berry was there," she said.

"I thought MEG wasn't doing their own raids anymore?"

"They let us do the raid to secure the building, then they came in afterwards with the K-9s."

"Sure wish it'd been that way when I was in MEG. So how's my old buddy Zack doing?"

"Same as always. Very brash. But he's nice, though."

"We shared a lot of good times together," Leal said. "So what else is happening?"

She looked down at her coffee for a moment, considering what else to say. Oh what the hell, she thought. This is Frank, after all. "Rick's thinking of moving to Minnesota."

"Oh yeah? What brought that on?"

"His brother Lance. He may get a chance at a plea bargain to turn state's evidence and get transferred to the federal penitentiary up there."

"Be a lot easier than doing state time," Leal said. "Some of them federal pens are like country clubs."

"He wants me to go up there with him."

Leal's dark eyes narrowed. "So you going?"

"I'm not sure," she said, looking down at her cup and saucer. She raised her head, hoping he wouldn't notice that her eyes were glistening. "I really care about him, but I've got so much here. My parents, my sisters, and my brother. The department, friends that I've made here. Rory. And you, of course."

Leal's smile was reassuring. Hart reached out and squeezed his hand.

"And I just hate the idea of starting over in patrol, up somewhere in a new city," she said. "Riding in a squad car for eight hours, having to prove myself all over again."

"Sort of difficult to pull up roots," he offered.

"Right," she said.

"Sounds like a real tough decision. I know I'll miss you if you go, but I'm sure you'll do well up there."

Good old Frank, always so supportive of her. "Thanks. I'll miss you too." She took a sip of her coffee and asked, "So how things been going for you? What's the latest on the Dick Forest investigation?"

"Oh, God, you had to remind me, didn't you?" he said with a grin.

"That bad?" she asked. "How's your new partner?"

"From bad to worse," Leal said. "He's fine when he's doing what he does best—talking about dogs. He's an ex–K-9 officer. That is when he's not talking to his hand puppet."

"Hand puppet?"

"Yeah, he calls it Oscar," Leal said.

Hart laughed. "Is Al still riding with you?"

"The king of the nerds?" Leal said. "Yeah, he's still with us. Now that he can't try and peek down your blouse anymore he's been trying to look up Linda's skirt."

"Linda?" she said, arching her eyebrows.

"Oh yeah, I guess I didn't mention her to you, did I?" he said. "She's with the tree police, working on the Dick Forest homicide with us. They found a dead hooker in the forest preserve. It was her print on the toilet seat at the Riptide Motel."

"Oh," Hart said. "What's she like?"

"She's nice," Leal said. "And it's good to have a woman's perspective on the investigation again."

Hart smiled. Sounds like more than that to me, she thought.

"Al didn't try to look down my blouse, did he?" she asked. "You're fibbing, aren't you?"

"Like hell," Leal said. "And he must have liked what he saw. Last week he came in with flowers for you."

She laughed again.

"What did he do with them?"

"He gave them to me," Leal said with a grin. "And I turned

around and dumped them in the trash."

"You didn't, did you?"

He nodded, taking a sip of coffee.

"So what else has been going on?" she asked.

"Well, that serial rapist struck again," said Leal. "You know, that guy who masquerades as a cop. Boy, would I like to catch that son-of-a-bitch. Got the ViCAP profile of him from the FBI the other day. And those motel bandits hit another place. There's talk of setting up an interdepartmental task force to try and go after them, but that's still at the talking stage. They'll wait till they kill somebody first."

"Sounds like you're swamped," she said.

"Yeah, and as usual Ryan ain't doing a fucking thing."

"Why am I not surprised?"

Leal sighed. "Well, we're supposed to go out later tonight and canvass some of the hotels in the area for those banditos, and Ryan said he'd come with."

"Wow. Talk about miracles," she said. "How's your finger?"

Leal held up his left forefinger, which was now covered with two overlapping band-aids.

"Cutting down on my typing speed," he grinned. "I'm supposed to get the stitches out Friday."

She touched his hand. "I felt bad that I was so mean to you on the phone when you were hurt."

"Ah, don't worry about it," he said, with a dismissive gesture. "I shoulda never asked Sean to go snooping around. It was my fault. Although he called me yesterday and told me something else that's real interesting."

"What?" she said, her eyes widening. Oh no, could word have leaked about her assignment?

"Old Sheriff Mike Shay might not be with us too much longer," Leal said.

Hart's brow furrowed.

Leal grinned. "Word has it that he's getting ready to throw his hat in the ring for President of the County Board. If he gets that, the next step is governor."

Hart raised her eyebrows. Thank God it wasn't about me, she thought.

"Then," Leal said, "that would open the door for Shay to appoint our very own Chief Burton, or Jack-off Burton, as most of us call him, to fill the vacant sheriff's position. When Shay's term expires in two years, Burton can run for re-election as the incumbent."

"Sounds Machiavellian," Hart said.

"Yeah, the worst part of it all is that Sean says that Burton is asshole-buddies with some dickhead captain from I.A.D. Probably appoint him to take his place."

That has to be Florian, Hart thought.

"Can you imagine what kind of a chief that guy'd make?" Leal said.

Her cell vibrated against her side. She checked the number and saw the code that Florian had given her after the number. A shiver went down her spine.

"So you don't have any leads at all on the Forest case?" she asked, changing the subject.

"Well, I still have the surveillance teams following that two-bit actor, but I'm expecting to go ten rounds with Card on that today when I go in. It's my one decent lead and he's pissing and moaning about the overtime. The only thing going for me is that I don't think the actor knows he's being tailed."

"At least you've got that much," Hart said. "On that raid Saturday, we came up empty. Almost as if they were expecting us and ditched everything beforehand." She began digging in her purse for some change. "I'll be right back. I've got to make a call."

"So use your cell. I won't listen too close."

She shook her head. "Low battery."

"Want to use mine?" Leal grinned.

Hart smiled back and stood up. "No thanks. It's personal."

"Anybody I'd know?" Leal asked with a smile, picking up his coffee cup.

She got up, not answering him.

If you only knew, she thought.

29
GREAT REWARDS

Hart had been both shocked and disturbed that Florian had told her that she would have to meet them at a Holiday Inn in Matteson for the update. That's the way he phrased it too: "the update." Luckily the hotel was right off the expressway, and she'd been told to go to the front desk and beep Florian.

He would then come down to the first floor, and they would meet in a conference room. The cloak and dagger routine seemed a little bit odd to her, and she told him so, but Florian assured her that it was absolutely necessary for secrecy. He and the Chief were preparing for the Shay fundraiser to be held at the hotel later that week, and it was imperative that they meet there.

"You can wait in the bar, if you'd feel more comfortable," Florian had said.

"No," Hart said into the phone. "I don't go to bars."

"You went to the Black Knight the other night, didn't you?"

His words hit Hart like fragments from a bombshell. Could they have been watching during the raid or at the bar afterward? He must have had her followed. Before she could respond Florian chuckled and said he'd see her at the hotel.

Now, as she waited at the front desk, she'd gotten over her outrage. It was part of the plan and not doing this assignment wasn't an option. Like she had a lot of choice in the matter. If she'd turned it down, they would have found some way to punish her. A transfer to the jail perhaps, or maybe to the far north side. And she could forget about staying in Investigations or ever making sergeant. Who knows what they would have done, and if word somehow leaked out about the investigation after she had refused to do it, she would automatically be suspect. No, she had no choice, pure and simple. They had her, and knew they had her, before they'd even asked.

She heard someone call to her and saw Florian standing by the elevators, which were perhaps 130 feet away, beyond the banquet rooms and foyer. She walked to him as he stood with his hand on the doors, keeping them from closing.

"Hi," was all Florian said.

She stepped inside and he let the doors close, then pressed number four. The elevator rose upward, leaving her stomach even more unsettled. When the doors opened, Florian exited and motioned for her to follow. He opened the first door on the left side of the hallway. Hart followed him into the room, which contained a large table made of fine wood, several plush chairs, and a long kitchenette. The drapes were drawn, but the overhead fluorescent lighting made the room appear very bright. It looked more like an office suite than a hotel room.

"Sit down, Olivia," Florian said. "Want coffee?" He stood at the counter. A large metallic urn with a spigot was on the counter along with two upended stacks of Styrofoam cups.

"Sure," she said, thinking how she hated him using her first name. "Black, please."

Florian nodded, grabbed a cup from the stack, and filled it. He walked over to the table and set the coffee in front of her, then took his seat on the opposite side. Leaning back, he regarded her with a lips-only smile. Hart watched the steam curl up from the cup.

The door opened and Chief Burton walked in carrying a manila folder full of papers. If Frank only knew what I was doing now, she thought. The Chief sat next to Florian and motioned toward the coffee pot. Florian got up and went to the counter.

"Get me an ashtray too, will you, Mark," Burton said. His fingers fumbled in his shirt pocket as his other hand opened the folder on the table. Florian returned with a cup of coffee and an empty cup. Burton looked up at him and Florian shrugged.

"This crazy smoking ban," he said. "It's a conference room, for Christ's sake." His finger snapped the button on a disposable lighter and the Chief stuck the end of his cigarette into the flame. Inhaling, he smiled at Hart and said, "Well, I see that you got your feet wet the other night . . ." His eyes dipped down to the open folder before him, then back to Hart, "Olivia."

She nodded and tried to smile, but the smell of the cigarette was making her feel somewhat sick. She hadn't touched her coffee.

"So, did you find out anything?" Burton asked, leaning forward. His shirtsleeves had been rolled up, and his tie had been loosened so that the knot hung away from his throat.

"Not really, sir," she said. "The raid itself was over quickly. We didn't find anything as far as drugs or money."

"Oh, Christ, I know that already," Burton said, pushing back in his chair. The movement caused the smoke to move away from her, but her nose and throat still felt tight.

"What the Chief means," Florian said, "is did you see anything suspicious on the part of the rest of the raid team? Could anybody have, say, scooped up something before anyone else noticed?"

"I don't see how it would have been possible for the part of the team that I was with," she said. "We moved in so quickly and had to worry about several suspects in the house."

Burton bent forward again. The tip of the cigarette glowed, and when he spoke he let the residual smoke drift out of his mouth with his words.

"Are you gaining their confidence? Do you think they've accepted you enough that they'd let you in on a special payday, maybe?"

"We don't want to overplay our hand too soon, Jack," Florian said. Hart noticed tiny droplets of sweat forming on his high forehead. "She did go out drinking with them afterward."

Burton sighed, blowing smoke through both nostrils.

"Yeah, yeah, you're right," he said. Then back to Hart, "We've been going over some of the financial documents of the team members. Now don't even mention this yet, but a couple of them are in over their heads."

Hart looked at him.

"Living beyond their means," Florian added.

"Garcia owns two cars, and has six kids," Burton said. "Stone's been married three times, and has kids from two of the marriages. He pays alimony and child support to each one. So they're both prime candidates for needing extra money. And that's not taking into account the black ones. They always bear watching." He inhaled once more on the cigarette and tapped the ash into the cup. Leaning forward again, he looked at her and asked, "Have you worked with any of those individuals directly, where they had an opportunity to do something?"

"Stone and I were together on the raid Saturday," she said. "If he'd picked up anything, I'm sure I would have noticed. I just don't think that there was anything to find."

Burton screwed up his face.

"That might be true on a few occasions, but goddammit, there's just been too many strike-outs lately."

"Seizures are way down," Florian added. "Money and drugs."

She looked at him.

"We're going to schedule more random urine tests for some of the team," he continued. The way he emphasized "random" made her realize that it was anything but. "We'll keep you apprised of anything that it might turn up, so you can keep an extra watch on those particular people."

"It's imperative that we get this cleaned up as soon as possible," Burton said. "Now, I've approved several raids for this week. I'm handling all these plans personally. In fact, you should do another one tomorrow night. Try to keep a special watch on those men we mentioned. Part of your job is to get in good with them." He leaned forward and his lips curled up over his teeth. "And this assignment is so important, I wouldn't mind *how* you did it."

"In other words, whatever it takes," Florian said.

Hart was stunned. Were they implying that she should sleep with them to find out if they were crooked? The assholes.

"Just what do you mean by that?" she asked, the anger welling up in her tone.

Burton blew out some smoke with a quick breath.

"Just that you're a very attractive young woman," he said, his hands fluttering in front of him. "You're single, too, right?" She stared at him a second before nodding. "Well, if they want to go out drinking or something, it wouldn't hurt to go along, would it? To gain their confidence."

"I did that Saturday," Hart said.

"We know," Florian said.

"Anyway, there'll be times that we aren't around to see anything," Florian said, "but you'll be up-close and personal."

"Win their confidence, Olivia," Burton said. "We're dealing with some rotten apples here. If we can't police ourselves, how can we maintain the public trust?"

The heavy smoky air was making Hart nauseous. Or was it the company? She wasn't sure. She only knew that she had to get out of there soon. Burton stood up, took one final drag, and stubbed the cigarette out in the Styrofoam cup, which made the odor even worse.

"Continue to report," he said as he moved toward the door.

"Are you coming to the sheriff's dinner tonight?" Florian asked.

Hart remembered hearing about it, but at one-hundred dollars a plate it had seemed overpriced. Besides, she'd always avoided political affairs.

"I didn't think it would be wise," she said. "I usually don't go to anything like that, and I didn't want to attract undue attention considering this assignment." She could think on her feet, too, she thought. Faster than he could.

Florian considered her statement and then nodded. "Good thinking."

Burton cracked the door, and, after peering down each hallway, held it open for her. Florian followed her to the elevators.

"Good luck," Burton said, smiling. She was sure that he was wearing a hairpiece now that she watched him step under the harsher hallway light. "Remember, there'll be great rewards for you after we've gotten rid of the rotten wood. Great rewards." His grin faded, and he turned and walked a few steps down the hall to one of the nearby rooms.

Florian, who walked up on Hart's left side, started to speak to her, saying how she'd be able to write her own ticket after this assignment. But as she turned her head to listen to him, she saw the Chief rapping softly on the solid door of the adjacent suite. She and Florian paused in front of the elevators, and he stabbed at the down-button with his forefinger. The door that the Chief had been knocking on opened inward, and Hart saw Burton's face relax into a gentle smile. As he went in, the double-doors of the elevator popped open and both she and Florian stepped inside the lift.

I wonder who he was meeting in there? she asked herself as the elevator descended.

30
DEAD DOG

The little man at the wheel of the Chevy Tahoe cut it abruptly so he could pull over to the curb in front of the gym. The guy sitting in the passenger seat regarded the smaller man with slit-like eyes. He was larger than the driver and much more heavy-set, with dark skin and short hair. His red beret was cocked to the right.

"That him, Pea?" the bigger man said, looking at the solitary figure walking toward them from out of the night shadows of the adjacent alley.

"Uh-huh," the driver said, slowing to a stop. At the curb Taji grinned at them and reached out for the rear door of the Tahoe. Pulling it open, he slung his gym bag onto the rear seat and got inside.

"What's happenin', bro?" he said.

"Marcellus, this is Taji," the driver said. "He that dude I been tellin' you about."

"My man Sweetpea here tells me you one bad dude," Marcellus said, extending his hand across the seat. They did the "brother handshake," which turned into the standard Soul Gangsta's dap at the end.

"Glad to meet you, Marcellus," Taji said. The Tahoe sped forward through a series of stop-and-go-lights.

"People calls me Raw Dog," Marcellus said, grinning. "So where you got these hos stashed at?"

Taji's lips curled up with a sly laugh.

"You don't mince words, do you?" he said. "A man after my own heart." He reached into his gym bag and withdrew a half-pint bottle of Seagram's, looked around, then unscrewed the top. "Hey, bro, head down a ways toward them preserves. I don't want no motherfucking cops stoppin' us and jacking us around." Taji tipped up the bottle and took a sip. "Ahhhh," he said, wiping off his mouth.

Marcellus eyed the bottle, and his tongue swept over his own lips.

Taji made a show of looking through the tinted rear windows of the Tahoe, and told the driver to hurry up. Then he raised the bottle again and took another sip.

"How rude of me," he said, grinning as he wiped his mouth a second time. "You want a blast, brother?"

Marcellus grinned and held out his hand.

"We gonna have a real good buzz by the time we get to where we goin'," Taji said. "That's fo' sure."

Marcellus unscrewed the cap and Taji put a palm on the man's shoulder.

"Wait till we get up on that road there," he said. "Less cars. Somebody might have a fucking cellular and call the cops about three niggers drinking in a car."

Marcellus nodded, keeping the bottle between his thighs.

"Turn right up there, Pea," Taji said. He reached inside his gym bag and began feeling around for something. "Shit, man, know what I forgot?"

"What?" Sweetpea asked.

"Ain't nobody around now," Marcellus said, putting the bottle to his lips, tilting his head back, and taking a long, slow series of gulps.

"Nevermind," Taji said. "I found it."

He watched as Marcellus, his head still lolling back against the headrest, lowered the bottle to his lap. Taji's left hand went up, closing over Raw Dog's face like a steel trap.

His right came up on the other side and pressed the short barrel of the Bersa Thunder to the base of Marcellus's skull and the gun popped seven times. Knowing the pistol was now empty, Taji placed it in his pocket with his right hand. His left still held the other man's face. He glanced around and, seeing no other cars on the road, let Marcellus slump toward the door. "Slow up," Taji said. "Cut your lights and pull over, but keep going real slow."

"Shit, man," Sweetpea said. His face was shiny with sweat, but he did as he was told.

Taji leaned forward, his upper body over the front seat, and pulled the door handle. The passenger door opened and Taji pushed Marcellus out the door. The right-rear tire ran over something. Taji leaned back in his seat, then told Sweetpea to pull up and stop. He opened the back door and got out.

"Clean up that blood there," he said, then turned and walked back toward the body. Sweetpea did as he was told. He tore open the glove box and scrambled for the box of tissues inside. Wiping frantically, he used spit from his own mouth to moisten the tissues to dab at the thick red stains. As he was doing this, he heard a loud shot that sounded like a clap of thunder piercing the night. Then Taji was getting back in the rear seat, and tucking a shiny automatic pistol into his belt.

"Wasn't he dead?" Sweetpea asked.

"I wanted to go through his pockets and see what all he had on him." Taji held up a fat wallet and some miniature bags of rock cocaine. "Besides, when I do somebody, I make sure they stay dead." He opened the wallet and began removing the currency. "Seen too many motherfuckers come back after being shot in the head with these small baby guns. That's why I always finish things Mozambique-style: One right through the head with Adolph."

"Adolph?" Sweetpea said, the octaves of his voice still fluctuating from nervousness.

"Yeah, Adolph," Taji said, pointing to the 9mm Sig Sauer in his beltline. "Ain't no motherfucker that's gonna live through that." He reached across and handed the driver half the bills from the wallet.

"Thanks, bro," Sweetpea said with a smile. He stuffed the money in his pants pocket and asked, "You gonna use all that rock too?"

"Forget that shit," Taji said. He didn't want to take the chance that this little motherfucker would turn stool pigeon if he got cracked with some dope.

"So you want me to go dump the guns?" the driver said.

Taji glanced at him. The thought of dumping Adolph was alien to him. He'd simply change the barrel. "You can take the Bersa," he said. "But not tonight. We gots another one to do tomorrow."

"Okay, Taji," the little man said. "What you want me to do now?"

"Take this fucking thing through the car wash," Taji said. "That full-service one on Cicero. And make sure they do the inside, and put one of them air fresheners in too. Strawberry mint if they got it. That motherfucker must have shit his pants." He laughed. "Unless that's you. But first, drive me back to the gym. I gotta wait for a phone call."

After being dropped off, Taji walked inside the main lobby of the gym. He nodded at the man behind the desk, who sat beside a telephone with a caller-ID monitor hooked up to it. The man shook his dark head. Taji frowned and grabbed the phone, punching in the number with savage pokes of his index finger. It rang twice, then Efron James answered.

"It's done," Taji said.

"Okay, I'll tell him," Efron said. "That was fast, bro. Any problems?"

"Just that that fuckin' bitch ain't called me yet," Taji said.

He listened to the high-pitched little laugh on the other end of the phone.

"Patience, brother, patience," Efron said. "She will."

Taji just grunted. Then said, "She better."

Efron James laughed again, then said, "Just don't forget to hoist the cue card tomorrow night."

"I won't," Taji said. "Later." He then hung up.

"This is something that you should write one of your papers on, Al," Ryan was saying as they turned right onto the parallel road that would take them to the front entrance of the Holiday Inn. Ryan was leaning over the front seat, talking to Tims, while Leal, who sat beside the intern, did a slow burn. Crazy Bob, at the wheel, was subdued as he pulled up in front of the hotel, and parked the car along the yellow curb.

"The day before my GI test I had to drink a gallon of this stuff," Ryan continued. "It looks just like water, but it tastes like crap." He grinned. "And that's what it makes you do, too, but don't worry, guys. I got it all out of my system."

"What did the tests say?" Tims asked.

"It finally confirmed that I wasn't full of shit anymore," Ryan said.

Tims bleated out his nerve-grating laugh just as they pushed through the front doors. His thumbs worked the keyboard on his smart phone again.

Leal smirked in spite of himself. He must be tweeting about the state of Ryan's colon. But I should tell him it won't take long before he's back on full again.

"So they find out why you were passing blood?" Leal asked.

Ryan nodded. "Been taking too many aspirins lately. Trying

299

to head off a hangover. They opened up a lesion somewhere in there." He turned to Tims again. "So let that be a lesson to you, Al. You can take an aspirin to get rid of a headache and still end up with a pain in the ass."

Tims was laughing so hard he could barely get his thumbs moving.

No truer words have ever been spoken, Leal thought. He glanced at Crazy Bob, who'd been silent the whole time. Leal caught up to him and asked, "You okay?"

"Oh, yeah, Frank, thanks," he said. "I'm just kinda down, is all. That dog—the one I took into the animal hospital, I'm wondering what's gonna happen to her."

"You can't save them all, Bob," Leal said. They were nearing the front desk. "Well, at least you gave it a real chance."

Crazy Bob nodded. "Maybe I should adopt her if she pulls through."

Leal reached into his pocket and pulled out his badge case, flipping it open toward the desk clerk. "We're police officers," he said.

"Oh thank God," the clerk said. He was a blond-haired white guy in his mid-thirties, and his face was pallid. "They're over there." He pointed toward two men. One was a barrel-chested black man, and the other was a white teenager in a gray hotel bellman's outfit. Leal looked at Ryan with a perplexed expression.

"Excuse me?" Leal said.

"You're here about the man with the gun, aren't you?" the clerk said. "Just talk to my security man." He pointed toward the two men again, and this time the big black guy smiled and came sauntering over.

"You guys police?" the black man asked.

Leal nodded and the black man extended his hand.

"Chester Himes," he said. "Hotel security." Leal grasped the man's hand. Himes seemed to pick up on Leal's querulous expression. "You guys are here about the man-with-the-gun call, right?"

"Why don't you fill us in," Leal said.

"Sure," Himes said. "One of my bellmen went into a room that was listed as unoccupied, and this guy pointed a piece at him. The kid's pretty shook up."

"How long ago this happen?" asked Leal.

"Just a couple of minutes," Himes answered. "I couldn't believe you guys got here so fast."

"This guy with the gun still here?" Leal asked.

Himes raised his radio to his lips and spoke into the mike. A garbled reply came back.

"As far as I know," Himes said. "I got one of my guys watching the room, but we ain't armed, so there's no way I wanted to go up there and open that door." He grinned, showing a pair of gold front teeth.

"You got a master key?" Leal asked.

"Sure do," Himes said. He turned toward the elevators, then paused to make sure the others were coming after him.

"Tell us what happened, son," Leal said as the elevator took them up to the third floor. At least Ryan had had the presence of mind to tell Al Tims to stay on the first floor, he thought.

The kid swallowed, then licked his lips.

"Well, Mr. Libby, the M.O.D., that's Manager On Duty, told me to go to room three-twelve and get the remote outta there, and bring it to room five-oh-two," the bellman said. "Three-twelve was supposed to be empty, and the people in the other room said their remote wasn't working." He swallowed again as the elevator jerked to a stop, and the doors popped open. "So I opens the door and I seen this big guy sitting in a chair, with this black chick on her knees in front of him. I just kinda stood there looking, then the next thing I know, this dude pulls out this gun and tells me to beat it."

"Can you describe him?" Leal said. They paused at the corner, and saw one security guard, in a blazer the same color as Himes's, peeking around the corner. "Was he white or black?"

"He was white," the kid said.

"What was he wearing?" asked Leal.

The young bellman took a deep breath and began to talk.

The doors to the second elevator slid open, and Captain Florian stepped out.

"Police officer," Florian said, holding up his badge-case.

"So are we," Leal said, holding open his own badge. "We got a situation here. Man in room three-twelve pulled a weapon on this kid."

"Hiya, Captain," Ryan said. "What you doing here?"

Florian turned toward Ryan, regarding him with narrowing eyes.

"You're . . ." he said.

"Sergeant Tom Ryan, Investigations South," Ryan said. "And you're Captain Florian, right?"

Florian smiled and extended his hand. "Right, good to see you again."

"Well, if you don't mind," Leal said, "we got a situation here."

"It's all a misunderstanding," Florian said. "We've got a fund-raiser downstairs in one of the ballrooms."

Himes glanced at him. "Oh, that's you guys in the Fernwood Room?"

"Right," Florian said. "This incident was just a slight misunderstanding."

"I see," said Himes. He extended his arm toward the bell-man, and when the boy moved forward, Himes patted him on the shoulders. The other security guard looked at Himes, then joined them as they moved toward the open elevator. Florian looked at the closing double-doors and exhaled through his nostrils.

He extended his hand toward Crazy Bob, who shook it, then towards Leal.

"What did you say your name was again?" Florian asked as they shook hands.

"I didn't say," Leal answered. "It's Leal. Sergeant Leal."

"Leal?" Florian said, blinking. "Francisco Leal?"

"That's right," Frank answered, thinking that he saw a momentary flicker of recognition in the other man's eyes. But he was sure he'd never met him before.

Florian rocked back on his heels and said, "This was, as I told them, a slight misunderstanding. An unfortunate incident. I've already checked it out." He leaned forward and said in a husky whisper, "No need to cause trouble for another copper, right?" He reached out and punched the down button with his index finger. When the doors to the second elevator popped open, Florian held up his arm against the door. "All we have left to do is to make sure everything's smoothed over, right?" He smiled. "Sheriff Shay doesn't need anything spoiling his fundraiser, now, does he?"

They got in and rode down to the first floor in silence. Florian nodded and moved off in the direction of Himes, the bellman, and the other security guard. Ryan said he'd go with him, "To make sure everything was copacetic."

"Who the hell is that asshole, and why is Ryan sucking up to him so much?" Leal said as the two of them walked away.

"You don't know him, Frank?" Crazy Bob asked, the muscles of his jaws bunching up. "He's I.A.D. One of the ones that took my dog away from me." He snorted. "Real funny him saying how he didn't want to cause no trouble for another copper, huh? Must be one of his asshole-buddies up in that room with some hooker, or something."

Yeah," Leal said. His cell went off. He glanced at the number and saw it was an emergency code to contact dispatch. He took out his radio and snapped on the volume, which they'd all lowered as they'd gone up on the man-with-the-gun call.

After identifying himself he asked what their traffic was. "You've got a homicide the 197th block of Central," the dispatcher's voice said. "Uniformed officers are standing by. Can you give an ETA?"

"Approximately five to ten minutes," Leal said. "Any suspect description?"

"No," came the reply. "Officers at the scene report that a body was found lying on the side of the road. Several gunshot wounds. Nothing further at this time."

"Sounds like a dump," Crazy Bob said.

"Aww, shit," Leal said. "Not another one."

31
ENLIGHTENING DIALOGUES

Leal waited until nine o'clock to call Linda LeVeille. She answered on the first ring with a crisp, "Investigations," but her voice changed to a soft purr after he told her who it was.

"Look, I know we had planned on lunch, babe," Leal said, "but I been up all night, and I'm running on coffee and no sleep."

"Oh?" she said. "Something break in the case?"

"No, I caught another one," Leal said. "A dump out on Central Avenue. Male black, several gunshot wounds to the head."

"Oooh. Sounds like it's gonna be another tough one, huh?"

"What's another unsolved murder to the guy who's saddled with the infamous Dick Forest case?" Leal said, mustering about as much humor as he could manage. "I'm still at the morgue waiting for my autopsy. The only break we have so far is that the victim had Raw Dog tattooed on his left forearm so we can probably get him IDed pretty quick. As soon as the autopsy's done, I'll print him, then get some sleep."

"Okay," she said. "You want me to try and get a sitter for later in case you feel like doing something?"

Leal rubbed the bridge of his nose with his thumb and forefinger.

"I'll call you," he said. "I still have to write up a preliminary on this one and make sure somebody runs his prints through AFIS as soon as possible."

"Sounds like you're in for a miserable day," she said.

"Yeah, well, the only saving grace of the whole thing is that I persuaded Ryan to make sure Card maintains that surveillance team on that actor dude for a few more days," he said. "Ryan's such a consummate ass-kisser that I have no doubt that he'll be able to accomplish that with no trouble."

Linda laughed. "Better him than you, right?"

"Yeah," Leal said. He thought about how much he liked the sound of her laugh. But it also made him realize that he was getting slap-happy. Time to hang up before he ended up putting his foot in his mouth. "Well, I'd better go see if they've started carving on my buddy yet."

"All right," she said. "I'll talk to you later then."

After hanging up Leal heaved a sigh and went back toward the autopsy room. He was dreading the smell that was sure to hit him as he opened the door. He continued breathing through his nose, knowing his senses would grow accustomed to the putrid odor. Doctor Gleason and Gavin were working on another body that was the one ahead of his. The technician flipped the corpse over on the stainless steel surface.

Raw Dog lay nude on another table. Leal slipped on rubber latex gloves and picked up the basket with the dead man's clothes in it. No wallet or IDs, no cash, except for some small change, and a pack of Kool cigarettes. Not much to go on. Dropping the clothes back in the container, Leal stood and ran his fingers over the forearm with the tattoo. Homemade. Probably stabbed out on some kitchen table or bathroom. He examined the body for any other telltale signs. The lids were halfway closed, exposing the bottom portions of lifeless brown eyes. They were a milky-brown. His lips had drawn back over his teeth in a desperate grimace. Leal pealed off the gloves, dropped them into a wastebasket, and took out his pen and notebook.

"We'll be ready for yours next, Officer," Dr. Gleason said. She smiled at Leal. "What happened to your finger?"

"Line of duty," he said. Then added with a smile, "Some guy bit me."

"Oh, my God. I hope you had a tetanus."

"Yeah, I did."

What's she doing working here? Leal wondered. She should be taking care of kids in a bright office somewhere.

"Oh shit," Dr. Gleason said, as her chart fell on the floor. "Nothing's going right for me today." She stooped to pick it up. "But at least I don't have to worry about this asshole biting me," she added with a giggle.

Maybe she is in the right place after all, Leal thought, and allowed himself time to grin.

Leal's cell woke him up. The first thing he did when he opened his eyes was roll over and glance at his bedside clock. Christ, it was seven-forty. He swung his feet off the bed and switched on the light. Shaking off the last vestiges of fatigue, he stood, stretched, and walked to the dresser to retrieve the cell. It was the office number with Crazy Bob's star behind it. Leal went to the phone and punched in the digits. Crazy Bob answered on the first ring.

"Yeah, Bob, it's Frank."

"Oh, hi, Sarge. I didn't wake ya up, did I?"

"Yeah, but I overslept anyway," Leal said. His head still felt a little fuzzy. "What's up? You run that victim's prints?"

"Sure did," Crazy Bob said. "And we got an ID. Marcellus R. Roberts, aka Raw Dog. Got the criminal history, and we're drawing up a warrant for the last known address now."

The name rang a bell with Leal. He blinked twice, trying to set his brain into motion.

"That sounds familiar," Leal said. "Where's he from?"

"Looks like the Heights," Crazy Bob answered. "I'm getting ready to check with the gang crimes unit."

"Yeah. And page Joe Smith. He should be working nights, but he was looking for a guy named Marcellus from that area in connection with a drive-by."

"Okay," Crazy Bob said. Then added, "You coming in?"

"Yeah, as soon as I shower and get something to eat," Leal told him. Maybe we can get a jump on one case, anyway, he thought, as he hung up and headed for the bathroom.

Joe Smith had seemed excited over the chance to search the dead Marcellus's apartment, in hopes that they might turn up something that would clear his drive-by case. Ryan had also showed up and agreed to come along to assist in a canvass of the neighborhood. In the car he told Leal that he'd talked to Lt. Card about the surveillance team earlier.

"And?" Leal asked.

"And, he's getting kind of antsy."

"Oh, Jesus Christ, Tom. That's the only decent lead I've got."

"I know, I know," Ryan said. "I convinced him to keep the team on him, but he cut it down by half."

"Shit."

"It was the best I could do, for Christ sake. It ain't my fucking fault."

Leal snorted and said nothing.

"Maybe something'll turn up soon," Ryan said.

It had better, Leal thought.

The search of Raw Dog's apartment turned up several things, including a stoned girlfriend, about thirty bags of crack, and a 9mm pistol that fit the description of the one Joe Smith's informant had told them was used in the drive-by. Smith was all-smiles as he dropped the gun into a plastic bag. Leal was smiling too, when his cell went off again. It was dispatch. She read off a number and told him to call the surveillance team assigned to Sax ASAP.

Leal felt a surge of hopefulness as he punched in the digits as quickly as he could.

"This is Sergeant Leal," he said into the phone. "What you got?"

"Yeah, Sarge, Vince Casey here," the other man said. "It may be nothing, but that actor guy we been shadowing . . . looks like he may be trying to score some dope. He got into his Firebird and drove to 159th and Pulaski. Met up with a couple of brothers and then followed them to a house in Harvey. They're all still inside now, but this area is shit. Lots of drugs."

"Where you at now?"

Casey gave him the address. "My partner's watching the back."

"We'll be right there," Leal said. "Keep an eyeball on him."

Leal drove like a madman to the surveillance team's location. A few of the turns caused Crazy Bob to take a white-knuckled grip on the dashboard, but he said nothing. They pulled up behind the dark black sedan of the surveillance team. Leal got out and went up to the vehicle, surprised to see only one person sitting in the passenger seat.

"Hi, I'm Frank Leal," he said, hopping in behind the wheel.

"Vince Casey," the other man said. They shook hands.

"What we got, Sarge, is that brownstone apartment building right there. Looks to be boarded up, but a lot of the local crackheads use it for a smoking house. Our boy drove over and waited in front till two brothers drove up in that blue Caddie there." He pointed to the dark blue Escalade parked in front of Sax's red Firebird. "Then they all went inside together."

"How long they been in there?" Leal asked.

"About ten, fifteen tops," Casey said. "When I called you."

"You said somebody's watching the back?" Leal asked.

"Yeah," Casey said. "My partner." He picked up his radio mike and said, "Hey, Paul, you got anything?"

"Nothing on my end," the voice said.

"Just the two of you?" Leal asked.

Casey nodded his head. "They cut us back."

"All right," said Leal, silently cursing Card for not maintaining a full complement of officers on the surveillance. "Here's the plan . . ."

Casey touched his arm. A well-built black man in a short leather jacket trotted down the front steps of the building and moved toward the Escalade. There was something vaguely familiar about the car, but Leal couldn't recall what it was.

"Shit," Leal said. "That one of 'em?"

"Yeah," Casey answered. He was peering through a small pair of binoculars now. "The plate's SPEARS INC." Leal scribbled it down on the tablet on the seat. "You want to stop it?"

Leal thought for a moment. "No, not with our target inside. Let's sit on the house and wait for him to come out. Then we'll grab his ass on something and hopefully catch him with some dope. My partner and I will set up down the block. What frequency you guys on?"

After returning to his own car, Leal and Crazy Bob drove around the block and parked down the street. They now had a unit facing each way in front and one watching the alley. Both men slumped down in the seat to be less conspicuous. Crazy Bob had a baseball cap pulled over his bald head. Although their car was an unmarked squad, Leal knew that the hardcore residents of the neighborhood would have little trouble picking it out as a police car. He wished that he'd had time to go pick up a surveillance vehicle like the one that he and Joe Smith had used last week.

"You're pretty quiet, Sarge," Crazy Bob said. "Think maybe this is it?"

"It's as close as we've come lately," Leal said. His mind raced trying to speculate what they might be able to gain if they stopped Sax and found some crack. Maybe they could lever him into talking about Dick Forest. He'd prayed for a break and knew that if he got one here he couldn't afford to make any mistakes.

"How we gonna handle this once he leaves?" Crazy Bob asked.

"We'll just have to play it by ear," Leal said. The stream of questions was starting to irritate him. God, he missed Ollie. They were always on the same wavelength.

"You know," Crazy Bob said, "my whole career I always dreamed about getting into dicks. And now that I'm here, I ain't got a clue on what to do."

Leal exhaled with a chuckle.

"Well, that makes two of us then," he said.

"No, I'm serious, Sarge," Crazy Bob said. "I know you been carrying me. That's why you called that Forest Preserve detective instead of me the other night. I can't blame you. I guess I just wasn't cut out for Investigations."

Leal felt a twinge of pity. "That's bullshit. You're my partner. We work together, and if we fail, we'll do that together too. And the reason I called Linda the other night had nothing to do with my not wanting to work with you."

"Really?" Crazy Bob asked, his mouth hanging open like an expectant puppy.

"Yeah," Leal said. "It was a rape case and I felt it would be better to have a female officer talk to the victim, that's all." Leal thought that if he told any more lies he was going to have to go to confession next Sunday.

"So . . . you don't have any reservations about working with me then?" Crazy Bob asked.

"No. None at all," Leal said, hoping he sounded sincere. It was definitely time to visit the confessional.

"But what about me not knowing what to do?"

Leal considered his answer, then said, "Just follow your gut, Bob. You'll do all right."

"Man, you don't know how good that makes me feel," Crazy Bob said. He folded his arms behind his head and stretched out as best he could in his slumped position. "You're the best partner I had since they took Brutus away from me."

"That was your dog?" Leal asked, grateful for a change in the subject.

"Yeah," Crazy Bob said with a wistful sigh. "Best damn partner a man could ask for. Saved my life more than once. I remember one time we were on this traffic stop when this car load of shitheads all bailed out and tried to jump me. I was wrestling with one of them, trying to get my piece out, when I felt this other one sneak up and start to unsnap my pistol. I managed to grab hold of it, but this other guy starts belting me in the face. I could only fight him with one hand, cause I had to keep the other one on my gun. But I managed to reach out with my thumb and press the button-opener on my belt that lowered the back window." A huge smile spread over his face. "Brutus was out that window in a flash and tore into those guys. Man, he had both of them chewed up in a matter of seconds. We used to work that scenario in training all the time, see." He stopped and nodded his head, as if envisioning the scene once more. "I'll tell you, that night I gave him the biggest, thickest steak I could find."

"Hey, Sarge," Casey's voice came over the radio. "Second suspect, small male black just exited alone." Both men waited for the next words. "He's looking around. He's entering the Firebird."

"He alone?" Leal asked.

"Yeah," Casey replied. "Want us to move on it?"

Leal thought for a second. "Negative," he said. "Maintain surveillance on house for main suspect. We'll tag the Firebird."

Down the block he saw the inverted lights flip open as the Pontiac pulled away from the curb. Leal did a U-turn and fell right behind it. The left turn signal activated on the Firebird. Leal stayed behind it.

"Let's grab him as soon as he turns," he said. "He's got to know who we are by now."

"Want me to call for a marked unit?"

"No time," Leal said. He nodded toward the floorboards.

Crazy Bob grunted and reached down for the red light. Both cars turned onto another side street. Leal grabbed the mike and told Casey that they were stopping the suspect on the next block. The Pontiac turned again, left this time, at the next intersection. Leal nodded towards the dashboard and flipped the toggle switch as Crazy Bob stuck the now oscillating light onto the metal plate right behind the windshield. The Firebird continued for half a block, then pulled to the curb.

"Hope he doesn't try to rabbit on us," Leal said.

Leal and Crazy Bob both got out and approached the car, Leal going to the driver's side, and Crazy Bob drifting up to the right rear door. Both men had their guns drawn, but held the weapons down by their legs.

"What you stoppin' me fo'?" the driver asked, his head bobbling up toward Leal, then straight ahead. He still had both hands on the wheel.

"You didn't use your turn signal back there," Leal said, trying to sound low-key. "Let me see your license."

The black guy snorted but took his hands off the wheel and reached for his wallet. He made a project of looking through it.

"Who's car is this?" Leal asked. "Yours?"

"No, it's my auntie's," the guy said, still poking through the many folded scraps of paper in his wallet.

"What's your name?" Leal asked.

"They call me Sweetpea. Pea for short."

"Tell you what, Pea," Leal said, grabbing the door handle and pulling it open. "Step out and give your real name. I'll just run a quick check on you. You ain't got any warrants, do you?"

"Me?" Sweetpea said, freezing his glance up at Leal. "No, I'm cool."

He stepped out. Leal pointed to the rear of the car where Crazy Bob was standing. "Put your hands on the car."

Sweetpea looked at him.

"Now!" Leal shouted, grabbing the small man's shirt and pushing him over the back fender. Crazy Bob moved forward and holstered his weapon. He grabbed Sweetpea's shirt, and Leal stepped back. Crazy Bob adjusted the smaller man's position so that Sweetpea was spread at an oblique angle over the trunk, arms outstretched. Lemack's big hands moved over the other man's body, feeling, squeezing, probing. He felt along the waist area and touched the hard metal along the inside of Sweetpea's belt.

"Looks like a ten-thirty-two, Frank," Crazy Bob said. He handed the stainless-steel Walther PPK over to Leal, who now trained his gun on Sweetpea's head.

"Don't fucking move," Leal said, enunciating each word.

He snapped the safety on the Walther and dropped it into his jacket pocket.

Crazy Bob had ahold of the small man's left arm and bent it behind him. Securing the handcuff in place over the slim wrist, Crazy Bob repeated the motion with Sweetpea's right hand. Then the cop moved him around to the rear of the car and down over the trunk.

"I'll call for a hook," Leal said, going up in front of the car and pulling out his radio.

"Hey, man, this ain't right," Sweetpea said. "I didn't do nothing, man. You cold-blooded."

"Shut up," the big bald motherfucker said.

"Yeah, shut up," a higher, forced falsetto voice added. Sweetpea suddenly saw the painted features on the white leather glove hovering before his face.

"What the fuck is that?" Sweetpea said.

"That's Oscar," the big cop said. "And I'm Crazy Bob."

"What you doin'?" Sweetpea asked. This motherfucker was crazy.

"I'm following my gut," Crazy Bob said.

"Yeah, he's following his gut, dickbrain. And the man told you to shut up," Oscar said. The small eyes seemed to stare into Sweetpea's own, and the red lips seemed to tighten into a thin line. The gloved hand canted toward the little man, then rotated back toward Crazy Bob. "This guy's a real asshole, ain't he?"

"Sure looks that way," Crazy Bob said.

The glove turned back toward Sweetpea's face a few inches in front of his eyes.

"You know, this ain't his auntie's car," Oscar said.

"I didn't think so," Crazy Bob said.

"Who's car is it really?" Oscar asked.

"I already told you," Sweetpea said.

"Don't lie to me, asshole." The glove moved closer to the small man's eyes, so that he had to arch his head back. Swaying there for a moment, Oscar tilted up toward Crazy Bob.

"You know what you ought to do?" the falsetto voice said. "You ought to just blow this fucker away."

Sweetpea jerked as if he'd been slapped.

"Just put a couple in his head, and loosen the cuffs," Oscar continued. "Say that he got loose, and tried to grab your piece."

315

The gloved hand turned toward the Latino cop, then back. "The Sarge'll back you up. He's seen the gun. Do everybody a favor. Shoot him."

"Hey, man, you crazy . . ." Sweetpea said.

The glove still loomed in front of his face.

"Shut up!" Oscar yelled.

"Yeah, shut up," Crazy Bob added.

"Hey, look man . . ." Sweetpea's voice cracked on the edge on sheer panic.

"Hey," Oscar said. "I got a better idea. Don't shoot him in the head. That'd be too easy on him. Shoot him in the spine, right below the base of the skull. That way he'd be alive for a while, but he wouldn't be able to move or talk. He'll die nice and slow."

Crazy Bob grinned. His hand rolled downward, until Oscar's painted orbs seemed to stare directly into the small man's eyes, the cold steel of the big Glock .45 pressed against the back of his neck. He screamed.

"Hey, Sarge! Sarge! This motherfucker's gonna kill me!"

Even to him, his voice sounded like a pitiful whine.

The other cop, the Sarge, was going through the car. He looked toward them, frowned, and looked away.

"Oooh, you shouldn't have done that. Say your prayers, motherfucker," Oscar growled.

The square block of the Glock's barrel pressed tighter against Sweetpea's neck. He screamed again.

"Okay, okay, wait. I got something to trade," he said with rapid desperation. "I got something to trade."

"What?" Crazy Bob asked, leaning forward.

"This car . . ." Sweetpea said. "It ain't my auntie's."

"No shit, Sherlock," Oscar said.

"The dude it belong to," Sweatpea continued, "he in the building back there."

"Tell me something I don't know," Crazy Bob said.

"He dead, but I didn't do him," Sweetpea continued. "It was Taji. He just told me to dump the ride and the gun."

The big cop leaned close.

"You better not be bulljivin' me, boy," he said.

"I'm not," Sweetpea said. "I swear to God I'm not. I'll take you to him if you want. Just please, don't shoot me. Don't shoot me."

Crazy Bob straightened up and called for Leal. Sweetpea felt a surge of relief as he felt the pressure of the Glock fade from the back of his neck, and he thought he was gonna piss his pants. Then the painted glove was in his face again.

"You just better be telling the truth, Pea," the gloved motherfucker said. "Or I'll be back."

32
EXTRA INNINGS

Hart lowered the shield down to the floor and looked around. Their second raid of the week and their second blowout. Nothing. No dope, no money, not even any suspects this time. The entire house, which showed all the earmarks of a typical crack-house, had been picked clean and evacuated before they arrived to break down the door. What made this even more inconceivable was that less than twenty hours before, when they'd done their scouting and threat assessment, it looked to be extremely busy. And the warrant was not even five hours old. At least the raid itself had gone like clockwork, but that didn't seem to help the spirits of the team.

"Man, we're striking out more than the Cubs," Elvis said. He had made the breach this time and absently nudged the battering ram with the toe of his boot.

Blackjack, who had helped breach the door and was the designated "tool man," stood in the uncarpeted living room leaning on the chrome Halligan tool. He got a sly grin on his face, then glanced around.

"Hey," he said. "Anybody check this?" He moved toward a television set that was on a small table. Lifting the bar, he brought the chiseled end down on the plastic rear shell of the TV, and sent it crashing to the floor. Big John Doscolvich and Sergeant Turner came running into the room. The two men looked at the shattered television, then to each of the officers standing in the room.

"What the hell?" Doscolvich growled.

"Rats, Lieu," Blackjack said. "Big one ran right by. Knocked the set off the stand."

Doscolvich scowled at him, letting his expression show his disapproval. "Listen," he said. "I'm just as discouraged as the rest of you. But it ain't our fault our intel was bad. Again."

"Again seems to be the operative word," TC said. "We keep getting shut out, Big John."

"Another whitewash," Lobo added.

Doscolvich started to say something when one of the containment guys called him on the radio. He adjusted his mouthpiece and barked a reply.

"A couple of detectives are calling on main band for backup a few blocks from here," the containment man said. "They got an apartment building that needs clearing. Supposed to be a shooting victim inside."

"Well tell 'em the cavalry's on the way," Doscolvich said, a big grin stretching across his face. "Containment, stay in place until the search team is done. Buzz, you're in charge here." The stout sergeant nodded. "React team, form up at the van. The game just went into extra innings."

Leal was out of breath from running all the way back to the surveillance site. He'd left the squad-car at the traffic stop with Lemack, so that he could guard their prisoner and wait for the tow truck. Leal didn't like leaving Crazy Bob alone with a prisoner back there, but the big man smiled and told him to go ahead.

"If he gives us any trouble we'll stuff him in the trunk," Crazy Bob had said. Leal wondered why he'd used the plural pronoun, but Sweetpea looked scared to death, so he wouldn't be a problem. As he was briefing Casey and his partner, the van pulled up with the Special Response Team. A big guy rolled down the window on the passenger side and addressed Leal. "Doscolvich, SRT," he said. "You called for a backup in taking down a place?"

"Yeah," Leal said, wondering if Hart would be with them. "It's that brown one right over there. We got one plainclothes on the back side, and the two of us here."

"Just stay on the perimeter and let us handle it," Doscolvich said. He brought a pair of binoculars up and studied the structure as he talked. "Run the whole thing by me again. There's possibly a shooting victim inside?"

"Right," Leal said. "A white guy named Bill Sax. The suspect we stopped on the next block says that another male black shot him and left him in there."

"So we don't know if he's still alive or not, is that it?" Doscolvich said.

"That's about it, Sarge," Leal answered. "It's unknown if there are any other suspects in the place or not, but I figure it justifies exigent circumstances."

"It's lieutenant," Doscolvich said. "But you're right about the exigency." He turned and shouted over his shoulder, "Okay, people, we've got an unknown situation here. We'll enter in the same formation with the exception of the breach. Blackjack, you hit the door since you've got a penchant for breaking things tonight. Watch your asses people. Clear and cover. That's the name of the game." The big head turned toward Leal. "You guys stay at the front door. We'll enter and clear. We'll call you when it's secure."

"Okay," Leal said, wondering just how badly they were going to mess up the crime scene if Sax was already dead. But there was still that slight chance that he wasn't, and if not, maybe Leal could get something from him. A dying declaration would be nice. A dying confession would be even better.

The rear doors of the van opened and ten people clad in

camouflaged BDUs jumped out and assembled behind it. Leal noticed that one of them was Hart.

"Hi, Frank," she said.

"Ollie," he said. "Look at you. You look just like Rambo."

"Naw, Rambette," the well-built dark-haired guy with the battering ram said with a grin.

"She's got a lot better build than Stallone," another one added, his tone salacious.

"Let's go!" the huge lieutenant grunted.

In unison, they did a quick jog across the sidewalk and turned up the steps in front of the dilapidated brownstone. The dark-haired guy ran up the porch steps with the ram, as a black guy passed him, and stayed slightly ahead of him. As they reached the top, the black guy ripped open the screen door and held it back, as the white guy planted his feet and let the ram swing into the solid wood of the front door.

Leal and Casey ran up the stairs as they watched the last of the SWAT team vanish through the door frame, their flashlights sending clear beams sweeping through the interior.

It was dark now, and Leal realized he hadn't even noticed that before. It had seemed to change from day to night in a few seconds. Shouting and muffled footsteps came from inside the house. He could hear them proceeding up the stairs to the second floor. More crashes as doors were kicked open. Shouts of "Clear!" could be heard from various points inside.

It took them a little over twelve minutes to secure the entire building. Doscolvich explained that they were going slow due to the nature of the call, but Leal couldn't help but be impressed at the precision with which they'd moved. The raids he remembered from his time with MEG had been Chinese fire drills compared with this one. Hart came up to him, taking off her helmet and shaking her head. Her blond hair, now loosening from the French braid, stuck out at odd angles in rag-tag fashion.

"You guys looked fantastic," Leal said, smiling. Hart's lips-only smile looked grim.

"A lot better than your buddy in there looks," she said, cocking her thumb back over her shoulder. "Several shots to the head. Better call for an evidence tech. Looks like you've got another one, Frank."

"Shit," said Leal. "I was hoping to talk to that guy before he expired. He was that actor I told you about."

"On the Dick Forest case?" Hart asked. "Was he your main lead?"

Leal nodded. "He's nobody's lead now."

"I'm sorry, Frank."

He blew out a tired breath.

"Hey, what's another murder between friends," he said.

33
THE OTHER OPTION

Rick's flight to Minneapolis had left at seven-thirty, which gave Hart more time than she wanted to get back to Maywood to have her meeting with the Chief and Captain Florian at ten.

She couldn't believe that Rick was leaving. . . . Giving up everything here just because his stupid brother might cop a plea and get to do federal time. She hit the steering wheel as she pulled into the massive parking lot adjacent to headquarters. Or was Rick simply trying to move on? To nudge her out of his life? Maybe he hadn't fallen for her quite as hard as she had for him.

Oh, God, she thought as she started up the steps to go into the building. I'll be glad when I'm through with all this.

Inside, the work-day was already several hours old, and people were bustling about, moving down the hallways with that mid-morning cup of coffee that would fuel their fingers for another hour or so. At the Chief's office Hart noticed that Janetta was murmuring into her cell phone, her computer screen lit with a long script. Janetta smiled at Hart and told the person on the other end to hold on. She opened a drawer and put something inside. Hart couldn't tell what it was, but the abruptness of the secretary's movement startled her.

"You can go right in, Olivia," Janetta said. "They're expecting you."

"What can I expect?" Hart said, hoping to get a little girl-to-girl hint of the Chief's mood.

"Expect the best," Janetta answered with a smile. "I always do."

She went back to her phone, and Hart reached for the doorknob.

When she entered, both the Chief and Florian looked up. "Your secretary said you were expecting me," Hart said in way of mitigation for entering without knocking.

"No problem," Chief Burton said, exhaling some smoke as he stood up. He stubbed out his cigarette and flipped closed a folder on the top of his desk. His smile looked tight and forced. "Come in, sit down." He indicated a chair in front of the desk. Florian's chair had been pulled around to the side. Hart sat down and looked at both men.

"We were just going over the reports from last night," Burton said. "I just finished Doscolvich's summary. From the gist of what I read, I gather it was another flop."

"Well, Chief, the raids went rather well," Hart said. She hadn't intended her reply to be as flippant as it sounded. Burton scowled at her for a moment.

"Raids?" he said, stressing the S. "I can only recall approving one for last night." The area between his eyebrows crinkled.

"We assisted the Investigative Division," Hart said, feeling that she'd suddenly been dropped into deep water. "It was a shooting victim inside an abandoned building." She spoke slowly, choosing her words with the utmost care, but she wasn't sure what to say or not to say. What was it that had upset the Chief so much? "We'd just completed the warrant and the detectives called for a backup to enter a building. We were just a few blocks away, so we went and helped them."

"How come I didn't see that in Doscolvich's report?" Burton demanded. He turned toward Florian and gave him a sharp look.

"Perhaps it's an oversight," Hart said. "I'll be glad to call the lieutenant and—"

"No," the Chief said, cutting her off. "Remember, as far as the SWAT team and the rest of world are concerned, these meetings never take place."

"You haven't told anyone else about them, have you, Olivia?" Florian asked. His use of her first name sounded like an invasion. She did not want to be friends with this man.

"Of course not," she said. "I don't know what I was thinking when I said that."

"Focus is important in a special assignment like this," Florian said. He smiled, but his teeth still had that feral look to them.

"Yes," she said. "Sorry."

"Well, regarding the warrant," Burton said. "What did you observe? Any irregularities? Anything suspicious?"

"Actually, no, sir," Hart said. "We entered the house and it was unoccupied. It almost looked like it had been," she paused, searching for the right word, "evacuated. We saw empty bottles of liquor and some half-eaten pizza, but no money or drugs at all."

"Could there have been some money or drugs laying around that one of the entry team might have grabbed?" the Chief asked. The hopeful expectation in his voice convinced her that he was an idiot, never having gone on one of these raids. She felt like telling him that she wasn't as stupid as he was.

"I really don't see how that would have been possible, sir," Hart said.

"How about the second raid?" Florian asked. "Anything on that one?"

"As far as suspicious activity, no," she answered. "We entered the apartment and cleared the building. There was a homicide victim in an upstairs bedroom. He'd been shot several times in the head."

"Then what did you do?" Florian asked, leaning forward.

"We turned everything over to the detectives on the scene and left," Hart said.

"Anybody pick up anything, handle anything in the house?" Burton said.

"No, sir," Hart said, shaking her head. "The building was deserted. It didn't look like anybody had lived there for a while."

The Chief pursed his lips then reached for the phone. He punched in a number, frowning as he looked at the receiver.

There was an intercom on the corner of the desk, and Burton leaned close to it and pressed the button.

"Janetta, get Lieutenant Doscolvich on the line, please," he said. "If he's not at his office, beep him." He hung up and muttered, "When you're off the phone that is." Smiling over at Hart, he asked, "Everything else going all right?"

"Yes, sir," Hart said. Now what was he trying to do, she wondered. A Father Flanagan imitation?

"Fine, fine," he said, standing up. "I guess that pretty much concludes our meeting today. Keep us posted as you have been doing."

"And keep your eyes open for any irregularities," Florian said. "On anyone's part."

Hart stood up. "I will, sir."

"You'll have another chance tonight," the Chief said. "I've authorized another raid. Let's see if we can get something on this one."

Hart nodded and went out of the office.

The two men looked at each other after the door had closed.

"What do you think?" the Chief asked.

Florian blew out a long breath through puckered lips. "I don't know," he said. "It's almost too strange. There have been entirely too many misses for something not to be going down. Something's rotten. Somebody's dirty. They've got to be pocketing it. There's just too much intelligence that couldn't have been wrong. We should be making three or four times the seizures we are. If you compare this year with last year . . ."

"I know, I know," Burton said. He heaved a sigh and shook a cigarette out of his pack.

"Something's going to have to break if we're going to stick to our planned schedule," Florian said.

"Ahhh, we should be all right," Burton said, holding the flame from his lighter to the end of the cigarette. He took a long drag, then said, "It'd be nice to have something next week, after the fundraiser, to show us as reform-minded."

"Nothing will do that better than burning a couple of dirty cops," Florian said with a sly grin. "So are you ready to consider the other option?"

Burton squinted at him through the haze of cigarette smoke before answering.

"You're sure you can get it set up in time?" the Chief asked.

"It's already in place, just waiting for your approval," Florian said.

The trace of a smile tugged at the corner of Burton's mouth as he exhaled smoke through both nostrils.

"Okay," he said after a moment of reflection. "Let's do it."

The preliminary interview of Sweetpea, aka Jerimiah Krump, had lasted well into the wee hours. Leal had called a halt to it at around two, telling Sweetpea to get some sleep, and that they could talk more tomorrow. The kid seemed to agree, as he sat there smoking cigarettes. Leal had him locked in on a statement admitting his complicity in Sax's murder, which Frank figured would be the lever to get whatever further cooperation that was needed. The kid had seemed eager to talk, as long as "Crazy Bob" was kept away from him, he'd said. Leal didn't know why Sweetpea was so afraid of Lemack, but he didn't question it as long as the suspect was flipping.

Now, after several hours of much needed sleep, he was ready to resume.

The major thing that bothered Leal was the lack of vital information on this Taji dude—the man that Sweetpea said had pulled the trigger. The name was all the little asshole could tell him. A black guy named Taji. He did body-guarding and executions for the Soul Gangstas. And he knew karate. Leal had told Crazy Bob to make the autopsy this morning, then to check the street-name file. He wanted to sew this one up in a hurry. There were too many open homicide files on his desk right now, and he needed a break, especially since his main lead in the Dick Forest case had become one of those open files.

He was mulling over his tactic for the opening interview with Sweetpea when his phone rang. He picked it up and said, "Leal, Investigations."

"Hey, it's Roxie, man," the voice at the other end said.

"What do you need, Roxie? I'm real busy."

"Man, I callin' to help *you.*"

Leal took a deep breath then said, "That's a familiar tune."

"Look, man, I ain't playin' this time," Roxie said. His voice was without the usual lilt of humor. "I gots to talk to you 'bout something."

"So talk."

"Don't know if you heard or not. My nephew got killed. Marcellus Roberts. He my sister's boy."

"Yeah, I'm working the case." Leal sat up in his chair. "I didn't know he was your nephew. I'm sorry."

"Yeah, well, thanks, man. I know he mixed up in some deep shit, but they didn't have no cause to go off and waste him like that."

"Who's they?" Leal asked.

"The S-Gs, man. Who you think?"

328

"How do you know this?"

"Look, I just know, all right," Roxie said. "Word came down that he was skimmin', but I know that's a bunch of bullshit, man. This is family, man. They had no call to do that." His voice cracked as he spoke.

"Can you meet me someplace and we can talk?"

"Okay, but I'm gonna go lookin' around some first," Roxie said. "I'm still in pretty tight with a lot of the old timers, from my days in Stateville, and they have me do things from time to time, you understand. So I'll do some checkin' and get back to you, okay, Leal?"

"You've got my cell number, don't you?" Leal asked.

"Yeah, I got it, man," Roxie said. "And I mean it. I really wanna do these motherfuckers for this." His tone was laced with an indignant rectitude.

"Just get me something I can use," Leal told him.

After hanging up he called over to the lockup and asked to have Sweetpea brought to one of the interrogation rooms.

He then beeped Crazy Bob to see where he was and waited. At least he wouldn't have to argue with Card about keeping the surveillance team on Sax anymore. And if he could close this one quickly, maybe he could get the prick to give him some more help looking for Gladis. She was the only lead left in the Dick Forest case. Linda would be counting on him to help close her case too. He had a lot riding on finding that damn whore.

When Crazy Bob didn't call back, Leal figured his partner must be stuck in traffic or something. Not that he would use him on the interview anyway. He was better off doing it alone. He really missed Hart. Suspects, witnesses, everybody seemed anxious to talk to her. He wondered how she was doing with her new assignment, and her "Rick problems." She'd looked great last night, he thought. And as far as the other problem, maybe it was better that she wasn't around to cry on his shoulder right now. He had too many things closing in on him as it was.

He brought the new pack of cigarettes into the interview room and tossed it to Sweetpea. Sitting down across from him, Leal let the small man take a few drags before he started talking.

"You get something to eat?" Leal asked.

"McDonald's," Sweetpea said with a smile. It was great how simple things were when your future was limited to four gray walls.

Leal re-advised Sweetpea of his rights, since this interview was technically on a new day. After the little man signed the new waiver form, Leal leaned back in his chair and asked him to recount the shooting again.

"What I gotta do that fo'?" Sweetpea asked. "I told you everything last night."

"Well, I want to know if you remember any more about this Taji guy. I'm having a hard time finding his real name."

Sweetpea thought for a moment, then shook his head.

"All I know him by is Taji," he said. "I ain't bulljivin'. He a bad dude. Fights in them full-contact karate fights all the time. Been in prison too."

Leal nodded. "Tell me again about when Bill Sax got shot."

"Bill Sax? Oh, that white dude?"

Leal nodded again. He'd purposely used the name to test the consistency of Sweetpea's claim during the previous interview that he didn't know the dead white guy by name.

"Ain't much to tell," Sweetpea said, sucking on the cigarette, then using it to light another as the ash burned down to the filter. "Me and Taji met up with him outside that house and went inside. He thought he was gonna score some shit. Taji told me before we went in that he was gonna ice him. I was supposed to take the dude's car and park it with the keys in it after

I got rid of the piece."

"Where were you gonna dump the gun?" Leal asked.

Sweetpea grinned. "I usually take 'em up to the Second District. They always got one of them gun collection things going on. You know, no questions asked, all you do is turn in the gun, and they give you the cash. One time they were givin' away new Air Jordans."

"Pretty neat set-up," Leal said. "Let the cops dispose of it for you and get paid all at the same time."

Sweetpea smiled and blew out some smoke.

"Why did Taji shoot this dude?" Leal asked.

Sweetpea shrugged. "He didn't say. I just figured it was orders from the top."

"The top, meaning who?"

Sweetpea looked down, hugging himself with his crossed arms across his dirty green tee shirt that had *BROTHERS OF THE STRUGGLE* printed on the front. Leal just kept looking at him.

"Who you think, man," Sweetpea said.

"Otha Spears?" Leal said.

Sweetpea nodded.

"Why would Otha order a hit on some white doper?" Leal asked.

Sweetpea shrugged again.

Leal was about to ask another question when he heard a knock on the door. Figuring it might be a good time for a break, Leal stood up and told Sweetpea that he'd be back in a few minutes.

"Can you bring me a pop?" Sweetpea asked.

Leal told him he would and went out the door, glad to get out of the smoky room, wondering now how he'd ever enjoyed the smell of cigarette smoke before he quit. Ryan was leaning against the wall grinning. He had an unopened can of Pepsi in one hand and an unlighted cigarette in the other.

"Guess what?" he said.

"Quit playing games," Leal said. "I'm ass-deep in homicides."

"Well the shit just got a little bit deeper," Ryan said. "That Cadillac Escalade that you had the type three out on . . . it's now listed as having been stolen yesterday morning."

"What?" Leal said. "That's bullshit. I ran the plate last night and it came up clear."

"Well, our buddy Mr. Spears reported it stolen, stating that he didn't realize it was missing until today," Ryan said, grinning.

"That son-of-a-bitch," Leal said. "He always seems to stay a step ahead of us, no matter what."

"And there's more." Ryan paused to gauge Leal's reaction. "The shitbird's lawyer is outside demanding to talk to his client."

"His lawyer?" Leal said.

Ryan nodded. He stuck the cigarette in his mouth and lit it. "Ronald Hollingsworth III," he said, punctuating his statement with an exaggerated frown.

"How the fuck did he get notified that the kid was here?" Leal asked. He glanced at the arrest log. "It don't look like he's made any phone calls."

"Maybe somebody gave him one and didn't log it," Ryan offered. "You gonna let him talk to him or what?"

"Who, the lawyer?" Leal asked. He thought for a moment, then turned back to the interview room, grabbing the Pepsi from Ryan's hand. "Not if he don't want to see him," he whispered.

Leal walked in and handed the can to Sweetpea, then sat down across from him. He considered his options, then decided that he'd taken this interview about as far as he could at the moment.

"So you want to call anybody?" Leal asked.

Sweetpea shook his head and took a drink from the can.

"You want to call a lawyer or anything?" Leal said.

Sweetpea shook his head again.

"Well, there's one outside here to see you," Leal said. "You want to talk to him?"

Sweetpea's head jutted forward and he swallowed hard. His eyes seemed to glaze over.

"Well, you want to talk to him or not?" Leal said.

"Who is it?" Sweetpea asked. "What's his name?"

"Hollingsworth," Leal said.

Sweetpea seemed to recoil from the sound of the name, then slumped.

"Look," Leal said. "It's up to you if you want to see him or not. I'm not going to tell you you can't, but if we're gonna deal, it's gonna have to be not."

"It don't matter none, now," Sweetpea said. "They know I snitched. I'm a dead man."

34
THE SET-UP

"This is our target," the heavy-set, balding guy said, showing them a slide of a rather seedy-looking structure he called the Evergreen Motel. He'd been introduced by Commander Bailey as Special Agent Devis of the DEA. Hart knew that multi-agency assists were quite common because each agency worked the same areas, guarding informants and targets until the periodic meetings during which the planned raids were set. Then it was determined if any other agency was involved, so as to avoid an inadvertent SNAFU. She also knew the team had done raids with the DEA before. This time, however, the agent was not known to any of them, claiming to be from the northern area of the city.

Special Agent Devis stepped forward and used a pointer to indicate rooms on both levels. "Our source has told us that the Soul Gangsta street gang has rented rooms on each of these floors. Large quantities of both drugs and money are believed to be in the rooms." He flipped to the next slide. It was another view of the motel. "As you can see, these rooms have only one door, one entrance. However, there are windows on the rear walls." The next slide showed the rear view of the motel. A long, fenced corridor approximately four-feet-wide ran along the back of the dilapidated structure. Even from the slide it was obvious that the area hadn't been cleaned in several years.

"Our approach will be from the north entrance here," he said, using the pointer. "We'd like two men per room. The containment team should be spread out back here and at these points to prevent any suspects from escaping."

"Which rooms are we gonna hit?" Marcus asked.

"These three rooms here," he said, indicating the upper level. "And these two down in this corner. Lieutenant, do you have anything to add?"

Doscolvich stood up and ambled toward the front of the room. "Okay, Buzz, you take this section at the corner here," he said, using his laser pointer to send a red dot to the northern section of the motel. "I'll be on this side." He indicated the opposite section. "Mike and Dick, you guys will be responsible for containment in the rear, here, and here." The red dot floated over the screen. "Special Agent Devis's men here will move in and conduct the search. And take charge of any prisoners, after we've secured them. His men are going to stay back to avoid any problems, since we don't know them by sight."

"My people have already been deployed," Devis added. "They're waiting for you. I'll contact them by radio and let them know when we're coming."

"Assignments are as follows," Doscolvich said, stepping in front so that part of the illuminated slide spilled over the left arm and shoulder of his fatigues. "Ollie and Blackjack, room twenty-two. Ray and Marcus, room twenty-three. Linc and PJ, room twenty-four. Those are all on the upper level." He indicated which room was which. "On the lower level, Elvis and TC will take room eleven, and Art and Lobo will take room twelve."

"May I say a few words, John?" Commander Bailey said, stepping forward. He grinned, showing yellowish teeth in the dim light of the overhead projector. Most of the older veterans of the department referred to Bailey as an "empty holster" who had avoided street duty his whole career. Now, in middle age, and after marching up the ranks by virtue of clout, favors, and ass-kissing, he liked to try and portray himself as an experienced street veteran.

Bailey cleared his throat with a "Harumph," then began speaking. "I don't need to remind any of you that this motel, as disreputable as it appears, is still a legitimate place of business."

Someone in the back of the room did an exaggerated imitation of Bailey's throat-clearing sound. Bailey paused and exhaled, then continued after licking his lips. "There may be innocent civilians in the area, men, women, and children, so use extreme care with your firearms." He paused and the throat-clearing imitator struck again. Bailey looked up, then continued. "And we expect that minimal damage will be inflicted on the motel itself. For that reason, only sledgehammers and Chicago-bars will be used." Chicago-bar was the street-cop slang term for Halligan tools, and several team members smirked when Bailey used it.

"So you more worried about us messing up some doors than getting in fast to avoid getting shot?" Marcus asked.

Bailey's face reddened. "Listen, I've personally inspected the doors on this establishment and they are not that sturdy."

"And just how'd you do that, Commander?" Blackjack whispered. "Take one of the administrative secretaries with you?"

"What was that?" Bailey scowled.

There was no reply. He cleared his throat again, which brought a smattering of snickers from several team members. Bailey strode over and flipped on the light switch. Doscolvich, who was standing next to Bailey, seemed to be having difficulty keeping a grin off his face. "As I said," Bailey continued, his eyes scanning the room, "the department will be liable for all damages done to the property, and individual officers will be held responsible for any unnecessary breakages. Any questions?"

Again, there was no reply. "Well, regrettably, I won't be accompanying you men out there to the field," Bailey said. "But good luck to all of you, and come home safe." He turned and left. Once he was out of the room someone blew a raspberry.

"All right," Doscolvich said, "let's head for the van. Buzz and Dick, you guys take one of the unmarked squads and come in from the north side. I'll pull the van in from the south."

The team members got to their feet and began gathering up their gear.

"Mama?" Chocolate said after her mother answered the phone. "It's me."

"Where you at, child?" Mrs. Brown said. "The police was here lookin' for you last week."

It felt so good for Chocolate to hear her mama's voice, but she had no time. "I know, mama, but it ain't nothing."

"Ain't nothing? You know what they told me?" Mrs. Brown let the question hang there trying to draw some response out of her daughter. "Little Dewayne is fine, in case you interested."

"That good," Chocolate said. She spoke with slow deliberation, as if concentrating on each word. "Mama, listen. This is very important. You know that suitcase I left there last week."

"What suitcase?" Mrs. Brown said.

"It's a silver one. I stashed it under Dewayne bed," Chocolate said.

"You did what?" her mother screamed in the phone. "When did you put somethin' in this house?"

Chocolate hesitated. A tear wound its way down her cheek. One of the men standing next to her opened the gas pliers and fastened the teeth over a fleshy part of Chocolate's arm, next to a half-dozen other bleeding welts that covered her arms, breasts, and stomach. He didn't squeeze this time. He just left it there so she'd know . . .

"Mama, please!" Chocolate screamed back. Her abrupt cry

337

silenced her mother's rebuke. "I need you to do something for me. It's very important."

"What you into child?" Mrs. Brown's voice was softer now. Almost a whisper.

"Mama, just take the suitcase," Chocolate said, speaking with deliberation again. "It locked shut, so don't try to open it."

"I wouldn't open it no way," Mrs. Brown said. "I don't wanna know what's in it."

"Mama, two men gonna come get it. I want you to just give it to them, mama, and don't be asking them no questions, all right? It's important you do it just like I tell you, okay?"

"I'll put the fucking thing outside my door right now. They can come and get it, but I ain't letting nobody in this place."

"That's fine, mama," Chocolate said, feeling the relief seep through her as the pliers slowly retracted from her skin. She crossed her free arm over her naked breasts. "Just do it for me, okay, mama. Just do it like I told you, okay?"

"Where you at?" Mrs. Brown asked, but the phone was ripped from Chocolate's hand and dropped in the cradle.

The man with the pliers shoved her back against the wall and stooped to unplug the phone. He glanced at her, watching her cower in the corner, and went out of the room. As he closed the door behind him, he slipped a padlock through the hasp that had been fastened to the doorjamb. Otha Spears leaned against the opposite wall, smoking a cigarette. His eyes were indistinct behind the dark sunglasses.

"Very good, Damian," Spears said. "Who'd you send for the case?"

"Couple of brothers I knew from the 'Ville," Damian said. "What you want me to do with her?"

Otha stared at the locked door. "Keep her alive for the time being. You can play with her if you want, but don't start hurting her real bad till Taji gets here."

"You want me to call him?" Damian asked. "Tell him we found her?"

Otha considered this, then shook his head.

"I think I want to watch this tape first," Spears said. Maybe even make a duplicate of it, he thought, in case he ever needed to hold something over Taji's head. Not that he thought he'd ever need to, but it was better to be safe than not. "I'll let you know when," he said. "Until then, enjoy."

Damian's tongue inched over his lips in anticipation as he glanced at the door, then back to Spears. "Thy will be done," he said.

35
THE MAN IN THE MIRROR

The office of the Evergreen Motel was separated from the target rooms by a walkway and a bar/restaurant. Doscolvich gave Mike Jahn and Dick Plutarch a few minutes to deploy to their positions in the rear and told them to verify that before the raid would begin. The inside of the van was hot and smelled like stale sweat. Hart could feel a droplet trickle down from her armpit.

Marcus said, "I got me a bad feeling about this one." His dark eyes flickered. "I asked that DEA cat if he knew Zack Berry, and he just looked at me, not saying nothing. Then I says Zack Berry from MEG, and he goes, 'Oh, yeah. Of course.' Sheeit, I don't know if this motherfucker's blowing smoke or what."

Doscolvich, who'd been listening, pulled the curtain back that separated the driver's compartment from the rear bay. "Everybody check your frequencies," he said. "Make sure we're all on the same band. And Marcus, knock off the negative commentary."

"Do you know this Devis guy, Lieu?" Marcus asked.

"I know that you're only as good as the guy standing next to you," Doscolvich said. "Whatever happens, don't forget your training. Our main goal is that nobody gets hurt. We're only as good as our intel, so it ain't gonna matter what we find, as much as all of us using the right techniques of room entry and clearing, so we can all go home at the end of the shift, okay?"

His comment was met by silence.

"Okay?" he repeated.

"OKAY!" came the unified response.

"Good," he said, cocking his head, "because Buzz, Mike, and Dick are there. Let's roll."

He put the van in gear and wheeled it down the driveway to the motel parking lot. As it screeched to a halt in front of the southern-most staircase, the doors flipped open and the team departed, each carrying a set of tools. Blackjack had the Chicago-bar slung over his back and carried the eighteen-pound sledge in his left hand. He took the stairs two at a time with Hart at his heels. Behind her were Ray and Marcus followed by Linc and PJ. Blackjack skidded to a stop in front of room twenty-two and positioned himself at a right angle to the door. He held the sledgehammer at hip-level and pivoted toward the door, slamming the hammer-head against the surface just under the doorknob. The door seemed to fly inward. Hart, who had her pistol out and pointed at a low angle out in front of her, yelled, "Police, search warrant," and swung into the room. Blackjack dropped the sledge and followed her inside, drawing his own weapon.

The room was lit by a pale glow from a lamp on a circular table. The television was on, soundlessly showing some pornographic movie. No one was in the room, which contained the table, a dresser, and a bed. Hart moved to the bathroom and kicked open the door. "Empty," she ripped back the shower curtain. Blackjack had up-ended the bed, sending the mattress against the wall. They turned their attention to the circular table, which was right in front of a window with drawn heavy canvas curtains. A large stack of currency, all hundreds and fifties from the look of them, was on one side. A scale, assorted small baggies, and a crusty mound of white powder rested on a sheet of slick paper next to the cash.

341

"Twenty-two is clear," Hart said into her radio mouthpiece. "We have dope and money, but no prisoners."

"Twenty-three clear," Marcus said. "Same for us."

"Ditto, Big John," PJ said.

The replies from the lower rooms were the same. Dope and money. No suspects.

"Lieutenant Doscolvich," Devis said over the radio. "Have your people stay in place for a few minutes until my men can sweep the bar and surrounding area."

"You heard the man," Doscolvich said. "Hold tight."

"Looks like a big haul," somebody said over the radio.

Hart relaxed slightly now that the adrenaline rush of the raid was beginning to subside. But she wanted to maintain a covert surveillance of her partner. She moved toward the bathroom, saying that she needed some tissue.

"Allow me," Blackjack said. But as he moved past the dresser, he slowed to a stop. He stood looking at his reflection in the oblong mirror.

"Shit, I sure do look good, don't I?" he said.

Hart smiled.

"I'll get my own tissue while you admire yourself," she said. She wanted to leave him alone in the room for a moment just to see what he'd do. "Besides, I have to make a minor adjustment on something." She glanced at him, then went into the bathroom and made a show of lowering the seat. Not that she intended on using the toilet, but she wanted to give him the impression that she'd be in there for a while. Then she'd open the door a crack to check his position. If he were near the table with the money and dope, maybe that would tell her something. She smiled and closed the door, waited a few seconds, took a deep breath, then opened the door and peeked out. Blackjack hadn't moved from his position in front of the mirror. He was holding his gloved finger against the front surface of the mirror.

Perplexed, Hart waited a few minutes more, flushed the toilet, and peeked through the crack again. He still hadn't moved. What was with him? Was he that much of a narcissist? She went into the room and stood next to him, glancing at their reflections.

"See anything interesting?" she asked as playfully as she could.

"As a matter of fact I do." He holstered his weapon and grabbed the sling of the Chicago-bar, lifting it over his head and arm. "What was that old Beetle Bailey said about collateral damage? About officers being responsible for it." He waved his hand directly in front of the mirror, then grinned.

Hart stared at their reflection, wondering what the hell he was doing. Blackjack moved around the dresser and leaned flush against the wall. He looked at the side of the mirror from that angle. The frame was bolted to the wall. Then, he centered himself in front of the dresser again.

"I'll take responsibility for this one," Blackjack said, swinging the Chicago-bar back, then slamming it forward into the top of the mirror. He raked the spiked end downward, shattering the glass and leaving the empty frame. Hart moved forward and saw that a small section of the drywall had been cut away. Two plastic discs formed concentric circles in the hole. Blackjack laid the Chicago-bar on the dresser and picked up the sledge-hammer.

"This is a job for Superman," he said, mimicking a radio-style announcer.

"What are you going to do?" Hart asked.

Without replying he swung the hammer forward, letting it sink into the drywall with a loud pop. He levered it out, creating an even larger hole, then used the Chicago-bar to widen it some more, leaving big flaps of the drywall hanging down. Taking out his flashlight, Blackjack leaned forward and looked into the hole.

"Just as I thought," he said, withdrawing his head from the wall. He pressed the transmit mike on his radio cord and said, "Hey, guys, guess what. We're on candid camera."

Hart was stunned. Had they orchestrated this set-up without even telling her?

"Say what?" Marcus's voice said over the radio.

"Blackjack, what the hell you talking about?" Doscolvich said.

"There's a camera behind the mirror up here, Big John," Blackjack said. "Looks like there's a space between the walls so they can work on the pipes and electrical. Must come up between the rooms from the basement, or something."

"What the hell's going on?" Elvis asked.

Doscolvich started to speak but stopped suddenly and said, "Everybody stand by."

When he did speak a few moments later his voice was laced with suppressed anger. "All right, listen up. Stand fast and prepare to be relieved by officers from I.A.D. They will be coming to each of your locations as I speak."

A man appeared in the doorway of the room, flashing his badge and saying "Internal Affairs."

"So?" Blackjack said. "You want us to genuflect or something?"

"No, just come with me," the man said.

As they left the room Hart looked down toward the bottom of the staircase and saw Captain Florian standing there in his London Fog overcoat. He was in heated discussion with Doscolvich.

"Just tell your people to assemble in this room here, Lieutenant," Florian said.

Doscolvich glared at him then held up his big arm and pointed the way. "You heard the man."

"This operation is now under the control of Internal Affairs,"

Florian said when the team had assembled in the room. "My name is Captain Florian. Those officers who were on outside containment during this operation may wait in the next room for instructions." Buzz, Jahn, and Plutarch got up and looked at Doscolvich. He nodded and the three of them shuffled out.

"What the hell's this all about?" Linc said.

Florian ignored him and looked around the room. Two more I.A.D men, both clad in the same style overcoat as Florian, stood at the door. Hart was glad their gaze didn't linger on her at all.

Florian took a deep breath, then said. "You will each step up here when your name is called and go with two of my personnel to the next room where a strip search of your persons will be conducted."

"What? A strip search?" Marcus said. "A complete strip search?"

Florian nodded. "Including a cavity search if necessary."

Marcus shook his head. "No fucking way, man."

"You will comply," Florian said. "Or face charges."

"What the hell's going on, anyway?" Lobo said.

"You are all being held as part of an internal integrity check," Florian said. "However, your failure to cooperate could have serious consequences, including being placed under arrest."

"We'll cooperate," Doscolvich said. "But show us please some professional courtesy."

"That goes without saying," Florian said. "And Officer Hart, I have a female officer standing by to conduct your search."

Hart stood up. Better to get this charade over with.

"Are those super-secret video cameras still rolling?" Blackjack asked. "I want to see the tape of her strip-search."

Hart glanced back over her shoulder at him and smiled. "Only in your dreams."

"Hey, what about that?" PJ said. "Are we gonna be videotaped during this search?"

"No," Florian said. "There are no video cameras in that room. You have my word."

"Bullshit," Ray muttered. "This is bullshit."

"Fucking right," TC added.

"Can it," Doscolvich said in a loud voice.

"Thank you, Lieutenant," Florian said. His face was becoming flushed. "Advice that the rest of you would do well in following." He stared at each face in the room, then turned back to Doscolvich. "You're excluded from the strip-search part, of course."

"No," Doscolvich said, crossing his arms. "Anything you're gonna do to my men, you can do to me first. Let's go."

"Oh boy," said Blackjack. "Now you guys in I.A.D are gonna get to see why we call him Big John."

Spontaneous laughter trickled from various team members. Florian's color deepened, and he leaned forward, pointing his finger in Blackjack's face.

"I've had just about enough of your fucking comments, Stone," he said in a low guttural tone. "And remember, you still have to answer for breaking that mirror, asshole."

Blackjack's grin weakened. A hushed silence fell over the room like a veil.

36
MINE'S A LOT BIGGER THAN YOURS

Hart kept the window down, letting the night wind blow her hair. She'd undone the French braid. Maybe it'll cool me off, she thought as she drove. It was near eleven o'clock, and Florian had saved her interview for last. During the humiliating strip-search that preceded it, the I.A.D. bitch had even made her spread her cheeks and "squat three times" after she'd disrobed. At least she'd been thorough, but Christ. Then Hart thought that if the other woman was an I.A.D. bitch, what did that make her?

But it's different in my case, she rationalized. I never asked for this. I was assigned. And then afterward, during his interview, Florian had the nerve to ask how her investigation was going.

"You see anything?" he'd asked when they were alone in the room.

Hart had waited a few moments to compose herself before answering.

"No, I haven't," she'd said in clipped tones.

"Look, I know you're upset about the strip-search, but, Christ, I couldn't take the chance that you'd be burned if I let you slide and searched the rest of them, could I?" Florian said. "Even my own people don't know about your involvement."

She'd said nothing. She hadn't really minded the search as much as the duplicity. This assignment was starting to grate on her and she said so.

"I know it's hard," Florian said with a sigh. "But it's important. There's nothing lower than a crooked copper, and we're trying to get rid of some real bad apples here."

But Hart really hadn't seen any "bad apples" in the time she'd spent with the team so far. Just good apples. Some a bit gnarled, maybe, but all good cops just the same. She'd learned a long time ago to trust her instincts, and something told her that Florian was barking up the wrong tree.

"Have you ever thought that maybe nobody's dirty on the team?" she'd said.

"Impossible," Florian answered back with a shake of his head. "Something's rotten here. Has to be. If you look at the list of our recoveries during the past year, compared to last year, you can't help but see the drop-off. No, we got us a bad one. No doubt about it." He paused to look at her, then said, "So you see anything or not?"

"No," she'd said. "I did leave Jack Stone alone in the room for a minute or so, but I didn't see him even go near the stuff."

"Yeah, we got that on tape," Florian said. "That asshole. How the hell did he figure out that the camera was in there?"

"These guys are pretty sharp," Hart said. "They're pros."

"Yeah, well, some of them are gonna be ex-pros when I get through with them," he'd said. "At least your cover is still intact. Keep at it, and maybe the polygraphs will tell us something tomorrow."

"Polygraphs?" Hart had said.

"Yeah," Florian had answered. "Everybody, except Doscolvich, has been stripped—temporarily suspended with pay, pending the outcome of the investigation. Or the integrity check, as we've been calling it. We've got to include you so it looks right. Get the picture? So give me your badge and ID and report to headquarters tomorrow morning at ten."

"Anything else?" Hart had asked, handing over her badge case.

"Not for you," Florian had said with a grin. "Just enjoy your paid vacation, and I'll get ahold of you next week."

She replayed the conversation in her mind as she accelerated around a curve. This assignment was really the pits. She couldn't remember one that she'd hated more. Usually she'd try to cheer herself up by saying things could always be worse, but could things get much worse? She'd been taken out of Investigations, she missed working with Frank, Rick seemed to be edging out of her life. What else could go wrong?

She knew a moment later when she glanced in the rearview mirror and saw the oscillating red light on the dashboard of the car behind her.

"Shit," she said as she pulled over to the right and felt the tires grip the gravel shoulder. A desolate spot for a traffic stop, she thought. An abandoned army housing project on the right and nothing but a grove of trees on the left. Why didn't he wait till the next subdivision so he'd have some street lights? And she didn't even have her badge to flash. I'd better just try to talk my way out of it, she thought.

"I need to see your license," the man said, stepping up to the side of her car. Hart could tell that he was white and about thirty-five. His face was somewhat obscure in the shadowy darkness, but she did manage to see that he had a mustache.

"You're not gonna believe this," Hart said, silently cursing Florian for taking her badge case. "But I don't have anything with me."

"What?" the man said. "Gimme some ID. Lemme see your purse." His insistent manner and demand to handle her purse set Hart on edge. Who the hell did this guy think he was, acting like this?

"Can you please tell me what I'm being stopped for?" she

asked. Then glancing back at the oscillating light of his car, she added, "And show me your ID while you're at it."

"Shut the fuck up," the man said.

Hart whirled her head back toward him and stared straight into the muzzle of the revolver. It looked to be a Colt snub-nosed, and she could see the gray ends of the hollow point bullets in the cylinder.

"What is this?" she asked. And then seconds later, as he opened her car door, she suddenly knew.

"Just shut up and I'll think about not hurting you," he said, sliding onto the seat, motioning for her to slide over. She did, and, as he got inside the car, he reached over and roughly squeezed her left breast, his pink tongue tracing over his lips. He got all the way in and, still holding the gun on her, reached in his pocket and withdrew a plastic wire-tie. The kind electricians use to secure bundles of wire. "Like I said," he muttered quickly, "do what I tell you, be nice, and I'll think about not hurting you. Run or scream and I'll kill you, you fucking cunt." His voice rose at the end of the sentence, so that it almost came out as a shout.

Hart had her hands down at her side, sliding across the seat. Her breathing was shallow and rapid. This was all so unexpected. Her right hand settled on the grip of the Sig Sauer, which was still on her belt. Thank God Florian didn't take that too, she thought. But she knew he had the advantage because his gun was pointed right at her. Still, she had to try.

Then he pointed the barrel of the snub-nose at the windshield momentarily as he grabbed the gear-shift to put the car in drive. Hart's left hand came up quickly and closed over the cylinder. She felt the pull against her grip as he tried to yank the gun free, but she jammed the barrel of the big .45 right up against his cheekbone, letting him see the massive bore in front of his eye.

"Police officer, asshole," she said. "Now let go of your gun right this instant, or I'll blow your fucking head off."

Frozen, the man let out a whimper.

"Release the gun now, or I'll blow a hole in your face!" Hart said, her voice a harsh rasp. She felt his hand go limp under her left palm, and suddenly the strong smell of urine filled the interior of the car.

Shit, she thought. This asshole peed in his pants. And in my car, too. She smiled. It was still better than the alternative, and she'd send the cleaning bill to Florian.

"Good boy," Hart said, seizing control of the revolver. "That was a smart move." She smiled and couldn't resist adding, as she nudged him with the Sig, "because mine's a lot bigger than yours."

37
REACHING OUT

Leal thought that he had exhausted all his sources, trying to get a real name to go along with "Taji." That was all Sweetpea had known, and after a full day of repetitive examination, Leal was ready to believe him. After stashing the little snitch in the protective custody section of the jail, Leal had tried the gang units and put out an inquiry on LEADS regarding information on a male black known as Taji. He'd also sent Crazy Bob down to Chicago PD, to check with their gang-crimes guys and their street-names file. So far nobody could find any reference to a Taji, but a couple said they'd check around and get back to him.

He reflected on the irony that in this age of high-tech, computerized law enforcement, he was reduced to waiting to see if somebody called him back with a tip. That didn't stop him from beaming as he looked over at Hart, who was busily typing up her report for the arrest of the "Phony Cop Rapist," as the press had called him. She'd let her hair fall around her shoulders in some relaxed-looking curls for a change, instead of wearing it up. Her black-knit top was sleeveless and fit snugly over the angular contours of her powerful upper body.

"Have I told you lately how fabulous you are?" Leal said, leaning back and putting his hands behind his head.

"Not for at least ten minutes," she said. The incredible speed with which she typed seemed not to slow at all as she spoke. The phone rang, and Hart said quickly, "If that's another reporter tell him I'm not in."

"What if it's Rick?" Leal said with a grin, reaching over to grab the phone. Hart glared at him sharply, but kept typing.

"Investigations, Leal," he said, continuing to watch her.

"Hi," Linda LeVeille said. "How are you?"

"Hey, babe. I've been up to my ears in work, but other than that, I'm okay. My ex-partner grabbed that rapist masquerading as a copper last night. You know, the one you helped me out on."

Hart paused for a second to look at him and raise her eyebrows, but he seemed not to notice.

"That's wonderful," Linda said. "Any of the victims ID him?"

"Yeah, two so far. We've got another line-up scheduled in about an hour."

"Sounds like you've really been busy."

"Yeah. I also caught another homicide yesterday, but looks like I'll be able to clear it completely if I can find out the shooter's real name. Ever hear of a guy named Taji?"

"Only in the movies," Linda said with a laugh. "Say, the reason I'm calling, Gladis's mother called me and left a message, and I just managed to get back to her."

Leal perked up. "What'd she say?"

"She said that two guys showed up to pick up a suitcase that her daughter left at the apartment." Linda's voice sounded strained. "She also mentioned that their visit was preceded by a call from Gladis."

"Sounds like dope, or something," Leal said. "She give you any more?"

"Only that she thought that Gladis might be in some sort of trouble."

"Well, we know that."

"I think she meant serious trouble," Linda said. "She told me she could tell from her voice. The way she talked."

"Why didn't she tell us about the suitcase before, when we went to see her?" Leal asked, anger creeping into his voice. He wanted this lead to be something hot but didn't think it would be.

"You know mothers," Linda said. "Anyway, I thought it'd be worth a trip over there to talk to her. What do you think?"

Leal sighed. "I don't see how I can right now," he said slowly. Maybe I could send Crazy Bob with her as soon as he gets in, he thought. "I'm still trying to trace down this shooter. I mean, I'd like to go, but . . ." He let it trail off.

"I understand." Her voice became coy again. "So . . . what's your schedule look like?"

"Busier than a one-armed-paper-hanger right now," Leal said. He was certain she was going to ask him over for dinner, and then he'd be forced into meeting her kids. He wasn't sure if that was the best thing right now. "Say, you want me to see if I can scrounge-up Crazy Bob to go with you on that interview? He's due in anytime."

"I'm sure he is, but I can handle it by myself."

"I just thought in that neighborhood . . ."

"In that neighborhood what, Frank?" she said, the anger rising in her tone now. "That I can't handle it because I'm a woman? The only reason I called you was that I thought you might like to spend a little time together, but I guess I was wrong."

"Wait a minute, that's not what I meant," Leal said. So far he hadn't seen this fiery side to her personality. Maybe I can still salvage things, he thought. But it was already too late.

"I'll talk to you later, Frank," Linda said coolly. "When you have more time." The line disconnected.

"Sounds like you handled that real well," Hart said, continuing with her typing. "Was that your new lady-friend?"

"How the hell can you sit there and be such a smart ass and still type so damn fast?" Leal said.

She stopped and stretched her arms over the top of the computer, causing the ripple of muscle to stand out in bas-relief along the backs of her arms and shoulders. Leaving her arms stretched forward, she leaned toward him and smiled.

"I'm ready for a break. Wanna get some coffee?"

"Sure," he said. "Why not. But is it permissible since you're on suspension?"

Her smile faded. Should she tell him what was really going on in her life? She considered it and decided that if she had to tell someone, it should be Frank. She took a deep breath. "I want to talk to you about something," she said.

"What's that?" He was getting up from his desk when his cell went off. He looked at the screen but saw it had gone to voice mail. Looking at the unfamiliar number, he frowned. It looked like a pay-phone listing. "This'll just take a minute."

Leal dialed the numbers on the display screen and waited. It was answered on the first ring.

"Yeah," a voice said.

"You called me." Leal said.

"Leal? It's Roxie, man."

"Yeah, what you need?"

"Man, I got somethin' for you," Roxie said excitedly. He spoke in hushed tones, as if afraid someone would overhear him. "About that dude I was talking to you about."

"Who's that? Otha?"

"Right," Roxie said. "I told you I was gonna try to get up next to 'em, and all. Well, they sent me and another dude on an errand. To pick something up."

"And?" Leal said. He couldn't help sounding a little bit impatient. "Get to the point."

"Well," Roxie paused and clucked his tongue, as if searching for words. "At his crib in Harvey, they holdin' this girl hostage."

"Hostage?" Leal asked. "How do you know this?"

"I seen her, man," Roxie said with a trace of indignation. "He keepin' her in the basement and they be rapin' her."

"Why are they doing this?" Leal asked.

"I don't know. Do it matter?"

"Well, I just want to be sure of the circumstances. If I call out the cavalry and she turns out to be some hooker, or just some broad coming down from a bad trip or something . . ."

"Send somebody over there?" Roxie said. "Man you gonna need the National Guard to take down that place."

"I don't know if I can call them out based on what you told me," Leal said. "Are you absolutely sure of this?" He knew Roxie wanted revenge against Otha, but he was just as certain that Otha would never consent to an inspection of his premises.

"Oh, man. You go sending some regular police over there, he ain't gonna give 'em the time of day. Then he gonna know it was me that said somethin'."

"How's he gonna know that?" Leal asked.

"Cause I seen her, man, just like I told you. After we made the pick-up one his boys asked me if I wanted to fuck her, or get a blow job or somethin'."

"Did you?"

"No, man, I didn't," Roxie said. "I mean, I went down there to get a little look-see, you understand, but she was all beat to shit. Blooded up, like they been torturin' on her."

"What's she look like?" Leal asked.

"Black girl. Medium skinned. Kinda pretty, maybe if she be fixed up."

"You know her name, or anything?" Leal asked.

"Un-uh."

"Are you sure you're not jazzing this up just a little to get some revenge for your nephew?"

"Awww, Sarge," Roxie said, sounding genuinely wounded. "All the time you been knowin' me, and you'd say somethin' like that?"

Leal considered this, still debating the options.

"Roxie, with what you told me, I don't know if I can do much," he said. "I can send a couple of marked units over there to check . . ."

"Aww, don't do that, man."

"Well what the fuck do you want me to do?" Leal said angrily. "You got anything else for me? What kinda pick-up was this that you made?" Maybe, if Roxie admitted it was dope, Leal could start a surveillance for a Bollinger warrant.

"It was some kinda video camera, or somethin'," Roxie said. "In a suitcase."

"A video camera?" Leal repeated. "What kind?"

"I don't know," Roxie said.

"That's going to do me a lot of good."

"Hey, man, relax." Roxie sounded almost wounded. "How long I been doin' this for you? I got everything written down, yeah, here it is. What you need first?"

"Got the brand, model, and serial number?" Leal asked. He wrote the numbers down as Roxie read them off to him. "What's this stuff from? A burglary, or something?"

"I don't know, but he was talkin' about some dude named Taji, and some tape."

"Taji?" Leal said. "You know the guy's real name?"

"Un-uh. I can try to find out for you."

"Okay, do that. What kind of tape was he talking about? From a VCR?"

"It was smaller than them old VCR tapes," Roxie said. "And it was with a big camcorder."

"Okay, Roxie," Leal told him. "Let me run these and see

what I can find out."

"You gonna get back to me, man?"

"Yeah, where you at?"

"A Walgreens," Roxie said. "There's a lot of people waitin' to use this phone too."

Leal gave him the office number and told him to call back in ten minutes. He then went over to one of the computers and called up a screen.

"It'll just be a second," he said to Ollie, then swore as the screen kept coming back *MESSAGE ERROR*. Hart giggled and walked over to him.

"Here, let me," she said. "What do you want to run?"

Leal handed her the information and leaned over the keyboard. She hit the transmit button and straightened up.

"You had an extra space there," she said, pointing to the format.

"The damn thing hates me," Leal said with a grin.

The message flashed across the screen.

"It's coming back stolen, Frank," Hart said.

"Oh yeah?" he said, leaning forward. He read the rest of the type-three response, then looked at her and said, "Holy shit."

38
SACRIFICIAL OFFERINGS

They'd set up the staging area behind the shell of an abandoned car dealership about half a mile from Otha Spear's apartment building in Harvey. It was late afternoon and the Raid Team had been ordered to remain out of sight to the general public, so most of them were huddled in or around the dark blue van that they used for raid deployment.

Several marked squads sat idling, keeping their interiors cool for the K-9s. A plainclothes officer passed out cups of Dunkin' Donuts coffee, but Hart and most of the others declined, not wanting to chance getting mobilized on a full bladder. Leal stood nearby, with Crazy Bob, Ryan, and Lt. Card, as Doscolvich punched in the numbers on his cellular phone once again.

"Any word yet?" Doscolvich asked, speaking into the flap of the receiver. He grunted, then said, "How's the operation going up north?" He grunted again, and told the other party to call him as soon as there was confirmation.

"So?" Leal asked impatiently. "What's going on?"

"The Chief's still ain't answered his page," Doscolvich said. He glanced at the officer with the box of coffees, reached over, and grabbed one. "Ah, shit, remind me to take a piss before we move out."

"Jesus H. Christ," said Leal. "We got a search warrant, a woman being held hostage, and proceeds from a high-profile homicide in the fucking house, and we're all just standing here pulling our pricks."

"I told you, Leal, I'm not sending my team in there unless the suspension's lifted," Doscolvich said, his voice rising in authority. "And until that's done, I don't give a shit what you do with your prick."

Leal glared back at him but said nothing. Card, who was looking more dyspeptic than usual, told Leal to settle down, but Leal didn't even look at him. He could tell that Doscolvich was nobody to smart off to, but he also knew that the big man was right. The Internal Affairs Division had stripped the team during the course of some bullshit investigation, and now they were needed and weren't available. And with the north team tied up on a barricaded suspect incident, they were the only game in town.

Doscolvich sipped the coffee, then tossed the remainder of the cup out. The big man licked his lips, then dialed another number on his cellular.

"Yeah, Vince, Lt. Doscolvich. What kind of activity you seeing over there?"

"Not too much, Lieu," Vince Casey replied. "Nobody in or out. Looks like they've got a bunch of shorties going up and down the block as look-outs with radio headsets on."

"Great," Doscolvich said. "Keep me posted." He flipped the phone closed and put it in the pocket of his camouflaged fatigue jacket. "Looks like we're gonna need a diversion when we do get ready to go. They got look-outs." He picked up his radio and keyed the mike. "Hey, Dick, Mike, talk to me."

"Nothing so far, Big John," Plutarch's voice came back. "Nobody on the roof."

"Clear from my point too, Lieu," Mike Jahn said.

"Surveillance team and my snipers report that everything's holding fast," Doscolvich said to Card. "Get me a marked unit over here. We're gonna have to dream up a one-act play."

"Christ," muttered Leal. He almost blurted out that he'd do the raid himself, without the Special Response Team, but the look in Doscolvich's eyes stopped him.

"Hey, Frank, there's Linda," Crazy Bob said. Leal looked up, and saw her walking toward them with Al Tims, of all people, tagging along. He walked over to greet her.

"Good," Doscolvich said before Leal moved out of earshot. "Maybe she'll keep you occupied for a while."

"Hi," Leal said. "You got my message, huh?"

"Yeah, how far is it?" Linda asked, her eyes widening.

"Right down the road a ways," Leal said, pointing south.

"Hey, Frank," Tims said. "They okayed me to go along. Even gave me one of these." He lifted his tie and tapped the plate in the Kevlar vest with his knuckles.

"You're supposed to wear that under your shirt, Al," Leal said. Then to Linda, "You got a vest?"

"No," she said. "But I'm hardly dressed for a raid, though." She lifted her right foot to display her high-heeled shoe.

"Those are pretty," Hart said, joining them. "Where'd you get them?"

Linda turned and smiled. "The Shoe Works," she said.

"That's one thing I really need," Hart said. "A decent pair of pumps. And those look like they'd go with just about anything."

"They do," Linda said. "That sort of made up for the price." She smiled. "Are you on the raid team?"

"Yes, I'm Olivia Hart."

"Not *the* Olivia Hart?" Linda asked. "Frank's ex-partner?" Her face turned back to him.

"Right," Leal said. "Ollie, this is Linda LaVeille, Forest Preserve Police."

"It's good to finally meet you," Linda said, shaking Hart's hand. "Frank's told me so much about you."

"Same here," Hart said, smiling at Leal.

361

"Congratulations on making that great arrest," Linda said. "I helped Frank interview one of the victims."

Hart nodded, said thank you, and cast another quick glance at Leal.

"Hi, Ollie," Tims said. He was grinning with that simpering look again, and Leal hoped he could get away from him before the inevitable, grating laugh honked forth. As if sensing this, Hart took Tims by the arm and led him off, saying that she wanted to introduce him to the rest of the team.

"He looks like a happy puppy," Linda said, watching them go.

"Yeah, but he'll be back," Leal said. "He can't look down Ollie's blouse with her wearing that BDU, so he'll come back and try yours. You want some coffee?"

"Love some. So catch me up on this."

Leal motioned at the plainclothes man with the box of coffees and held up two fingers. The guy looked inside the box and smiled. He began to amble toward them.

"My informant called me right after you did this morning," Leal said. "He gave me the serial number of a camcorder that he delivered to Otha Spear's building. And get this," his voice became more animated. "The serial number matches the one I put a type-three out on regarding the Dick Forest case. Forest used his credit card to have it repaired a couple of weeks ago." He muttered a thanks to the coffeeman, handed one cup to Linda, and took another for himself. "My snitch also told me that he'd picked up the camcorder, which was in a metal suitcase, from a woman in an apartment in Harvey."

Linda's eyes widened over the rim of the paper cup, and she swallowed the sip of coffee with sudden quickness. "Gladis's mother?"

Leal nodded, smiling.

"There's more," he said. "They're holding a black, female

hostage in the basement of the building. He doesn't know why. And that tap we put on mama's apartment showed that the call yesterday came from Otha's."

"Oh, Frank, that's great," Linda said. "We're so close."

"And yet so far," he said sardonically. "If we can ever get in there, maybe we'll be able to fit all these pieces together. The north team is tied up on a barricaded suspect, and the south's waiting for a suspension to be lifted before they can serve the warrant." He glanced at his watch. It was ten to six.

Chief Jack Burton rolled over in the bed, and heaved a sigh of ecstatic exhaustion. He reached to the nightstand for his cigarettes, but found the pack empty. Crushing it in his palm, he looked over at the smooth, dark features of the face beside him.

"Ahhh," he said. "Nothing like making love in a classy hotel right before a big fundraiser, huh?" He smiled. "If only I had a cigarette."

"Ain't this a no smoking room?" Janetta asked. She pulled the sheets up over her.

"I'm the man. I can do anything I want."

"So I suppose you want me to go over and get you one outta my purse, huh?" Janetta said. The silky softness of the sheets felt good against her breasts, and she hated to move. "Gimme some Kleenex, then," she said, and watched as Burton leaned over and grabbed a box of tissue from the stand. He handed it to her, and she snatched a wad and adjusted them in her crotch. Then she ripped back the sheet and swung her legs over the side of the bed, knowing he was watching her ass as she walked. She caught the reflection of his gaze in the mirror and swung her hips in an exaggerated fashion.

Burton smiled.

"So you want to shower first or what?" she asked, unsnapping her purse and taking out her cigarettes. She withdrew two from her pack, then searched for her lighter.

"Yeah, I guess I'd better," Burton said. "Got to make an early appearance."

"She gonna be here?" Janetta asked.

"Ah, Rose? Yeah, my brother's picking her and my kids up," Burton said quickly.

"Well, I guess you don't want me stickin' around then," she said, flicking the flame of the lighter over the ends of the two cigarettes. "Hey, your cell's vibrating."

She unclipped the cell phone from his belt, and moved back toward the bed.

"Yeah, I had it vibrate because I didn't want to disturb us," Burton said. He took the cell, pausing to kiss her on the lips, then pushed the button. "Shit, it's a 9-1-1." He hit the redial. Janetta crawled over beside him, pressing her breasts against his back, and placing one of the smoldering cigarettes between his lips.

"Yeah, this is Chief Burton," he said into the phone, listening intently. "What? Of course I know who Otha Spears is. What? You what? He what? Oh Christ." He was puffing on the cigarette rapidly now, hot-boxing it. Janetta ran her tongue over the back of his neck, then laid her head on his shoulder. "Uh-huh. Of course I'll lift it. Right this very minute, consider it done. But keep me posted on this. This could be . . . big . . . just what I'm looking for." Burton crushed the remainder of the cigarette in the glass on the nightstand and stood up. Janetta's arms fell away from him as he did so. "Right. They're in position now? Good. Call me when it's done. And good luck."

He set the phone back in its cradle and smiled broadly at her. "This is the most fantastic development."

"What?" she asked. She rolled over onto her side, pulling the sheet over her breasts.

"That wildman Leal's got a search warrant for Otha Spear's place in Harvey," Burton said, licking his lips. "They're holding some girl hostage, and it all ties into a homicide case. Can you imagine how big a feather it'll be in my cap if I can get on the ten o'clock news tonight announcing that we took down the head of the Black Soul Gangstas?"

Janetta smiled briefly. "They gonna do it now?"

"Yeah," Burton said. "As we speak." He went to her purse and got another cigarette, lit it, then moved toward the bathroom, not bothering to close the door. The mirrored wall reflected his protruding gut as he pissed, not bothering to lift the seat.

Janetta felt a surge of desperation. "You putting on a little weight, baby?"

He frowned and shoved the door closed.

Burton sucked his gut in a little, imagining how he'd look in a suit on the evening news. Smoothing and adjusting his hairpiece, he took a long drag on the cigarette, then exhaled the smoke. Glancing at his watch, he decided a shower was out of the question and smeared a quick dab of deodorant under each arm.

"Here's looking at *you*, kid," he said to the reflection in the mirror. As he opened the door, he heard Janetta whispering and came around the wall. When she saw him her eyes widened in surprise and she snapped the cell phone shut.

"Who were you calling?" he asked.

"Oh, nobody," she said quickly. "Just wanted to tell my mama that I'd be a little bit late is all." She smiled and moved across the bed on her hands and knees. "We got time for another go 'round, baby?" She moved her palms over his chest, and around to his rather flabby white butt.

Burton sighed.

"The spirit's willing, but the flesh is still weak," he said watching their reflection in the adjacent mirror. "I'd better start getting ready for that dinner."

"Oh, that's too bad," she said, pressing the side of her face against his right hip. "You know I can never get enough of you." He saw the reflection of her unsmiling face staring back at him.

Taji parked the black Ford Taurus in front of the apartment and watched as one of the kids whizzed past on the roller blades. Another shortie shot past, and Taji glanced down the block to see that a couple of county cops had two brothers pulled over and leaning against their car. One of the honkies was yelling at the top of his voice, and a small crowd was gathering to watch the show. Taji spit in their direction to show his contempt for the police, then trotted up the stairs quickly. His whole body felt nervous. Anxious. Just like before a fight. He had to watch that tape to be sure it was the right one, then he'd deal with that fucking bitch. And he'd make sure the retribution was nice and slow.

He flashed the sign as the door opened and answered appropriately. The two hall guards relaxed, and one stepped out, his 9mm Glock dangling loosely by his leg.

"The Great Leader is waiting for you, brother Taji," the guard said.

"His will be done," Taji said, nodding. He could barely contain his excitement but didn't want to let them see that. Once he got his hands on that motherfucking tape, he'd be off the hook. He moved down the hall, past the two guards. Each had a small table in front of him, with two semi-autos, ammunition, and cans of pop. Cigarettes smoldered in crammed ashtrays, alongside spare magazines. Taji heard Efron James's high-pitched giggle and saw him wheeling himself down the hallway from the first floor bathroom. In Efron's "computer-room" the huge monitor screen was frozen with the image from some sort of game.

"Hey, Taji," Efron said, stopping right in front of him. "Didn't I tell you, bro? Didn't I?"

"Tell me what?" Taji asked, looking down at the little man.

"We got her," Efron said. "That caller ID monitor showed us where she was calling from, and all we had to do was set up on the phone and wait. Course it was my great computer work that showed where the pay phone was."

Taji smiled. "I owe you one, little man. Have to buy you something special for Christmas, or something."

Efron wheeled past him and went to the computer. He pressed a button and then grabbed the mouse and began moving it over the pad. The image of several playing chess pieces readjusted.

"No *problemo*," Efron said. "Oh, shit, that reminds me, I got to check my voice mail." He wheeled his chair over toward the table and picked up his cell phone.

"Later, bro," Taji said. He was anxious to find Otha. See that tape. And Chocolate.

Otha stood as Taji entered the last room on the right, and the two men exchanged a ritualistic handshake that culminated in an embrace.

"I owe you my life, Great Leader," Taji said.

Otha smiled. He went to the center table and picked up a small video cassette and held it toward Taji.

"I believe this is what you want," he said.

Taji reached out and took the tape from Otha, holding it in both his hands.

"Would you like to review it in private?" Otha asked. "You'll have to watch it on the camcorder. It don't fit in any of my machines."

Taji nodded.

Otha smiled. "I have Chocolate for you too. As a sacrificial offering."

Taji smiled too. A predator's smile. Then he heard a shrill yell coming from one of the other rooms. Both men's heads turned, and they saw Efron frantically wheeling himself out into the hallway, screaming. His thin face looked panic-stricken.

"What?" Otha demanded.

"They're coming for us!" Efron screamed. "The police. I just found out they coming for us now!"

39
REUNION

The team swayed against the heavy metal side as the van careened around the corner. Up the street they knew that the phony traffic stop was being enacted to draw the attention of the look-outs. Hopefully, that would give them the edge as they stormed the front door. The outside containment was also moving into position now. Everything had to be synchronized: the front and back covered simultaneously, as the van pulled in front, and they made the breach. Hart's grip tightened on the handle of her ballistic shield. No one spoke. Finally Marcus said with a grin, "I wonder if we gonna have video cameras on us again?"

"Not that asshole Florian's," Lobo said. "Wouldn't get his skinny ass anywhere near a hot situation like this."

Everybody laughed

"Unless it was to Monday-morning-quarterback us, and tell us what we did wrong," PJ said.

"That asshole couldn't critique two dogs fucking," Linc said. That brought another chuckle, but more subdued than the first. They were closer now, maybe only two blocks away.

"Okay," Big John said. "Containment's in position. Check your frequencies." He paused while they did so then transmitted the next part over the radio. "I'm proud of all of you for showing up when I called. Especially in view of what happened. I want you to know that. And I want you to know that you guys are the best." He paused. "This ain't gonna be no cake-walk, so remember your training, and I'll see you on the other side."

Hart looked at Blackjack, who was seated right next to her. He clutched his shield with equal determination. They were to be the first two through the door, followed by Marcus and Ray.

"So how did you know about that camera behind the mirror, Jack?" she asked.

"Simple," he said, forcing a grin. "I just used my x-ray vision."

"Actually he's psychic," Art said.

"You mean physic," added Elvis, which brought another strained chuckle. The van made its final turn, and Big John told them to get ready. This meant that they had about thirty seconds.

"A regular mirror has about a quarter-inch depth to its reflection," Blackjack said to Hart, leaning close and placing his hand over his mike, his voice was barely a whisper. "One-way glass doesn't. I saw it on TV once. A special about people spying through mirrors at sleazy motels. Lord knows I been in enough of them."

"Thanks," Hart whispered back. "I'll have to watch for that."

The van's brakes began to squeal, and the vehicle rapidly decelerated. Doscolvich yelled for them to go, and Marcus popped open the back doors. From the pre-raid briefing, they all knew it was the apartment building on the right, and they ran single-file between two parked cars, across the barren parkway, and up the sidewalk. The porch was five cement steps that recessed back to a solid-looking steel door. Elvis had the ram, so Lobo grabbed the screen door and yanked it back, as the bigger man positioned himself.

"Police! Search warrant," Elvis yelled as he swung the ram up behind him. He let it sail forward, and it smacked into the door, leaving a large circular dent. But the door held.

"Hit it lower, hit it lower," Marcus shouted. Elvis brought the ram up again, but crouched as he smashed it into the door. It hit several inches below the first impact point. This time the door jutted inward, off its hinges. Elvis threw his massive body against it, still holding the ram, and flew through the opening. Hart and Blackjack entered right behind him, their ballistic shields up, but Hart had to flatten against the wall to step around the prone Elvis and the ram. Marcus brushed past her as the first shots rang out.

"Shots fired!" someone yelled over the radio.

Hart heard Marcus grunt, then saw him stumble. A black hand reached around a corner of a wall down the hall. A round zinged off her shield, sending a shock of terror through her.

The explosions of rounds going off was deafening. Another zipped by her, like an angry hornet. Blackjack fell, clutching his stomach area. Oh, God, did it go through his vest? She held the Sig out around the shield and began squeezing off the rounds. One of the assailants showed his head momentarily, and Hart shot at it. More bullets zipped by, and the hallway was suddenly filled with a smoky haze. She knew they had to move . . . fight through the ambush, but there was nowhere to go. Then Doscolvich's voice yelled behind her. "Ollie, down. Stunner."

She stepped in front of Marcus and Blackjack, lowering her shield and crouching protectively behind it. Over her shoulder came the booming sounds of Big John's automatic shotgun, tearing chunks of plaster from both sides of the walls in front of them.

"Buzz!" Doscolvich yelled, and the nimble old sergeant gave a quick underhanded toss to what looked like a black ball. The stun grenade exploded a moment later, sending a concussive wave inside the house. Hart had prepared herself for it so she wasn't as disabled as she hoped the two gunmen would be.

"Go," she heard Doscolvich yelling as he stepped over Marcus and Blackjack. "Police! Search warrant."

Hart stepped up and went around the corner, gun-first. One

of the gunmen lay on his side, his Glock still clutched in his hand, his body quivering. Hart saw the flicker of his hand as the gun started to raise toward her, and then the convulsive jerk as the big forty-five round from her weapon struck him. She moved forward and stepped on his gun-hand. Buzz was behind her in a moment and ripped the weapon from the man's grip.

"We've got officers and a suspect down," Buzz shouted into his mike. "Two officers and a suspect." He wrenched the man's arms behind him and snapped a pair of handcuffs over his wrists. Hart moved to the corridor in time to see the rest of the team moving past her. The roar of more stun grenades accompanied by the sound of shattering glass came from farther down the hall.

"Adjust the containment and get me two backups in here," Doscolvich shouted into his mike. "I need evac for two wounded officers. Get those paramedics up here."

Taji ran and looked out the basement windows. Outside by the alley the two pigs were still there. Hadn't moved since the party started. Probably wouldn't either. And one of them had a fucking police dog. Shit, it wasn't enough that he got there just in time for this motherfucking raid, but now there was a fucking dog to chase him. He heard the sounds of more shots, followed by the loud explosions. The concussion had blown out an upstairs window so there was glass all over the sidewalk. They ain't gonna notice a little more, he thought as he grabbed a broom and broke out the glass of one of the basement windows on the sidewall. Tossing the broom down, he grabbed the sill and pulled himself upward, carefully wiggling through the opening. Shards of glass cut his hand, but he managed to crawl out between this building and the one next door while still clutching the tape. It was a narrow sidewalk, and the shadows from the two structures made the area seem cool. He heard somebody yell at him to stop, but he was already running toward the back, figuring there'd be fewer of them back there.

Otha had a large wire cyclone fence around his property, but Taji managed to scramble over it. He ran across the next yard and scaled that fence in a quick vault. Angling through the yard after that, he went toward the alley. He slipped open the gate and started down the alley when he heard the voice-command to stop. Plus snarling and barking. That motherfucking dog was close. Too close to run.

"Police. Drop what you're holding and lay face down," a voice instructed him.

Taji turned and glanced at the cop. The pig was holding a gun in one hand and the dog's leash in the other. The cop looked old and fat. Probably got slow reaction time.

"Okay, man, okay," Taji said, pretending to cooperate. "Just don't let that dog bite me, okay?"

"He won't bite unless I give him the command," the officer said. "Now drop that, and lay down on your face."

Taji realized that the guy was talking about the tape.

Christ, he couldn't let them get ahold of that. He smiled and began to squat.

"How 'bouts I set it down real easy so it don't break," Taji said, watching the cop's eyes follow the movement of his left hand. With his right Taji grabbed the 9mm from his belt and twisted as he shot. He saw the man's head jerk back and knew that he'd hit him in the face. The dog snarled and lurched forward, but the cop fell, curling the leash under him. The dog jerked to a sudden stop and Taji began to sight in on the animal, but thought better of it as the dog assumed a protective stance around his fallen master.

"I'll let them decide if they want to shoot you, motherfucker, if they want to treat your buddy," Taji muttered. Keeping the pistol in his hand, he ran into another yard and through it.

If he could just get clear of this shit, he had the tape, he'd be home free. His only regret was that his little reunion with Chocolate had to be so short.

"Christ, it sounds like Afghanistan in there," Crazy Bob said.

Leal nodded grimly and worried, knowing that Ollie was in the thick of it.

Lord, please let her be all right, he prayed. Sirens wailed in the background. Both he and Crazy Bob were dressed in gray raid jackets, with *POLICE* stenciled on the back and front in large white letters. When the containment got adjusted to replace the wounded officers, one of the rear guard had moved forward, leaving the back sparsely covered. They moved down the alley and saw a uniformed officer frantically waving at them.

"I need help," he called out. "I got an officer down over here."

Leal and Crazy Bob ran down the alley to the patrolman. He was standing about ten feet away from a large German shepherd, which was snarling and growling at him. The officer had his pistol out and pointed at the dog. Behind the dog, the K-9 officer lay on his side, a pool of dark blood widening around his face. The back of his head was also streaked with crimson.

"I think I'm gonna have to shoot that dog," the officer said. "I can't get near him to check the copper."

"Don't shoot him," Crazy Bob said. "It's just an instinctive action on the dog's part. Protecting his master."

"Yeah, well, I got no choice," the officer said, leveling his gun at the snarling face.

"No, wait," Crazy Bob said. He moved forward, shouting hissing commands in German. The dog continued to bark and snarl for a few moments more, then abruptly stopped. Crazy Bob shouted another command and took off his hat. The dog looked frozen in place, then the large head twisted as the brown eyes stared at the big bald-headed man approaching him. Crazy

374

Bob held out his hat, and the dog barked again, then sniffed it. Suddenly the shepherd emitted a low whine, and began wagging his tail. Crazy Bob extended his hand and rubbed the huge animal's head and throat. The dog's long tongue lashed out with a few tentative licks toward the bald head and face.

"How's he look, Bob?" Leal asked.

"Not good, Frank," he said as he stood and pulled the leash, leading the dog away from the body. "But I'll be . . ." He stooped and wound the leash around his hand, then reached out for the dog's heavy leather collar. His fingers twisted the silver medallion affixed to it. As Leal moved forward to check the fallen officer, Crazy Bob cried out, "God damn!"

Leal checked the fallen K-9 copper, then stood up. "He's dead."

But his partner seemed not to hear him.

"Frank, you ain't gonna believe this," Crazy Bob said, tears running down his face. "But this is Brutus. My old dog."

40
THE DIXIE SQUARE

"Which way did the fucker go?" Leal asked.

"He ran that way," the patrolman said, pointing north. "I took a shot at him."

"You hit him?"

The patrolman shook his head. "Don't think so. The guy could really move."

"What'd he look like?"

"Black guy," the patrolman said. "Short hair, dark skin. Moved like an athlete. Dark pants and shirt."

"Come on, Bob," Leal said, and started moving in that direction. Then, to the patrolman he called, "You stay on the perimeter."

"Frank, wait," Crazy Bob said. "You'll mess up the scent."

He issued another command and Brutus sat down obediently. Lemack stooped over the fallen K-9 cop and unsnapped a long leather leash from the dead man's belt. "Let's go," he said, and repeated another command to the dog.

They moved cautiously down the alley, guns drawn, Brutus eagerly following some unseen spore. Leal saw droplets of blood on a section of sidewalk by a yard. The dog barked, and Crazy Bob opened the gate. On the garage siding Leal noticed a round bullet hole. It must have been the shot that the patrolman had taken. Brutus moved quickly through the yard. Leal radioed their location, and that they were trailing a suspect wanted for the shooting of an officer. The dog continued across the street and over an expanse of asphalt overgrown in spots by tall weeds. Broken glass was everywhere. Leal saw a few more blood droplets.

"He must be cut or something," he said.

"No doubt where he's heading," Crazy Bob said, pointing toward the looming structure of the old Dixie Square ahead of them.

"That place is abandoned," Leal said. "It's got to be boarded up."

"Don't look like they did too good a job," Crazy Bob said. Brutus was pulling on the leash harder now, moving toward a large section of the building that had apparently housed a nightclub of some sort. Broken neon letters spelled out *CITY LIFE* in partial red relief. Beyond it was an indented section that was overgrown with high shrubbery and small trees. The wooden plywood on the wall had been peeled back and broken. Inside they saw patches of light.

"You'll be all right with Brutus as long as you come through the door with me," Crazy Bob said.

"Wait," Leal said. "He could be anywhere in there. Maybe we'd better wait for backup."

"But there's no time, Frank," Crazy Bob pleaded. "He'll get away for sure." He moved closer so his breath seemed to strike Leal's face as the words came out. "We can get him. I know we can. Just the three of us."

Leal regarded him for a moment, then said, "Okay, partner." Crazy Bob crouched and snapped the thirty-foot leash on the dog's collar. He let Brutus go in first, extended the leash, then crouched by the opening. He slipped through and flattened out. Leal followed. As soon as they entered, they heard a rapid flapping noise and their eyes went immediately upward. A flock of pigeons circled the ceiling area, the sound of their wings echoing, then shot out a large space that had once been a skylight.

Patches of the late-afternoon sunlight filtered in through the space, illuminating the otherwise dark area.

Their feet crunched on pieces of broken glass scattered over a rough cement floor. The musty smell of decay was everywhere. It looked to be the main corridors of the old mall. Empty-framed windows of abandoned stores, the glass and doors long since gone, on either side. Ruptured conduit pipe hung down through the metal skeletons of ceiling-tile frames, spewing forth bundles of wire like synthetic spirals of some gigantic web. Most of the tiles had fallen, leaving assorted piles of congealed pulp in various places along the floor.

Brutus was about twenty feet ahead of them now, still sniffing, still following the scent. He looked back periodically at Crazy Bob, as if for reassurance, then forged ahead. They passed an old Thom McAn store on their right, its sign still mostly intact. What ceiling tiles there were in the store hung in twisted distortion from the dilapidated frames. An unnamed store next door had a half-lowered security gate draped across its entrance, as if somehow guarding its vacant interior.

Brutus continued forward, leading them toward a center section that was better lit by the sunlight. Glancing in the large shell of the department store to his left, Leal saw a vast empty space, dark, and filled with the debris from the decaying structure.

The fucker could be hiding in any one of those places, he thought. Waiting to ambush us, and I'm in here on a K-9 reunion.

"Don't worry, Sarge," Crazy Bob whispered. "He'll alert when the scent gets strong enough, and he knows where the asshole's at."

For once, Leal hoped that his partner was right. And maybe, if the dog could draw him out, Leal could get off the first shot . . .

The dog led them into the center section of the mall, past some bare concrete pillars and a set of triangular-shaped plywood supports, on which someone had spray-painted *JESUS SAVES*, followed by the Soul Gangsta's crescent moon and five-pointed star. More sunlight shone in from a larger hole in the roof. A new group of birds abruptly flapped away. Leal and Crazy Bob moved cautiously forward, their feet making more crunching sounds. But it was impossible not to step on something.

Brutus stopped, his head jerking, as he apparently caught a whiff. He emitted a low growl, and then began moving toward one of the larger stores. The broken plastic letters seemed to spell out *MONTGOMERY WARD*. They looked beyond the broken-out sections of the large picture windows and into the vacant twilight as the dog suddenly jumped over the low brick wall and went inside.

Doscolvich watched as the ambulance carrying Blackjack and Marcus took off in a wail of red lights and sirens. He bit his lip and started back inside the house. Hart was telling a uniformed officer to stay with the wounded suspect that the paramedics were taking out on another stretcher to a second ambulance. She looked at Doscolvich as he strode up the steps.

"They going to make it?" she asked

"Hard to tell, but what we got to worry about is shock." He frowned. "That can kill even with a superficial wound. All rooms secure?"

"Yes, sir," she said.

They re-entered the house and saw two members of the raid team, Lobo and Elvis, bringing a handcuffed Otha Spears down the hallway.

"Look who we found trying to flush all this here dope down the shitter, Big John," Elvis said, holding a knapsack full of brick-sized, plastic-wrapped white powder. "It was up on the second floor, but I figured that I'd better haul this down here and give it to you. It's kinda wet up there."

"And pretty soon it'll be wet down here too," Lobo said.

Elvis grinned. "Had to shoot the toilet bowl."

"Mess with me, and you're all dead motherfuckers," Spears said, his bald head gleaming with sweat.

"Aww, shut up, Otha," Doscolvich said. "I'll be waving to the bus when they take you back to prison."

"Hey, Lieu," Linc called from a room farther down the hall. "You'd better take a look at this."

Doscolvich and Hart moved down toward the voice. A shrill scream accompanied it. Inside Linc stood over a skinny man next to a wheelchair on its side.

Spit was foaming at the corners of the man's mouth as he spoke unceasingly.

"Wait till I tell my lawyer that you guys knocked me out of my chair for no reason. Picking on a cripple."

"Shut up," Linc said, then to Doscolvich, "look at these, Lieu. Copies of some of our police reports."

"Those are public record," the skinny guy said quickly. "I can get those through the Freedom of Information Act."

Linc put his boot on top of the scrawny throat, causing the slender man to gurgle slightly.

"What the hell," Doscolvich said, paging through a sheaf of printed papers. "These are copies of my memos to the Chief on the raids we did this past week." His brow furrowed. "How the hell did this little fucker get 'em?"

"Yeah, he was fussing with the buttons on that computer when we cleared the room," Linc said. The screen was solid blue.

"Don't you touch my machine—" the skinny guy said. Linc

leaned more of his weight on his foot, choking off the rest of the sentence.

"Anybody a real computer whiz?" Doscolvich asked.

Hart shrugged, and Linc just smiled, but an unfamiliar voice said, "Yeah, I am."

Al Tims, still wearing his bullet-proof vest outside his shirt with the garish necktie dangling over the front of it, moved into the room.

"Oh, yeah," Doscolvich said. "You're our intern. Well, go ahead, college boy. Have a go at it." He held his big hand, palm outward.

"Don't you touch that! Don't you touch that!" the skinny guy screamed.

"Cuff that little asshole, search him real good, then take him and his chair out to one of the prisoner vans," Doscolvich said.

"I already erased all the files, I already deleted all the files," the skinny guy taunted. "Even from the recycle bin. You ain't got shit."

Linc snapped some cuffs over the guy's wrists and lifted him by his collar and belt.

"Might still be in the hard drive," Tims said. He worked the mouse, then his fingers flew over the keyboard. A couple different screens popped up and Tims moved through various ones, clicking and checking. After a few moments more, the screen lit up with columns of numbers, detailing accounts, dollar amounts, and dates of transactions.

"That looks like something that Financial Crimes might be interested in," Doscolvich said. "We'll take his computer, but can you save that for us, Al?"

"Does a bear go to the bathroom in the woods?" Tims said, punctuating the sentence with his honking laugh. "What's your email?"

Doscolvich recited it for him and Tims hit the keys with a

flourish, like a pianist finishing off a concerto.

"Hey, Big John," PJ said, coming down the hall. "You'd better take a look downstairs. There's a body down there. Black female. Looks like the one we were supposed to rescue. We called the ambulance for her. She's in pretty bad shape, but she's still breathing. Been shot in the head."

"Well, Christ, get one of them stretchers, and let's get her to the hospital then," Doscolvich said. "Ain't nothing gonna go easy with this one?"

"Hey, Lieu," a uniformed patrolman shouted. "We got another officer down in the alley. Looks like a D.O.A. Two plainclothes dicks are chasing the shooter somewhere in the neighborhood."

"Shit. Find out where they're at," Doscolvich yelled. "Then get hold of some marked units to set up a perimeter. And see if you can raise Air One on ISPERN." He turned to Hart and muttered, "That's gotta be your friend Leal, leaving me to clean up a mess like this, while he goes running off after some bad guy."

"That does sound like him, doesn't it?" Her smile was grim.

Brutus sniffed at the pile of brown ribbon, then started forward again. Leal's foot dragged over it, and he reached down instinctively to clear it from his shoe. Then he saw what it was: recording tape. The thick kind, for a video. He shone his flashlight in a small arc over the floor and found the broken shards of a small, plastic cassette nearby. He rolled the tape into a loose ball and stuck it in the big pocket of his raid jacket. The sweat was pouring off him now, from the weight of his vest and the heavy nylon coat. Crazy Bob was about ten feet ahead, making just as much noise as Leal was, but how could you help it? The floor seemed covered with all kinds of junk.

Metal scraps and broken glass, ceiling tiles and discarded

bottles. Occasionally a large mouse, or a small rat, could be heard scurrying away from their looming presence. Leal just hoped that they found the human-sized rat before he saw them.

Brutus stopped suddenly, his head straightening toward a set of thick cement pillars near the middle of the room. Large stacks of scrap, scattered pell-mell over the floor, were illuminated as Crazy Bob swept his flashlight beam over the area. He moved back toward Leal and whispered, "He's close."

Before Leal could ask what that meant, the dog lurched forward toward a section of pebbled wall. A drooping section of cyclone fence hung curled-down from the ceiling. Beyond the wall was solid darkness. Brutus began barking and growling as Crazy Bob followed with the leash. The flash and pop of several gun shots exploded followed by a shriek. The barking stopped suddenly.

"If you shot my dog you're dead, motherfucker!" Crazy Bob bellowed, charging forward, his automatic spitting fire. Leal ran to the edge of the wall, saw movement deeper inside the room, a muzzle-flash, then felt a round ricochet off the wall near him. He fired three spaced shots at the muzzle-flash, then heard a grunt. Leal swept the area with his flashlight and saw a prone figure, but Crazy Bob was already converging on it. Running forward, he called out, "Bob, watch it."

Crazy Bob's flashlight beam lit up the figure, who was now raising his hands and flapping his arms.

"I'm shot," the man rasped. "Don't shoot no more. I'm shot."

"So was that officer you left back in the alley, asshole," Crazy Bob said, leaning over the wounded man, and jamming the barrel of his Glock against the man's temple.

"It was an accident, man," the man said. "Didn't mean to do it."

"Where's your fucking gun, asshole?" Crazy Bob asked, the muzzle of his weapon still pressing downward.

"I don't know. I dropped it."

"There it is," Leal said, stopping to grab the shiny 9mm from a spot on the floor several feet away. His flashlight swept over the form of Brutus, who was lying on his side, his legs working uselessly, each movement accompanied by a convulsive quiver. The dog struggled to raise his head, then fell back again from the effort. Moving forward, Leal holstered his gun and took out his cuffs. He snapped one over the man's outstretched right arm at the wrist, bent the arm back, and then secured the other arm.

"Can't feel my legs," the man grunted.

Leal shone the beam over him. There was a large, gaping hole in his upper back.

"Looks like an exit wound," Leal said.

Crazy Bob nodded, then suddenly looked around. "Brutus?"

"He's over there, Bob," Leal said. "You'd better go check on him."

Crazy Bob was up like a shot, running back swinging his flashlight back and forth. Suddenly he stopped and knelt down, cradling the dog's head in his arm.

"Frank, he's been hit."

"I know," Leal said, coming over to him. "How bad does it look?"

"Looks like the bullet hit him here," Crazy Bob said. "Oh, God, Frank, we've got to get him to a vet right away." He stood and started to strip off his jacket. "Gotta keep him warm."

"Here, take mine," Leal said. He ripped his off, grabbing the tangle of tape from the pocket. He handed his partner the radio. "Call for a marked unit to meet you outside the north entrance. Tell him I said to go lights and sirens to the vet's."

Lemack wrapped Brutus in the heavy jacket and picked the dog up. Leal watched the bouncing of his flashlight beam over the ragged interior of the abandoned store. When they had disappeared from sight, Leal strolled leisurely back to the man, who was still lying face down on the harsh concrete.

"All that shit about some fucking dog," the man said, "when I'm laying here bleedin'. You better get me some motherfucking help now, motherfucker."

"What's your name?"

The man gritted his teeth. Leal repeated the question.

"Taji, man. All right? My motherfucking name's Taji. Now you gonna get me some help, or what?"

"Oh, I'll get you some help, all right," Leal said. He walked over and shone his light over the expanding red puddle. "But first you're gonna give me the last few pieces of the puzzle, starting with this." He let the tangle of brown ribbon droop in front of Taji's face.

"I ain't got nothing to say to you 'bout that."

"Okay, how many people you killed lately?" Leal asked matter-of-factly.

"Fuck you, man."

"Wrong answer, asshole," Leal said. "See you around."

"Where you going?"

Leal shrugged. "Got to check this whole mall area out. See if there's any other suspects hiding inside. Might take me awhile, too."

He started a slow walk toward the front wall of the store, where the fading sunlight streamed in from the broken skylights above the main hallway. He was almost to the old broken-out windows when he heard Taji call, "Wait."

41
DIRTY LAUNDRY

The first traces of dawn were starting to filter in through the windows of the office as Leal hung up the phone. He'd told Linda that he was going home to get some sleep, then he'd be by later that night to take her out to dinner. And she'd told him that since it was now Friday, her ex would be picking up the kids, so he should just get some sleep, then come over to her place after five.

"Bring some wine, and I'll fix you something," she'd said. "We'll celebrate you closing the Dick Forest case and me solving my first homicide."

It had sounded good to Leal and suddenly, just thinking about it seemed to energize him. He heard footsteps and looked up to see Hart.

"Hi," she said. "I hear the techies are working on restoring your videotape."

Leal grinned. "Yeah. Luckily it was commercial grade and very resilient. Should be totally recoverable."

"Great. Need any help typing up the reports?"

"For once I just wrote out a bunch of notes," Leal said, standing. "I'll let the secretary worry about typing it all up. Including a letter recommending that Al Tims be awarded the civilian service award for his help."

"That's sweet of you, Frank," Hart said.

"Sweet? Are you kidding?" He flashed a tired grin. "All that stuff he recovered on that computer has got the Financial

Crimes Unit drooling. Remember, I told the boy that if he stuck with me he'd have a helluva paper to write. So how are your guys?"

"Looks like they'll both pull through," she said. "Jack got hit in the abdomen under his vest. Marcus got shot in the thigh."

"You been at the hospital?" Leal asked.

"No, I've been with the state's attorney and Internal Affairs," she said. "I got cleared of the shooting during the raid."

"Great," Leal said. "They can do mine when they can track me down next week." He paused and smiled.

"How's the dog?" she asked.

"Looks like he'll make it too," Leal said. "He'd better, or old Crazy Bob will track down Taji in prison and blow him away."

"I'm glad for the pooch."

"He's through as a police dog, but Crazy Bob is already pushing to adopt him. I told him I'd ask Sean to pull a few strings." Leal shrugged. "After all, I still gotta depend on that nut to back me up on my shooting board. And I don't want him to bring in Oscar to testify."

She smiled. "All things considered, you could've done a lot worse for a partner."

"And a lot better too." He looked at her. "So are you coming back to Investigations?"

She lowered her head.

"I'm not sure," she said slowly. "But there is something you should know . . . before you hear it from somebody else."

He waited for her to go on, but the booming voice of Big John Doscolvich interceded.

"Hey, I been looking all over for you," he said as he stepped into the office. He nodded an acknowledgment to Leal. "I just wanted to tell you that you did a great job today, Ollie."

"Thank you, Lieutenant," she said.

"Hey, it's Big John, remember?" Doscolvich extended his

hand toward her. "I wanted to personally give you these. You earned them."

Hart looked at his hand. It was a *1** pin and four patches.

"You can wear the pin on your collar. The patches go on your left sleeve, up here." He slapped his massive upper arm. "It's a place of honor."

Hart looked at the patches and pin in her hand and took a deep breath.

"Thank you, but there's something you should know."

"What?" Doscolvich smiled. "That you were planted in my unit by Internal Affairs?"

Hart stared at him. "You knew?"

"Let's just say I surmised," he said. "Christ, the timing gave it away. I been asking for people for the better part of a year, and all of a sudden our recoveries drop, and they give me you."

"If it makes any difference, she was ordered to do it," another voice said from the doorway. Captain Florian stood in the jamb. "Reluctantly, I might add."

He walked forward toward them.

"Leal, you have to report downstairs for a shooting hearing," he said. "The state's attorney's standing by."

"Not till I get some sleep I don't," Leal said. "I'm so physically exhausted, Captain, that I don't recall a thing."

Florian looked at him, licked his lips, then turned to Doscolvich. "Your team's been exonerated," he said. "We found the leak."

"Oh?" Doscolvich said. "Who? And don't tell me I haven't earned the right to know."

The I.A.D. man licked his lips again, but this time his gaze was on the floor.

"It was the Chief's secretary," he said quickly. "She was emailing Spears all our target sites and raid plans as soon as they were submitted for the Chief's approval. We found a trail of emails on her laptop." Florian paused and compressed his lips. "We also checked her cell phone. Apparently she called them just before the raid and tipped them off that you were coming. That's probably why they reacted so violently."

"Ain't no 'probably' about it," Doscolvich said. "We walked into a fucking ambush."

Florian compressed his lips and nodded.

"So what you gonna charge her with?" Leal asked. "Murder? Conspiracy? Obstructing?"

"No." Florian took a deep breath. "She'll be fired, of course. Apparently she has a brother in the prison system who is under the control of the Soul Gangstas. Spears was using him to extort information from her." He shrugged his shoulders. "She was no more than a pawn really."

"A queen is more like it," said Leal. "That was them that night at the hotel, wasn't it? She was jumping the old man's bones, too, wasn't she?"

"I'd watch your mouth if I were you, Leal," Florian said. "Now are you going to report downstairs, or what?"

"No, I'm not."

Florian flushed. "Are you disobeying my direct order?"

"With all due respect, Captain," Leal said. "You can take your direct order and blow it out your ass, *sir.*" He gave heavy emphasis to the last word and then brought his hand up to his chin mimicking a thoughtful pose. "You know, I could do a photo line-up with that bellman in the hotel. I got a reporter friend who wants to do a story on those hotel bandits, but he specializes in political figures who abuse their authority."

Florian took in a breath with a sharp hiss. He seemed on the verge of saying something, then paused, stared at Leal, and turned to walk out.

"I'll deal with you later, Leal," Florian said over his shoulder as he left.

When he had gone, Doscolvich said, "Jesus, Leal. And I thought I had balls. I hope you have an attorney on retainer."

"Nah, I hate lawyers." Leal grinned. "Besides, Florian ain't gonna do squat. He knows if he tries to bring me up on charges, the Chief's little indiscretion will come out. And Florian's involvement in covering it up at the hotel. If it's one thing I've learned about administrators, they don't like to air their dirty laundry in public."

Doscolvich laughed. "Well, I personally think Burton's finished. The sheriff will need somebody to point the finger at for a fuck-up of this magnitude, so he'll offer up Burton as a sacrificial offering." He turned to Hart. "Well, Ollie, like I said, you did a hell of a job, and I'm proud to have you on my team."

"Wait a minute," Leal said. "I just about had her talked into coming back into Investigations."

They both looked at Hart.

"Hell, at this point, you can write your own ticket," Doscolvich said. "It's your call."

"Well, Lieutenant," Hart began.

"Hey, it's John, remember? After all we been through."

"Okay, John," she said, pausing to take in a breath. "In view of all that's happened, I think it would be better if I did go back to Investigations." She started to hand him back the patches, but he held up his big hands, palms outward.

"Un-uh, lady," Doscolvich said. "I already told you that you earned those." He paused and stepped forward, draping a big arm over Leal's shoulders. "Can I buy you two some coffee? You know, I could use a guy like you on my team, Leal. It is Frank, isn't it? And, Ollie." He draped the other arm over her shoulders, and steered them both toward the breakroom. "If you could make say, two or three training dates a month, I could carry you on the roster as an alternate. I'll need all the help I can get, seeing as how both Marcus and Blackjack are gonna be out for a while . . ."

His voice continued to drone on as they all walked, like three weary musketeers, toward the coffee machine.

ABOUT THE AUTHOR

Michael A. Black is the author of sixteen books and more than seventy short stories. He has a BA in English from Northern Illinois University and a MFA from Columbia College Chicago. He was a police officer in the south suburbs of Chicago for more than thirty years and worked in various capacities in police work, including patrol supervisor, SWAT team leader, and investigations. He has also written two novels with television star Richard Belzer of *Law & Order SVU*. His recent books include, *The Incredible Adventures of Doc Atlas* and *I Am Not a Psychic!* In 2011 the second Leal and Hart book, *Hostile Takeovers*, won the Readers' Choice Award for Best Police Procedural Novel. His hobbies include the martial arts, running, and weight lifting.